Black Wat

Sean Watkin was born and raised in Liverpool and studied a BA and MA in Creative Writing at Liverpool John Moores University. He has been shortlisted for Fresher Writing Award, Book a Break Prize and Bristol Short Story Prize. His writing has been featured in *The Gay UK* magazine, and *The Content Wolf* e-zine, as well as other LGBT+ publications. Sean lives in Liverpool with his partner and two dogs.

SEAN WATKIN
BLACK WATER RISING

First published in the United Kingdom in 2025 by

Canelo, an imprint of
Canelo Digital Publishing Limited,
20 Vauxhall Bridge Road,
London SW1V 2SA
United Kingdom

A Penguin Random House Company

The authorised representative in the EEA is Dorling Kindersley Verlag GmbH. Arnulfstr. 124, 80636 Munich, Germany

Copyright © Sean Watkin 2025

The moral right of Sean Watkin to be identified as the creator of this work has been asserted in accordance with the Copyright, Designs and Patents Act, 1988.

All rights reserved. No part of this publication may be reproduced or transmitted in any form or by any means, electronic or mechanical, including photocopy, recording, or any information storage and retrieval system, without permission in writing from the publisher.

No part of this book may be used or reproduced in any manner for the purpose of training artificial intelligence technologies or systems. In accordance with Article 4(3) of the DSM Directive 2019/790, Canelo expressly reserves this work from the text and data mining exception.

A CIP catalogue record for this book is available from the British Library.

Print ISBN 978 1 83598 130 6
Ebook ISBN 978 1 83598 131 3

This book is a work of fiction. Names, characters, businesses, organizations, places and events are either the product of the author's imagination or are used fictitiously. Any resemblance to actual persons, living or dead, events or locales is entirely coincidental.

Cover design by Andrew Smith

Cover images © Shutterstock

Printed and bound in Great Britain by Clays Ltd, Elcograf S.p.A.

Look for more great books at
www.canelo.co
www.dk.com

To my grandparents: Win and James, Kath and Des; whose stories I'll keep alive for as long as I can.

Chapter One

The thing about dead bodies is that they've nothing to do but wait. Winifred de Silva was in no hurry as she walked through Paradise Street bus terminal. The 82A that would head to Liverpool John Lennon Airport boarded passengers with their suitcases, and U-turned onto the main road.

She crossed Strand Street toward the Albert Dock area, where string lights twined around trees and glittered, where seagulls circled the still water of Canning Dock and clacked to each other. De Silva wasn't prepared. You've never experienced cold until you've been down the docks at night, when the wind rushes in from the Irish Sea and thunders down the Mersey, uninterrupted. She was so unused to the cold these days.

It was pretty there. A little changed since her last visit, now that old-fashioned buses and carriage carts had been turned into eateries and places to drink. The sun hadn't risen yet, but the place was bright. The water lapped against the ancient dock walls and winter snuck in to choke out the last amber glow of autumn. Rain came down, a light haze, the kind that doesn't fall but floats. She wished she'd remembered her coat.

It's so quiet. Almost tranquil. Police tape blocked off the road between the entrance to the Pump House pub and the merry-go-round. The horses were frozen in pose, blue light pulsing over them in waves. Two cars were parked next to it: a squad car, lights on, and a silver BMW with a cream leather interior. O'Brien's. He must have come straight from his bed, too.

'I'm sorry,' he'd said on the phone half an hour ago, 'but I told you. We need you, de Silva.' She'd lain there completely still for a full five minutes before she'd bolted out of bed and dragged on some clothes.

De Silva didn't recognise the PCSO at the cordon. She reached for her warrant badge, old habits die hard, then remembered. That was another life. She took out her phone instead and went to her call list. Rows of missed calls from O'Brien over the span of two weeks.

The PCSO approached her, a young woman without a line on her face, hair perfectly tucked into a bun below the rim of her hat, the way de Silva used to wear hers. 'You okay, love? Can I help you?'

Love. 'The Detective Superintendent asked me to come down. I'm Win,' she said. 'Winifred de Silva.'

'Oh!' A flicker of recognition on the PCSO's face, and de Silva wondered what she might know about her: was she the hard-boiled detective or the one who vanished and never came back to work? The PCSO reached for her radio. 'Could you let O'Brien know his guest is here?' She watched de Silva closely as she waited for a response. She said, 'They'll send someone down now to escort you. I'd take you myself, but I'm the only one this end.'

'That's fine, I don't mind the wait.'

De Silva looked beyond the cordon, to the cobbled path, shiny and slick with rain. From there, she could see the black anchor she'd played on as a kid. A relic from the HMS *Conway*, which ran aground on the Menai Straits in the fifties. It made her think of her dad, of visits to the museums on days they couldn't afford to do anything else. It felt like yesterday and centuries ago at once.

De Silva saw the tall, broad hulk of him, a silhouette under the yellow lights.

For God's sake. Of course O'Brien would send him. Guilt pulsed in her like a second heartbeat as DS Benjamin Barclay nodded to the PCSO and lifted the cordon. For two weeks after it had happened, Barclay had come ringing the doorbell. Finally, when he eventually understood she wasn't going to answer, he gave up.

Barclay was by the book. He followed correct procedure, and even though most detectives didn't bother with them, de Silva knew that underneath his jacket, he'd be wearing his standard-issue harness; cuffs safely stowed to the right next to his PAVA spray, baton tucked away near the radio klick-fast. However, this morning, his jacket didn't bulge or pucker on the left, so she determined he wasn't wearing his radio. Probably in his pocket.

'Are you coming?' He avoided making eye contact, and de Silva was surprised that she felt hurt.

'Sorry, yes.' De Silva dipped under the cordon. 'I didn't expect to see you here. O'Brien didn't say.'

'Why would he?'

De Silva didn't know how to answer. Instead, she asked, 'Why am I here? Do you know?'

Barclay shrugged. 'I wondered the same thing when I heard you were coming down.'

Up ahead, the dark was split open by the bright white light of crime scene rigging. Bile rose in her throat. This was not her world any more: death and blood and scene preservation kits. She'd put it behind her after Ritchie. Since death crept into her house and slung itself over the banister, hard and still.

She felt like the tide was coming in and she was unsure whether she could swim.

'I tried to call,' Barclay said. 'A lot.'

'I know.'

'I won't pretend to know what you've been going through.' He stopped and looked at her.

De Silva was sure the last three months hadn't been kind to her face. It had dried out quickly when she stopped taking care of herself. Her clothes hung from body, loose and shapeless. She wanted to speak to him, to unload the agony she'd felt, but her mind was a dam, a reservoir of guilt and pain. It would stay there.

'There's CCTV cameras there and there.' She pointed over to the Tate then the old Piermaster's House. 'From those angles though, I'd say the view will be limited. But they might have picked up something.'

'We're on it.' Barclay tilted his head to the left. 'O'Brien's over there.' He walked away.

De Silva felt even colder than before, but she hadn't time to think or process. She knew that sooner or later she would have to make good with Barclay. She decided then that it would have to be later.

O'Brien ambled over to her, took her hands in his. 'I'm sorry for waking you up so early, de Silva. I know you need your rest.'

De Silva wrested her hands from O'Brien's light grip. 'It's a female, you said. A girl.'

'Yes, that's right. Just like the others.' O'Brien walked toward the bright crime scene, and de Silva followed. 'Oh, I know you'll say it, that your time at crime scenes is over. Yes, yes you've said it and I've heard you. But I want your perspective here. Just your perspective, then you can go home and put your feet up. Is that okay? Good.'

They passed a young woman speaking with two uniformed bobbies. She was dark-haired, taller than average, and in reflective activewear. De Silva noted that her trainers were clean, despite the weather, and wondered if they were new. The woman cried into the palms of her pink hands.

'She discovered the body?' In de Silva's experience, those who discovered bodies either sobbed uncontrollably, or stood still in shock, skin like chalk.

'Yes. Poor girl.' O'Brien sighed. 'Stay with her for life.'

Yeah, they always do. They passed the Liverpool Mountain sculpture in Mermaid Court, and even those brightly coloured rocks seemed muted.

'You'll need to put these on.' O'Brien reached into the side panel of a Scientific Support van and held up a white paper suit. 'What am I talking about? You know this stuff like the back of your hand.' He picked up a torch from the van.

De Silva slipped into the protective suit and put the overshoes over her battered trainers. She felt as though she was redressing herself in a costume that was so out of her character, she didn't know how she was supposed to act or feel.

The bright lights blasted specks and dots across her vision; she stood, dazed, at the edge of the crime scene. She didn't want to leave the safety of the gloomy dockside, didn't want to step into the clinical light where the dead lay waiting for her.

'Barclay, get over here and get these on,' O'Brien said. 'We'll need you.' He looked down at himself, tried to pat out the wrinkles in the protective suit and looked to de Silva. 'You ready?' He moved to her side, a smile on his face.

You don't know what this will cost me. Her stomach churned and she wanted to turn back and go home to the quiet of her house. But even there, in the shadows of the place she had shared with Ritchie, the dead waited for her in every corner. In the bathroom when she showered. At the dinner table while she ate her microwave meal for one. In the hall where the banister was, where Ritchie's swollen face had looked down on her.

Even now as she closed her eyes to steel herself, she could see it. Feel it. The cobbled stone scraping against naked flesh, skin torn off and left there, to be washed away by the rain. She couldn't know whether the girl had been dragged to her final resting place, not yet. But this was it, the thing O'Brien wanted. De Silva's imagination. Her gut, her instinct. Her feelings. Whatever.

She opened her eyes, let the image drain out of her into the night, tied her hair back, and took a deep breath.

This is it. Sink or swim.

She stepped into the crime scene.

Chapter Two

'I called in Underwater Search already,' Barclay said. 'They're on their way.' He studied de Silva's face for a reaction, some sign that she approved, or had at least heard him. There was nothing. Her dough-white face was blank. It all made him uncomfortable: de Silva shouldn't have been there, not at an active crime scene. *What is O'Brien thinking?* He took a breath. O'Brien had experience, rank, respect. All the things Barclay admired. Craved. He trusted in that.

O'Brien had woken him with a phone call an hour earlier. 'Dead body down the docks,' he'd said. 'Young woman by the name of Olivia Mc... Mc-something found the body. Preliminary witness statement makes it sound like... like it's another one. One of *his*.' O'Brien had made no mention of de Silva then.

Barclay had hung up and called for reinforcements to help preserve the scene as he pulled on jeans and a jumper. His coat and shoes were by the front door. Nick didn't even stir as Barclay left the bedroom; he'd peeked in on Sarah as he crossed the landing. On her back, fast asleep, in the peaceful, untroubled slumber that only children know how to have. She'd looked happy.

He'd called dispatch to check that Scientific Support were on the way, but found that O'Brien had already made contact. They arrived just after him, and the support bobbies had set up a perimeter. There were three obvious entry points to the swing bridge: one down by the Museum of Liverpool, one near the M&S Arena, the other by the Pump House. He'd requested cordons be put up at all three points initially, then extended it out to incorporate access points from the building on the south side.

While officers paid house visits to the apartments there, he'd asked others to speak to the hotels to inform them that a crime scene had been established nearby. He was surprised that rag, the *Liverpool Journal*, hadn't caught the scent and shown up with flashing cameras.

Barclay and de Silva crossed the swing bridge together, O'Brien close behind them. At high tide it would open like a jaw and let the Mersey into Canning Dock, but that morning it was fastened shut.

O'Brien's phone rang out, loud in the quiet of the dock. 'Excuse me,' he said. 'Here, you'll need this.' He handed Barclay a large torch and walked off to the other side of the bridge.

'Who's coming?' De Silva stopped at the railing overlooking the dock water, her back to the river, and took in a deep breath. Her hands trembled and Barclay wanted to say something to her, some words of comfort that would make her shoulders relax, her jaw unclench.

De Silva closed her eyes, the way he'd watched her do so many times before, and waited. Sometimes, she'd come up with something, some titbit another detective would miss. He didn't know how she did it.

This is wrong. She shouldn't be here. She's not ready. He said, 'Brennan's coming down himself.'

She nodded. They'd both worked with Brennan numerous times. He was the best area forensics manager they could get their hands on. He cared about the victim. None of the usual budgetary and bureaucratic crap. If Brennan said to get it done, then it got done.

'She's over this side, here.' Barclay waited for de Silva at the other railing, looking out over the river toward the lights of the Wirral. They shone in the early morning like thousands of watching eyes. She joined him and looked down, gripped the railing and almost balked. She reminded Barclay of someone with severe vertigo.

Barclay felt the same. Images of his own daughter flashed in his mind. Fast asleep at home, her tiny chest rising and falling, unaware of the horrors outside of her front door. Not knowing the things her dad saw every day. He wondered whether the darkness stuck to his clothes and hair and went home with him. He shivered.

The tidal river had ebbed away and the bank was a plane of brown mud. The girl's naked skin caught the moonlight and shone the colour of pearls. Her legs were caked in river filth, but even from this distance, the bruises and lacerations to her arms and torso were clear.

Barclay looked back for O'Brien, but he was talking on his phone, so quiet that he couldn't make out what was being said.

De Silva's eyes were all over the scene now. He'd watched her do this countless times before, in the MacNeil case, and the Richards one, and others. He knew what was coming, but he let her go with it. Maybe O'Brien was looking at a bigger picture Barclay knew nothing about.

'Could you aim that light down there, please?' De Silva didn't look at him as she spoke.

He turned on the torch and watched de Silva's face. Other than a slight frown, it remained unmoved by the sight below.

The girl's blonde hair spread about her head, bright, even in the wet dark. Her ankles and wrists were blue and purple. Her mouth was open and twisted. Her eyes were turned up to the sky and had already begun to turn white. On the side of her head, a mess of black. Her skull had been caved in.

Just like the others.

De Silva looked away from the body. 'Do you know who it is?'

'Erm…'

She looked at him and blinked.

'I'm not sure how much I'm supposed to tell you.'

'I was asked to come, Barclay. I didn't want to come. O'Brien asked me to offer some insight.'

'Offer it then.'

De Silva's mouth fell open, just for a moment, but Barclay caught it. 'I'd think it's the missing girl from the news,' she said. 'Kelly Stack. Thirteen years old. Went missing from Kirkby three or four days ago, I think. I've not been following it closely. I'd say her head's been caved in by some blunt instrument.' She turned back to look over the railing. 'Like the others.'

Barclay knew she'd have seen the posts on Facebook, too. Everyone had. *Concerns grow for much-loved local school girl, Kelly Stack*, they'd said. *If you have any information, contact the local police.*

'It's difficult to tell from here, but that bruising…' de Silva trailed off.

'She suffered, didn't she?' Barclay tried to swallow, but his throat was dry.

'Yes,' she said.

His tone turned flat and tight. 'It's him again. Isn't it?'

De Silva nodded. 'Based on the previous two victims, I think you're right. It's a safe assumption there'll be a sexual element to this. A violence. A rage he's turned outward. Onto her.' De Silva drew a breath. 'This is the third, isn't it?'

Barclay stared at her. 'I'm not sure how much I can say.'

'I'd like to see the case files.'

'I'd have to ask O'Brien—'

'Whatever she needs,' O'Brien called from his spot opposite before continuing his phone call. 'No, not you. Though I'm sure you'll get what you need. It's nearly Christmas, isn't it?'

'I'll take you back to the station, show you what we've got so far,' he said. 'It's not much, I'll tell you that.'

'Chase Underwater Search for that team,' de Silva said. 'We need to get her out of the mud before the tide turns.'

The drizzle had stopped and the clouds separated. For the first time in days, Liverpool would wake up to skies blushed by the sun, not shadowed by rainclouds. That meant no more deterioration of possible evidence in the surrounding areas, footprints or fibres, tyre marks.

Tyre marks. The body would have been too heavy to carry. True, she was a small girl, but to get a body down to the dock, you'd need something to move it with. Something substantial with a decent-sized boot or cargo space. Something he could climb into if he needed to, to drag her body inside and secure it.

Body. He felt sick. Barclay reminded himself that the victim was a person. That she had family and friends and people she loved. How quickly the job had changed him. Bodies had become evidence, the people who once inhabited them already beginning to fade.

'Come on,' he said. 'We'll go back to the station.'

They walked out of the crime scene limits and removed their protective gear. O'Brien was still on the bridge. 'Has anyone contacted PVPU?'

Barclay struggled to keep from frowning. The Protecting Vulnerable People Unit was where all of this started. Where the investigation into the disappeared teenage girls was run by DCI Mike Crosby, de Silva's long-time friend and colleague. Where he and his team had failed to find them before the suspect murdered them and left them somewhere along the banks of the Mersey.

'I tried, but no one is at the office,' Barclay said.

'I know Crosby instigated the investigation, but was he still leading?'

'Yes.'

Something flickered across de Silva's face that Barclay couldn't quite make out. But, he was sure, something in her changed. 'You should give him a call personally, instead of the office. Let him know you'll be taking over. This is a murder investigation now.'

'I'll call him on the way to the station.' Barclay didn't know Crosby well, but he knew him enough. The man was married to the job; he'd be devastated.

'It feels weird, doesn't it?' Barclay stopped and looked back to the swing bridge.

'What does?'

'Leaving.' He hoped that hit a chord with her, and he felt guilty for that. For wanting her to feel something after all that she'd been through. But that first case had laid heavy on his mind. The first case she'd let him take the lead on, the man in the woods at Freshfields, and she'd left him. *Abandoned me.* They'd found no evidence they could use as a lead and nobody had stepped forward, so many unanswered questions. They didn't even know the victim's name.

He thought of the girl they believed to be Kelly Stack. She was alone now in the water, with officers stood at either end of the bridge like sentinels. Scientific Support snapped shots of her still body. If the witness hadn't seen her, she could have been swept away when the tide came in. They'd never have found her. They had assumed that this was the third victim, but given the suspect's pattern of dumping his victims, used and beaten, somewhere along the Mersey, Barclay knew they couldn't be sure.

There could be more of them out there, caught on the riverbed, tangled on a shopping trolley, or spinning out toward the Irish Sea.

His skin crawled.

Chapter Three

De Silva sat in silence in the messy white Ford Kuga that, she was sure, used to be clean. Her head pounded, and her sobs came heavy and agonising. She told Barclay she would follow him back to the Operational Command Centre. Speke wasn't too far of a drive, and she'd need the short time alone. Time away from him, from the dock, and from the cold before she continued any further.

Surprised as she was at her reaction to the body, she'd known it would be difficult. It had been months since she'd last seen a dead person, and the violence of it would never leave her. *This is why you're not fit for the police any more. You haven't got the stuff any more.* When she closed her eyes, the victim's stared back, clouded white.

Her watch vibrated on her wrist, told her, *It's time to stand up!* Even Apple was on to her. She checked her hair in the visor mirror. She'd done her best with a ponytail, but it still looked like wire wool. Her dad's hair. She took a half-packet of Wrigley's from among the coppers and small change in the cup holder, stuffed two into her mouth and started the engine.

It took just fifteen minutes to get to the OCC and there was light traffic even at that hour, before seven. The roads were wet, black rivers veined between buildings, old and new.

She dried her eyes and looked up to the OCC, in which she'd not set foot since before Ritchie. Barclay stood at the entrance, saw her looking back, and dropped his gaze. *Great. That's all I need.* She checked her face in the mirror. There was no way to pretend otherwise: it was obvious she'd been crying. Her reputation as unmoveable, hard and cold had been important to her. It was a defensive wall. If they thought you'd take no shit, they'd give you no shit. That all came crashing down when she found Ritchie.

She walked toward Barclay, wishing that O'Brien had assigned the case to anyone but him.

'I, er, I'm sorry. I didn't mean to stare,' he said. 'I was just...' His brows pulled in close over his bright eyes.

'That for me?' She eyed the lanyard in his hand – *Visitor* printed in big white letters. He handed it to her.

She didn't feel like a visitor, as much as she tried. She knew that when she stepped into that office, she'd not be able to step out again easily. It was in her, that need to understand what happened to people and why. The justice of it was just an interesting by-product to her. She knew that sometimes justice isn't always done. The guilty walk away, the innocent serve lifetimes behind bars and the victims never get their lives back.

'Come on, I'll take you down to the incident room.'

The corridor on the ground floor had recently been painted grey; it smelled sweet and chemical. The walls were lined with photos of officers from the force's fifty-year history. Rows of tiny watchful faces, officers in their prime. All long since buried or in care homes, gnarled and forgetting the cases they'd worked on. If she looked long enough, she was sure she'd see her dad. After three years, even that felt too fresh to look.

They passed Olivia McNaughton, the witness who found the body, as a uniformed bobby escorted her out toward the interview rooms. De Silva recognised the officer; he nodded and smiled at her and she returned the gesture. Anything else would be too far, too familiar.

'Do you think we could interview her?' de Silva said to Barclay quietly.

Barclay nodded. 'Jenkins,' he called down the corridor to the uniformed officer. 'We'll take Ms McNaughton from here. Do you have a copy of the statement?'

'No worries.' Jenkins handed Barclay sheets of handwritten paper. He turned and headed back down the corridor. 'Nice to see you again, ma'am.'

De Silva felt her face flush. She hated when people called her *ma'am*. It was de Silva, and it always had been. 'Interview One?'

'Yeah,' Barclay said.

Interview Room One smelled of lemon-scented bleach. Olivia's face was red, her eyes bloodshot. She hugged herself and de Silva felt a pang of sympathy. She knew that for the next few days, Olivia McNaughton would wake up in the night screaming, or crying, or both.

'Take a seat,' Barclay said. 'This will be just a quick chat, so don't worry. I know you've already given your statement, but I just want to go over it again for peace of mind.' Olivia's eyes flitted between Barclay and de Silva. 'Sorry, this is Det— This is Winifred de Silva, she's a detective chief inspector with Merseyside Police. She's here this morning in an advisory capacity.'

Olivia nodded, and some tension in her shoulders uncoiled itself. She sat back in her chair. De Silva scanned the statement quickly.

Barclay took out a pen and a notepad. 'So, you left your house at what time?'

'About four. I've got work at six. I should be there now.' She looked at her watch and grimaced. 'I'm the one opening up today – no one else has the keys.'

'We'll get you out of here soon as we can,' Barclay said. 'Where do you live?'

'City Quay.'

'Up near the Land Rover showroom, yeah?'

'Er, yeah.'

De Silva put down the papers. There was missing information from the witness statement, key questions hadn't been asked, and she'd have to feed that back to O'Brien later. She leaned forward. 'What do you do for work, Olivia?'

'Retail. Is that important?'

De Silva shook her head. 'Retail. I bet that keeps you busy, doesn't it?'

Olivia let out an uneasy laugh. 'Yeah. Long days, always on my feet.'

'But you run,' de Silva said. 'You're into keeping fit. God knows I need to take a leaf out of your book.'

Olivia smiled at her, warm and genuine. 'I do my best. I think it's important.'

De Silva cleared her throat, a tactic she'd learned early on in her career. A pause to give the interviewee an opportunity to fill the silence. Sometimes, they rambled when they were nervous, remembered or said something they wouldn't ordinarily. There was nothing on Olivia's face except an awkward smile and flushed pink cheeks, and she kept quiet. 'So as you passed the body, it was on your left. Is that right?'

Barclay scribbled on his notepad.

'No, the girl would have been on my right.' Olivia said *girl* pointedly. 'Do you know who she is yet?'

'She was on your right? So that means you were heading back toward City Quay rather than away from it?'

'What do you mean?' Olivia rubbed her temples.

'Were you on your way back home to City Quay when you found the body?'

'Yeah, I was.'

'So you left your home at exactly four, or is that the time your alarm went off?'

'You're making me feel like you think I've got something to do with this.' There were tears again, threatening to fall beyond the brim of her eyelid.

Barclay put his hand on de Silva's arm and leaned forward. De Silva knew she'd gone too far, overstepped the boundaries of her adviser capacity. It's just that… things needed to move faster. The third girl in as many months. The media would be all over it soon.

'Sorry,' Barclay said. 'These are just standard questions. It's important for us to establish a clear timeline. If you left at four rather than leaving at four fifteen, for example, it narrows the timeline. See what I mean?'

Olivia wrung her hands, but smiled. Barclay had that effect on people, de Silva remembered. They were drawn to him. His good looks, his height, his calm and charming way. But he was married, and he doted on his husband.

'Yeah,' Olivia said. 'I get it. Sorry, I'm just… Look, I'm shaking.'

'We'll be done shortly, I promise.' Barclay beamed at her. 'So…' Barclay looked down at his notes, pen poised.

'So what?'

'Did you leave at four or later?'

'Sorry!' Olivia rubbed her forearms. 'I can tell you the exact time because I've been using that running app everyone went mad for during lockdown. Hold on.' Olivia swiped through her phone. 'Twelve minutes past four is when I left the apartment building.' She held it up for Barclay and de Silva to see.

'Ah, I've got that app. It's great, isn't it?' Barclay grinned.

'It's all right like. Can't make it past week two.'

'It times you, doesn't it?'

De Silva sat back and watched. Barclay had his own approach to interviews, but he was good at it. Something buzzed under her skin and she subdued a smile. Pride in him. He'd come so far, even in the three months since she'd been gone.

'Yeah. I think I was on target to complete my run in thirty-five minutes today. Until... you know...'

'It notifies you when you get to the halfway point of your run, doesn't it? That little ding-dong sound always makes me happy.' Barclay chuckled and de Silva watched as Olivia eased even more. 'Could you tell me what time you got to your halfway point?'

Olivia held up her phone, a map that tracked her run via GPS. She'd looped around the Liverpool Museum and at the far side, a marker read ½. The halfway point. Seventeen minutes.

'Could you screenshot that and email it to me? I'll give you my email address when we're done.'

De Silva took Barclay's pad and pen and wrote down *four thirty to four thirty-two?* and said, 'Did you notice anything out of the ordinary on your way past the swing bridge, toward the museum? Keep in mind now that the body would have been on your left at that point – if it was there.'

'Like what?'

'Like anyone hanging around?'

'Well, I did see red lights down near the Pump House. They went off as I got to the bridge, but I remember them because they were so bright.'

'Did you see a car?'

'No, it's a bit of a way from the bridge.'

De Silva nodded. 'This could be really important, thank you. Did you see the body on your way toward the museum?'

'No.'

'Are you certain?'

'Well, I didn't see it. I mean, I'd have stopped, wouldn't I?'

'I need you to be really sure.'

'Who goes out running keeping an eye out for dead people?'

Me. I do. Did. When she got into bed at the end of every day, she imagined Ritchie. She'd see his face, swollen and purple. She'd see the faces of every dead person she'd ever investigated. Eyes open, skin pale, lips blue as glacial ice. 'Thanks for your time, Olivia. We've got your contact details if we need to be in touch.'

Barclay handed Olivia a card and she flushed pink. 'Get in touch if you remember anything else,' he said. 'My email is at the bottom there for you to send that screenshot. Drop those keys at work and take yourself off home. You'll need some time for yourself.'

'I doubt they'd pay me for it. Tough times, isn't it?'

They escorted Olivia out to reception, and Barclay handed her some leaflets with contact numbers for support. When she left, he held up his phone to de Silva. Crosby – ten missed calls. 'Next stop?'

De Silva swallowed hard. She'd not planned on seeing Crosby today. She just wanted to get to the case files, to offer her advice and leave. To fulfil her obligation to O'Brien. 'Okay,' she said. 'Let's go.'

Chapter Four

De Silva stepped into the lift and pressed *B*. The doors hissed open into a corridor that was bitterly cold, like the open-front freezers they used to have in Kwik Save. As a kid, de Silva would blow out her breath and watch it steam in front of her face, then disappear into the cold.

In the small room, there were whiteboards lined up next to each other. Across them, three different timelines for each of the three victims, from disappearance to finding the body – the point where the Protecting Vulnerable People Unit would have handed the case over to CID. Kelly Stack's story remained unfinished.

For now.

Crosby paced in the middle of the room, surrounded by the three girls, and chewed gum – a habit he'd always had. He was never without a packet of Wrigley's. He'd spun around as soon as de Silva and Barclay had entered the room. He looked straight to de Silva, ignored Barclay completely. 'Is it her then?' She could smell the spearmint on his breath.

He looked as though he hadn't slept for days, and knowing Crosby the way de Silva did, she knew that he hadn't. He was the detective chief inspector over the PVPU. He could have delegated – he definitely should have – but he was so hands-on. That was his way. So dedicated to each vulnerable person case that came into his unit.

De Silva picked up Crosby's *World's Best Daddy* mug from his desk and switched on the coffee machine. 'Let's sit down and have a hot drink.'

'I don't want any coffee!' His face was red and wet. 'I'm sorry,' he said. 'I'm sorry, I'm just…'

It had been months, but de Silva had never seen him this bad. He had, in the past, taken cases personally, but nothing like this. He'd been different since a particular case three years ago. The way they'd found the little boy's body had been too much for Crosby. The damage done was massive. He'd needed de Silva then. *He needs you now.* But she couldn't open herself to that again, that's not what she was there for.

'We don't have a positive ID yet,' Barclay said.

'Oh, swerve the bullshit, Barclay. Is it Kelly, or isn't it?'

The percolator bubbled in the quiet, and finally, Barclay nodded. 'I'm sorry.'

'Fuck!' Crosby kicked the plastic bin at the side of his desk, and it cracked on the wall. 'I promise I did everything I could. We just didn't have the manpower. The evidence just wasn't there. At first, we thought she was a runaway – it happens all the time…'

De Silva's heart broke for him. She rolled an office chair to him. 'I know,' she said. 'I know how hard you'll have worked on this.' He'd always put everything into any case he got across his desk.

Crosby sat down. 'So, it's over to you lot now, is it? After everything I've put into this.' He rubbed at his already red eyes.

'You know that's not Barclay's call, Mike. Come on. This is murder. It belongs with CID now.'

'And you,' Crosby said. 'What're you doing here? How did O'Brien reel you back in?'

'It's temporary. I'm here to offer some advice, that's all.'

'Make sure it is, de Silva,' he said. 'Get out of it soon as you can and don't look back. I wish I could.'

De Silva flushed; the skin on her chest felt as though it was on fire. *He's right, I shouldn't have come back into this.*

Crosby stood up, picked up some notepads and his mug. He looked to Barclay and said, 'You'll be wanting a brief?'

'We can work with the case files,' he said. 'If it's too difficult for you, I mean.'

'You're welcome to it. Just promise me you'll find who did this to them.'

'I'll do my best.' Barclay was earnest, de Silva knew.

Crosby left, and the room grew instantly gloomy. De Silva looked around at the photographs and witness testimonies, the files and folders. Kelly launched herself from the boards as though she'd been waiting for de Silva to arrive.

Kelly had disappeared on 25 November, and as the days wore on, de Silva saw it on the news and knew that there was a very real possibility that she would turn up dead. It was a statistical probability, and she had been right. When Crosby rang her the day after Kelly disappeared, she knew it would be about the Stack case. But she hadn't had the energy or the time to give him. If she had, things may have been different. That throbbed in her like a fresh wound.

You could have helped save Kelly's life.

De Silva felt no control over her emotions, her moods; instead they controlled her, they swelled inside her and she'd do her best to stay afloat. Sometimes they'd surge, and she'd be pulled under. She'd hold her breath and wait, and wait, for the ebb of the tide.

She'd seen Crosby on the news at a press conference just yesterday. 'We're exploring every avenue of investigation,' he'd said. It could have been straight out of a textbook.

'Such as?' asked Joel Matthews from the *Liverpool Journal*. 'Do you think this is connected to the other disappearances? The murders of Lynsey Renshaw and Danielle MacDonald?'

'I have to keep that information confidential for now,' Crosby had replied, 'to preserve the integrity of the case.'

Barclay sat down on a chair near her and said, 'I suppose I'd better start getting all of this moved upstairs.'

'Waste of time,' de Silva said. 'Set up your incident room here.' De Silva searched the cupboards for another mug and found a clean one. She poured some fresh coffee and wished she could have sneaked some whisky into it. Give it some fire.

'I'll go and arrange it,' Barclay said. 'I'll get someone to do a breakfast run. Want anything?'

The breakfast run. She smiled despite herself. 'My waistline hasn't missed that. Just a cheese bagel, though, please.'

When Barclay left, de Silva turned on the heating and wrapped her hands around the hot mug and let the heat seep into her skin and bones. She followed Kelly's timeline. After school, she and her mother, Patrice, left Dovecot to visit family in Kirkby. Kelly met some friends there and they went to hang around near the brook on Headbolt Lane, according to the girls she was with. They spent maybe two hours there before the girls went home for dinner. They said goodbye to Kelly at the bridge, where they headed off to the Northwood area, and Kelly would have headed back to her aunty's in Tower Hill Park. She wasn't seen again until she was found in the Mersey.

De Silva used to play near that same brook as a kid. She and her friends would dare each other to jump over it, which in those days seemed as wide as the Mersey itself. They'd run through what they called the Turtle Tunnels, which were probably part of the sewage system. They'd found a ferret there once, wet and shivering. None of the other girls went near it, but it walked straight toward de Silva. Unsure at first, it had a good sniff of her outstretched fingers and let her pick it up.

She shook herself from the memory. *Focus, girl*. The white spaces along the timelines of Kelly and the two other victims, Danielle MacDonald and Lynsey Renshaw, concerned her. So many gaps. The other two girls were thirteen and fifteen years old respectively. They were all young teenage girls, all with the same hair colour, similar soft features.

So, he likes blondes.

Kelly's school photograph, provided by her mum, stood out. That awkward smile, and her bright green eyes. She'd been failed. Danielle and Lynsey had been failed. De Silva didn't care how or where that failure had happened. She took a deep breath, found a marker pen and detailed the discovery of Kelly's body on the board.

—

O'Brien's office smelled of tobacco. The kind of reek that soaked into the paintwork, the fabric of the chairs, and lingered on your skin hours after leaving the room. De Silva rapped on the door and entered as he tried to waft the smoke out of a window opened only a slither. She'd known something was up when the blinds were drawn.

'Ah, you caught me,' he said. He took a bottle of Oust from his desk drawer and sprayed the very strong, sweet smell across his desk. 'Don't tell the wife. Or the boss.' He tried to open the window wider, but it wouldn't budge. A suicide prevention measure introduced in the nineties. *In time everything in this job becomes a potential method for harm, a possible weapon. Even a window, open or closed.*

'Bloody things.' O'Brien sat down and de Silva sat opposite him. 'Sorry I had to take that call earlier. Are you up to speed now?'

'No,' she said. 'More reading to do.'

'So, what can I do for you?'

'I'm going to get access to the case files, which is fine.' In saying it, she knew this would take more of her time than she'd wanted. 'Barclay's going to need help down there, O'Brien. Three cases. All girls under the age of sixteen. The media spotlight on this is going to be huge. Already is.'

'I hear you, you don't have to tell me.'

'Okay, well get him some bodies. I'm only here temporarily. Few hours, we said. That's it.'

'That's it,' O'Brien repeated. 'Yes, I remember. I could see about rearranging some DCs from other cases. But we have a small team on that unidentified man in the woods, remember?'

'The one from Freshfields?'

'Yeah,' he said. 'Truth is, we don't have the usual manpower any more.'

'Have they found anything?'

'They're working on it.'

'No leads, suspects, possible ID?'

'They're working on it.'

De Silva nodded. She'd have to try again in a few days. Something about that case had always stuck with her, though she couldn't ever say why. 'If there are no detectives readily available, is there anyone in uniform we could borrow?'

That was how she got her own big break years ago. When the detectives were stretched, swamped with work, they called her in off her beat.

O'Brien nodded. 'You should be sitting this side of the desk, and I should be sunning myself, me and my Kath, on some tropical island where there are no crimes. Where there are no other people. Except a chef and someone to make the drinks.'

'No power on earth would get me behind your desk.' De Silva stood. 'I'll leave you to it. I've got some reading to do.' She stopped at the office door. 'If I see you with another ciggie, I'm telling Kath.'

O'Brien's face dropped. 'You wouldn't dare.'

She laughed. 'Spark up and find out.'

Chapter Five

The incident-room door was wide open, light spilling out into the gloom of the basement corridor. There were unused rooms either side of Barclay as he exited the lift. The darkness beyond the open doors unsettled him; like it had housed the ghosts of criminals and victims and witnesses, of crimes committed, investigated and tried. He resisted the urge to button up his coat and headed for the light in front. Heat rose from the greasy brown takeaway bags in his hands and he was thankful for it.

De Silva sat at an empty desk, reading. She looked up when he came in. 'You all right?'

He wasn't all right. They'd been close before Ritchie, and now it was as though they'd only just met. He was a firm believer in doing the right thing, in following the orders of his superiors. The things he'd learned in the navy and earlier than that, in the lessons his mum taught him.

He believed in treating people with respect, especially friends; to not treat them as though they were rubbish. His mum had once caught him giving cheek to Mr Bell, the old man who lived on the corner. A ball had been kicked over into his garden, and he came out and burst it. Barclay, made brave by the presence of his mates, piped up, 'You're a... a twat!'

He'd felt the heavy, hot palm of his mum's hand on the back of his head like the blow from a hammer. He hadn't even heard her approach. Later, when she'd calmed down and the ache had gone from his scalp, Barclay crept downstairs and offered to make her a cup of tea. She nodded but didn't look up from her sewing. She sewed things back then. Curtains, trousers, socks, that type of thing, for the neighbours who were willing to pay.

As Barclay put the tea down in front of her, steaming, she cleared her throat. 'You know, you can't go about talking to people like that.'

'Mum, everyone calls him it. He's miserable. We have to buy a new ball every week.'

'So why are you playing outside the man's house when there are playing fields five minutes' walk away?'

Barclay had looked at his feet, a habit he still had now.

'You too lazy to walk?' She looked up from her sewing then, fixed him with her dark eyes. 'You can't go about speaking to people the way you did today. No matter who else does it. You hear?'

'Yes, Mum,' he'd said. He hadn't realised at the time that she was protecting him. The things our parents do and say to protect us aren't always right.

His mother hadn't taught him to forgive Mr Bell, but she'd taught him a way to make sure that he himself would never need forgiveness from anyone. He looked at de Silva then, worn out and looking ill. She'd lost her husband, and Barclay wondered how he'd forgive her for abandoning him in the aftermath. He felt cheap, dirty.

'Barclay?' De Silva was on her feet, stood in front of him.

'Yeah. Sorry.' He held up the bag. 'I got breakfast. Had to go myself in the end.'

She took one of the bags from him and smiled. 'Thank you,' she said. 'I've been to see O'Brien on your behalf, I hope you don't mind.'

What? And behind my back... He put on his best professional smile and said softly, 'No, I don't mind.'

'I just suggested you're going to need some help.' She tucked into her bagel and wiped stray crumbs from her black jumper. 'Some heads down here.'

A knock at the door. Barclay recognised the uniformed bobby, but couldn't think of her name. 'Sorry, sir. We're still working on the rest, but I managed to get the CCTV footage from the Pump House. I've uploaded it to the PNC and dropped you an email, but wanted to give you a heads-up.'

'Thank you, uh...' He raked his mind for her name, but came up empty.

'McGarry, sir. PC McGarry.'

'McGarry, of course. Thank you. That's good work.'

PC McGarry nodded and left.

'Do you want to watch this now?' Barclay moved to a computer on one of the empty desks.

De Silva's face stiffened and she stopped chewing. The bagel sat in her mouth. She tripped over her words. 'I'd love to finish these case files, but okay. I'll take a quick look.'

They huddled around the computer and waited for the thing to warm up and log in. He looked at her and felt words form somewhere in the back of his mouth, but he kept them there. He needed to talk to her about how he'd felt not hearing from her for so long, how he felt she had turned her back on him, to air everything once and for all, but first he'd want to talk to Nick. Nick was his sounding board, his conscience, he'd tell him if he was in the wrong, and support him if he felt Barclay was right. If he spoke to her before that, it would come out garbled and childlike, like when Sarah tries to tell him about her day, but there's too much to say all at once.

Barclay navigated to the Police National Computer and into the CCTV footage that McGarry had dropped there for him, and wondered if de Silva still felt a sense of responsibility for him. For his work. For how others saw him and treated him. She didn't know, but Barclay had heard her defending him when someone had commented that he'd 'only got the job as an exercise in diversity'. It had pissed him off.

'You'd last a week in CID,' she'd told the uniformed bobby, loudly, so everyone could hear. The bobby had been in uniform for decades, and had never sought to advance his career. Still, the fact that people thought that about Barclay sometimes kept him awake at night.

'Olivia McNaughton's movements place the dump at about four thirty,' de Silva said. 'That is, if the body wasn't there on her way across the bridge the first time.'

'You saying you don't believe her?' He pressed play and skipped forward toward 4.30 a.m.

'No, no, I'm not saying that. I'm trying to work out the timeline. The museum isn't far from that bridge, so he'd have to move quick to make the dump if he did it when she'd already gone past.' She shrugged. 'Never mind. Oh wait!' She put up her hand. 'Rewind it.'

The footage was in colour but grainy, made worse by the haze of rain and the dark, everything looked shiny black. Barclay recognised the exterior of the red-brick Pump House and could make out the edge of the carousel across the cobble road.

There's nothing there.

'Look,' she said. 'There.' She pointed it out. The brake lights illuminated the dark cobbles in deep red. 'You can see some of the reg plate there, see.'

'Yeah,' Barclay said. 'Can't quite make it out.'

'Will anyone from Visual Evidence be in yet?'

'Sure, someone will be. I usually see Goodwin, but he's visiting family in Somerset.'

'Ask for Stephens. Let him know he still owes me. He'll know what you mean.'

Barclay wanted to ask what she meant, but that wasn't their relationship any more. His watch vibrated and told him he'd had a perfect exercise goal week so far, to continue that momentum. 'I'll give them half an hour – it's still early.'

'Let's watch some more, but the quicker you get it enhanced, the sooner I can…' de Silva trailed off, and Barclay was sure he saw her flush pink. Her eyes flashed across the screen, eager to glean more information from the footage. A cat after a pigeon.

The red lights went out and the car seemed to wobble. The top of someone's head passed at the lower edge of the frame. Couldn't tell if it was male or female, but they had light hair and they moved awkwardly. The driver left the car for some time.

'That's him, isn't it? You can't tell properly, but the way he's walking… almost like he's carrying something.'

The seconds ticked off too slowly. He wanted to suggest that they skip ahead. He wanted to get to it, to the very heart of it, but he knew better. If they took the time now, analysed the frames carefully, they wouldn't have to revisit it later.

'I think it's a four-by-four, look. You can make out some of the tyre there,' de Silva finally said. 'It's a light colour, blue I think. Could be silver.'

The driver returned and climbed in. This time they could make out their physique. Tall but slim, dressed in a T-shirt and jeans that were splattered with what looked like paint and torn at the knees. They had shaggy hair grown out to about jaw-length, and Barclay was sure he could make out facial hair. 'It's a man,' he said. The car rolled out of sight.

'Okay, let's get this upstairs.' De Silva stood up. 'Could we get in touch with any uniforms still down there? See if they've had any luck getting more footage? Be a good place to start. The rain's probably washed away any tyre marks already, but speak with Scientific Support, see if there's anything they can do—'

'Hold on,' Barclay said. 'He's come back.'

The car reversed outside of the Pump House. The driver climbed out of the far side and stood at the boot of the car, in the brake lights. The man held his head in his hands and his shoulders shook.

'What's he doing now?' Barclay leaned in closer. 'Is he... crying?'

'It looks like it.'

The suspect stopped suddenly. His head snapped up, and he ran back to the car and the lights went dead. The car sloped off the screen.

Barclay paused the footage. 'What spooked him?'

'Olivia McNaughton,' de Silva said. 'Looks to me like we've caught the moment he's dumped the body. Olivia arrives just moments later, which narrows things down for us. You'll want to ask Stephens to scan the rest of the footage – our suspect may have come back between that time and the time police arrived on scene. He needs to go over it very carefully.'

'Yeah,' Barclay said. 'Yeah, that's fine. I'll do that now. But I have to go and visit Kelly's parents.' He dragged out the last word and arched his eyebrow.

'Not a chance.' De Silva shoved her phone into her trouser pocket. 'I'm not coming, Barclay. No way. I'll stay and look over the other two cases, but that's it.'

De Silva's hands shook as she stood and moved to the boards. Barclay didn't want to push her too hard. Not yet.

'Go softly with her first,' O'Brien had told him. 'She's worse than we thought.'

Chapter Six

Barclay had printed off the case notes and left them on an empty desk before he'd left. De Silva stared at them until the coffee mug in her hand was cold. The sheets of paper had a weight all their own that pulled at de Silva's gut. A few months ago, she'd have jumped straight in among the dead, but now she wasn't sure she could do it. She wiped her clammy palms on her jeans.

She found a small room off the main corridor with a sink and toilet. De Silva tipped the cold brown coffee into the sink, turned on the tap and watched until the water ran clear. If only everything was that easy. She pressed the soap dispenser and scrubbed at her hands until they were warm and pink from her efforts.

A hot drink would help. Back in the incident room, the percolator bubbled and dripped coffee into her clean mug, and she turned to the case files on the empty desk. She took a deep breath, slumped into an office chair and turned the page with her free hand. She was glad that Barclay hadn't put the crime scene photos on top. Their edges stuck out at the bottom; she could make out a bush, a bench, the blue-black of fingers, which reached out around the pages and beckoned her in.

The first victim, Lynsey Renshaw, was fifteen years old. A bright girl, the report said, doing well at school, decent friends. On 18 September, she and two of them had walked to Stanley Park from her home on Burrell Street, just a five-minute walk away. According to Samuel Daley and Delilah Spinks, the friends she'd been with, they'd spent about two hours at the park then headed down Walton Lane onto Goodison Road, stopped off at the cafe there for a bottle of Coke. The three split up and went their separate ways home. The quickest route for Lynsey would have been to return down Walton Lane, but, according to the report, CCTV footage obtained from the buildings and traffic lights showed her turning right at Priory Road toward the cemetery there. Nothing after that.

The questions were obvious, but she saw no sign of them in action in the reports. What made Lynsey go that way? Why didn't she go home? An appeal to the public returned nothing in the way of eyewitnesses. Nobody saw anything? *Unlikely.*

The body was found four days later when the river's tide pulled out, near the Britannia Inn on Riverside Drive, almost six miles from where she was last seen. The postmortem revealed that the victim had been restrained by her ankles and wrists. She'd been beaten and brutally raped. Semen found didn't match any known offender in the databases. The coroner stated that given the damage caused to the body, an instrument of some kind would have been used. The tearing and splinters found were consistent with something wooden.

De Silva closed the file and turned to the evidence boards lined up behind her. The photograph provided looked like a family snap, enlarged and grainy. Behind the girl's dark blonde hair, the colour of straw, de Silva could make out a blue sea and wondered where they'd gone and whether that was their last holiday as a family.

What are you seeing in them? It goes beyond hair colour and faces. Who are these girls to you? De Silva imagined herself out of the basement, as Lynsey at Stanley Park. She put herself in the scene and looked around. Visualised Lynsey's movements, the sound of her laughter, how she interacted with her mates. She got in there close and caught a whiff of Lynsey's perfume, something sweet and spicy, too mature for her. Probably her mother's.

A random grab is unlikely. They're too messy, especially in broad daylight. Too many witnesses about and CCTV footage would be clearer. No, he had planned this. He'd seen her about. Watched her. Studied her movements. Knew her routes, her habits, her vulnerabilities. Knew the reasons why she'd go down Priory Road rather than go home. De Silva shivered. She needed to understand more about Lynsey. Her after-school activities, hobbies, places she went in the evenings and weekends. All of the things that were missing from the pages in front of her.

Danielle MacDonald's timeline sat directly below Lynsey's, eerily similar. She was taken on 3 November, and her body was found just a few days later on 6 November. She looked older than thirteen. She'd already started to wear make-up, from what de Silva could see on the selfie taken from her WhatsApp profile. The coroner report said she measured in at five foot two. She was very slim, de Silva could see that from the post-mortem pictures.

Her brain hurt. The girls didn't go to the same school, their schools weren't even in the same area. Something was underneath the surface of this whole thing and de Silva knew the right questions hadn't been asked at the right time.

O'Brien had bet on the wrong horse. That thing she used to have, that insight into the criminal mind, it was gone. Her training and experience all came to nothing in the end, when she stood in Ritchie's swaying shadow. It meant nothing. She hadn't seen it coming, but she knew, without doubt, that it was her fault. She knew that there would have been a decline in his ability to cope and she'd missed it. Been too busy. Too focused. His death was on her conscience day and night, his blood had stained her hands. Hers and Crosby's.

Chapter Seven

Barclay turned off the radio, needing space to think. Sometimes the words or melodies of the tracks they played got into his head and would stay there for hours, repeating over and over. He wouldn't be able to think of anything else. But he needed a clear mind for this. He stared at the road ahead, driving on autopilot.

I'm very sorry, Mrs Stack, but we have found your daughter, he imagined himself saying. It seemed so formal, so impersonal. No, no, think of something else.

He drove past the Church of the Holy Spirit on the corner of East Prescot Drive. His mum came here to pray sometimes. Some Sundays, she liked to visit churches other than her local one; he'd supposed it was her way of keeping things fresh. To him, they'd all smelled the same.

Kemsley Road was a cul-de-sac of red-bricked narrow houses. The ones who could afford it had painted their houses cream or white. Even though every available drive had a car on it, the street was lined with them, which made it hard to get through. He drove carefully and braked hard as a kid ran across the road chasing a ball and giving him the middle finger. *Little git.* He pulled up outside number thirty-six and struggled to parallel park in the gap between two cars.

Patrice was in the bay window and pulled open the office blinds when she saw Barclay's car. She ran to the front door and dragged it open before Barclay had even got to the old, almost vintage Fiesta that sat on the drive. Patrice looked a wreck, her skin grey with dark bruise-like circles under her eyes. She was skeletal, her eyes red, raw and sunken.

'Have you found her?' Patrice threw a cigarette stump onto the floor and squashed it with her dirty pink slipper. 'Come on, lad, open your mouth.'

'Can we go inside?' Barclay looked around the street. Neighbours came out of their houses and stood at their front doors or their gates. They watched and waited. 'Please?'

Patrice turned and went back inside, her head in her hands. Barclay felt that was the moment that Patrice knew that her daughter was dead. With the comparisons in the media between her disappearance and Danielle and Lynsey's, how could she not? Barclay followed her inside, her shoulders shaking and tears falling in loud sobs. All that she waited for now was confirmation.

The house had an aroma to it: cigarettes and the warm, stale smell of cooking oil. The kind from a bottle with pictures of sunflowers on and a yellow lid. It smelled like Barclay's childhood home before his dad left. Above where Patrice sat, the ceiling was stained yellow. He imagined her, night after night, sat in that very chair smoking. On top of the peeling marble fire surround, there were small painted ornaments: a mouse running through grass, a bird perched on a tree branch, watchful, and at the far end, a wolf stalked them both.

Barclay stood, hands behind his back, near the living-room door. This wasn't the time for formalities, he told himself. *Sit down.* The couch was white once and sagged in the middle. It was covered in cat hair and crumbs, but he took a seat anyway.

'Go on then.' Her hands trembled as Patrice lit up another cigarette. The partner came in from the kitchen and put his hands on Patrice's shoulders. Andy Dee, Barclay remembered. She took a ragged tissue out from the sleeve of her tiger-print jumper and held it to her swollen and sore eyes. It looked like she'd cried sea salt. 'She's dead, isn't she?'

A pause. He should have rehearsed this more in the car. He'd have given anything for de Silva to be there then. She was better in these situations than he was. 'A body was found in the early hours of this morning,' he said, finally. 'A runner spotted her off Canning Dock and called the police straight away.'

Patrice's cries roared through the house and Andy threw himself to her, held her tight. Through the window, Barclay could see neighbours shake their heads and wipe their eyes; one of the older ones crossed themselves and turned back to amble into their house. *Kelly was well liked.* The street would mourn.

'What happened to her?' Andy asked. His face was like ash, but he didn't cry, and Barclay thought that Patrice would appreciate his stoicism.

This was difficult. They needed and deserved answers, but the ones that Barclay could give them right then wouldn't satisfy and that would break their hearts into pieces, like smashed tempered glass. 'She was in the water,' Barclay said.

'What was she like?' Patrice drew hard on her cigarette and held it in for the longest time. She needed that momentary pause before smoke slid out through her nostrils. 'What did she look like?'

'I'm sorry?' Barclay asked. 'What do you mean?'

'How had they done it?' Andy asked. 'That's what she's asking.' He had small eyes that seemed really close together and his brow hung over them so they were always in shadow.

The inevitable question, given what was being said in the media. 'Third victim of serial snatcher' and 'When will police stop another girl like little Kelly being taken?' They all alluded to the fact that she would show up dead – they'd already given up on her when Crosby and his team hadn't.

'I think we can discuss that later,' he said, then looked at Patrice directly. 'If you want to know' – Patrice nodded – 'we'll need to wait for the coroner's findings to make a determination of death.'

Patrice clung to her partner and his T-shirt was wet through from the tears.

'I'm really sorry to have to say this,' Barclay said, 'but I have to ask you not to speak to anyone about this until we've had evidence returned to us. We can give you as little or as much information as you want then.'

She nodded again, but Barclay wondered whether she had even heard him. In her position, Barclay supposed that he would be incapable of thought. *If Sarah…* God forbid. 'We will need one of you to come and identify the body,' he said. 'It doesn't have to be right now. But this morning. The earlier, the better.'

'I'll go,' Andy said.

'No, you won't.' Patrice sounded cross, a new firmness in her voice. 'She's my daughter. I'll go.'

Andy frowned. Not the angry type, the other kind, when someone's words have cut you deep. Barclay wondered whether Andy saw Kelly as his own daughter, and whether he had other kids with someone else.

He thought of his own parents. The dad who'd abandoned him when he was a kid, and the mum who turned cold on him through his teenage years. He'd heard stories of how parents knew about their child's sexuality years before they came out. If his mum had known, it didn't make his coming out any easier. He still felt her hot, heavy hand on his cheek when he thought about it.

'I'll come back for you shortly, then we'll go and see her. She's in Alder Hey,' Barclay said. He could take Patrice then, but he knew they'd need space to start the grieving process. Some privacy to air their pain between themselves.

'I'll make my own way there. It's just up the road. I could do with the air.'

Barclay nodded and waited for what seemed like an acceptable amount of time, an adequate amount of silence. 'I'll see myself out,' he said softly. 'A family liaison officer will be touch. You can ask them any questions you have, talk to them—'

'Talking won't bring her back, will it?' Patrice snapped.

No. You're right. Andy followed Barclay to the front door and grabbed the handle before Barclay could get to it. Barclay spun around quickly. What the hell did this fella think he was doing?

'The phone,' he said. 'Kelly's.' He tripped over his own words. 'There's photos and stuff. It'd be important to Pat to have it back.'

Barclay nodded. They'd found the phone in some grass on Headbolt Lane, tying in with the last time her friends saw her. 'It's still being examined,' he said. 'Soon as we can release it, I'll ring you.' Barclay glanced down at Andy's hand, trembling on the handle, until finally he pulled open the door. 'A family liaison officer will be in touch later today.'

'Yeah.' Andy closed the door with a slam.

Barclay walked toward his car on the street as what remained of the neighbours watched from their front gardens. Young women with perfect hair, kids on their hips; old people propped up by walking frames and sticks; young lads in black tracksuits, their hands down the front. All watching.

Barclay grew up in a community like this. The houses in Skelmersdale were newer than those in Dovecot, built hastily in the sixties to rehouse those displaced communities from the inner-city region.

He imagined that, later on, the neighbours would bring over Tupperware filled with scouse or curry and rice, maybe a jar of red cabbage or beetroot. That was what people in places like that did. They didn't have much, but they shared it with those who needed it.

He climbed into his car and fastened his seatbelt. As the crowd dispersed and returned to their lives, he let out a long and tired breath.

Chapter Eight

'You all right?' Barclay stood next to her. She hadn't heard him come in. Hadn't heard the ping of the lift, or the office door squeak open.

'Yeah, sorry,' she said. 'Just thinking.'

'Looked deep in it.' There was an iciness to his words that de Silva had expected but was unsure how to resolve.

'How did they take it?' De Silva took a seat and watched Barclay.

His massive hands shook and he jammed them into his pockets. 'I hate doing that,' he said. 'Part of the job, I know. Never gets easier, does it?'

'I know.'

'The mum was devastated. I'm meeting her soon for an official identification. Just wanted to make sure you were okay.'

She felt a small tug in her chest at that. Something shifted and began to thaw out. 'I've been reading,' she said.

'Has that famous insight come up with anything?'

'Not yet, no.' She glanced at the three girls on the boards then at the desk and the pages spread out in front of her. 'Three bodies across three months. No evidence. No wonder Crosby is the way he is.'

They'd made a conscious effort, early in their partnership, to put the victim first. They had names and families.

They were alive once. They'd respected that, but over the year, it had disappeared. Keeping hold of that attachment was too difficult, it got in the way of the work.

In her therapy sessions, it was described as 'dissociation', the inability to discuss her experience finding Ritchie's body. She hadn't found him, she'd found what remained. She hadn't realised until that moment that she'd brought that with her.

Barclay hadn't seen the things that de Silva witnessed these fifteen years. The drunken fights on Matthew Street during the night shift; the rape kits she'd taken into evidence from the Royal; the black-eyed, split-lipped partners who'd come to the station to tell how they'd fallen down the stairs, how their partners had a temper but didn't really mean it. She wanted him to see these things how she saw them now.

He's come so far. Miles to go, though. She wondered how Barclay would have fared on the first case she had gotten as a detective. Jeanette Armstrong, the domestic-violence victim murdered in her bathroom. De Silva had almost slipped on the white tiles slathered with red.

Man, as a species, has a knack for violence. A need to destroy. Jeanette Armstrong was one of those destroyed things, like Kelly, Lynsey and Danielle. All just bodies in the end. Like Ritchie. *That's all any of us are.* Dust scattered on the wind, or food for bugs and bacteria.

'There's no real pattern in his choosing to take them. You see?' She pointed at the timelines. 'Danielle and Kelly were taken just three weeks apart, give or take. But Lynsey, she was in September.'

'What does that tell us?'

'He's disorganised enough to take them on a whim, or when the opportunity comes along. But he has a type. Blondes, young, early teens. That's all we have to go on.'

'So there's something about these girls, about young blonde girls, that he likes?'

'No, not *these girls*. In cases like this, where the victims look so similar, it's never really about those girls. Not all of them, at least. It's usually about one girl in particular. She could be up on the board here, or she could be someone we don't know about.'

Barclay chewed his lip and looked at his watch. 'I'm going to have to go and meet Patrice Stack at Alder Hey. I'll speak with O'Brien when I'm back. I'd say you've given us more than we had in the PVPU investigations. So, is that you done?'

De Silva looked at the girls on the boards. It swelled in her chest, that old resolve to catch the perp. To hunt. For the family, for the victim. These three girls deserved that. The killer needed to be caught before another little girl became another little body.

'I'll come back in the morning,' she said.

Barclay eyed her, a frown on his usually smooth brow. 'Really?'

'Just for a few hours,' she said. 'I'll meet you back here at nine.'

—

She parked on the drive next to the *For Sale* sign. Turned the key in the front door and pushed it open. Whenever she came home, she'd kept her eyes on the grey carpet of the hall floor since that day with Ritchie. She never looked up again until she was safely in the kitchen, living room, or up the stairs. It was a habit she was all too aware of.

The mind is weird. My mind is weird.

All the things she'd studied those long years ago, the science of the mind, she pushed away and buried so she didn't have to confront what was truly happening to her. No, it was better not to think about it.

In the kitchen, she took the already opened bottle of Pinot Grigio from the fridge, dropped the lid on the floor and with shaking hands poured the wine into a wide, thick-stemmed glass. She didn't care that it was produced in the village of Monteforte d'Alpone, or that there were undertones of lime and almond. These things she'd read on the bottle when she bought it, so she didn't look to any passers-by in the supermarket as though any wine would do.

There are no problems here, she'd wanted to say out loud. *See, I'm considered.*

She just wanted to feel the sharp tang on her tongue and in her throat. She let out a long breath and her shoulders relaxed. The weight of carrying herself, keeping herself together, finally lifted.

It calmed her, that was the truth of it. Whether it was wine or whisky, beer or cider, the chaos in her quietened down. She'd picked up a bottle from the shelf after the police had taken Ritchie's body out of the house, and she'd drunk ever since. In the past, she'd enjoyed a drink socially, dinner with friends or after work, but she'd never drunk like this.

She drank because beyond her guilt at Ritchie's death, there was an anger she knew she was completely unjustified in feeling. But, if Ritchie had spoken to her about everything, his feelings, about finding out that de Silva had been unfaithful, he could have still been alive. He didn't have to die. He didn't have to leave her. Even if things couldn't be fixed between them, if their marriage couldn't be saved…

He could still be here. He should be!

She stood at the fridge door and swallowed. Gulp after gulp until the glass was dry. She poured another, put the remnants of the bottle back into the fridge and headed upstairs and across the landing.

She saw it like she saw it every day, the fat line where the paint had come away, the naked blonde wood underneath, raw and knotted. She ran her finger along it slowly and looked down into the hall.

She'd found Ritchie on the second day of a new case she and Barclay had landed. The day before had bled into it, as it usually does at the start of a new investigation. She'd been exhausted from the previous day spent out in the rain at Freshfields woods where a body had been found by two local dog walkers. The male dog walker, Edward Bradley, had stood silent, held their dog in his arms; a little Pomeranian called Bear. His wife, Karrie, wailed and sobbed and at one point vomited from her exertions.

The body was badly decayed, almost skeletal, the shallow grave it was found in offering no protection from the elements. From her experience, de Silva decided the body had been there for years, possibly decades but they'd had to wait for the post-mortem report for confirmation. She itched to know what had become of him.

The next day she'd spent with the newspapers and TV channels. She felt dirty in the same clothes as the day before, but had managed a shower at work, and to brush her teeth with the old pink toothbrush she kept in the bottom drawer of her desk.

'Any leads?' That man from the *Liverpool Journal*, Joel Matthews, had said. His face was shiny, pockmarked and his eyes looked black. He reminded de Silva of a rat, ever scavenging for scraps, feasting on the fallen.

'There were no means of identification, but we are still combing the area. The area around Freshfields, the woods and the beach there will remain cordoned for the time being.'

'No leads.' He laughed. 'I see. Bit of a theme for you lately, isn't it?'

'Does anyone have a question pertaining to this case?'

A hand. 'Julie Price from the *Su*—'

'Next question, please,' de Silva said.

'What will you do next to find out who this person is?' Matthews again. 'Can you talk us through it?'

'No,' she'd said. 'I can't do that. What I can tell you is that we'll do all that we can.'

'We'll do all we can' went out the window when she pulled up onto the drive that night. Unusually, for after eight in the evening, the house was dark. The windows were open and she could see right through to the living room: TV off, couch empty, cushions perfectly plumped.

When de Silva looked back on those few moments, she swore she felt it. That intuition she relied on at work, felt the weight of what was beyond the front door before she saw it. Like he was waiting for her all that time. For hours.

She pushed on the handle, but found the door was locked. She unlocked it, pushed it open, and called, 'Ritchie?' She heard the creak before she saw him. Slow, steady. His boots, covered in the house's shadows, then his legs. His torso and head, backlit from the window on the landing. His face. Ritchie's face. He hung there, his body rigid and lifeless. She wanted to scream but couldn't. Wanted to move to him, to pull him down, but she was frozen. That was how she'd felt every day since then – frozen.

The place was different without him. A house instead of a home. That was behind her decision to sell, but who wants to buy the local suicide house? *I'll be here forever. Trapped here.*

She went into the bathroom and turned on the hot water, watched it tumble into the tub. She stripped off and climbed in while it filled.

She thought of the bills she needed to have altered, to remove Ritchie from them. The council tax and energy company accounts. How she'd been advised to contact his life insurance provider to inform them, and how it felt grotesque to her. There were things that needed to be sorted. Paper that needed to be signed, folded and stuffed into envelopes. She didn't want to think about that then. Didn't want to think about it ever.

The steam curled off her skin in thin wisps. The water was hot, the way she liked it, and she'd begun to turn pink. She slid down the bath, held her breath and let the water wash over her head. Eyes open, she saw bubbles float above her, and from down there the ceiling light looked like a hazy sun. She thought of the victim, of Kelly Stack. She'd been alone in the water so long her eyes had turned white.

De Silva imagined the killer, Kelly's head bobbing as he carried her, probably over his shoulder. The swing bridge was glossy with rain, glowing in the orange of street lighting. He'd have stopped at the railing, perhaps looked dockside first, before deciding it would be best for her to go in the river. She could be washed away, dragged out by the tide and never seen again.

He'd have slung her over the railing and into shallow water. She'd have splashed and he'd have watched for a moment, before he turned away and left her there. He'd have looked down and seen her there, the water would have lapped at her hair and shifted it. He'd have felt something.

Not remorse, not guilt. Not anger at himself. He'd have felt the loss of her.

Why?

Her white eyes would have looked back at him.

De Silva sat up, took in a sharp breath and reached blindly for the towel to dry her hands. It didn't make sense. It didn't make sense and she'd missed it. It was obvious.

Chapter Nine

The sun was half an hour from disappearing behind the other houses on Oaktree Road when Barclay turned the corner onto the street. He loved the way the light poured through the front windows of his house and turned everything the colour of marmalade. It was his favourite time to be home.

The afternoon with Patrice Stack had been hard. She'd positively identified her daughter's body, laying there on a metal slab, a white sheet covering most of her injuries. She'd cried and wailed and Andy held her from behind, hands on her shoulders, but couldn't look up. That image would stay with them forever, but she had insisted.

He pulled up onto the drive, and for the first time that autumn, he realised how desolate the front garden looked. The petunias and sweet peas gone to seed. The rose bush – Nick's pride and joy that he'd grown from a cutting he'd taken from his nan's garden after the funeral – trimmed right back.

Sarah was at the window, her tiny fingers splayed and her face squashed against the glass. Nick would be furious, he'd get the Windolene out straight away, but it made Barclay laugh. She beamed back at him, the widest smile Barclay had ever seen. His heart melted, and she bolted from the window.

He pushed open the front door, kicked off his shoes in the vestibule and slipped out of his jacket, feeling the heavy layers of his day come away piece by piece.

The porch door swung open and Sarah jumped up at Barclay. 'Daddy!' She squeezed him tight. 'You weren't here when I woke up.'

'I'm sorry, princess. I had to go to work. A little girl got hurt and I had to help.'

'Will she be okay?'

Barclay looked into her face, at her pale skin and into the depths of those big brown eyes. He couldn't contemplate telling her the truth, that no, Kelly would not be okay. That her parents would not be okay. That the two before her, Danielle and Lynsey, and their families would not be okay. That there was a chance that they would not catch the bad man before he took another little girl.

They'd adopted Sarah when she was three years old, and since then her life had been comfortable. Safe. Even before that, before they were a family, she'd been in a loving foster home. The Smiths visited every now and then, even though Nick had initially protested. She was young when her parents died, but had a photograph of them on her bedside table. She never spoke about them or asked about them, or the rest of her family. Barclay was thankful for that; none of them had expressed an interest in taking her in. It was the only loss she'd experienced in her short life and she didn't remember it.

He kissed her cheek instead and said, 'Where's Dad?'

'In the kitchen.'

'Okay, well, why don't you go and play. I'll help Dad with tea, all right?' He put her down and watched her walk back into the living room where she'd stacked jumbo

Lego blocks one on top of the other. 'See if you can build me the biggest tower ever.' *Where I can keep you safe.*

'Okay, I will. The biggest, biggest tower.'

The kitchen was hot and Nick rummaged in the fridge. 'Oh, you're home then,' he said. Barclay felt the place turn instantly cold.

'I'm sorry,' Barclay said. He leaned against the counter and watched. 'Is there anything I can help with?'

'No.' Nick didn't look at him. He turned to the chopping and placed some carrots in a row. 'I'll do it.'

'How was your day?'

'Fine.'

'Oh.' It hung in the air between them. He'd pissed Nick off – his job had gotten in the way again. He'd chosen it over them. He'd heard it all before. In his mind, Nick and Sarah were safe at home, but at work, the people he came across were rarely safe. Rarely at home.

'So let's just get it out the way,' Barclay said. 'You're pissed off I'm home later than I thought, that we were going to go out together. Alone.'

'I don't know what you mean.'

The dismissive approach. He'd used this more and more lately. The intention was clear: Nick wasn't the one with the problem here. 'Of course you don't. There's still time, we can get ready and go.'

'I've cancelled my mum already.'

'Oh.'

'But what would you care?'

'About what? You and Sarah? I do care, but I have to work.'

'Then prove it. Keep the plans that you made. Don't miss things that you've promised.'

'Look, I have to work, Nick. I won't apologise for that. That work helps pay for all of this stuff we have.'

'Oh, here we go,' he seethed. 'My saviour. Whatever would I do without you?'

Barclay sighed. There was something else behind all of this. These last few months, maybe a year, Nick hadn't been himself. 'That's not what I meant and you know it. You don't want to speak to me, you want to rage at me. For working.'

Nick stopped what he was doing and glared at Barclay.

'Not that you've asked, Nick, but my day was pretty awful.' He'd love to be there to pick Sarah up from school, or have dinner with them both at a normal time every night, or read her a story before bed. But he couldn't always be that. Couldn't always be Daddy to Sarah, and a husband to Nick. 'We found another body,' he said.

'No,' Nick whispered.

'What?'

'I can't hear this,' he said. 'I don't want this in my home. Please. You turn that corner onto the street and you dump it there until you go back to work. I'm sorry, but...'

But what? Barclay waited for Nick to look at him instead of the ceiling spotlights. He wanted to scream to Nick that it was their home. All of theirs. His work was important to him. More than that, it was what he'd wanted for years, to be exactly where he is now. *This isn't working out. Oh God, this isn't working out.* 'I'm going for a shower.'

The bathroom window was open and Barclay felt goosebumps pop up on his arms. He sat on the toilet seat and unfastened the laces of his Balenciagas. They'd cost a bloody fortune and he'd scuffed them already. Nick had said, 'Don't wear them to work, they'll get ruined.' He'd been right.

The slate-grey tiles felt warm and comforting on his bare feet – at least the underfloor heating was worth the money. He padded to the shower, switched it on and watched the water swirl down the drain, turning around on itself. He should have gone to the gym. Worked off all this tension. He'd have been better equipped to deal with Nick, he knew that. How many husbands felt as though they needed to be equipped to deal with their other half?

The glass shower screen hazed with steam as the water ran hot. The reflection of his frame disappeared first as he quickly undressed, then his face, and he wondered whether the steam could erase him, too.

He worked shampoo gently through his tight curls and into his scalp. He'd tried to grow the top for months, but it snapped when it got to an inch or so. He thought of Kelly then, and her soaked hair that would have smelled of the river.

They say that a person's olfactory senses can bring back memories, sharp and clear. Whenever he smelled whisky and Chanel cologne, he found himself back in his room that night, so many years ago, aboard the HMS *Iron Duke*. Unable to fight back. Unable to say no.

He squirted shower gel onto the rough edge of a sponge and scrubbed hard at his skin until he turned red. He rinsed off the suds and stepped out, cleared the mist from the medicine-cabinet mirror with his hand and looked at himself. The tiredness didn't yet show under his penny-coloured eyes, but he knew it would come in time. If the case went unsolved. He breathed in deep, then let it go. He felt better after the shower, as though the water and suds had washed away more than sweat and dead skin.

He rubbed cocoa butter into his still damp skin and walked through to the bedroom with the clothes he'd strewn on the bathroom floor. He fished into the back pocket of his Armani jeans and sat on the bed as he took out his phone. Three new emails and a missed call from an unknown number. He hated that.

He slipped into some loose-fitting loungewear, and for a moment, he felt guilty. For Nick and for Sarah, but mostly because he knew his time would have been better spent back at the incident room. He knew there was nothing he could really achieve until tomorrow, but he wanted to be there. He'd been promised the digital analysis from Kelly's phone.

Nick walked in the bedroom, face red, eyes wet. 'I'm sorry,' he said as he got down on his knees in front of Barclay.

'What's wrong, Nick?' Barclay held his husband close to him. 'What's happening? You can talk to me.'

'Nothing,' he said. He pushed Barclay away and looked up at him. 'I'm sorry I'm a crank. I love you and I love Sarah, and I love our home. I just feel so tense... I'm still trying to work out why.'

'Do you want to talk? It might help.'

'Not now,' Nick said. 'Dinner will be ready. Sarah's starving, she keeps telling me.'

'Got to love a girl with an appetite.'

Nick laughed. 'You can talk to me, too,' he said. 'I'm sorry.' Nick stood up, wiped his face dry and walked to the door. 'You coming down?'

'I'll be down in a minute.'

Alone in the room, Barclay threw himself back onto the bed and let out a long breath, relieved they'd cleared the air between them. Still, he wished the soft quilt would suck him in and completely cover him. He could sleep for a week. He thought again of Kelly in a refrigerated unit on a metal tray in the morgue.

He wondered whether they'd closed her eyes or left them open.

—

Barclay didn't sleep that night, and at last, when the sparrows chirped somewhere in the trees at the back of the garden, he rolled out of bed. His mum would say, 'Morning chorus is coffee for the soul. Sent straight from God.' He would settle for actual coffee.

Nick lay on his back, and for a moment, Barclay saw the man he'd fallen in love with. His face was kind and his expression soft. Barclay missed the man he'd married. The one who'd hung feeders in the garden so the birds had something to eat all year round. The man who'd once booked a cabin in the middle of the Lake District for New Year's Eve, and they'd spent it alone. Kissing, walking on the fells, and fucking. He didn't recognise the man who flew off the handle and cried apologies on his knees. Barclay needed to figure out what was going on.

He snatched his phone from the charging cradle and pushed it into the pocket of his grey dressing gown. Downstairs, he turned on the percolator and waited as it bubbled and dripped down into his favourite mug. He couldn't say why it was his favourite. It was a white mug with a chip on the handle, nothing special about it.

He checked his phone as he sipped at the black coffee. Another two missed calls from an unknown number and three text messages. De Silva. His heart pounded in his chest.

Tried to call you earlier, are you awake? at nine last night.

Then, *Message me when you're awake* just after two this morning.

And another, *I'm on my way to the office. Can you meet me?* sent just ten minutes ago.

Barclay's head was fuzzy and dull. *Coffee first.* It was Barclay's belief that coffee fixes everything. *Don't run when she clicks. She's not your boss any more.* He'd eaten scrambled egg on toast, showered, and left before Nick was awake.

De Silva was already outside headquarters when he arrived. He was glad to see she had on a thick coat and an umbrella to protect her from the rain. He looked at his watch. It wasn't even six. He climbed out of the car and headed to her.

'What couldn't wait?'

'I'm sorry, did I wake you up?'

'Yes,' he said. He wasn't sure why he lied, why he wanted her to feel some small amount of guilt over that at least.

'Sorry,' she said again. 'Shall we go inside?'

Barclay nodded, swiped his pass on the panel next to the door and pushed it open. She entered first, ducked under his arm and waited at the receptionist's desk. 'Morning, San. Could I have a visitor badge for Winifred de Silva? She's a guest of O'Brien's.'

'Morning. Access to anywhere?'

'No,' he said. 'That won't be necessary.'

San handed de Silva a lanyard and security card. She slipped it over her neck. 'I had a thought last night,' she said.

'O'Brien will be pleased.' He hadn't taken the sarcasm from his voice quite as well as he imagined. They headed toward the lift.

'So her eyes were white from being in the water.'

'Yeah, I know.'

'Except she wasn't in the Mersey long enough for the water to have turned them white.'

Barclay stopped walking. 'What are you saying?'

'She was dumped just before the body was found – we saw that on the CCTV. There's no way the water could have done that to her eyes.'

'So, she was kept in water before she was dumped. Is that what you're saying?'

'No.' The lift pinged and the doors slid open. 'I did some research this morning, just from some of my old journals and volumes.'

Barclay imagined her sat there, dust pluming from the old books she'd not touched in months, maybe years. She'd relied on instinct and ability, not the knowledge of others.

'It's so obvious. You know this, I know this.' She laughed. 'Eyes don't just turn white from prolonged exposure to water. They turn hazy after just a few hours following death. Opaque over the next two days. So he's killing them quicker than we thought, but keeping hold of them for a bit longer.'

'We need that preliminary report from Brennan,' Barclay said.

'And the crime scene photos.'

Chapter Ten

He needed to open a window. The bedroom smelled like cigarettes and beer, and on the towel next to him, the faint reek of cum. He hadn't been able to stop last night, but sometimes touching himself in that way was needed. He was told it was a bad thing as a kid. That some people would say it was naughty, an evil thing that the devil made him do. The thing that whores and queers did. Bad, they'd said, but only when he did it alone.

But it feels so good.

The room spun and tilted around him as he opened his eyes. He was thankful that the curtains were still drawn. He could hear the rain like stones against the window and he rolled over to look at the time, felt sick rise into his chest but swallowed it down. The old digital clock's red LED lights flashed *10.13*. Late for work again. His boss, with her mullet cut and Hush Puppies shoes, would love this. She'd probably be waiting with his P45, a smile on her stupid face.

He rolled off the bed, kicked over a half-empty can of Stella Artois. It fizzed and sat on the top of the rough, brown carpet. The drawings he'd made with pencils caught his eye from the far wall, where they fluttered in a draught from somewhere. That place he'd hated, the place that was so bad he could only ever scribble it in dark pencil. He'd hated it, but he was obsessed with it. With the memories. With the pain.

He looked away, ashamed of them. There was stuff everywhere. Bottles, cans, food wrappers, dirty clothes. He needed to do a run to the baggy.

You'll have to now. That was your only clean towel.

He grabbed it anyway and stumbled through to the bathroom. The bathtub was still full from days ago, the cold of it stinging as he reached down to pull the plug. It still smelled like lavender bubble bath, and he thought of her there, her eyes wide under the water. He shook the memory from his head. The bathwater swirled down the drain, strands of hair along with it. He'd need to clean it later. Properly. With bleach.

He showered quickly, dried himself on the already-damp towel and pulled on some battered jeans, splattered with stains from God knows where and God knows when.

The state of you. You look a mess.

He had to pull hard on the front door so that it would close properly. He hadn't bothered reminding his landlord it still needed fixing. The concrete stairs and landing were freezing cold and smelled of piss.

He walked out of the building and climbed into his battered old RAV4. It was blue once, but now it was scratched and grazed and rusted.

He found his phone in the drink well and turned it on, an older iPhone he'd bought in Cash Converters on London Road for twenty quid. The screen was cracked from that time he tried to update it and it wouldn't work. He'd thrown it against the wall. Three missed calls, a voicemail, and a text – all from Jackie. The text read: *Meet me at head office. Need to talk.*

He flicked on the radio. A news announcement. '*The body of Kelly Stack was found early yesterday morning, and Merseyside Police say they're working every line of inquiry they're given. Kelly's body is the third found in as many mon—*'

He turned off the radio and smiled. *They found her. So what? Doesn't mean they'll find you.* The thought of her made him hard. What they'd done together, how she'd begged him for it and he'd finally given it to her. She'd cried, like. They always do. But she'd wanted it. She'd wanted it and he'd wanted it. He'd given into her. To himself. He wondered then whether the old bird on the ground floor had heard them at it. That made him harder.

You had to punish her. For trying to leave again.

The traffic lights turned red, and that's when he saw her. She was gliding down the road from the direction of Everton and Walton in her school uniform. It must have been lunchtime, or else she was bunking off.

What do we have here?

Her hair was blonde, bright in the gloom of the day, and tied back in a ponytail. He caught her looking at him through the windscreen, her eyes met his and he held his breath. The way she wore her skirt, high on her thighs just for him. It was cold out, but she'd undone the top three buttons on her blouse, her blazer tossed over her shoulder.

She wants you.

He was hard again. He needed to get to know her, and then he'd take her.

She'll get you into trouble…

Chapter Eleven

'I'm sure the SOCOs will have uploaded the photography by now,' Barclay said. De Silva sat next to him and he was sure he caught the faint smell of alcohol. Could be Listerine. He couldn't believe he hadn't caught this. It was so blatant. This is why she's here. This is why O'Brien wanted her around. She's good at this. *Better at this than me.*

'How are things?' de Silva asked.

It came out of nowhere and surprised him. He fidgeted, then sat up straight, to attention, and said, 'What do you mean?' He could have kicked himself. He knew what she meant, he just couldn't think quick enough.

'You know, with Nick and Sarah? Your life away from all of this.'

Barclay tapped at the keyboard and waited for the pictures to load. 'We're all fine. Sarah was six last week. Doing well at school. We think she's going to be an artist.'

'I remember you saying she likes her drawing.'

'And colouring in the wallpaper. Nick was fuming. She's a little cow.' He laughed. 'Knows her own mind already.'

'She sounds amazing.'

'I've got some new photos here – hold on.' He fished into his pocket for his phone but then the crime scene folder popped up on the computer screen. He remembered why they were there and put his phone away.

He flicked through close-ups of Kelly's body, hands, legs and feet until finally he found her face. Her eyes were fully opaque. 'You were right,' he said.

'She was dead a day or two before the body was dumped.' De Silva sat back in her seat.

'So, why's he keeping her for twenty-four to forty-eight hours before moving her...?' Barclay said to the screen. To Kelly, as though she could tell him the answer.

De Silva's lips were a straight line. 'Because he couldn't bear to part with her.'

Silence.

She continued, 'You find out why he couldn't let her go, you find out everything about him.' She stood and paced. Thinking. 'I'm going to be honest here, I don't think you're going to need me around much longer. You're heading in the right direction.'

'I haven't done anything.' Shame made the skin on his neck and cheeks flush hot. 'You got all of this, not me.' He realised he sounded desperate, pleading almost, as though he needed her. He'd never wanted her to go in the first place.

Things happen. Things happened to her, to her loved ones.

He'd tried to understand it these last three months and had failed. 'Not that I can't cope without you.' He wanted to say that it had been nice, like old times, but couldn't. There was too much there between them, unspoken.

'It's okay,' de Silva said. 'It's been like it was before.' She stopped pacing and looked at him. 'Do you want to talk? Doesn't have to be now.'

'O'Brien wants to see me.' Barclay held up his phone even though the screen was locked. 'I'm sorry.'

'No, no,' she said. 'Work first. I get it. Go on.'

'Talk when I get back?'

De Silva nodded. Her eyes were downcast, her face pale. She paced again. *She's hurt*, Barclay thought. He wanted to say that he was sorry, but it would have to wait. It would open up the can of worms between them and its contents would writhe.

O'Brien's office smelled like stale smoke and was thick with an air freshener that did nothing to mask it. Barclay coughed. He'd knocked and waited to be invited in, then stood there, hands behind his back until O'Brien said, 'Jesus, sit down will you? You're reminding me of my mother-in-law. You know, the night after I married my Kath, her mother came into our room and stood just like you did. We were up to all kinds, the usual newly-wed stuff. Threw holy water at us. I digress, I know. I'm guilty of it.'

'Did she think she was saving your mortal souls from sin, sir?'

'If only it were that simple, eh?' O'Brien cast his eyes down to his desk. Kelly's crime scene photographs across it, bloodless but raw like meat at a butcher's. Just last year, they would have made him balk. But now, things were different. He was different. They called it 'desensitisation', but he found these things no less shocking, no less horrific. He'd just learned to steel himself. 'How is she? De Silva, I mean.'

'Well, sir. She came back.'

O'Brien's eyes opened wide. 'And…?'

'And she seems invested,' Barclay said. He shifted in his chair, uncomfortable. He didn't want to overpromise or misread de Silva's intentions. She may have come back so that her life had at least one piece of closure. He didn't know for sure. 'In fact, there was a breakthrough.' Barclay told O'Brien about the discovery of Kelly's white eyes, and what it potentially meant for the case; Barclay told him of de Silva's insights into the mind of the killer.

O'Brien nodded, listening. 'But how is she?'

He got it now. Barclay had never seen this side of O'Brien before. The caring, protective father figure. He wondered whether she felt the same way. He'd always been warm to Barclay, asked him about his family, but professionally. Distantly. Like a senior officer should, Barclay had told himself. 'She seems well, sir. Capable and in the moment.'

'Good,' he said. 'Good, I'm glad.' O'Brien took a long, ragged breath that reminded Barclay of when he last saw his dad. In a hospital bed in the Royal, a mask over his mouth hissing air into his body. He'd held his dad's pale hand, bruised from a cannula, and watched a tear fall from his grey-blue eyes. He'd thought how they'd lost their sparkle. In the harsh white light of the hospital, they'd looked grey and dull. Like O'Brien's. They'd never had a great relationship, but in that moment, Barclay felt pity for the man that left his mum for another woman.

'Can I ask you a question, sir?'

O'Brien rolled his eyes and nodded. 'Fine, fine. Hurry up, I've got an appointment with Benson and Hedges and a security window.'

'Do you think that I'm incapable of solving this case? I mean from the get-go, before I had it, did you think I was capable? When these passed through Crosby and PVPU, you were on about de Silva and getting her back to work. Now I have them, you're even more determined to have her back.' He desperately wanted to ask, *Am I not good enough?*

'You want me to massage your ego while we have a killer on the loose, is that it?' O'Brien stood up from his desk, took out a packet of cigarettes from his pocket.

It was an insecurity that had plagued him his whole life. He had never felt good enough. Not for his parents, not for his friends, not at school, and not in the navy.

'I'll bite, Sergeant,' O'Brien said. 'You were headhunted from uniform and trained by me. Appointed to detective by me.' There was a long pause where neither of them spoke. 'So, Sergeant, get back to work.'

He wasn't sure that was an answer, not a full one anyway. But, with O'Brien being how he was, it would have to do. For now.

'There's one last thing I needed to ask you.'

'See, you really are a detective.' O'Brien smiled, his teeth stained yellow. 'What is it?'

'Is there anyone you know at the coroner's office? I really need to get Kelly's post-mortem sped up somehow. I can't move the case forward without knowing exactly what happened to her. If it matches Danielle and Lynsey, we know we're after the same guy. For certain, I mean. A pattern isn't enough for me. Not when he's out there, probably looking for his next one. Could have even found her.'

'Okay, okay,' O'Brien said. 'Enough with the dramatics, please. I get it.' He took a deep breath and thought. 'I know Scott Grindon over there. He'll more than likely perform it himself. I'll give him a call. When do you need it?'

'Yesterday, sir.'

O'Brien chuckled and it sounded wet, like he needed to clear his throat. 'Fine, fine. I'll see what I can do. Now get out of here before I incriminate you.' He held up his box of cigarettes.

Barclay felt foolish. He took the stairs down to the basement, hoping the shame would disappear from his face. *He's your superior. Not your dad.* He knew that O'Brien owed him nothing, least of all validation.

There was laughter from the incident room when Barclay stepped out of the stairwell. De Silva's laughter. He'd not heard it in such a long time and it made him smile.

'Oh, here he is!' Holden shouted. 'O'Brien's boy wonder.' Holden headed up the digital forensics team for Merseyside Police, even though he dressed like someone attending a comic-con.

'Hardly.'

'Don't be modest.' Holden threw an arm around Barclay's shoulders and he could smell the sweat, sweet but sickly.

'I'm not.'

'He is,' de Silva said. 'He's doing a great job.' She looked away from him quickly and added, 'Holden and me were just catching up. The world of digital forensics really is as boring as I thought.'

Barclay willed his face not to blush, but wasn't sure if he'd manage to maintain a cool exterior. He gestured to the laptop in Holden's hands. 'I take it you've got something for m— us?'

'Not much,' Holden admitted. His countenance changed. His smile faded from his eyes and they narrowed behind his thick glasses. He wiped his hands on his bright shirt, something with cartoon characters on it that Barclay didn't recognise. 'There were a few calls to and from a phone number that wasn't saved into her contact list.

We tried the number. Disconnected. Unregistered, too. Probably a pay-and-go SIM and could be nothing.'

'So not much means nothing?' Barclay said. He needed a break, something to click in the case beyond the fact that Kelly had died days before she was left at the dock. Square one.

'Well, no. If I meant nothing, I'd have said nothing.' Holden tapped a few keys on his laptop and pulled up an image. 'Recognise this?'

Barclay leaned in closer. The brown outline of a bear's head and two green trees either side. 'No,' Barclay said. 'What is it?'

'It's an app we found on her phone.' Holden tapped a few more keys. 'We couldn't find it on any app store. We're going to need to look into it. Getting into it has been difficult, though. Not like an app I've seen before. Whoever designed it wanted to keep their doors locked up tight.'

Kelly's phone had been found in some grass off Headbolt Lane. But the way it was found… the placement of it so perfectly on top of some flattened grass, it had always felt to Barclay as though the phone was placed purposefully. If it wasn't with Kelly, she couldn't be tracked. The killer was smart enough to have known that.

'Every time we break through a wall, we come up against more encryption. Layers and layers. We're peeling it back slowly.'

'How long do you think?'

'I couldn't say, I'm sorry.' Holden's thin-lipped smile was sincere. 'I've got people working on it right now. It could be in the next five minutes, it could be a week.'

'Do you know anything else about it?' De Silva asked.

'We think we found its name,' Holden said.

'What is it?'

'The Woulds,' he said. '*W-O-U-L-D-S*. Not like the woods, as in a forest.'

Barclay felt de Silva's eyes on him and he looked back. She frowned, and he could sense the thoughts ticking away behind her eyes. There was no connection to anything they'd seen before. DFU hadn't found a similar app on Danielle or Lynsey's phones.

'When you search phones, you can find what was on it previously, can't you?' Barclay asked. 'What may have been deleted?'

'Yes, we would do a full scan of the device. A deep dive if you like.'

'And nothing like this was found on Lynsey Renshaw's phone?'

'That's right,' Holden said. 'Look, this is probably nothing. It could be a random social-media-type thing. App stores are full of them.' Holden looked at his watch. 'I'll get back to it and give you a ring when I've cracked it.'

'Thank you,' Barclay said.

'Ms de Silva, lovely to catch up as always,' Holden said. 'Come and visit us upstairs soon. The lads would love to see you.'

'Nice to see you, Holden,' she said. 'When this is all over, we'll go for a drink.'

'Sounds good.'

When this is over. Barclay felt hopeful that she would stay and see it through for O'Brien, whatever he had in mind. It felt so unusual though, to bend the rules for de Silva. What was his endgame? He couldn't guess, didn't want to. He was just thankful that de Silva was here. But that app gave him pause.

The Woulds, he thought. *Would what?*

Chapter Twelve

De Silva put down the file and rolled her head to stretch out her neck, sore from looking down at the pages.

'You all caught up?' Barclay nodded to the pile of printed case files sat on the desk in front of de Silva. She hadn't been reading. She'd been faking it and instead wondered whether the moment had gone, whether O'Brien's interruption earlier had cost them both the opportunity to speak. For her to offload about Ritchie, and for him to vent whatever it was he needed to say.

'Almost,' she said. She wished to God none of this had happened, that she could have gone on with her life as it was. *And what was that, girl?* Being drunk by 10 a.m. and spending the rest of the day in a black pit? Letting herself go until she was almost unrecognisable, even to herself? 'I just have Danielle's file to read over, but I'm still stuck.'

'With what?' Barclay moved from behind the desk he'd made his own. Mug, stationery, it was just missing a photograph of his lovely family. Something that was always just out of her reach.

When she and Ritchie were trying for a baby, the doctor had told her in no uncertain terms, 'There's a twenty-nine per cent success rate for someone your age.' She'd not turned thirty at the time, and to her, the numbers seemed unjust.

'You okay?' Barclay asked.

'Yeah,' she said. 'Yeah, sorry. I'm fine.' She decided to lie. 'I was thinking about Lynsey, the first victim. I've got many questions I need answering, but the thing I can't get away from is the moment she was taken.'

'Oh yeah?'

'She left her friends. They all went home. She didn't. Why? Did she plan on going somewhere else? Meeting someone? Did she have other friends in the area? None of that's in here.'

Barclay shook his head. 'Been thinking the same thing.'

'Something doesn't feel right.' People had laughed about her feelings all through her career, those straight, white men who had had no real need for instinct their entire lives, but Barclay seemed earnest. His nod was one of encouragement, a please-do-continue. 'The files here, I noticed something. Lynsey had a mobile phone, didn't she?' she said. 'You ordered the digital forensics analysis of Kelly's phone, didn't you?'

'Yeah,' Barclay said. 'I requested it after we found her body. When the case came to CID. It was sat in the lab. Crosby never asked for it to be sent anywhere else.'

A miss from Crosby? The man had a stellar career, an impeccable reputation, so why not follow it through? De Silva stood up and looked Barclay in the eye. 'I've known Crosby for years, I'm not saying he's been perfect. You'd know more than I would recently, but it's not like him to neglect something like this.'

'I don't really know him at all. Worked with him once or twice, but that's it.' Silence sat in the space between them. 'Do we go to O'Brien with this?'

'No!' She realised she'd shouted and lowered her voice. 'No, no. The analysis has been done, and besides, if I know O'Brien, he's probably already got plans for Crosby.' She sighed. 'This case.' De Silva shook her head. 'No matter how many years I've done this job, I'll never get it. Why anyone would harm a kid? Or how they could?'

'Paedophiles,' Barclay said. 'There's the everyday bad shit we deal with, then there's them.'

'Ephebophile,' she said. 'He has sexual interest in those aged fifteen to nineteen. He straddles that line between legality and illegality.'

'Fifteen and dead feels pretty fucking illegal to me.'

De Silva nodded. 'So what does this tell us about him?'

Barclay bit his bottom lip and looked to the photos of the three girls on the boards across the room. He seemed unsure, almost embarrassed to answer.

De Silva held his gaze. 'Couple their age with the blonde hair, the similar features, what else do we learn about him?'

He twisted the wedding ring on his finger. 'He's definitely focused on one girl. Whether it's one of our victims or someone else, like you said. He knows them then, doesn't he? Or gets to know them. That's how he knew Lynsey wouldn't go straight home after leaving her friends. How he got her.'

'He could know them, yeah, in the sense that he's seen them around, but we don't know that yet,' de Silva said.

His phone rang. 'O'Brien. Again.'

'I remember those days well.'

'I'll be right back.'

'Yeah, okay.'

De Silva paced when Barclay left the room. Her phone bleeped in her pocket. A text from Crosby:

> Can I see you? Usual place?

She replied yes, and fired off a text to Barclay, said she'd run out to get some coffees, knowing perfectly well that he'd question why she didn't use the machine in the office. She'd think of that excuse later. That was her habit whenever she saw him. Excuses and lies.

—

Crosby was sat in the back corner of the Caffè Nero on Bold Street. It was busy, but there was no one waiting to order. De Silva ordered two Americanos and took the seat opposite him. He looked awful. She wondered whether that was what people thought about her, too. Skinny and pale. *Death on legs.*

'You can't just message me whenever you'd like, you know.'

'What?'

'You just click your fingers and think I'll come running.' *And I did.*

Tears brimmed in his red eyes. 'I know, I know. I'm sorry.'

He reached across the table to touch her hand. She snatched it away, hid it under the table on her lap and looked about to see if anyone had noticed. Nobody had. 'Don't do that.'

'Please.' De Silva had never seen anyone actually plead before. He was desperate. He needed her and she wanted to give in to him. Again.

'No,' she said. 'That's done. Why did you want to see me?'

'Because I messed up the case so badly. I let them all down. Lynsey, Danielle, Kelly. God knows who else. I couldn't connect the dots with it all.'

'Will you stop snivelling? What's happened to you?'

'Ann's left me,' he said.

De Silva's mouth opened but nothing came out. She hadn't expected this. She had always supposed it would be a matter of time before Ann left him. There was a period, years ago, when they would all go out for dinner or drinks, the four of them. They'd been close. Then de Silva and Crosby got too close after work. Too close again in a cubicle at the Ship and Mitre, and again and again in various hotels around town.

She had craved Crosby once, felt the need for him to touch her so strongly. At first, she didn't understand why she felt so much for him, that burn of sexual attraction deep in the pit of her body. But then, she understood it. After they'd finished one night in a meeting room, as Crosby put on his top and she did up her zip, she realised that the thing she wanted wasn't Crosby's hands. It was anyone's hands.

Ritchie hadn't wanted to have sex in months. Something in him had changed, and that fire between them died, starved of oxygen.

Ann must have known what was happening, de Silva had always thought. And Ritchie... well, Ritchie happened.

'I'm sorry,' she said. Crosby sat in front of her, broken. Both of their marriages in ruins. Her next words could shatter him, but she needed to know what he knew. 'I can meet you later to talk about it, but I've got other things to focus on right now.'

He wiped snot from his nose with a napkin and didn't look up from the table. 'Go on... How's it going?'

'You know I can't tell you that.'

'Come off it – this is me you're talking to.'

'I know that your work was slipping, Mike. The report says the prints the lab found on Lynsey's phone couldn't have been hers, but didn't say why.'

'Too big. Probably a man's prints,' he said. 'Didn't match anything on record.' He took a quick sip of his coffee and wiped at his eyes again. 'We sent the phone off to Digital Forensics for them to take a look at it.'

'No, you didn't,' de Silva said. 'Barclay did that.'

His mouth formed a small 'o', and de Silva couldn't read his face. 'What did they find?'

'Nothing of any interest,' she said.

'Now I know I sent Danielle's phone off,' Crosby said. 'That's in the report.'

Something was going on here, de Silva knew. These inconsistencies in Crosby's approach to the investigation had had a detrimental impact on the case. *It's good you've quit*, she thought. She wanted to share that with him, but instead she said, 'Come back to the station and show me the bits that are missing from your reports, Mike. I need it.'

'I can't.' He looked down again. 'I've quit.'

She felt for him. This job had been his life for so many years, and he'd thrown it all away. She wanted to tell him that she was sorry to hear it, but if she entertained any warmth to him, she wasn't sure where they would end up. She couldn't do that again. 'Can you get your emails on your phone?'

'Not this one, no.' He held up his personal phone. Not the one he used to message her from. 'Work phone's been handed back. Warrant card, too.'

Jesus. Crosby hadn't wasted any time. For a fleeting moment, she caught herself in the act of preserving his reputation, his character; of wanting to go to O'Brien and argue his case, to beg him to ask Crosby to come back.

She'd defended Crosby before. Countless times with other bobbies, and that one time in the toilets at Baby Squid on Castle Street. Ann had known then that Mick had been unfaithful and de Silva had talked her around. Said it wasn't possible. She saw how much it was tearing Ann apart.

She'd promised herself that night that they'd not see each other again, not like that. Not sweaty and moaning behind closed doors. They'd lasted two weeks.

She'd never told Crosby about that conversation, and Ann had never mentioned it again. De Silva looked at Crosby now and he looked smaller, older. Less like him, like the man who'd gripped her and made her cry out his name.

'I'll sort it,' she said. 'But Mike, if there's anything you remember, you tell me. Anything that comes to you.'

'You wouldn't want to hear it.'

'About the case, I mean.'

He nodded and snorted a laugh from his nose. 'I know. I know.'

'I need to ask,' she said. 'Did you actually look at the victims? Think about why he was selecting them? How?'

'We didn't know at first. There was nothing linking them except their age. But two victims is a coincidence, isn't it?'

'And three is a pattern,' she said. 'Didn't it occur to you that they look alike?'

'No.'

Then it's a good job you've quit. 'I need to go.' De Silva stood up and headed for the door.

'Win,' he said. 'I'm sorry.' He took a deep breath and relaxed his face. 'About Ritchie.'

'Yeah,' she said. She was sorry, too.

When she got back to the office, she went straight upstairs to see Holden in the Digital Forensics Unit. It wasn't that she mistrusted Crosby, it was more that his behaviour seemed erratic. Unreasonable. It felt entirely feasible that he could have missed something.

Holden sat in an open-plan office. Some of his team looked up from their computers to say hello or smile at her. She recognised most of them, but there were a few fresh faces.

'Twice in one day,' Holden said as de Silva sat down next to him.

She leaned in close, elbows on his desk, and lowered her voice. 'Listen, I need you to check something for me.'

'Why does this feel a bit 007?'

'I need you to listen to what I'm about to say very carefully.'

'Oh shit,' he said. 'Nothing that follows that can ever be good.'

De Silva moved in even closer, almost to his ear, and said, 'I need you to get into the emails of an officer here.'

'De Silva!' he hissed. 'I can't do that. Do you suspect someone?'

'No,' she said. 'I just need to be sure that nothing was missed.'

'No way, de Silva. I respect you, but not this. Sorry.'

'How can I convince you?'

'You can guarantee I won't get the sack if I'm caught.' He put up his hands, as if by not touching the keyboard he'd set his mind. 'No, no. I can't. It's unethical. It's wrong.'

She said nothing, just stared at him.

'God's sake, de Silva. You know I can't deny that bloody face.' He turned back to his computer. 'Who is it?'

'Mike,' she said. 'Mike Crosby.'

Chapter Thirteen

The atmosphere between Barclay and de Silva strained under the weight of unspoken things. Like where de Silva had been, what she'd done while Barclay went to see Holden. Since she got back, de Silva had busied herself with Danielle MacDonald's case file, and Barclay sat behind his desk, tapping away at his keyboard. He didn't look up, couldn't bring himself to look at her. That same burn he felt in his chest when she didn't return his calls and texts was there again, and it raged.

He'd tried to call her so many times. It would ring for a few seconds, then go to answer phone. He imagined her sat there, watching his name on her screen, then pressing the big red *End Call* button. With each unanswered text, every dodged phone call, every time she pretended not to be home, Barclay felt more and more betrayed. He felt himself slip from worry and concern to sympathy, spiralling down until finally he hit the rocky bottom of his feelings for de Silva: hatred. Resentment. And in that deep dark place, his guilt took root.

He'd seen her leave the building from the window near O'Brien's desk. He knew instinctively that she'd purposely lied to him. *She must know that I know. Must be able to tell that something isn't right.* He took a deep breath, swallowed down his anxiety and said, 'Are we going to talk about it then?' Barclay didn't take his eyes from the computer.

De Silva put down the file. 'What do you mean?'

'No, don't do that.' Barclay slammed his hand down on the desk, a loud sound that was almost like a crack. 'Don't act like you don't know what I'm talking about.'

He felt so unlike himself, so angry. The old de Silva would have asked who the hell he thought he was speaking to, but instead she sat there quietly. It would all come out, and there was no way to stop it. His issues with her coming back to help him, the things that had gone unsaid. It wouldn't be the right time, not the right way, and it would ruin the progress they'd made together. *She's just started thinking of you as a good detective. You're going to mess all of that up.*

'Why did you lie to me?' He looked at her then. Her face was expressionless, her shoulders hunched. He thought for a moment that she looked embarrassed, ashamed. He wondered whether that was because she'd frozen him out. He pressed on. 'You didn't bring any coffee back, so I can only deduce that you didn't want me to know where you were going.'

'And you were right,' she said. 'Because it's none of your business.' There was an edge to her voice, a frown over her blue eyes, a readiness to fight. 'I don't need to explain myself to you.'

'That badge around your neck doesn't entitle you to swan in and out any time you like.'

'Why don't you tell me what's actually wrong? You're not this wound up because I went out of the office without telling you. And let me remind you I'm the DCI here, not you.'

'You're no DCI.' He spat out the words. 'You're just a civilian with a visitor badge.'

De Silva's face turned to stone.

'I knew this would happen,' he said. 'I told O'Brien it would go this way. I said, "She won't be ready," and here we are. You shouldn't be here when you're on a leave of absence until... God knows when...'

'Yeah, I suppose you would think that,' she spat back. 'Because that's what good little boys do, isn't it? Follow orders.'

'I follow rules,' he said.

'Oh shut up, you follow orders.' Her voice boomed loud in the basement incident room. 'What rule says that a former detective can come back and work on an important active case? What rule says that you should babysit her and compromise your own career?'

'Compromise my career?' He shouted now, too. 'The only career I see compromised is your own. You're lucky Holden rang me instead of O'Brien.'

Her face fell. 'What?'

'He rang me before you even set foot in the lift back down here. I'm going to have to ask you to leave the building now,' he said. 'I'm speaking with O'Brien about this whole mess you've made. I won't work on this case any longer if you're involved. I just won't.'

'Barclay...' de Silva altered her tone. Lower, softer.

'No,' he said. He walked toward the door, held it open and waited there. He couldn't look at her face, he felt disgusted in her actions, ashamed that he'd ever thought of her as someone to aspire to be. 'You think you can walk in and pick up where you left off. Well, you can't. *You* left.'

'Just get it out, Barclay,' she said. 'Whatever you've got to say, say it and let's get it over with.'

He slammed the office door and yelled, 'You left!' He put his hand to his forehead, a shield from the harm his words might do.

'My husband died!' she screamed. 'Move out of the way. I'll go.'

He ignored her. 'I respected you. Looked up to you. You were my...' He felt embarrassed to say it out loud and hoped his face hadn't flushed and betrayed him. 'I needed you.'

'I needed to grieve.'

'All the ale helping you grieve, is it? Or does it just make everything numb and manageable? Because God knows being cold and numb is better than feeling anything for anyone, isn't it?' He hadn't meant to say it, but it flew out so quickly.

'You what?' Her eyes were narrow now, thin lines that seethed at him.

'I'm—'

'Move!'

He pulled open the door again, and she ducked under his arm and stormed out. She wiped at her face and headed down the corridor to the lift.

It felt done to him, that he'd destroyed any trace of friendship that may have remained between them. He felt a weight on his shoulders and his back; those girls on that evidence board might never get justice, their families may never know peace.

Chapter Fourteen

O'Brien wasn't in his office when de Silva arrived. She had knocked, but when she heard nothing from him, she decided to let herself in and sit down. If she waited in the corridor and gave herself the time to think, she knew that tears would come, and that wouldn't do.

Inside the office, she could smell his cigarettes and the cotton-scent air freshener he'd used; it smelled nice. Familiar. Comforting. The small window was ajar, the blinds twitching in a slight breeze. Traces of ash smudged the windowsill. She could see his fingerprint in one of them.

Her row with Barclay had been building since yesterday, she knew that. She also knew that part of the reason she'd avoided Barclay's calls for so long was because she didn't want to explain herself to him; didn't want to have to say 'I'm fine' when she wasn't. Didn't want him to see her weak. She hadn't expected it to happen like that.

She realised then that her hands were shaking. She couldn't remember the last time she'd raised her voice. Her life since Ritchie had been uneventful; she'd been lost in the quiet that follows the death of a loved one where nobody wants to bother you or cause more pain. Everyone, she realised, except O'Brien and Barclay. They'd kept at her. Tried to make sure she was okay. Even Laney, her sister, had backed off.

In truth, Laney stepped away years ago. Way before de Silva's mum went into the care home, before the stroke and the falls and the calls from neighbours at three in the morning. She'd left everything to de Silva ever since their dad had died. She had walked away and lived her life, and de Silva was chained to it all. *For God's sake, girl. She's your mum, not something you're chained to.* She felt horrible, sickened at herself.

Barclay had accused her of leaving. She hadn't officially left her job or the police, but she hadn't exactly been open to returning to work. She couldn't face the 'Oh, there she is, poor de Silva', or the speculation about what had happened. She knew why Ritchie did what he did, she felt it swell in the pit of her stomach like a black hole: he'd found out about her affair with Crosby. It dawned on her the day of the funeral.

His mum, Sheila, a little woman with grey hair. In her black dress, she could have been out of a black-and-white film, where no one was ever happy and they never turned on the lights. She'd wondered whether Sheila would ever be happy again.

'Why did he do it, Win?' she'd asked. She wiped at her eyes with a white handkerchief, then tucked it into the sleeve of her blazer. 'He loved you,' she said. 'He loved his work, his mates. I don't see why.'

She wanted to say that they may never know why, that sometimes people have secret struggles they know nothing about, but she knew Ritchie like the back of her hand. They'd grown up together on the streets of Kirkby, and yes, they went their own ways when he was shipped off to some special school for troubled kids. But they always found their way back to each other. *Not any more*, she'd thought. She opened her mouth to speak to Sheila when she saw Crosby leaned against the side of his car. He wore black like everyone else, he could have blended in easily, but she felt him watching her and she watched him back.

You. It was you. It was both of them. He did what he did because of them, because of their affair. Her seasoned-detective brain kicked in. Had Ritchie noticed a text message, a missed call that could have suggested anything? No, they kept in touch only through their work phones. That was risky in itself, but what's a disciplinary when the other option is the death of a marriage and a relationship they'd spent decades building?

She'd wondered whether Crosby had thought the same at that exact moment, when their eyes locked across the still-open grave of Richard James de Silva. It pulled at her, like the hole in her stomach, she could feel it writhing below her feet and waiting for her. She wanted to succumb, to jump in with Ritchie and lie there while they threw earth over them both. She'd loved him. She'd slept with someone else and she'd lost Ritchie. And what she'd done meant that Ritchie's mum had lost him too, his cousins and his family and friends.

Sheila had turned away to talk to someone else, someone she might get some sense out of. In de Silva's experience, funerals were strange. They were not really a celebration of life, though some pretended that they were. They were the last agonising hours of a drawn-out official process.

The death came first, the reporting of it second, then the paperwork and organising; the phone calls and letters and emails and sympathy cards. The post-mortem and the investigation. The instructions to not send flowers. The priest and the passages and the plot. She thought, it's a lay-by on the way to the actual grief, which only comes when you try to eat eggs on a Sunday morning, or call to your friend's for a cuppa, or comb your hair in the bathroom mirror. When you try to live your normal life without them.

It dawned on her then. Barclay wasn't mad that she had left work; he was mad because he felt as though de Silva had abandoned him. 'Jesus.' She told herself that no, she shouldn't take that on. That she was not responsible for his hurt feelings.

She wanted to go back down to the incident room, to just look at him and tell him she was sorry. She'd spent her career placating the feelings of men, it was so engrained in her. She didn't even feel two ways about it any more. It was the usual way. *Men never stop needing a mum to kiss their grazes and plaster their cuts.* They never stop needing to feel like they matter to someone.

She wondered whether that's how Ritchie felt in his final moments. Whether, when the belt pulled tight and his chest ached for air, he'd wanted his mum to make it all right again; or whether, in agony, he'd thought of his wife.

The tide of her anxieties swept in again and her head went light, her mouth dry. *Breathe. Just breathe.*

She felt exhausted and remembered that there was one last bottle of wine under the kitchen sink, but she'd stop for more on the way home. She needed it. Deserved it.

—

O'Brien never did show up, so de Silva decided to head home. As she pushed open the front door, she felt the cold of the house rush toward her, unwelcoming. On the drive home, she had the news station on. A reporter said, '...*is that all three of the victims were almost identical. They looked the same! Look at them. Go online, on social media, and look at their photographs. Tell me you don't see it...'*

She turned off the radio. The media were on to it now, too. She wanted to call Barclay, give him the heads-up, but thought better of it.

She realised as she approached the house that she'd forgotten to switch the heating on through the app before she got in the car and drove through rush-hour traffic. She'd fought off the tears and was thankful that she'd managed to keep them at bay. At the command-centre reception desk, she'd briefly spoken to a young man she didn't recognise and returned her visitor pass.

'Will you need it again tomorrow?' His face was expressionless, a clear smooth mask that gave nothing away.

'No.' She'd left the building and didn't look back.

She went to the thermostat and turned it on high. She didn't care about the rising energy bills right then, she just needed to feel warm. O'Brien hadn't turned up to his office, and she assumed he'd left for the day. She put her phone on silent and pulled a blanket around her shoulders and slumped into the couch. She didn't feel like drinking any more, despite the two bottles she'd got from the corner shop; didn't want to make dinner or watch telly. Instead, she stared at the wall, a dusty-looking blue that Ritchie had chosen. The only decision he'd made about the house's decor. It was chipped and she'd marked it when she moved the couch around. An attempt to change things up a bit. She'd pushed it back to its original position after fifteen minutes.

Her eyes felt heavy and stung. She rubbed them and thought about asking Laney to come over for dinner and a chat, or Chris, her best friend since high school. She'd not seen him since the funeral. That was a pattern in her life. Everyone showed up for her then and she turned her back on them all. Guilt, she decided. If she looked any one of them in the eyes, they'd know the horrible, stinking truth. That she was responsible for her husband's death; her and Crosby.

She couldn't say how it started. A flirtatious comment here, a slight touch there; it must have started slowly, almost unnoticeable. The first time they'd kissed, she felt horrible. She'd Listerine'd for ten minutes, thinking Ritchie might somehow be able to taste another man on her tongue. Maybe he had.

She tried not to think about it, to not let her mood sink even lower. Enough had happened already that day. She'd caused it all. She wasn't sure what Barclay would do about what she'd asked Holden, or how far Holden had gotten with her request before his conscience had caught up with him. He lived by the book, Barclay, and never deviated from it. It was his world and his world was structured.

They were inescapably different the pair of them, and she supposed that was why she enjoyed working with him, why they worked so well together. Opposite sides of the coin, maybe. But right then, she felt like a penny to Barclay's fifty-quid note. Worthless.

She took out her phone and ordered chicken chow mein and egg fried rice, some spring rolls and seaweed from Jade Garden. She'd keep half of it for lunch tomorrow, the half that Ritchie would have eaten. Uber Eats said her order would be there in one hour. Enough time to have a shower and get into some pyjamas.

De Silva drew the living-room curtains and switched on the lamps, thankful the place was finally heating up, and walked up the stairs. As she crossed the landing, she felt the left side of her body prick, as though the banister was electrically charged. She saw it flash in her mind, his face, him rocking on the belt. The crack as it snapped and the dull thud as his body hit the carpet. He didn't move. She didn't move. The stillness had felt like hours.

She held her breath and hurried across the landing and into the bathroom, and in the safety of the shower cubicle, she finally breathed again. She rubbed at her upper arms, a method her therapist had taught her to ease out of her anxious state. 'It'll defuse your brain's fear centres,' she was told. 'It'll promote soothing.' Sometimes it worked, sometimes it didn't. She was pleased that on that particular night it did.

Her food came thirty minutes early – she barely heard the doorbell over the hairdryer. 'Thank you,' she said and closed the door. She poured a large glass of Malbec and didn't wait for her food to cool down before she started eating. It burned the roof of her mouth, but she didn't care.

Later, when the food was gone and the dirty dishes were left in the sink and de Silva's mouth and teeth were stained from the wine, she sat waiting. She'd wanted to speak to him about it all, the man she'd craved, to get it out in the open, and right then seemed as good a time as any. She wasn't that pissed, she could still string a sentence together. By the time the doorbell rang for the second time that night, she'd drunk two more glasses and opened another bottle.

Chapter Fifteen

The bleach made him retch. He'd used too much of it, more than the bottle said to. If anyone came sniffing around, he couldn't leave any scent for them to follow; no hairs, no blood. Nothing.

The underwear was different. He put them in a ziplocked freezer bag and put them with the others in a petty-cash tin in the broken drawer under his bed, underneath the old, unusable now, porn mags.

He scrubbed the walls of the bath until his fingers throbbed and his hands cramped, but he was used to hard physical work.

Once the bath had been cleaned, he threw the cloths and scrubbing brush into a bin bag. He found an old razor, the blades orange from rust, and shaped the hairs on his cheeks and neck into a tidy-ish beard. He checked himself in the mirror.

You'll look sound when it's time. She won't be able to say no to you.

He held the razor in his hand and looked down there. If he trimmed some of the hair back, it would look bigger. Nicer. He'd considered using hair removal stuff once, but that was for queers and birds.

When he was done, he dried himself and threw the towel into the pile he'd take to the baggy tomorrow. Next on his list. He looked around at his handiwork: the bin bags near the door stuffed full of the crap that had accumulated all over the place in the last few days. He'd felt so pathetic when he'd had to stop the last one from getting away, useless and lonely. He'd always felt some level of loneliness in his life. As a kid, in his mum's bedroom, at the school, or in that wet, stinking place he couldn't stand to think about.

He needed to pick out his clothes for tomorrow before he did anything else. He flicked through the rail in the corner of his room near the window. He had nothing there that would show the thickness in his arms and shoulders, the strength he had in him that he knew these little sluts loved.

He settled on his cleanest pair of dirty jeans and a hoodie. He pulled some other bits off the wire coat hangers and added them to the pile for the baggy. He wasn't sure if they were clean or dirty, but either way they smelled of must, like they'd not been dried properly. He made three trips to the car before he came back for the dirty washing.

He bundled them up in another bin bag and took them down the stairs, almost tripping over his own feet. The corridors and stairs were cleaner than the day before; there was no stink of piss, but still it was cold. A breeze blew in from the downstairs door and howled around the banisters.

The old lady from the ground floor was there again with that stupid smile on her face, as though all the world didn't know she had falsies in. They slipped around her mouth as she spoke. 'Evenin'. You movin' out?' She laughed at her own little joke, which he didn't find funny.

It was getting late and it surprised him to find her there at this hour. 'No,' he said. *Careful with her. Nosy.*

'You're lookin' all posh,' she said. 'Going to meet your lady friend?'

He felt his face burn hot. He wanted to say, *Yes, I'm meeting her tomorrow*. 'Fillin' my car up to go the skip tomorrow,' he said. 'Just rubbish.'

'Oh,' she said. 'Well, that's good timin' for me.' She chuckled to herself. 'You couldn't do me a favour, could ya, love?'

'No,' he said. 'Busy.'

'I've just got this roll of old rug I need throwing. I spilled tea all over it and I'm not what I once was. Can't get down and scrub any more. You couldn't take it with ya, could ya, lad? Sorry I wouldn't normally ask but our Mick hasn't been 'round for weeks.'

Mick. The daft-looking one who only came over whenever she got her pension. Maybe he was dead. Maybe that needle he stuck in his arm most days finally went in too deep and bumped him off.

He grunted, but dropped the bag of clothes on the floor and followed the old lady inside her flat.

'It's there, love.'

It had already been rolled loosely, so he picked it up and put it over his shoulder. It wasn't heavy, and it didn't smell like tea. It smelled rancid. 'Got to go.' He turned and was out of the door already.

'No, no,' she called. 'Here you are.' She handed him a fiver. 'Well, take it, soft lad.' She laughed. 'You're doin' me a good deed.'

'No,' he said. No one had ever thanked him for a single thing he'd done in his life, and then this old woman whose name he didn't even know offered him a fiver from whatever money she had left in her purse. 'It's okay,' he said. The whole exchange made his skin crawl. He wanted to be out of there so badly, to get on with what he needed to do.

There was something on her face that he didn't recognise. Something behind her eyes seemed to soften and she nodded. He wondered whether she had ever heard someone say thank you either.

She smiled and her loose dentures slipped to the right. 'I don't think we've ever chatted in all the years we've lived here,' she said. 'Well, I'm Phyl.' She clapped him on the back. 'You'd best be off or you'll be at it all night.'

He ambled out to the car, the rug over his shoulder, and the bin bag, knotted shut, in his free hand. He felt something inside himself that he couldn't give words to. He wanted to go back inside and see if Phyl needed anything else. To clean up maybe, or go get some milk for her tea. It made him uneasy. He didn't recognise it and it scared him.

Don't let her draw you in. All women are bad. Gutless and evil. They just want to see you fail and get in trouble.

Chapter Sixteen

Dinner had been nice. Nick had started work on carefully seasoning some duck for roasting by the time Barclay kicked off his shoes in the porch and padded through to the kitchen. He took Sarah in his arms straight away and kissed her cheek. Even Nick was pleased to see Barclay home before six.

They'd sat down for dinner together as a family and then Barclay took Sarah for her bath and read her a story about a girl who'd got lost in the woods. She was found in the end – an old man had come chopping wood and said he'd take her back to the village; to her parents. The story ended there and Barclay wondered whether the little girl ever did get home.

She'd fallen asleep before he got to the last page, but he hadn't noticed until he closed the book. He kissed her forehead, took the book with him and left the door ajar; the landing light left on.

He'd gone back downstairs and found Nick at the kitchen table with two large glasses of red wine. Barclay sat down and let himself sink into the chair. He took a sip of his wine, warm and fruity, and looked across the table at Nick. There was no frown, no look of complete contempt, he looked like the man Barclay had married. The perfect smile, his small hand on top of Barclay's, which stroked his skin ever so gently. Above all, he seemed happy to see Barclay. Really, genuinely happy.

'You okay?' Nick asked.

Barclay felt cold and at any moment he could cry. 'No,' he said. 'I'm not.' He took a deep swallow of his wine and placed it onto the table with a clunk, watched it slip down the steep curve of the glass.

'You can talk to me.'

'Can I?' He felt himself bristle, but knew there was no need to. Nick had already apologised about last night. 'I think you need to talk first.'

'I'm sorry,' he said. There was something in the way Nick squeezed Barclay's hand that seemed genuine. He took a deep breath. 'I'm unhappy.' Then the tears came, a hot and heavy stream down his face. The wine couldn't have kicked in already. This outbreak of emotion had been building for some time, Barclay could tell, and it worried him. 'I'm sorry, I'm sorry… you go first.'

Barclay moved to him, squatted on the cold kitchen floor and held Nick's hand. He'd always been the protector. Had always looked after Nick, and Barclay knew, in that moment, that it would never change. He'd always take care of him. Always want to. 'What's going on?'

'I didn't think it would be like this. Having a kid.' He pulled away from Barclay and looked at the table, his face mottled pink. 'I feel ashamed. I've wanted a kid for as long as I can remember, and we have Sarah. She's sweet and smart and she's…'

'She's what?'

'She's hard work.' They both laughed and Barclay felt the tension break. 'It's "Can I have this or that?" or she needs something. As soon as I'm awake until I go to bed.'

'She's a six-year-old. She does need and want things. If we need to look at bringing in some help, we will.' Barclay moved and sat on the chair nearest to Nick. 'I'm trying to get home early when I can. It's been non-stop since de Silva walked out, and I don't see that changing any time soon.'

'I think I want to go back to work,' Nick said. 'Adoption leave was great, but I never should have resigned after it. I miss it. I miss talking to adults. Having a conversation about art and lighting and placement.'

Nick had worked in an art gallery in town. It had been a successful one, and they'd bought some pieces over the years that hung in their home. They looked like splotches and drips of paint to Barclay, but Nick had assured him, 'She's celebrating spontaneity and improvisation. Going beyond the paint brush. It's physical, look.'

Barclay had looked but didn't see the beauty that Nick seemed to get from it. Barclay felt more comfortable at the Walker Gallery than in the Tate, and even that comfort was an uneasy one.

'You should do it,' Barclay said. 'Go back to work. If Stefan still has an opening.' In truth, Barclay never liked Stefan. He couldn't ever tell whether that discomfort was on a personal level or something he felt in the almost sixth sense he'd honed as a detective. Maybe it was both.

Nick's smile was wide and his eyes shone in the low light of the kitchen. 'But—'

Barclay shushed him. 'If you say "but anything", you'll talk yourself out of it. You need to make you happy.'

Nick beamed. 'I'll call him tomorrow.'

'Good,' he said. 'We'll figure something out for Sarah. People do it all the time.'

Nick put down his wine glass and let out a puff of air. 'So why don't you see things changing any time soon? I thought de Silva was back?'

'She's not back. Not officially.' Barclay reached across the table to grab his wine. 'I don't know where to begin. She's hard work, too.'

'You always looked up to her,' Nick said. 'The way you spoke about her was like… I dunno, like she was who you wanted to be.'

Barclay hadn't realised that Nick had noticed that. Didn't think he'd cared. 'She's a great detective, sharp-minded. But she's an idiot sometimes, too. She did something today that I can't go into, but she compromised everything.'

'You did always say she was strong-willed.'

'This is beyond that. Next level.'

'Did she do whatever she did with the best intentions?'

Barclay thought about that. 'Yeah, I believe she did.' Still, he couldn't excuse it. 'She put my career on the line, the career of someone else. Her own, too.'

'That doesn't sound very sharp-minded to me.'

Barclay huffed and laughed through his nose. 'No, it doesn't, does it? I'm so torn about it.'

'What are your options?'

'I do what's right and by the book. I talk to O'Brien about what happened and end her career for good.'

'Or?'

'Or I keep it to myself and we crack on as we were. The thing is, what she planned didn't even come off. I stopped it before it could happen.'

'So no harm was done then?'

'No, I suppose not.'

'I think you've already got your answer, DS Barclay.' Nick leaned in and kissed his husband's cheek.

'I said some really hateful stuff to her. Accused her of leaving.'

'Well, she did,' Nick said. 'With good reason. She couldn't work and mourn her husband at the same time.'

'That's not even what I meant.' Barclay felt a lump swell in his throat and he felt hot. 'I meant that she'd left me.'

Nick half laughed and scanned Barclay's face quickly. There was no joke there. 'You what?'

'I know,' he said. 'I must be such a bad person to feel that way and to say it to her face...'

'Come here, you soft sod.' Nick took hold of Barclay's hand again. 'You can't help how you feel. The fact that you even feel bad about how you're feeling says a lot. You're not a bad person, you've just realised that de Silva isn't an idol on a pedestal. She's a human, God love her. She messed up and that's that. We've all done it.' He moved to sit on Barclay's lap, kissed his neck. 'You just have to choose how to react.'

Barclay couldn't think about de Silva any more. His attention had shifted to Nick, now straddling his lap. He was hard, and it had been so long since they'd touched each other like this, that he wanted to tear off Nick's clothes. His hair smelled like that aftershave he wore, citrus and bergamot and something else. He lifted Nick and carried him upstairs.

—

Nick had gotten up and had Sarah ready for school by the time Barclay woke from a dreamless sleep. He lumbered down the stairs in his dressing gown. 'Morning.' He kissed

Nick on the cheek and lifted Sarah into the air for a quick squeeze.

'Morning, Daddy.' Her little arms looped around his neck.

Nick was busy putting Sarah's packed lunch into her *Frozen 2* lunch box. She'd been obsessed since she'd discovered how to use Disney+ by herself. 'What do you want for dinner tonight? Any ideas?'

I've got a few ideas. Barclay gave Nick that half-smile he first used on their third date, when they were sat on Nick's couch. When they knew they wanted each other.

Nick laughed; it was almost like he read Barclay's mind. He shook his head.

Barclay took hold of Nick's hand and held it. 'Why don't I take us out for dinner instead? Be ready for half five?'

'Oh, I don't know,' Nick said. He bit his lip. 'Cost of living and all that. Have you seen our last gas bill?'

'Never mind all that,' Barclay said. 'We work hard all of us, so we deserve to treat ourselves. And if the worse comes to the worst, we can build an ice castle.'

'Like Elsa?' Sarah asked.

Barclay put her down on the ground and she ran off singing some song he didn't recognise – he always fell asleep before the halfway point. He moved to Nick, opened his dressing gown and pulled him in. 'Don't worry about any of that, all right? We're sound.'

'Why are you still here?'

'I'm going in late today,' Barclay said. 'Taking Mum to the cemetery.'

'Ah, I'm sorry, I forgot it's your dad's anniversary.' Nick kissed Barclay on the mouth. 'You going to be okay?'

'I'm fine,' he said. He wasn't exactly sure how he felt about his dad. He'd left them both and started a new family with another woman and had new kids with blue eyes and blonde hair. Two girls. Mum never mentioned them so neither did Barclay. 'I'd best go and get ready,' he said. 'Thank you for last night.'

'Oh God, please don't thank me for sex,' Nick said. He winced and pulled away, zipped up Sarah's lunch box.

'That's not what I meant.'

'I know. Now go and get ready and brush your bloody teeth.' Nick walked through to the living room and said, 'Right come on, love, into the car. Let's go.'

When the door shut and Nick's white Clio rolled off the drive, there was quiet. Barclay couldn't remember the last time he'd been home when there was silence. It felt strange. Too strange. That wasn't his life any more. He had Nick and Sarah to look after. They were both noisy people, and he was thankful for that. In the quiet, too many things would sneak in. De Silva, the whole sodding case, his dad and what happened there, and the HMS *Iron Duke*. It was always there, somewhere at the back of his mind, a small but hard kernel of a truth he had never felt ready to crack.

—

He was outside his mum's house within the hour, a bit earlier than they'd planned. The traffic had been light and any roadworks along the route had disappeared. The council's budget spent. She came out of the house, bundled up in a thick coat, a scarf wrapped around her neck and mouth, and the thickest set of mittens Barclay had ever seen. She somehow folded herself into the passenger seat.

'Bloody hell, Mum,' he said. 'You going on an Arctic expedition or what?'

'I'm perished.' She slipped off her mittens. 'I haven't had a second to myself to get flowers. We'll have to stop on the way.'

'Tesco isn't far,' he said.

'Now never mind the Tesco,' she said. 'We'll go to Boutique Bouquets, like we always do.'

'They're expensive.'

'Turn it in,' she said. 'It's for your father.'

'Fine.' He pulled off from the house. 'Have you eaten anything?'

'Not yet.'

'I'll treat you to some breakfast if you want?'

She didn't answer and stared out of the window. This day was always hard for her, no matter how long she and his dad weren't together for, or how long he'd been dead. She'd loved him, even when he stopped loving her. She'd never once thought about moving on and that broke Barclay's heart. But on the day that his dad left, something in his and his mum's relationship changed. She was colder toward him. Not awkward or anything; truth be told, he couldn't quite put his finger on it. It was just... different.

The cemetery was quiet and Barclay was still reeling that the flowers Mum wanted had cost him almost fifty quid. They were bright shades of purple and blue and pink. 'Beautiful,' she'd said. She'd sniff at them and nod. It seemed so wasteful to Barclay. In a few days, they'd wilt, and shortly after that, they'd fall apart and turn brown, then they wouldn't be beautiful any more. He thought of Kelly.

His mum opened up the cellophane wrapping and took scissors from her handbag. She cut the stems at a sharp angle and placed them delicately in the pot on the slab below the gravestone. She pulled off most of the leaves and said over her shoulder, 'You have to take them off. They contaminate the water.' It was a reminder that Barclay heard every year, and every Mother's Day.

They stood on the muddy path and looked down at the grave. She linked his arm, which surprised him, she hadn't done that in years. She shook, but whether it was from the cold or something else, Barclay didn't know. He found it all a bit too odd, this ritual. To stand at the graveside of a person who's rotting under your feet and to say nothing. Just to think. He didn't get it, but he knew it meant something to his mum. He just didn't know what.

'So,' she said. 'That breakfast you said about?'

Barclay smiled. 'Come on then, old girl.'

'Old girl?' Her eyes went wide. 'You're not too old to go over my knee, you know.'

He laughed. She would say that to him as a kid. His phone pinged, a message from O'Brien:

> I know you're with your mum. Thought you'd like to know the Stack PM will be tomorrow with Grindon.

'How's Sarah?'

'She's good,' Barclay said. 'A little madam sometimes, but good as gold.' There was a pause then, where a normal mum would have asked about Nick. But she never really accepted him, never asked after him, never passed over a card for his birthday or Christmas.

'Nick's fine, too.'

'Mm-hmm,' she said. 'You should bring Sarah for a visit.'

'Yeah, me and Nick will bring her over next weekend.'

'Right.' She took a breath. 'Could it not just be us?'

He stopped and looked at her, unlinked her arm from his. They'd danced around this conversation for years. 'What's the problem with him, Mum?'

'Don't start.'

'No, Mum, you don't start.' He kept his voice even and light. Any indication of aggression and she'd have him. 'I'm married, Mum. To a man. He's my friend, yeah, but he's something else. You need to get used to it or don't. I love you, Mum, but...'

He couldn't bring himself to finish the sentence. He knew that if he left her, she would have no one. There was a circle of abandonment in his family that he wasn't eager to fulfil. He loved her, she loved him; she adored Sarah, but she'd never made the time to get to know Nick.

'It'll be Christmas soon, Mum,' he said. 'I'd love for you to come for dinner in our home. But you're going to have to accept Nick. For me, Mum. I love him.'

He knew this was nothing personal against Nick. She was from a different time, an older generation. Gay men were a lesson to be learned from, something Jesus wouldn't have approved of. And if it went against the risen Jesus Christ, it went against everything she knew. Men weren't gay, or if they were, there was something inherently wrong with them.

'Times are changing,' she said, almost to herself. 'It's hard, you know... when you get to my age, it's hard to keep up with everything. It all changes so fast.'

Barclay had spent his life reading between the lines of the words his mum said. This wasn't an apology, it wasn't acceptance, it was a promise that she would try. That was all he could ask of her for now. There was a comfortable quiet between them then, and he felt no need to fill it.

They headed to his car as two blonde women walked toward them, each with a small and modest bunch of flowers, all shades of white or cream. His mum concentrated on her feet, on not slipping in the mud. Barclay glanced back over his shoulder and watched the women stop at his father's grave. They looked back too, but Barclay kept walking. In a few weeks, it would be his dad's birthday, and he wondered whether the flowers they'd just placed would have had the time to turn to mulch when they came back.

All through breakfast, he thought about the upcoming post-mortem, and about contacting de Silva. His phone felt hot as it sat on the table next to his knife, clean and unused. Before he got to Kelly Stack, he needed to do a post-mortem of his own.

Chapter Seventeen

The quiet of the incident room rang in Barclay's ears like so many Sunday church bells when he was a kid. It had been years since he'd been to kneel and pray and ask for forgiveness. *Probably too late anyway.* He thought about last night, the way Nick's small fingers pinched Barclay's nipples. How Barclay pushed into him and how it felt warm and soft. How could it be wrong? A sin? *It can't be.*

He thought about calling de Silva on the way into the office, to see if she wanted to talk. He decided against it. He wasn't sure that he'd be able to look her in the face. Besides, she hadn't contacted him, so he assumed she didn't want to talk. After all, she was in the wrong, so it should be her that picked up the phone to make the first move.

Barclay looked around at the evidence boards he'd stared at for hours on end, at the case files he'd printed off for de Silva, all read. He felt it swell around him, a high tide and, just for a moment, he wanted to stop swimming and let it pull him out to the sea. He told himself that answers were coming. He just had to wait.

He sat down with a cup of coffee and read over all three of the case files again. He stopped and lingered over every sentence and tried to wring it for some hidden truth he knew wasn't there. He was reaching. If there was something there, more than the stuff with Crosby, he'd have caught it. De Silva would have for sure.

He thought about going down to each of the sites where they were found, to see if something would come to him, something instinctual that he'd not picked up before. But that wasn't him. He dealt in facts. He moved them about and sifted through them until he saw a pattern. But there was nothing here beyond age and their looks. Nothing.

They didn't go to the same schools, they didn't have anyone in common, they lived a few miles from each other and didn't even know the others existed. Lynsey was taken from the Walton–Anfield area, Danielle from Ormskirk, and Kelly from Kirkby. They were the closest in proximity, Danielle and Kelly.

He thought about that. There was something sticking out of the mud in his mind that he couldn't quite make out. Couldn't reach out to grab. What was it that de Silva had said? That he was probably watching them, studying them, learning their movements. So if those girls were taken so close together, geographically, is that where they should focus their search for him? Was he in that north Liverpool area?

Such a large area of the city to focus on. They didn't have the resources, and he doubted O'Brien would spring for the overtime. De Silva had also talked about how the girls looked so similar, something PVPU missed. If they were similar in looks and around the same age, the natural conclusion would be that they remind the killer of someone at a particular age.

His first?

'This is useless.' Barclay threw himself into his chair.

'Talking to yourself while you're alone in a basement room? Do I need to order you a psych evaluation?' O'Brien stood at the office door. God knows how long he'd been watching.

Barclay dropped his phone to the desk and stood up, hands behind his back. 'Good morning, sir.'

'Oh, for God's sake, sit down, Sergeant. This isn't the navy, and it makes me bloody nervous when you do that.' O'Brien shuffled into the incident room, and Barclay caught the redness of his eyes and the dark circles below. He was sure that O'Brien had on the same shirt as yesterday, but couldn't be certain. 'It's like you're about to pounce. Sit down, sit down. I won't keep you a moment.'

Barclay sat down and, with sweating palms, held his phone. He needed to step back into that thought process, there was something there unfinished, a thread of thought he needed to pull on.

'Where is she?' O'Brien asked. He looked around the office theatrically. 'Is that it? Has she gone and won't be coming back?'

Barclay's throat was dry, and he had to clear it before he could speak. 'She's sick,' he said. 'Some stomach thing. It's probably a twenty-four-hour thing.' Barclay shrugged.

O'Brien's eyebrows arched so high that he reminded Barclay of an owl. 'Oh,' he said. 'I see. So nothing to do with what de Silva asked Holden to do yesterday?'

Barclay went cold. 'How did you—'

'I know things, Barclay.'

'She...' Barclay couldn't think of the words. He didn't want to drop her in it. Nick had been right, everyone makes mistakes. De Silva was like this; she took chances and leaps and didn't follow the rule book. He and O'Brien knew that. She pushed and pushed until the thing got done. It was why O'Brien wanted her back, Barclay had assumed. But what she'd asked Holden to do was extreme, even for her. He took a breath and said, 'Don't worry, I spoke to her about it.'

'Oh,' O'Brien said. 'The DCI that I put my job on the line for asks Digital Forensics to do something for her which is not only against our protocols, but is, in fact, illegal. But you know, you're right. I shouldn't worry. You've spoken to her.'

Barclay got it. It wasn't his to have a conversation about. O'Brien was her mentor or whatever, had been her boss, and would be again if she ever came back. 'I'm sorry, sir,' he said. 'I didn't come to you straight away because I didn't want to ruin your relationship with de Silva. I needed to be sure.'

'About what?'

'How I felt about it.' Barclay stumbled over his own words and found he couldn't think quickly enough. 'Sometimes we do things with the best intentions. Yeah, they're wrong, and against protocol... She was trying to stop another girl from dying, sir.'

O'Brien held him in his glare for so long that Barclay felt uncomfortable. He wanted to look away, to give in to him, but he didn't. He stared back. Finally, O'Brien took a long, rattling breath and said, 'Anything like this happens again, Barclay, and I'll give this case to someone else.'

'Yes, sir.' Barclay wasn't sure whether O'Brien knew what he was doing with that. Whether he knew that Barclay couldn't handle failing at this. He'd had to prove himself all through his life to his parents, his friends, his colleagues, to the Royal Navy Police all those years ago. 'I am sorry, sir.'

O'Brien stood and headed for the door. He didn't turn back as he said, 'Get back to work, Sergeant. And if she rings you, tell her to ring me instead.' He stopped at the door for a moment and looked over his shoulder. 'I'll send some bodies down to you. They'll be uniform bobbies, so they're needed elsewhere too. Can't spare any DCs, I'm sorry. They're on the unidentified-male case. Do what you can.'

He was gone. It seemed to Barclay that having every available DC staffed onto a cold case while this was so active was a waste of resource. But who was he to argue? O'Brien knew what he was doing – there was a reason he was in charge.

Barclay felt sick to his stomach, and he knew that his face glowed red. He'd been caught trying to cover for de Silva and it could have gone worse. O'Brien could have suspended him, but he didn't. Barclay knew that this was his last chance to prove himself to O'Brien. To de Silva. To everyone.

He had to push that guilt aside; he would deal with it later. There was work to do.

He turned his mind to the case, to the girls waiting for him to help solve their murders, and a thought half-formed in his mind. Something about the killer's past, what if there was something there? Hidden away. Something ancient. This girl that was the blueprint for the relationship he had with the other victims… Who was she?

A knock at the door. 'All right, Barclay?' DC Zoe Woods pushed the door open and walked in, her ginger hair bouncing beyond her shoulders. She had the widest smile Barclay had ever seen.

'My God, Woods,' he said. 'I didn't realise you were back.' He stood up and walked to her, took her in his massive arms. 'You look fantastic, when did you get back?'

'First day,' she said. 'I thought I'd miss him, but, to be honest, I'm thankful for the break.' She laughed but her forehead and eyes didn't move. 'I'm joking,' she said. 'My little Thom is the light of my life. I'll show you some pictures later if you've got time for a coffee.'

'Ah, I dunno.' He winced. 'Things are mad here and I'm on my own.'

'Oh, someone said de Silva was back.' Her mouth tightened. 'Shit, isn't it, what happened to her?'

Yeah. It is shit. 'She's just not here today,' he said. 'She's not feeling well.'

'Oh, well, look, let's try and go out for a coffee later?' She touched his shoulder. 'Be nice to have a catch-up. You can tell me about Sarah, and I promise I won't do any baby talk.' She laughed.

'That sounds nice,' he said. 'I'll let you know.'

'Sound.' She lifted up a brown envelope and handed it to Barclay. 'We enhanced some stills from the CCTV footage you got. You're lucky, we got a partial reg.'

'Thank you.' Barclay tried to keep the excitement from his voice. 'This is great work.' He slipped the image out of the envelope and looked at it. Clear as day, the last two letters of the vehicle registrations: *WL*.

'It's gonna take some time searching through the PNC. You gonna be okay?'

'O'Brien is sending some people to help,' he said. 'Looks like I won't have time for that coffee today after all.'

Zoe laughed. 'No worries,' she said. 'Listen, I'll leave you to it. Give me a shout if you need anything else.

Oh, we're already analysing the other CCTV we've gotten through. Nothing so far, but I'll let you know.'

'Thanks, Woods.'

She smiled at him and left him alone. Barclay couldn't take his eyes from the image. It would take some time, but those two letters right there could turn this case around for him. He needed time to think, to get it right in his head.

'No, you knock.' Barclay heard the whisper from the corridor, and then another voice say, 'No, you!'

He rolled his eyes. 'Somebody knock, for the love of God.' It went quiet out in the corridor until finally a brunette-bobbed head came around the door frame. 'Yes?'

'I'm PC Maloret, sir,' she said. 'DSI O'Brien asked us to come down to lend a hand today.'

'Well, come in then,' he said. Two others followed Maloret into the incident room. Three of them. He needed to thank O'Brien in person later. 'What're your names?'

The man, the tall one with arms that rivalled Barclay's, put his hand up and said, 'PC Carmichael.'

'Lawrence,' said the other. She had a straight face that showed no emotion, and people like that made Barclay nervous. 'What do you need me to do?' Straight to it. Barclay liked that.

Barclay explained to Lawrence and Maloret the urgency in matching the partial number plate from Woods against registrations in the Police National Computer. 'We think it's a four-by-four, but best to check all vehicles you find,' he said. 'I need a list of the vehicles, descriptions, complete registrations, owner and address. Start with the Merseyside area and work your way outward. Massive undertaking, I know.'

Maloret sat down behind an empty computer and got to work, and Lawrence pulled up a chair on the desk next to her.

'Carmichael, did you say?' He turned to the stocky man, almost as tall as Barclay himself. 'I need you to go through that list of sex offenders in the Merseyside area again. You'll be at it a while, but when you're done, help Maloret and Lawrence. I'll need names, addresses, whether they have jobs at the moment. If so, what do they do? Cross-reference it with the reg lists.'

'No worries, sir.'

Barclay breathed out long and slowly and felt his hunched shoulders drop a few inches. Things were moving now, but he needed a sounding board. Someone to speak to who could understand where Barclay's brain was going with all of this. He looked at his phone: no missed calls or texts from de Silva. He bit his lip and wondered whether he should ask to meet her.

He'd taken de Silva's suggestion that these girls themselves served a purpose for the killer – that they were just a link to, or a template of, someone from the killer's past – and he wanted to run with it. He knew that de Silva could help. She had those skills, that knowledge other detectives didn't seem to have. An instinct.

Barclay said to the others, 'I'll be back soon. Ring me if you need me.'

He sat in the car park for fifteen minutes before he started the engine. He wanted to speak to her, but he wasn't sure what to say. Whether she'd want to speak to him after the things he'd said.

The case was too important to hang about and wait. He started the engine.

Chapter Eighteen

De Silva took a deep breath, but found she couldn't open her eyes. They were too heavy, didn't want to open, almost as though they didn't want to face the consequences of de Silva's decision to drink. How many times she'd been in this position, she couldn't guess.

She knew it was light outside already and from the orange hue of her eyelids, she assumed she'd left the curtains open again. Probably forgot to lock the door or clear away the takeaway. It would be sat downstairs right now, the chips would be cold and hard, the sauces turned to gloop. Her stomach twisted and her mouth felt suddenly wet.

No, no, no. Not that. She would have given anything right then to go back to sleep, to ignore the fact that at any moment she was going to vomit. She lay still and slowed her breathing, but her heart beat hard and fast. Her skin burned hot and then she felt it. A movement on the mattress next to her.

The vomit rose quickly and she launched herself out of the bed into the en suite. She slammed the door shut and just made it to the toilet as everything she'd drunk and eaten the night before spilled out into the toilet bowl. Rice swirled in a froth of red wine and sauce, and as she saw it, she vomited again. That awful type of wretch that feels as though your soul is going to leave your body, like it's being raked up from the pit of your stomach and hurled out, screaming in agony.

She lay down on the tiles of the bathroom, rolled onto her back; the cold made her feel better instantly. She'd be fine in half an hour or so; she always was. But waking up was so difficult. Had been since Ritchie. Sometimes, when she woke up and found autumn rain beating against her window, she wished that she'd not woken up at all.

She'd dream of him sometimes. Not the terrible dreams where she walked into the house and found him hanging, or the ones where she almost saved him. The lovely dreams, where he was happy and safe, and they kissed and cuddled and had sex. Those were the worst because for just a moment, she could feel him again. Alive. In those dreams, she could smell him. The warm and woody aftershave he wore from the bottle the colour the sky turns when the sun is almost gone.

She'd kept the aftershave, and sometimes she'd spray it on his side of the bed. She hadn't done that in days, but she could smell it now. In her hair, on her skin.

Mike.

Tears streamed down her face and into her hair. Since the funeral, she'd become an expert at crying without making a sound. She never wanted anyone to see her cave.

A phone pinged, sharp and clear, somewhere beyond the door. Three or four times. She peeled herself off the floor and flushed the toilet, then crawled to the bath and managed to turn on the shower. She hoped that by the time she was finished, he'd be gone from the bedroom and her house, and they could do what they always had done. Not speak about it or acknowledge it had happened at all. Until next time. *No. Not a next time. Not again.*

She climbed into the shower, and as the hot water hit her cool skin, she felt safe, even if it didn't last long. She'd felt that way before, but since Ritchie, those moments were few and far between. Sometimes she felt that way in bed, wrapped up in her thick duvet, or on the couch with the lights off, staring into the dark. It was always temporary, always fleeting. She'd push it aside and sink back into her misery, or she'd flinch at the creak of a floorboard and imagine him hung over the banister, rocking toward her, away again, then back.

She lazily worked shampoo into her hair and wished she'd never met Crosby. If she hadn't have met him, if they hadn't had those few drinks that first time, Ritchie would still be here. She was worthless, she decided, a slut and a failure. That's what they'd all say if they knew. The woman who let her husband die while she slept with another man. It wrenched at her and she hated herself.

She felt a lump in her throat and those familiar thoughts flashed in her mind: her holding a sharp knife in the kitchen, covered in blood, her own blood; her lying on the floor next to an empty bottle of prescription antidepressants that she'd never taken; or perhaps hanging from her dressing-gown belt over the banister, in the same place as Ritchie. But who would find her? Who would care to come around if they'd not heard from her? Not Laney. Not Mum, she couldn't. Now she'd messed up everything with Barclay and O'Brien, there was no one else left.

She knew in her heart that she would never do anything to hurt herself, but that didn't stop the torrent of thoughts. They were torturous, and when she slipped back into the darker place, constant. She'd try to stay afloat in those rising black waters, but her own voice in her head would dare her. *Do it. Just do it. No one cares. You don't care. Just do it.*

She rinsed out the shampoo and thought how she didn't want to be this way any more. She didn't know how to make it stop, how to swim against the tide. She should never have stopped going to therapy, she knew that, but she hadn't been ready for it either. It was too soon; she hadn't organised her own thoughts or decided how she felt about the death of her husband, so how could she ever talk about it? How could she ever heal?

This isn't healing either. This isn't healing at all. This behaviour was destructive, and so were the thoughts she had about herself; but somewhere deep inside her was an understanding that she deserved everything she got.

'It's guilt,' her therapist had told her. 'Pure and simple. Your guilt feeds your trauma and your trauma feeds your guilt.' She'd paused, clicked the button on top of her pen and looked down at her page, scribbled some notes. 'We can work together to make it easier for you.'

She hadn't wanted it easier. If she deserved everything she got, she deserved to feel the pain and misery she'd caused Ritchie. She left her session that day and never went back.

There was a tap on the door. 'You okay?' His voice sounded like rasping metal through the wet gush of the shower. He tapped again. 'Win?'

She wanted to shout for him to go, to leave her house. Instead, she said, 'I'm fine.' She heard him shuffle away from the door and let herself breathe normally again. De Silva knew she couldn't stay in the bathroom forever, hide out until he'd gone, but she didn't know what else to do.

The embarrassment would be all too evident on her face when he looked at her. The last time they'd had sex was in an office at OCC the night before she found Ritchie. She knew she would be pulling an all-nighter, and Crosby dropped in unexpectedly with coffees and sweet things in cardboard boxes for her and the team. They ate with relish, but de Silva asked if she could have a word with Crosby before he left.

They'd laughed and played the can-we-touch-here? game and she could smell the alcohol on his breath; it was dangerous, but the excitement was worth it. If anyone wanted to look at the building's CCTV, they'd know they were having an affair. They got into the office and Crosby closed the blinds, slammed the door and he lay her down on the desk. It didn't last long. It didn't need to. She ran to the loo and cleaned herself up before she went back to work. He went home to his wife.

She climbed out of the shower and dried herself, scrubbed hard at her skin with the towel and walked out into the bedroom with it wrapped around her. The bed was empty. None of his clothes were here. His phone wasn't on the bedside, but he'd left a packet of Wrigley's spearmint chewing gum. *Thank Christ he's gone.* She went through her drawers to find some clean underwear.

Smash!

Something downstairs. A mug or a glass. *He's still here. He's in the kitchen doing God knows what.* De Silva wanted to get back into bed and cry and wait until he'd gone. She picked up her phone, but the light from it made her head swim; there was a single missed call from Barclay. *What does he want? To tell me off even more than he already has? To let me know that O'Brien never wants to see me again?*

She tossed it onto the bed and let it get lost between the sheets and duvet, then slipped into a comfortable tracksuit and her dressing gown. She needed all of the comfort she could get.

Crossing the landing, she looked at the wall to her left, where all of the photographs once hung in white frames. They were in the loft now, gathering dust. She didn't know how to prepare herself for seeing Crosby in the light and ached with the need for him to leave. Now.

But, in the kitchen, she found Barclay pouring boiled water from the kettle into two massive mugs. Seeing him made her shoulders jerk in surprise, but it subsided quickly and she found his presence more of an annoyance. 'What the hell are you doing in here?'

He turned to her but didn't smile. Didn't seem warm at all. Two faint lines ran parallel between his eyebrows. 'Crosby let me in.' There was an air of something in his voice. Accusation, maybe?

'Oh,' she said. She took one of the mugs from the side, and even though the coffee was scalding, it was exactly what she needed. A hot coffee and a cold Coke Zero was her usual hangover cure. That would sort her out until she could stomach food. 'What are you doing here, Barclay? I haven't got the energy to argue with you. So if it's that, just go.'

He looked at her and she felt him taking her in. Her hair was slapped up in a bun, still wet. She knew he'd never seen her in a tracksuit before, let alone her dressing gown. She hadn't even thought to look at her face in the mirror, but she could take a guess that it wasn't good.

'Are you all right?' His tone was one of concern, and he put a big, hot hand on her shoulder. 'De Silva, what are you doing? With him, I mean. You can talk to me.'

She wanted to cry. She wanted to collapse in his arms and let everything out until she was too exhausted to stay awake. She felt it on the tip of her tongue, the fact that she'd killed Ritchie. Her actions. She almost said it, swallowed it down.

'You need to stay away from him,' he said. 'He's bad news.'

Barclay didn't know the half of it. She wanted to tell him she knew and disclose all the nasty things they did together. All the ways they'd destroyed their own marriages. Instead, she said, 'What do you want, Barclay?'

Barclay took in a deep breath and let it out, sipped his coffee then set it aside. 'I'm sorry,' he said. 'The things I said to you... they weren't very nice things to say. Or to hear, I'd imagine.'

She nodded and stared past him at the egg-shell tiles of the kitchen wall, focusing on the one that was just off centre in the top right corner of the splashback behind the hob. If she looked at him, she'd give in and apologise too. She wasn't ready for that. 'Is that all you're here for, to say sorry?'

'I thought you might want to talk.'

'I don't. I'm done with it. With you, O'Brien, the whole pack of you. I don't want to think about you or this case any more. I'm finished.'

'No, you're not.'

'Don't tell me what I am or what I'm not,' she said. 'I've made my mind up. I'll find something else. But I can't go back to the force.'

'Why?'

'Look at me.' Her voice was calm, but underneath it, her anxiety uncoiled itself from the centre of her chest. 'Look at the state of me. I'm a mess.'

Barclay moved closer, put his arms around her, and for a moment they felt like Ritchie's used to. She pulled away.

'If I let you say what you've got to say, will you go?' she said.

Barclay shook his head. 'Okay.'

He explained to her his feeling based on her theory, that there was something lurking beyond the shadow of the killer. 'I keep coming back to what you said the other day, about these three girls.'

De Silva nodded. 'Someone from his past.'

'But where do you start with something like that? Missing persons? From when?'

De Silva's head rattled with every word Barclay spoke, with every step down into the murky waters of the crime scenes of those three victims. The theory had merit, but she didn't want to have this conversation, didn't really have it in her. But if she co-operated, Barclay would go away and she could go back to bed.

'It's a good place to start,' de Silva said finally. 'The girls don't just have their looks in common.'

'They're all similar ages.' Barclay nodded, apparently eager for her to continue her thought.

'So you have that as a search criteria. Missing girls aged between thirteen and fifteen.'

'Even that's so wide. We don't even know if he's from Liverpool. The North West. He might not even be from England.'

'The typical age of serial killers is late twenties, early thirties. But that's not an exact science. He could be older, younger.' She waited for a reaction but there was none. His face was stern, intent, but listening. Open. 'These urges he has, they're not the needs of a newborn, are they? They're out of his control. Impulsive. He's developed them when he's had some level of self-awareness. You can see the loss of control in the spacing between the victims.

Over a month between the first and second, then almost three weeks before he took the third. He's not perfecting his approach, not getting any tidier. He's angry and he's angry with her. Whoever *she* is...' She cut off and took a sip of her coffee. It burned her lip. '*She* was in his childhood, like I said. That, coupled with the typical age of serial killers, might help to narrow the search criteria.'

'I could start by looking into previous cases of unresolved murders in the last twenty to twenty-five years, maybe? Cross-referencing victim type and style.'

'Exactly.'

There was quiet between them then, but de Silva could almost hear Barclay's mind at work; thinking of possibilities, scenarios and potential outcomes. *It doesn't matter. As long as the killer's out there, then another girl is as good as dead.*

'I'm going to have to lie down,' she said. 'Show yourself out.'

'Wait.' It blurted out of his mouth hard and quick. 'Listen, O'Brien knows about what you asked Holden to do. I didn't tell him. I wasn't going to. He just knew. I think you should ring him.'

'No, thanks.' She felt herself withdraw again, like after the funeral. She wouldn't mind that right now, being left alone. Disturbed by no one. 'All that's done.'

'It isn't,' Barclay said. 'I think there are some things you need to sort out, for definite. But after that – days, weeks, months from now, whatever it is – you should come back to work.'

De Silva couldn't say anything. She was empty inside. 'I'll give it some thought.' The words sounded as hollow slipping out of her mouth as they had in her head. 'I'd like you to leave now.'

She didn't wait for him to say anything more, just turned her back and headed upstairs. As she got into her bed, she heard the front door close, heard him call the incident room and ask someone to begin a search for missing or dead young teenage girls from cold cases. Heard his car door slam and the thrum of his engine disappear slowly. The house fell silent. It was the most welcome sound de Silva had ever heard.

Sat up against the headboard, the coffee in her hand, she could easily fall asleep and forget this whole messy event for just a few hours. Then she saw it. The shoebox sticking out of the wardrobe. The box from the last pair of Nike's Ritchie had bought. The lid was halfway off, the way she'd left it weeks ago. She'd stuffed papers inside it and now they stuck out, untidy. She put down her coffee and took the shoebox back to bed with her.

They were Ritchie's things. Mortgage papers, some school certificates and reports, life insurance. She touched the parts where his signature was on an old contract he'd had drawn up for a client, as though it somehow connected her to him again. It was all the stuff she hadn't wanted to deal with these last three months. She closed her eyes and took a deep breath, then picked up her phone.

Chapter Nineteen

Barclay's head pounded as he drove across the city toward the hospital. Town was busy. Roadworks everywhere, all the way up Strand Street and onto the junction at Brunswick Road. A tatty-looking micro industrial estate squatted in the middle of the circular junction in faded, old sixties-era buildings.

There was so much he'd wanted to say to de Silva, but she gave nothing away, brushed his apology aside. Still, she'd made him think. The killer would be out there, stalking his next victim. Barclay imagined him as a black shadow, the silhouette of a man, outside a school or community centre or park. He shivered.

He parked in the multistorey beneath Alder Hey hospital and took the stairs up to the lower-ground floor to get his blood pumping. He thought of the incident room in the basement of the Operational Command Centre in Speke and wondered whether society needed subterranean floors to bury all the horrors of the world.

He felt cold. He told himself that the chill was caused by the adrenaline coursing through his body. He'd never attended a post-mortem, and he was worried how he would react to it. De Silva had been to plenty on O'Brien's behalf, and she'd always said, 'They never get any easier. Just don't eat breakfast until afterward. If you can stomach it.'

Barclay came out of the stairwell into the main corridor. A short man, handsome in an older-guy kind of way, with almost-white hair, bounded over to him, his hand outstretched.

'You must be Detective Sergeant Barclay,' he said. 'O'Brien told me to look for the massive guy. "He looks like a bobby," he said, "can't miss him."' The guy chuckled to himself.

'Oh.' Barclay was unsure whether to laugh or not. He shook the man's hand anyway. 'Dr Grindon, isn't it?'

He nodded cheerfully. 'Come on, it's this way.' Grindon led Barclay into a small room where he scrubbed his hands and forearms. 'You won't need to scrub. Just stay at the back of the room. Have you attended a post-mortem before?' He dried his small pink hands on a crisp white towel.

'No,' Barclay said.

'Well, I won't lie to you, it isn't pretty. If you feel sick or like you're going to faint, just come outside. Don't be embarrassed, it's common.' He retied a loose knot in his drawstring scrubs and Barclay caught a glimpse of abs.

Sweat had already started to bead on Barclay's back, he could feel it soak into his shirt. Grindon slipped into the rest of his gear, the gloves and visor. A much younger woman came in through an entrance at the back of the room. 'This is Dr Clara Newman, my APT,' Grindon said. 'She'll be assisting today.'

Barclay had read somewhere that anatomical pathology technologists were the ones that did all of the dirty work, so to speak. Still, Newman looked much younger than she must have been to be at this stage in her career; fresh-faced and pale. The kind of skin that was suited to work in the dark, cold rooms of hospital sub-levels. Barclay thought she looked almost haunting.

'I'll be giving instruction and taking some photographs,' Grindon said. 'So there will be flashes. I'd ask you not to take any photographs yourself. This isn't standard practice, I'm doing this as a favour to O'Brien, so please don't compromise anything.' He chuckled again, but Barclay knew he meant every word. 'One last thing. There are some scrubs over there. You'll need to put them on.'

Barclay obliged without a word, and pulled on scrubs, gloves and a hairnet. He followed Newman and Grindon into the examination room. It smelled of nothing in particular, and that struck Barclay as odd, just a faint whiff of cleaning chemicals. On a bench in the middle of the room, the ghost-shape of Kelly Stack lay under a white cotton sheet. Various utensils and devices were on top of a steel table off to the side. Next to that was a marble bench, bright white under the harsh lights. Barclay imagined the veins in it almost pulsed.

Barclay's head banged. He couldn't remember when he'd last drunk some water. *You're dehydrated. That's all.*

Suspended above Kelly was a cable and a microphone. Newman and Grindon moved into place, and he reached up to press a button to start the recording. 'The date is the thirtieth of November 2022. The time is' – he looked at a digital clock on the far wall – 'one fifteen p.m. The following are post-mortem notes relating to the case of Miss Kelly Stack, fifteen years of age. The post-mortem will be completed today by Dr Scott Grindon, Forensic Pathologist for Her— His Majesty's Coroner. Assisted by Dr Clara Newman, Anatomical Pathology Technologist for the Liverpool region. Please duplicate report for

Detective Superintendent Thomas O'Brien of Merseyside Police.

'I'll begin with an external examination.' Grindon removed the sheet and the sound of it reminded Barclay of when his mum would hang bed sheets on the washing line in summer. *Flap.*

Kelly's feet and hands were covered in clear plastic bags and tied off with elastic bands. 'There is no evidence of malnourishment, indicating the body's basic needs for food and water were met before the time of death.'

He feeds them. He cares enough to feed them. Grindon's camera flashed and it made Barclay flinch. Click and flash. Newman took a long piece of measuring tape from the steel table. Grindon held the top near Kelly's head and Newman took it right down to the feet.

'Body is approximately one hundred and sixty centimetres in length, equalling around five foot and three inches,' Newman said. 'The skin is raised and pink on the lower legs and across the chest and arms. There are two, four, six, seven lesions, blue in colour. Crime scene observations reported the presence of jelly fish in the area where the body was found. Stinging may account for the rash and lesions. There are obvious contusions to the throat, chest and breasts.

'The more obvious injury here is to the left side of the head. Would suggest a blunt instrument has been used more than once. The skull is almost completely obliterated in this region.'

Click and flash. Click and flash.

Barclay stared at Kelly's chalky skin, at the purple and blue bruises that stood out like shadows in bright sun. He imagined the killer on her, squeezing, pulling, groping. His stomach contracted.

Click and flash.

Newman had her measure out again. 'Contusions are different sizes, but averaging about one to two inches,' she said.

Grindon looked across the examination table at Barclay, kept his tone flat and professional and said, 'Size and shape of contusions are consistent with finger marks left behind in previous cases of death by strangulation and cases of sexual assault.' *Click and flash.* He put down his camera, looked to Newman, then and said, 'Could you help lift?' Together, he and Newman twisted the body to reveal her back. 'Hold her there, please,' he said. He lifted his camera again and took photographs as he spoke. 'You got her? Good. More raised and pink skin and some grazing of the scapulae. Consistent with being dragged.' They both lowered the body. Newman carefully removed the evidence bags from the hands and feet. 'Nail samples were not taken from the body at the crime scene, but we will complete the process today for both left and right hands and feet.'

They got to work. 'Nails appear mostly clean of debris, consistent with being kept in water. Moving on to an external examination below the waist,' Newman said.

Kelly looked small lying there and Barclay thought of Sarah. He loved her so much and wondered how anyone could do that to a kid. The hate they had for something so innocent must be so powerful. Incomprehensible.

'Toxicology may show some hormonal reaction to these stings, so take extra care during processing.' Grindon was in his flow now.

Click and flash.

Grindon let out a hard breath. 'There is tearing to the exterior of the anus.'

Click and flash.

Barclay wanted to turn away and face the wall. This was all too much. The examination was so clinical, more so than he'd expected. They handled Kelly as though she was... Barclay couldn't think of the word. *Meat* felt too callous, too coarse, but it crept back into his mind time and again. His stomach churned and he felt the urgent need to cover the girl up, to tell them to stop what they were doing and leave her alone. She'd been through enough.

'There is similar tearing here to the vaginal opening, the labia majora.' He moved across to the table of utensils and dragged it closer. One of the wheels whined and Barclay winced. 'We will continue on with the internal examination now. Clara, could you start, please?'

The lights seemed harsh in the room, like they were getting brighter, more intense. Barclay wiped sweat from his brow. There was a smell somewhere between sweet and putrid. His stomach gurgled.

Click and flash.

'Liquid in the cavities,' Grindon said. 'Could you get a sample of that, Clara? Lungs are inflated, but the water smells... it smells like soap. Just like the others.'

All the victims had been cleaned before they were left out somewhere along the Mersey. His brain buzzed with a hive of questions he may never get the answers to. His legs felt like jelly, but he tried to focus. He was learning first-hand what had happened to her – he needed that to steel him, to make him remember that this wasn't for nothing. He turned away from it all, tried to find a speck on the wall he could focus on. To calm his breathing like his therapist had said. But there was none.

There was a high-pitched whirr, snaps and cracks behind him, and his chest constricted. He couldn't catch his breath. He reached out to grab the wall to steady him, but it was too late.

Click and flash.

The room turned black.

Chapter Twenty

'She's in the courtyard,' Sue said. She must have been in her late sixties already and de Silva wondered why she wasn't retired yet. 'Are you okay going through yourself? Got my hands full with a code brown in room six.' She sniggered to herself and pushed the mop bucket away down the corridor.

De Silva nodded and even managed a polite smile. She felt as though her entire body jangled, and she hadn't been entirely sure it was safe for her to drive. She didn't really care. All worry and concern had left her the moment she realised, yet again, that she was a failure.

She'd sat with Ritchie's things on her lap, the phone in her hand, ready to dial the first phone number. She couldn't. To say those four words out loud would mean that there was nothing left that she needed to do for him. *My husband is dead.*

She'd been trapped in a state of mourning and that would come to an end, and maybe, she assumed, the healing would start. She wasn't ready. She'd packed it all back into the shoebox and closed the wardrobe door tight.

She'd still not eaten, and her stomach ached and grumbled, and sometime soon she'd have to feed it. *It can wait*, she thought. Whenever she felt sick as a kid, she would go straight to her mum. Marie would say, 'Lie down here.' She'd tap her lap and de Silva would snuggle down. Marie would run her fingers through her girl's auburn hair and de Silva would drift off to sleep, far away from how she felt.

If she sat down and rested her head on her mum's lap right then, de Silva didn't know if Marie would stroke her hair or ignore her completely. That was the horrific unpredictability of her mum's condition.

De Silva pushed open a glass door and stepped out into the cold courtyard. Her mum sat on a bench in the far corner under a lattice-work trellis covered in a vine-like plant de Silva had never noticed before. It twisted in and out of the wood, held on tight, and in the breeze, the wood creaked. The sound of Ritchie twisting from the banister.

She stood at the door and watched her mum for a moment. She stared ahead at nothing, a mustard-and-grey blanket over her knees. It would have killed her dad to see his beloved wife in here, but there was no other choice.

De Silva moved to the bench and sat down. Her mum didn't even know de Silva was there. She could have been anyone. The leaves on the trellis trembled in the breeze. 'You all right, Mum?'

It was as though someone had clicked their fingers in front of Marie's face. She started and her trance was broken. Marie broke into a smile so bright that it lit her eyes, the colour of copper. The frown softened and her eyes focused. 'Win, love.' She put her hands on her daughter's face and they felt warm. 'Where've you been?' She looked about and leaned in close, almost conspiratorially and said, 'They haven't let me watch *EastEnders* in a fortnight. Grant's down in the pit – Phil found out about him and Sharon.'

'You don't need to wait for them to let you watch it, Mum. You've got a telly in your room.'

'That thing? No thank you – I don't know how to work it.'

De Silva took hold of her mum's hand and Marie lifted the blanket to put it over both of their laps. It was in those moments, those tiny actions that would mean nothing to anyone else, when de Silva knew that Marie remembered how to be a mum. That she was a mum. *My mum.*

When they were kids, in the summer, they'd go to the beach as a family. They'd drive down and park where all the big trees were. In the evening, when the sun would burst red and hover above the sea like it was never going to set, Marie would cover them all in an old ragged blue blanket. De Silva remembered hoping that the sun wouldn't set, that the moment would last forever.

The sun did set. The moment didn't last.

De Silva slipped down and lay her head on her mum's lap. Marie's fingers felt different in her hair, but also the same. They were thinner, less supple, but the effect was just right. Tears came easily and soaked into the blanket.

'Ah, there, there,' Marie said. She patted her daughter's shoulder with her free hand. 'Poor little girl.'

'Oh, Mum!' De Silva couldn't help herself from blurting it out. Her whole body tensed, her chest tightened, and the agony was wrung out of her, silent and sodden. The guilt of everything she'd done or said, her sins.

'What's the matter, love? Come on, you can tell me.'

She could have told Marie everything. *But you'd forget.* De Silva sat up, dried her cheeks, and faced her mum. De Silva took her mum's arm and pulled her up from the bench. 'Come on in, it's cold.' De Silva tucked the blanket under her arm and they ambled slowly back toward the door. 'You hungry?'

'My stomach thinks my throat's been cut, love. Have you seen the slop they're serving in there?' She gestured toward the dining room, where the other residents sat and ate or were fed. 'Wouldn't give it to a stray. And have you seen that cook? Filthy nails, and I'm sure she's from Birkenhead.'

De Silva burst out in laughter.

'Come on,' de Silva said. 'We'll put some clothes on and go and get some chicken. Girls' night out.'

'Ruthie will be so jealous.' There was an urgency in her steps then as they got to the door and de Silva didn't have the heart to tell her mum again that Ruthie, their neighbour when de Silva was young, had died last year. 'I'll race you.' She started off, slow but deliberate, and de Silva walked behind in case she fell, just as she'd watched Marie do with Laney when they were young.

In the end, we become the parents of our parents.

—

The night came on freezing cold. Frost had already gripped de Silva's garden wall, the grass she hadn't managed to cut before the end of summer, her car and everything it could find. De Silva wrapped herself in a thick woollen blanket that usually sat folded on the back of the couch and watched the night happen.

The doorbell rang and she ignored it, prayed for whoever it was to go away, but it rang again. *Bing-bong-bing. Bing-bong-bing. Shut up.*

'I know you're in there, de Silva.' O'Brien's voice. 'I can smell your greasy head from here.' He came to the front window, hands at his brow like a visor, and glared through. 'Don't make me ring for a team to break in. I just want to talk to you.'

De Silva wanted to pull the blanket up over her head and dissolve into the couch. He'd go away eventually, she told herself, but he was already back at the doorbell.

Bing-bong-bing. Then heavy banging on the door.

She grunted in frustration, threw the blanket onto the floor and stomped to the door, her feet slapping against the tile in the hall. She pulled the door open and let it clatter against the wall. 'For God's sake, O'Brien. You'll have the neighbours ringing the police.'

'Well, I'm already here, so I've saved them the effort.' He stepped into the hall. 'Can I come in?' It didn't sound like a question, but de Silva closed the door behind him. 'Oh, I was joking just now, but you really do smell greasy.'

'What do you want?'

'Well, I'll tell you what I want, but you have to promise to shower right after I've said my piece.'

'If this is a lecture, save it. I'm not in the mood.'

O'Brien frowned. She hadn't seen that look since her early days as a detective. It was the look he gave her whenever she was in trouble. 'Well, I suggest you get in the mood,' he said. His face softened again, brow relaxed. 'I'll have a cup of tea. Do you have those caffeine-free tea bags?'

De Silva walked off toward the kitchen and gestured that he should follow her. 'Just the normal kind,' she said. 'Will that do?' She was already putting one into a mug and switching the kettle on to boil.

'It'll have to,' he said. He took a seat at the small round dining table and looked out of the window into the back garden. 'So all of this business... the thing with Holden.'

She knew why he was here, but as he said those words, they felt like a kick in her stomach. Right in the spot where the guilt and shame lived. 'I know,' she said. 'I'm sorry. I was limited in what I could do, you know with my lovely visitor's badge, and I grasped at anyone I knew could help. This isn't Holden's fault. It's mine.'

O'Brien cleared his throat; that frown was back on his face. 'You chose for it to be a visitor badge, like you chose to ask Holden to do something you both knew was against protocols. If he'd have gone to anyone else, but me...'

She knew. Never mind a leave of absence, she'd have been given her P45 and never been allowed to serve with the police again. But that's what she wanted... wasn't it? She wasn't so sure when faced with it properly. She nodded.

'I know what you're going through is terrible, de Silva. One of the worst things there is, I know.'

'No, you don't know.' The kettle popped behind her, the steam hot against her back.

'I do.' His voice was soft, almost a whisper. 'Kath isn't very well.'

De Silva's breath caught in her chest. She hadn't expected this. So wrapped up in her own problems, she'd not seen that the people around her were sinking, too. 'What's happened?'

'I didn't come to talk about that,' he said. He wiped his face with the sleeve of his woollen coat. 'We need to sort this out. Sort *you* out.'

She brought his tea to the table and sat down next to him. 'Tell me what's going on.'

He sighed. 'Pushy, just like your dad. Dog with a bone that one.' He chuckled but de Silva stared at him until he gave in. 'Fine, fine,' he said. 'She has cancer.'

De Silva felt sick. The piece of her heart that held fondness for Kath and O'Brien cracked. 'I'm sorry,' she said.

'They've done everything they can they say.' His voice was thick. 'But, well, it's not looking good for us.'

Kath had been so lovely after de Silva's dad had died. She'd sent food and flowers and cards, and came to visit. 'There has to be something they can do.'

'They'd have done it by now,' he said. 'No, there's nothing. We've asked. I've spent hours researching. She's just... I mean, she didn't even drink. Where's the fairness in that? I smoked like a trooper for years, and what? I'm a picture of health.' He tapped at the paunch that hung over his waistband. 'See?'

'I'm so sorry, Thomas,' she said. She put her hand on his and tapped it. 'I'll go and see her.'

'Yes,' he said. 'Seeing you looking like the Crypt Keeper will cheer her right up. Have yourself a wash before you visit, and get a pan of scouse down you, for the love of all that's holy.'

They sat in a comfortable silence. De Silva thought of Kath and of the pain they must both be feeling. It's one thing to come home and find your husband dead, but another to watch them go slowly. She wondered if Kath and Thomas felt the pull of the tide going out. Time. Their time together, ebbing and flowing, until finally... Just like she'd felt those last few weeks with her dad.

'And you.' His voice trembled and de Silva wondered what he'd thought about in those silent few moments. 'What are we going to do about you?'

'I don't think I can do it any more,' she said. 'It's so bleak. I've had my fill of it.'

'You used to see the job differently.' He removed his hand from the table, from her touch, and let it sit on his lap. 'You saw yourself as a helper, someone who looked after people who couldn't look after themselves.'

'Until *I* became someone who can't look after themself.'

'I won't argue with you there,' he said. Quiet again, more strained this time. He sighed and said, 'But this thing you have... that instinct, whatever you call it. I'm struggling to see it.'

'It's gone.'

'It's not gone, you just don't want to access it because you're scared of what you already know: it's what you were made for. You see these victims, in their lives, imagine how they came to their end. And ninety-nine per cent of the time, you're right... I've done the stats. Your dad would be proud.'

She hadn't expected this either. She felt something throb in her chest. She wanted to tell him not to talk about her dad, that he was hers to grieve; but that wasn't true. O'Brien and de Silva's dad had worked together for years, decades even; he was just as much O'Brien's to grieve, to remember, as he was de Silva's. That's the thing about grief. It belongs to everyone and everyone does it in different ways.

'Not because you can't look after yourself now,' O'Brien went on. 'But because of what you've achieved. The things he didn't quite manage. Oh, he loved his job, but you were going somewhere.'

She looked at him then, the word *were* stuck in her mind like a hook. 'What do you mean "were"?'

O'Brien wound the reel. 'You spent the last three months showing me that this is it for you, de Silva.

That you're out. I hadn't listened to you.' He paused, gestured with his massive hands, the fingers stained yellow. 'I should have listened to you, and I'm sorry. Everything with Kath and what's happened in the case the last few days, I don't have it in me to fight with you any more.

'You win,' he said. 'I get it. You don't want to come back. I'll fill your post.'

De Silva's throat went dry. 'Who will you get?'

'I'll have to interview, but I'll see if there's anyone laying around that I can borrow. Manchester or Lancashire maybe.'

'Oh.'

'Of course,' he chuckled. 'If you changed your mind...'

She wondered what hoops he would make her jump through to get back to work. 'What are the terms?'

'You'd have to meet regularly with an appointed therapist,' he said. 'Once a week, non-negotiable. Just to help you deal with everything that's happened.'

De Silva's stomach churned. The thought of speaking with another professional about Ritchie... She couldn't. Could she? Could she get back to work, stop drinking in the day, move forward with her life? The truth was that she'd missed it. Those two days with Barclay had made her realise how much. But she was still wrapped in her private grief for Ritchie and it had settled on her now, like the fuzz of a warm blanket.

She took a deep breath, looked O'Brien in the eyes and said, 'No.'

O'Brien sighed and nodded. 'That's fine, de Silva. I'll move on.'

They'd spoken more about the old days, when de Silva's dad and O'Brien were young and they worked as street bobbies, until de Silva had felt her eyes closing and O'Brien finally said his goodbyes and left after ten. She crawled into her bed and tried to picture them all in happier days. Her mum young and present, Laney still involved with the family, Dad still alive and well. And Ritchie.

They were all gone now, in their own ways. Not all of them to death, but gone nonetheless. Only memories in those that care to remember them; and after that, when the last person who knows them stops remembering, they'd be truly gone. She felt like the keeper for her loved ones, that keeping them alive was her responsibility, and that was heavy.

She wondered whether Barclay felt the same about the girls from his case. Whether he felt responsible for keeping their memory alive, keeping the next girl alive; whether he would catch a break in the case.

If the killer's MO was anything to go by, they'd have just a few more weeks before the next girl showed up dead somewhere along the Mersey. She wasn't sure that Barclay would catch him before that happened; she wasn't sure if she could be any help to him either.

What she was sure of was that she had to try.

Chapter Twenty-One

He pulled on his big coat and locked the front door, took the stairs two at a time and when he reached the ground floor, expected the old hag to be at her door. She wasn't.

The car smelled of rubbish, old food and stale ale, and the piss from the rug Phyl asked him to get rid of. She said she'd spilled tea, but she'd lied. Like all women lie. It was thick and rancid, the type of smell that hits you hard in the back of the throat and makes your eyes water. He needed rid of it now.

He checked his watch, the old silver thing with the cracked face his mum had said was his grandad's. He didn't know for sure, because he'd never met him. Probably dead now.

On the day his mum had sent him away to that place, he'd taken it from her top drawer. She visited him only once in term time, screamed at him to give the watch back. He denied everything. She, he knew in the pit of his belly, was where it all started; where women slithered into his life and showed him what they were. She would stagger in, hit every wall to her bedroom with a man's hands on her hips. He'd hear them through the walls, the moans and the headboard bang-bang-banging. He used to think at least she loves someone, and he'd force himself to sleep.

But some nights, when she had the money to, she'd ask Lisa to sit with him. Lisa was the perfect girl. He'd loved her, wanted to be with her, but she met that lad and changed.

Suddenly, you were the problem, you're weird, you're messed up. She didn't want to know you. She's a slag, too.

They were to blame, all of them. Not him.

'All of this is holy,' he remembered one of the men saying in that place. He wasn't one that worked there; he was a priest, the only one that had ever visited. Everyone else was nameless, normal-looking men. The priest would say, 'Your body, my body. It's God's. And you worship God, don't you?'

He would answer, 'Yeah, I do.' He wasn't entirely sure that was true, but it was expected of him. Beaten into him.

'God made this.' The priest would stroke his own little pink dick. 'And this.' He touched Lewis. 'We should worship, shouldn't we?'

Some teachers would show up after, in their dressing gowns, and take all of them through to the shower block. It smelled of mildew.

He pulled into the household waste and recycle centre in Bootle, parked his car next to a line of open skips, separated by low concrete walls. He launched the bin bags into any old skip, didn't bother to read the instructions on the wall about what should go where, and returned to the car for the stinking carpet. He hefted it over his shoulder. But he stopped. He'd be late if he stayed here any longer. He threw the rug into his car and left the skip, wound down the windows and let the cold winter air in. He'd have time to park around the corner and get to St Mary's. He doubted anyone would recognise him, he'd always felt invisible in those corridors.

The school doors opened and they teemed out, almost identical except for their hair and the bags they carried. He didn't see her. His heart pounded hard, she could have slipped by him.

Fuck. You've messed this up, dicking about with a stinking rug.

He might have missed his opportunity, and could have to wait until tomorrow.

He breathed out and realised he'd been holding his breath for a long time; his chest was the panicked beating of caged birds.

He could leave now and go home to wank, or he could stay here and wait for her. There was a chance she might come out later than the other kids, or he could just be wasting his time. He decided to go and walked back down toward the school and his car. It was nearly dark already, the sky turned deep shades of blue that he couldn't name.

He could find her again tomorrow, and he knew that he would think about her all night and wonder whether she thought of him at the same time. He twisted the car key. It didn't start first time, but the second time, it rumbled and spluttered to life.

Then he saw her. It was like seeing a ghost.

These games she's playing. She's messing with your head. Do it.

She walked past the car in her hockey kit without even a second glance. He willed her to turn around, but she never did. She was talking on the phone.

The car tyres bumped off the kerb and he rolled forward slowly, then moved in front of her. In the mirror, he could see her; she'd noticed his car then and she frowned. She was dressed like all the others. Short skirt showing most of her leg.

It's her, and look at her. Take her. Do it. Do it. Do it!

He heard her voice and it sounded so different, softer maybe. 'I'm on my way to the bus stop now, Mum... It's fine, it won't take me long... Yes, I know. I'll text you when I'm on the bus... Yes, and when I'm off it, too... No, I'm not walking home. I'm going to the bus stop, like I said. I'll cut through the park the other side.' She sighed. 'See you in a bit.'

A bus pulled around his car. She noticed it and ran to the stop, her arm outstretched to flag it down. It stopped for her and she got in.

Follow it. Follow it and see where it goes to.

He tailed it past the gym, around the roundabout and onto Moor Lane. The journey took no more than a few minutes, and she got off the bus and walked through some side gates of Walton Hall Park that he'd never seen before.

He stopped on the road and let her walk ahead a bit, then turned down the small dirt path. Bollards blocked any further passage in a car.

His cock was hard in his jeans, harder and bigger than he'd ever felt it before. He never thought he'd see her again, had never known what had happened to her, but he wasn't going to let this chance pass by. He opened the glove box and rooted. Shit, he hadn't brought the chloroform with him. He leaned over the seat and reached into the back into the small bag that carried his tools. His hand rested on the long, oily shaft of the ball-point hammer. He usually didn't use that until later.

Just do it, you pussy.

One quick blow and then it's all over.

He slipped off his shoes, pushed open the door gently. It creaked, but she didn't seem to hear it. He left it open. It would take four lunges to get to her. He looked around quickly. No one about. No passersby, and no cars behind him. No cameras at all on this tiny stretch of path.

Smack.

She fell down to her knees.

Smack.

He caught her.

Smack.

Chapter Twenty-Two

De Silva woke up before the alarm she'd set and had managed to shower, dry her hair and put make-up on for the first time in months before the clock hit seven. Breakfast was two pieces of toast with butter and a cup of coffee. Milk, no sugar.

Dressed in smart dark denim jeans, sensible heeled boots and a casual blouse the colour of wet sand, she slipped on her police-issue harness and looked in the mirror. It looked ridiculous to her, a prop from some 1970s police show her dad would have watched. She took it off, put the PAVA spray, extending baton and handcuffs into her handbag. She'd never returned the stuff when she took her leave of absence, and she was thankful for that.

Not practical, but it'll do.

She couldn't decide on a jacket, so instead found a loose-fitting blazer, the navy one she'd bought on the trip to Loch Ness with Ritchie. In her bedroom mirror, she realised for the first time all the damage she'd done. Her body had changed; she looked weak and sallow.

Despite the make-up, she looked ill. She was. She had been. She spent yesterday weighing up her options. She could live this half-life in an endless cycle of grief and trauma, a shroud of mourning that protected her from the world outside, or she could pick herself up and get back to work.

She'd had moments of strength like this before, where she felt untouchable, like she was back in control of herself. Of her life. It was always temporary. She'd walk outside onto the drive or get into town, and she'd crumble.

It was O'Brien that made her set her alarm for six that day. It was him and Kath and the knowledge of what would come next for both of them: the bloody awful inevitability of untreatable cancer. It was Ritchie. It was Barclay and his love for the work. It was Lynsey and Danielle and Kelly. It was the poor girl plastered over the news the night before when she couldn't get to sleep. The one who looked so much like the others.

De Silva had turned to the Liverpool local channel when the national ones had moved onto another news story about a Tory MP who hadn't paid taxes and had had sex with his child's nanny during the Covid lockdowns.

Joel Matthews's face, the one de Silva had so desperately wanted to smack over the years, streamed live from some cheap-looking studio. Probably in the basement of some building. There was a faint smile on his face as he told of how Amanda Maclennan had gone missing. People like Joel Matthews revelled in this stuff. They loved it. Lived for it.

De Silva knew that if Barclay didn't move quickly, Amanda would turn up dead too. Barclay needed her. She had turned the TV off and expected a phone call or text from O'Brien, but none came through. Somewhere between hearing about Amanda and waiting for Barclay or O'Brien to contact her, she'd managed to get some sleep.

With still no word from Barclay or O'Brien that morning, she got into her car and made a mental note to have it cleaned professionally. The seats needed shampooing and the carpet was filthy. She reached into the glove box for her sunglasses and found a half-empty bottle of whisky on top, shining like amber in the winter sun.

The bottle had a gravity all its own and pulled hard at her. She reached for it, unscrewed the lid and sniffed. She thought the smell might relax her, or placate her at least, but it didn't. She put it to her mouth, ready to knock it back, when she caught sight of herself in the rear-view mirror. Hunched over a bottle of alcohol before eight in the morning. *What have you become, Win?*

There were lines on her face, around her eyes and mouth, that weren't there before Ritchie. Before the bottle. She got out of the car and poured the whisky onto the grass then threw the bottle into the blue recycling bin. The clatter as it dropped in reminded her just how many bottles she'd gone through. Luckily, there were no neighbours about to hear it.

De Silva got into her car and set off for the OCC. As she sat in the usual rush-hour traffic through the city, she was aware of how hard her chest pounded; so hard it made her feel lightheaded. She didn't know how well she'd be received, if she'd be received at all, but she had to try. She knew that she could help, could add value to the case.

Barclay's words came at her full force. Before he'd come to see her, before his apology that she didn't return, he'd said he wouldn't work on the case if she was. Said he could smell the ale on her. She'd been mortified but couldn't show him that. Couldn't dare show that his words had hit a place where the truth she'd tried to escape resided.

It must have taken some strength to come to her after that and apologise. And what had she done when he did? Turned him away like he was in the wrong. That was wrong, she'd known it all along. But in those mornings that had started with whisky or wine, everything was fuzzy, everything meant nothing. Throwing out those bottles earlier had almost been cathartic, symbolising a new beginning. This was the first morning alcohol hadn't clouded her judgement in such a long time. She hoped that she could keep up that momentum. Later, she'd jangle for it. Thirst for the bitter taste of some sort of ale. But that was later.

Her phone rang through the car's speaker system. She pressed the green button on the touch screen. 'Barclay,' she said. 'Where are you?'

'At the office,' he said. 'Have you seen the news?'

'I've seen it,' she said. 'What're you thinking?'

'That I could do with your help.' Barclay sighed. 'Just a few hours, I promise. I think I'm on the right lines about this fella, but I need to hear your thoughts.'

'I'm already on my way in,' she said. She smiled in spite of herself and was thankful. *You've not ruined everything after all*, she thought. 'Meet me at reception?'

'I will.'

'Ben, I just wanted to say... I'm sorry...'

The line went quiet. She couldn't even hear his breath. After what felt like an age, Barclay said, 'Okay.' Something in his voice, the tightness of it, made de Silva feel that it wasn't okay at all. 'I'll see you soon.'

Traffic was heavier than normal and she got to the OCC almost thirty minutes later. At the gates and all along the edge of the car park were news vans, reporters setting up for live TV and cameras aimed at the building. *They're like vultures. One sniff of meat and they descend.* But that was why she was there too, attracted by the scent of a dead body.

She closed her car door and heard the shutters clap from the many cameras. She'd never experienced anything like this before. But then, she'd never worked a case as high profile as this one. A reporter headed toward her, her heels clicking on the tarmac. Her camera operator, a young woman in combat trousers, in tow.

De Silva couldn't take the chance that she was caught out here alone. She wasn't the lead detective on this case. She wasn't even sure what she was right then, but she had no business appearing on the news. She turned toward the Operational Command Centre building and walked quickly.

Up the steps, she tripped over her own feet and almost hit the ground, but saved herself. Her wrist and forearm rang in pain. The door swung open in front of her; Barclay was there and rushed out to her.

'Are you all right?' There was a warmth to his voice; he sounded genuinely concerned. 'I saw you go.'

'I'm all right,' she said. 'Caught myself, but my wrist…'

Barclay's tight face, so full of concern for her, gave way to a massive smile and a laugh that came from him that she'd not heard in months. He had a laugh that sang from his belly. 'I'm sorry,' he said. He tried to compose himself. 'I'm so, so sorry. Falling isn't funny.'

'No, it's not,' de Silva snapped. 'I could have broken my neck.'

Barclay erupted again and it made de Silva laugh, too. 'You should have seen your face,' he said. 'Absolute picture.'

'I'm sure I heard the cameras going as well.' De Silva checked herself for dust or grit.

'Oh Lord, I'll have to ask Nick to record *Granada Tonight* just in case.'

'Oh, thanks!'

'What's the joke?' O'Brien stood there, big and bold, and looking tired. 'De Silva, it's nice to see you, but if you're not here to help, let Barclay get back to work.' He didn't wait for them to respond, but de Silva was sure she saw the hint of a smile before he loped off.

They walked to the lift and Barclay called it. They waited. 'Are you actually okay, though?' Barclay asked.

'I think I'm at the age where falling isn't funny any more,' she said. 'Where it's genuinely scary.' She chuckled. 'I'll be all right.' Her wrist throbbed and she rubbed it. The lift doors opened and they stepped inside. 'So, where are you up to with all of this?'

'We're working on lists of local sex offenders,' he said. 'We have some resources and we've started working through it.' The lift opened on the basement floor and they walked out toward the open door at the bottom of the corridor. 'I've got someone cross-referencing sex offenders with registered vehicles, seeing if we can come up with a match to the partial reg. That list of missing girls, too.'

'Any news from Holden?' She knew she was pushing her luck asking him, but it needed to be asked. 'The app he found on Kelly's phone.'

'I'm catching up with him today.'

'I'll do it,' she said. 'You'll be called for a press conference in the next few hours. So you'll want to prepare for that.'

'How do you know?'

Experience, she thought. 'Just a hunch,' she said.

'I don't think it's wise you meeting with Holden on your own.'

'I'll take one of your team members with me,' she promised. 'Besides, I owe him an apology too.'

'About that...' He looked down at his shoes. 'I'm sorry too.'

She wanted to give him a squeeze to let him know it was okay. That she was okay. That they were okay. To ride this high for as long as she could. The doom voice she often heard in her head using her own voice chimed in. *It's temporary*, it said. *You'll be back to crying on the bathroom floor, thinking of ways to kill yourself by tomorrow morning.*

She pushed the voice aside and tried to focus. There was work to be done now, things that needed her attention. Barclay needed her and she needed this more than she could ever tell anyone. The sense of purpose, the distraction; to help work on something and bring it to a resolution. If nothing else in her life could be resolved, at least she'd have tried with this case.

She needed it.

De Silva nodded and swallowed down the lump in her throat. The corridor felt freezing now, even through her jacket, as though a breeze blew in from the incident room. 'I get that I hurt your feelings,' she said. 'But it wasn't personal. It wasn't like I'd selected you and decided to ignore you. It was everyone. O'Brien, my sister, I didn't even visit my mum in weeks. Ritchie's family. Everyone. I didn't want to be around anyone.

'It's hard to explain,' she said. 'I didn't want to be here. Not that I wanted to hurt myself or anything, just that I didn't want to exist.' She thought of how much stronger that inner voice became. The shift from, *You'd be better off not here, everyone would*, to the violence and aggression of what it had become. What she hoped would, one day, disappear.

'You don't have to explain,' Barclay said. His eyes darted across her face and his hand felt hot on her shoulder. 'You know, when you didn't answer me, my texts, or you know… the front door… I just wanted the opportunity to be there for you. Christ, de Silva. I don't just think of you as someone I work with or to look up to. I don't care if you feel the same,' he said. 'You're my mate. But that makes me selfish, doesn't it?' He paused and looked at his shoes again. 'Like really selfish. I was mad at you because I couldn't be there for you. It's stupid.'

'You wanted an opportunity to be there for me, and that's lovely,' she said. 'I mean it. But I wanted the opportunity to grieve my husband. I'm still in the middle of that, and I'm not apologising for pushing people away. I get that you needed to be there, but I needed you not to be. Needed *everyone* not to be.'

'Oh.' Barclay looked away. 'Maybe I shouldn't have said anything.'

'You should,' she said. 'It's how you feel. And I've told you how I feel.'

'And when you've offered your expert advice or whatever, what's next for you then? Back to yours and ignoring everyone?'

She shook her head no. 'I don't think so,' she said. 'But there's something in being on your own, you know? For one, this type of stuff doesn't happen to you.' She gestured to the incident-room door.

'No,' Barclay said. 'That's already happened to you.' He sighed. 'Jesus, I shouldn't have said it like that. I'm sorry.'

'It's fine,' she said. 'I get what you mean. I don't know what's going to happen after all this. How I'll feel when it's over. But something's different, I can't explain it. God, I must sound like a wet lettuce.'

He chuckled. 'You don't.'

'Good,' she said. 'I've got a reputation to maintain and if you tell anyone about this little heart-to-heart, I'll break your legs.'

He smiled. 'I'm here you know,' he said. 'If you need me.' He walked off toward the incident room as his phone rang. 'Hello?'

Press conference.

'Yes, sir,' Barclay said. 'I'll be right up.' He put his phone away in the pocket of his leather jacket. 'All right, Psychic Sally. I've got a briefing for a press conference upstairs.' He gestured to the incident-room door. 'All yours.'

De Silva moved toward the light of the doorway, different from the harsh light on the docks just days ago. *Still cold, but… almost inviting.*

She listened to the buzz inside. The chatter. The click-clack of keyboards.

And closed the door behind her.

Chapter Twenty-Three

It felt like a strange day for Barclay. Like things had started a little differently to a normal Thursday, moved quicker. De Silva had come to offer her help, nobody asked her or begged or tried to sway her. From what he saw of her interaction with O'Brien in reception, not even he knew she was coming. Which meant there was hope that she'd come back to work. That she'd be okay, start to move on with her life without Ritchie.

The case itself moved at its own pace; sometimes slow and painful like the throb of toothache, but he had a team now. They were working hard. There wasn't any one system that could cross-reference a partial reg to a registered address and match it with that of a known sex offender. It needed to be done manually. It would take time. Time they didn't have. Time Amanda Maclennan didn't have.

Barclay had to work on the logical assumption that Amanda was the latest victim of their suspect, given her similarities to the previous victims. But in truth, they weren't, and couldn't be, certain. PVPU would run their investigation because, as far as anyone knew, Amanda was still alive.

Barclay headed toward the interview rooms and saw O'Brien ahead of him. There was something about him today that seemed different; the shine in his eyes had gone, replaced with a dullness that Barclay couldn't put his finger on. 'They're in here,' he said. Even his voice sounded different. There was no energy there, like he begrudged every word.

Barclay turned into the interview room, past the uniform bobby stood at the door. The room was one of the larger ones, with a sofa and comfortable chairs. The parents were on the couch, they held hands and the woman sobbed into a wad of tissues. He whispered to O'Brien, 'What are their names?' Things had moved so fast he hadn't had time to prepare, hadn't had time to collect his thoughts.

'He's Craig,' he grumbled. 'She's Eileen.' He turned for the door. 'You've got this, haven't you? You have, I'll leave you to it.'

Barclay turned to the bobby at the door and said, 'Could you sit in with me? Take some notes?'

'Yes, sir.'

'It's Watts, isn't it? Jay Watts?'

'It is, sir.'

'Barclay's fine.'

Barclay took the lead and went to the couches. He sat down opposite the couple, red-faced, eyes so distant Barclay wasn't sure they'd be able to focus. 'I'm Detective Sergeant Barclay, this is PC Watts.'

'Hello,' Eileen said. Her voice took Barclay aback. She wasn't local; sounded posh, really well spoken. She wiped at her eyes. 'We were asked to bring some photographs of Amanda with us.' She took three photos of her daughter from her handbag. The obligatory school photo and two from family days out.

'Thank you,' Barclay said. 'These will help.' Amanda was blonde like the others, the same plump cheeks and thin nose. She'd inherited that from Craig's side of the family, Barclay could tell. A handsome man for his age, pale skinned, with green eyes.

Barclay took a deep breath and put the photo aside. 'I've been asked to come in and speak to you before I speak to the press. We're hoping that we can find Amanda, and to that end our Protecting Vulnerable People Unit are involved. They'll be leading this really, and someone will be along from that unit to speak to you. I'll be doing the press conference with them. I just wanted to speak to you first.'

The parents nodded and Barclay was unsure they were hearing him. He'd seen this look so many times before: the thousand-yard stare.

'If PVPU can't find her over the next few days, if she doesn't come home – which is what we're hoping for, isn't it?'

'Yes,' Craig said.

'Good. If she doesn't, then you might hear some things that aren't very nice. I'm sure you've read in the papers, seen on the news, the stories about what's been happening these last few months.'

'The girls...' Craig said. His eyes darted to Barclay's face then back down to the linoleum floor. 'The missing ones. The de—' He cut himself off. For his own sake or his wife's, Barclay couldn't tell.

'That's right,' Barclay said. 'I just want to get some information to add to our files in case... and we're still hopeful she'll come home by herself. Kids her age, sometimes they go off. Need space.'

'Not Amanda,' Craig said.

Barclay nodded. 'Can you tell me more about Amanda?'

'What would you like to know?' Eileen asked.

'What her interests were. Did she do anything after school? Did she have a boyfriend? Any friends she would have gone to instead of coming home?'

'Do you think she could come home?' Eileen wiped at her eyes with tissue.

'I don't know,' he said. The raw honesty of it hurt his own heart. 'She might be there now. She could have lost her phone, or broken it. She could have stayed at a friend's and not thought to contact you.'

'No,' Eileen said. 'Not Amanda. She isn't like that. She's a very conscientious young woman.'

Barclay nodded. 'Okay. So...'

'She had a hockey match after school last night. Just an hour.' Craig looked at Barclay now. 'She goes twice a week to that.'

'Did she have her kit with her?'

'Yeah, she would have done,' Craig said. 'Her PE kit, hockey stick. All of it.'

'Do you know who leads the practice? Is it a teacher at the school?'

'Yes,' Eileen said. 'A Mr Beckett.'

'That's great,' Barclay said. 'Does she have any particular friends in that group?'

'They're a pretty close group,' Craig said. 'They're pally outside of school, too. Parties and such like.'

'Is there anyone there that she's closer to out of the group?'

Eileen looked to Craig, her eyes swollen with grief. 'Yan?'

Craig looked to Barclay, then to Watts scribbling notes at his side. 'Yan,' he repeated. 'Yan Peng. She's in all of Amanda's classes. They're always together.'

Well, they weren't together last night. 'Okay, we'll make sure we speak to her.' He cleared his throat. 'Did Amanda have a boyfriend?'

'No,' Eileen said.

'Well, we didn't want her to,' Craig said. 'But there was a boy. Connor Lambert. He doesn't go to her school, but they've been in some community plays together. She was Calamity Jane once, while he was Wild Bill.'

'Where's Connor from?'

'Maghull, I think,' Craig said. 'Could be Aintree. I'm sorry, we don't know much about him. I think he goes to Deyes High School – I think I remember Amanda saying.'

'That's really useful, thank you.' Barclay wanted to reach out and put a hand on Eileen's knee, to tell her that he understood. As a father, he could only imagine what they were going through, but as a detective… well, he'd seen this so many times before. The agony of not knowing, the pain of waiting, the glasslike shatter that happens when the news finally comes in. 'We'll find her,' Barclay said.

One way or another.

Chapter Twenty-Four

De Silva had noticed a change in Barclay after he came back from the press conference, and it was even more prevalent as they drove out to Maghull in silence.

De Silva had watched the coverage live on the local Liverpool channel. The entire incident room had stopped what they were doing and watched. She wondered how many of the uniform bobbies wanted to become a detective, how many of them took mental notes as Barclay navigated the questions thrown at him as though it was only his most recent press conference, not his first.

When Barclay had come in a few minutes after it had ended, his small team had said things like, 'Well done, sir' and 'You did great'. He'd flushed. De Silva had shown him the local channel, hosted by Joel Matthews, and had said, 'They're playing him on a bloody loop. The same shit over and over again.'

'Oh.' Barclay sat at his desk and didn't say another word until he asked de Silva to go with him to visit Connor Lambert.

He'd asked for an update from the team before they'd left and the sharp one, the one with dark hair that didn't smile, told him they'd found vehicles with partial matches and were cross-referencing known sex offenders on the PNC.

De Silva worried that it was getting too much for Barclay, the pressure that can feel like walking through quicksand. Then, without warning, lightning will hit and you're racing toward some sort of resolution. Some sort of break. This case didn't feel like that though.

Scientific Support found blood and a broken mobile phone on the pavement after yesterday's suspected kidnapping, but both were still being analysed. De Silva knew in her gut that they both belonged to Amanda, but without confirmation from the lab, they couldn't pursue it properly. She looked so much like the other victims that, for de Silva, it was a foregone conclusion. The same person who took Amanda had killed Kelly and the others.

There was an urgency in his taking her how he did, something animal. It was there in the violence of the kidnapping, the blood and the pace of it all. The killer was escalating, taking his victims quicker each time – but she expected at least a week between finding Kelly and him taking his next victim. Not days.

Who was this girl? What she represented to the killer de Silva couldn't guess. Yet.

'What are you thinking?' Barclay turned down the radio in the car.

'Hmm?'

'You were thinking, I could almost hear it. About the case? The killer? Do you think it's him that took Amanda?'

'I do, yeah.'

Barclay nodded, an acknowledgement that they were on the same page.

'From what I've read in the reports, we're talking about a very damaged man. All the usual stuff, white male, twenty-five to thirty-five years old. His childhood will have been one of neglect, one where there was an oppressive female dominant presence in his life. Abuse, maybe.'

'Why abuse?'

'The violence in him, the rage. He's reacting to something. There's some sort of violence in his past. If there's no history of him committing acts of violence, there will be history of those acts against him. He's turned that rage inward for too long. There's only a finite amount of time that could have continued, before…'

'Before he turned that rage outward.'

'Yeah.'

'This girl, the one he's fixated on. Do you think she's the one who perpetrated the abuse?'

'Not necessarily, no. It's likely more complex than that.'

A moment of quiet between them. Barclay bit the inside of his cheek and focused on the road.

'I didn't like doing that this morning,' Barclay said finally.

'The press conference?' De Silva shook her head. 'No, they're not a nice experience, are they?'

'All those questions. All those eyes and lenses.' He tapped the steering wheel in quick succession, a rapid beat only he knew.

'You did really well, though,' she said. 'I watched it. I wouldn't have done anything differently.'

'Really?' His voice was oddly high-pitched for him.

'Yeah,' she said. De Silva looked out of the window as they crossed Switch Island. 'What're you expecting to find out here? From this Connor lad, I mean.'

Barclay shrugged. 'I'm not sure.'

'Was he with her last night?'

'I don't know. That's why we're going to speak with him.' There was an edge to his voice, sharp as a knife.

'I understand,' she said. She wanted to tell him that their time would be better spent back at the incident room, helping with the cross-referencing. It could take days. They could have sent a uniform bobby out to take statements and followed it up later.

'I feel like there's something you need to say.' Barclay chuckled this time, the atmosphere changed.

'Well, usually I'd go out and get statements myself,' she said. 'But we're in a situation where the killer is either losing control or is stepping up his game. Or both.'

'I get that,' he said. 'I need answers from this boy though, and I don't want to read it on paper. I want to see it. I need to see it.'

De Silva understood that. She got it. 'I know,' she said. 'That's fine.'

'But?'

'But nothing,' she said. 'I get your thinking.' There was more to this, she knew. Barclay's insistence of him coming to see this lad felt like a waste of his time. Someone else could be doing it while they focused elsewhere. She watched him gripping the steering wheel tight, his jaw clenching and unclenching in an unsteady throb.

De Silva chose to zone him out, and looked through the window at the other cars, trees, and people going about their day as they zipped past them. In the quiet, her brain whirred into action. She knew that a killer's behaviour rarely came out of nowhere. In this killer's past, there will be other victims; animals or people who wouldn't have been missed.

She wanted to go back to OCC and help trawl through old files of unsolved murder cases. There would be answers there. Somewhere. Her mind screamed: *Take me back to the station!*

Stay focused, girl. Stay present. She took in a deep breath and let it go. In and out. In. Out. She felt calm spread over her like warm bathwater; it soothed and relaxed her. Soaked her. The anxiety, the stress of wanting – needing – to do two things at once subsided. That instinctual, erratic part of her brain quietened.

They stopped outside of the house on Deyes Lane, two cars on the drive; one shining red sports car that reminded de Silva of clichéd midlife crises and affairs with secretaries, and a family car with a roll door on the side. De Silva decided who Connor's parents were. The wife did most of the driving, ferrying kids to footy practice or dance class; the dad would be a senior manager in a high-performing business, perhaps an independent. Sales, maybe.

Maghull was the kind of place where every house had two cars on the drive and had their hedges cut perfectly square. Where they spoke with a Liverpool accent, but by the time they hit their thirties and had kids of their own, begrudged it. At least, that's what it had been like when she was a kid. All middle class and dinner-table manners. People from Maghull always liked to remind her that she was from Kirkby, from the council estate, and they'd say it as if they had shit on their shoes and the smell made them ill. The towns were about five minutes' drive from each other, but could have been worlds apart.

As she walked up the drive of the Lambert residence, she wondered whether they were any different at all.

Barclay rang the doorbell and de Silva eyed the plants in the porch, all tall with massive leaves, and healthy shades of green. She couldn't keep plants alive in her house, they just didn't seem to like it there. *Everything in that house dies.*

She shook her head, tried to dislodge the doom voice. She couldn't deal with that today, not now.

Barclay rang the doorbell again. A tall, skinny young lad came to the door in his school uniform, his dyed-black hair combed down over one of his eyes. She'd gone to school with kids who dressed like him, and the style hadn't changed much. He reminded her of the younger goth kids, the ones who were bullied and called witches.

'Connor Lambert?' Barclay pulled out his warrant card from his inside jacket pocket and showed it to the lad. 'I'm DS Barclay, this is... this is de Silva.'

The lad stared at them both, and de Silva could see the redness in his eyes, the chalk colour of his skin. 'I'll get my mum,' Connor said.

Barclay was impatient now, eager to get in there and get his questions answered, almost as keen to wrap this up as de Silva was. There was other work that needed to be done.

Connor's mum came to the door, flustered and pink-faced. 'You're the police?' She moved out the way of the door and said, 'Come on in. Excuse the mad house.' They walked through into the hall where a little girl stood, her hair wild.

'Hello.' Barclay beamed. 'What's your name?'

The girl turned and walked away slowly.

'Forgive her,' the mum said. 'She's like that with strangers.'

Good. She should be. Even with police. 'We're sorry for the intrusion,' de Silva said. 'We really would like to speak to Connor.'

'Well, yes, that's fine,' she said. 'But his dad and I would like to be in the room.'

'It's nothing serious,' Barclay said. The softness to his voice now sounded reassuring. 'We just want to talk to him about Amanda Maclennan.'

'Yes, we thought you might,' she said. 'We were thinking of bringing him in last night. To get all of this out of the way so it wouldn't interfere with his school. I asked him to come straight home for lunch.' She passed Barclay and de Silva and headed into the kitchen. 'Come through, we'll talk in here. I'm Georgina, by the way. This is my husband, Mark.'

Mark stood up, white shirt perfectly pressed, blue trousers with a crease ironed in and brown brogue-effect shoes. He swaggered over to de Silva and Barclay, walking with his shoulders. He reminded de Silva of a silver back in documentaries narrated by David Attenborough. 'Will this take long?' His accent was a local one, but he'd spent years trying to mask it. 'I have a meeting with a client shortly, and I'm afraid I can't miss it.'

De Silva shrugged. 'How long do you have to talk about the disappearance of your son's girlfriend?'

Mark's eyes went wide, held de Silva's gaze for a little too long, then looked away. 'Fine,' he said. 'Let's get on with it.'

'You can leave, Mr Lambert,' Barclay said. 'We don't need you here.'

Barclay had taken an instant dislike to him, too, de Silva could tell. Mark had the air of someone who thought of himself as an alpha male, the Andrew Tate type.

'No, Mark,' Georgina said. 'I need you to stay.'

He didn't look at his wife. 'Connor!' His voice boomed through the house. 'Get down here!' He took a seat at the kitchen table and waited. Georgina scooped up the little girl and they sat quietly together. The girl played with the earrings dangling from her mother's ears, which looked as though she'd made them herself.

Connor lumbered into the kitchen-diner, head down. 'What?'

'Could you take a seat?' Barclay asked. 'This could take a while.'

Mark sighed.

Connor did as he was told, sat on a chair in front of his mum, the opposite side of the table from his dad. De Silva could feel the tension between them. This was not a happy home.

Barclay took the last seat at the round table and de Silva stood, leaned against the door frame. 'How long have you been going out with Amanda?' Barclay took out his little notepad.

'We've been seeing each other for a year.'

'That's a long time,' Barclay said. 'How did you meet?'

'We did a play together,' he said. 'Then we saw each other at a party, and... that was it.' Connor fidgeted in his seat.

'Are you aware that Amanda is missing?'

'Come on,' Mark said. 'It's all over the news. This is a waste of time.'

'I'm sure Amanda's parents wouldn't think so,' de Silva said. Mark Lambert didn't look at her.

'Yes, I know she's missing,' Connor said. 'It's on the news, everyone is talking about it in the group chat.'

'Which group chat?'

'Just the drama kids,' he said. 'We have a group chat and talk a lot.'

'What are they saying?'

'How sad it is.' Connor couldn't look at them. 'Some of the girls are saying how scared they are, that anyone could be next.'

'Next?'

'They think he has her.' Connor folded his arms across his stomach. 'You know, the killer.' He looked at Barclay for the first time since they met at the door. 'Is it him?'

'We don't have any evidence of that, Connor.' Barclay scribbled into his notepad. 'Do you know of anyone who'd want to hurt Amanda?'

'No!'

Georgina cleared her throat. 'She was a lovely girl,' she said. 'Whenever she was here, she was so polite. So kind, even with this little terror.' She tickled her daughter's belly and she giggled.

'I have to ask you, Connor.' Barclay took a breath and looked up from his notepad. 'Where were you last night after school?'

'Are you for real?' Mark was on his feet now. 'That's enough now. You people! Think you can barge into peoples' homes and ask anything you like. Well, not in my house.' He folded his arms. 'I'd like you to leave.'

'Mark!' Georgina was up now. 'Just let them finish. Let Connor tell them.'

'Don't say another word, Connor!' Mark glared at his son, his eyes wide. 'They want answers, they can wait until I speak to my solicitor.'

'Mr Lambert.' De Silva stepped forward. 'A girl is missing. Someone your son cares about. If he can tell us anything that might help, you should let him speak.'

He didn't look at de Silva, but spoke to Barclay. 'I'd like you to leave.'

'If we have to come back and take Connor in officially, then we will.' There was a hard edge to Barclay's voice. 'He'll be taken to the station from your home in a marked vehicle. Now I know he goes to school on this road. Do you want that for him?'

'Are you threatening us?' Mark growled.

'Mark!' Georgina was on her feet now. Her daughter pulled at Georgina's jumper, wanting to be held again. 'Please, you're making this worse.'

'Connor,' Mark said. 'You're going to be late for afternoon registration. Get going.' Connor left without another word.

'He hasn't even eaten anything, Mark, for God's sake!' There were tears in Georgina's eyes. 'Just calm down.'

'Don't tell me to calm down,' he roared. 'I don't need to calm down. These two need to leave my property like I've asked.'

The little girl started to cry, and Georgina picked her up and left the room. 'There, there, love.' De Silva heard Georgina thud up the stairs.

'We'll go, Mr Lambert,' de Silva said, 'but we'll be back.' She smiled at him. She knew it would get to him, piss him off. She was used to dealing with men like that, the kind that didn't like it when women spoke up, spoke out, spoke against him. She could see him in his life: inappropriate comments to female co-workers; homophobic, probably racist, jokes with the men. It's what lads do, isn't it? Boys being boys. De Silva hated him.

The front door slammed behind them. 'Well,' Barclay said, 'that could have gone better, couldn't it?'

'Not with a man like that, no.' De Silva stopped at the car and looked back at the house. Georgina watched from an upstairs window. She wanted to go to her, tell her not to take that shit from him. There's only one direction relationships like that go: violence. One day, Georgina Lambert would have to make a choice between standing up for herself, or accepting her existence with a husband like Mark. De Silva hoped it was the former.

'De Silva, look...' Barclay gestured down the street. Connor stood there on the corner, his school bag over his shoulder.

'Move the car down a bit,' de Silva said. 'Around the corner, maybe. Don't want soft lad in there wondering what we're up to and coming out.'

Barclay nodded and got into the car, disappearing around the corner from where Connor stood. De Silva moved quickly to the edge of the street just as Barclay got there.

She said, 'Are you all right?'

'I'm fine,' Connor said. 'He's always like that. I told Mum, she should... well, she never will, I don't think.'

'Did you want to speak to us?' Barclay asked.

Connor nodded. He was different out here, away from the house. There was eye contact and he stood up straight. 'Yeah,' he said. 'I went straight home after school yesterday. I usually have a piano lesson, but when I got home, Mum said it had been cancelled, so we didn't end up going.'

'Are you okay?' De Silva put a hand on his shoulder. 'Your dad seems... he seems very angry.'

'He's never hit us, or Mum, if that's what you're getting at,' Connor said. 'He's just, well he's home a lot lately, I suppose.'

'Oh, I see.' De Silva got it straight away. He'd lost his job, hung about the house more. Maybe left in the morning and came home early in his flash car and perfectly pressed shirts.

'She's not my girlfriend,' Connor blurted. 'We've never been seeing each other. We're just really close.'

Barclay frowned. 'Why did you lie?'

Connor took in a long breath and let it out again. 'I don't like girls. I say I'm with her when I'm not. She comes to mine sometimes for dinner, and I go to hers, but... neither of us are interested in that way, if you get me?'

'Are you saying that Amanda is gay too?'

'Yeah,' he said. 'But you can't say anything! Her parents wouldn't get it, and my dad deffo wouldn't.'

'It's fine,' Barclay said. 'No one needs to know.'

'You're gonna find her, aren't you?' His brows knitted together, his lips trembled. 'Before anything else happens to her?'

De Silva wanted to say that there were no guarantees. They couldn't make any promises. Given the blood on the pavement, it didn't look good. De Silva knew the killer had Amanda, but she couldn't say that to Connor. They'd know for certain soon whether the blood they found was Amanda's and then she would be his fourth.

'We'll do our best, Connor,' Barclay said. 'I can promise you that.'

The faint chime of a school bell. 'Ah, shit, err, sorry... I'd best get going or I'll be marked late again,' Connor said. He turned around and ran down the street, his backpack bouncing against his shoulders.

'Seems a nice kid,' de Silva said. They headed for the car and got in.

'Being gay in secondary school.' Barclay shook his head. 'It's hard.'

'Things have changed since we were at school, though.'

Barclay started the engine. 'Yeah, I know. Maybe it was different for me.'

'Why?'

'I didn't really have mates in secondary, one or two like. When I was younger, it was different. We didn't think about gay or straight. We were just kids and got on with it.

'But secondary hit different. The things I'd be called, and then when I came out, it just got worse.' He pulled away from the kerb and bounced over a speed bump. 'Fag, all of that.'

'I'm sorry that happened to you.' De Silva was unsure why Barclay told her these things. She felt certain she'd never heard any of these stories before, but he needed to speak. She let him go with it. 'I can't imagine how difficult it must have been.'

'It wasn't just at school,' he said. 'The lads I played footy with stopped knocking for me. I could see them outside at the front of my house. Everything changed the day I got caught kissing Chris Wilson in the toilets before chemistry.'

'Did your mum ever find out?'

'She knew,' he said. 'She never spoke about it. Pretended it didn't happen. She still does.'

'I'm sorry to hear that, Barclay.' De Silva was unsure what else to say. Her best friend, Marco, had had a completely different experience. He'd always hung around with girls, and when he told them he was gay, they took him in even closer. He was one of them. 'I thought you and your mum were close.'

'We are,' he said. 'As long as there's no gay talk.' He gripped the steering wheel so hard that his knuckles turned white. 'Anyway... back to the station.'

De Silva felt like they were leaving something unresolved. Not that opening up about his relationship with his mum could solve anything for Barclay, but she knew that just talking helped. That conversation would have to happen on his terms, in his own time.

'Yeah,' de Silva said. 'I want to get my hands dirty.'

—

The office was loud with noise from the telly when de Silva and Barclay walked into the incident room. Barclay's team were crowded around it, but stood up when they heard de Silva and Barclay arrive.

'Sir,' Lawrence said. 'We were just...'

'You're allowed to take a break,' Barclay said. 'Anything new?'

'That Joel Matthews is on the local news channel,' Maloret said. 'He's saying about how heartbroken Amanda's family are by her disappearance.'

'I'll bet he is,' de Silva said. 'Tory behaviour.'

'What do you mean?' Barclay moved to his desk and slumped into the chair. He looked tired.

'Don't you remember how he reported on Kelly Stack's disappearance? That her mum was out robbing at the local shop while her daughter went missing. That she was pissed and on drugs. Can you see the difference between Kelly and Amanda's parents?'

'Amanda's are middle class.'

De Silva nodded. 'Tory behaviour.' She typed into the PNC any keywords she could think of to bring up files that might relate to the current case. *Unsolved. Rape. Murder.*

'He mentioned you by name,' Carmichael said.

'That's no surprise,' Barclay said. 'He was there at the press conference.'

'No, not just you,' Carmichael said. 'De Silva, too.'

'How does he know I'm involved?' de Silva said.

'Probably because you nearly went arse over tit in front of all the cameras,' Barclay said with a wide smile.

De Silva's face felt hot. 'Great,' she said.

'That's not all, sir,' Lawrence said. 'We're still working on it, but we found a match on the lists. A partial reg match on a blue 2006 Jeep Cherokee.'

De Silva stopped her search and listened.

Carmichael continued. 'The PNC has the owner listed on the sex offender register, too. We checked him out,' she said. 'Multiple sex offences against girls, all underage.'

Chapter Twenty-Five

Barclay bumped his car onto the kerb on Stepney Grove. The street was two rows of red-brick terraced houses, some painted white or magnolia. It was the type of street where the front doors opened onto the pavement. No front gardens. People walking past could see right in to you having your dinner, or watching *Coronation Street*. Squad cars were parked around the corner, Barclay would radio them when he was ready. The last forty minutes had moved so quickly, he'd barely had time to think.

He'd pulled de Silva aside in the incident room, out of earshot of the others. 'I need your advice.' His whole body had hummed, his pulse had pounded in him, a drum beat that built and built to... God knows what. 'We don't have time to dick about.'

'No, I know that,' she'd said.

'I've never worked on anything like this before,' he'd said. 'But this could be it. This could be him.'

'What are you asking me?'

'Do we take this slow, or do we go for it?'

De Silva smiled and Barclay hadn't been able to place it. She hadn't been amused, hadn't found anything funny. It had been that half-smile he'd seen her use sometimes when she'd been thinking. She'd asked, 'What's your gut telling you to do?'

'That I should already be in a car.'

'Why?'

'Because, if he's got her, we have maybe twenty-four, forty-eight hours before this sick fuck leaves Amanda somewhere along the Mersey.' He had felt tension build in his chest, across his shoulders and down into his arms. He'd been ready to move. Ready to go.

'Follow your gut,' she'd said. 'Do you want me to come?'

'Yes, I do.'

'Good.'

Barclay and de Silva watched number thirteen from the car, the curtains drawn against the low winter sun. Against prying eyes. Barclay didn't know how long to wait; he'd never had to do this before. On the way here, he'd called O'Brien. More to steady his own nerves, to check in, than to offer any sort of update.

'I trust you,' O'Brien had said. His voice had sounded weary, exhausted. Defeated. 'You know what you're doing.'

He'd wanted to say that no, he didn't know what he was doing. This was all alien, and someone else should have taken charge. But there he was, leading everything, pulling resources to a property he was completely unsure was connected to the case.

'You know what,' de Silva started. 'I hadn't realised before, but this is Walton. Lynsey Renshaw lived right by here. Just a few streets away.'

'It's him, isn't it.' He'd said it out loud, but he was talking to himself. 'It adds up. The reg, the sex offenders register, the location. It's all here.'

'How do you want to handle this?'

'Quietly as I can,' he said. 'Knock at the door.'

'What if he runs?'

'I've got a team ready to move in.' He took the radio from the klick-fast on his harness and pressed the green button on the side. 'Are you in position?'

He stared at the red button on top while he waited for the return call. It's what you pressed when things got out of hand, when there was trouble you couldn't deal with. It would call in every bobby within the vicinity. He'd not pressed it once in his career.

Finally, a crackled response. *'In position and awaiting your go.'*

He stowed the radio safely on his harness.

Barclay got out of the car and made a beeline for the front door. He heard de Silva behind him, her shoes slapping against the tarmac as she hurried to catch up.

He was at the tatty-looking door before he knew it. It was an old wooden one, the paint chipped and peeling, the small windows in it covered up with yellowed newspaper.

Barclay rang the doorbell and waited. And waited.

'I don't think there's anyone home,' de Silva said.

Barclay leaned in closer to the door, certain he could hear movement beyond. A shuffle and a scrape. He tried the doorbell again, and the sound he had heard stopped. 'No, there's someone—'

The door flung open and someone flew past them, knocking Barclay backward into de Silva and they both hit the floor. Barclay reached for his radio. He screamed, 'Move in! Move into the front!' He got to his feet, pulled de Silva up and saw the suspect getting into his car. 'No, no, no.'

Barclay launched himself forward, bounding toward the Jeep and pulled on the handle. The door was locked. Barclay banged on the window, but the driver was focused. He revved the engine and raced for the junction and then it happened.

Barclay wasn't sure what he heard first, the slam or the crack as the car hit someone, or the terrible groan as they hit the ground. He couldn't tell who it was, but he was on his toes, running straight to them.

Everything seemed to move in slow motion. The car disappeared around the corner, the smell of burnt rubber in the air. The suspect gone, Barclay turned back to look for de Silva. She was on her phone and headed for him. The other officers appeared. One of the squad cars zipped past the junction, lights flashing and siren blaring, and one of his own team lay on the pot-holed road. PC Carmichael. Blood, deep red, spilled out of him from somewhere, but Barclay couldn't tell where.

Barclay heard de Silva's voice somewhere far away, echoing and tinny. 'Are they breathing?'

He couldn't move to check. His hand gripped Carmichael's as he lay still in the road.

'Barclay!'

Her voice snapped him back into the present. Every sound was sharp. He was aware of everything around him. He reached down and pressed his fingers into the officer's neck. A dull, slow, pulse. He took out his phone and held it in front of their mouth. The screen misted instantly. 'They're breathing,' he said.

He repositioned himself and moved to the other side.

Carmichael's eyes were open wide. The skin on his face was… Barclay wanted to turn away, but couldn't. Carmichael looked terrified. 'You're going to be okay,' Barclay said.

'The ambulance is on its way,' de Silva said. She was on her knees too and said to the others, 'Just stay back and tell me someone's gone after that car.'

'Two units, ma'am,' Lawrence said.

Good.

But Carmichael didn't look like he was in a good way. He shivered and there seemed to be blood everywhere, but Barclay couldn't figure out where it was coming from. He dragged off his coat and put it over Carmichael. His big hand held onto Barclay's.

'Talk to him,' de Silva said.

Barclay didn't know what to say. Words bumbled around his head, snippets of conversation he couldn't quite grab; nothing would feel right. 'We've sent someone after him,' he said finally.

Carmichael nodded, a shuddering nod that Barclay almost mistook for a convulsion. He pulled on Barclay's hand. 'Get... the fu... fucker.'

Barclay smiled. 'We will, Carmichael. Just stay with me, because you're going to want to look him in the eye when this is all over, aren't you?'

'I... I'm... c... cold.'

De Silva put her coat over him, too. 'Just hold on, all right? The ambulance is on its way.'

'Am... I... I... dy—?'

'Nah, you're not,' Barclay said. Spit flew from his lips onto Carmichael's face. The least of their worries. 'You're gonna be all right.'

The sound of sirens somewhere, getting louder. Carmichael's grip on Barclay loosened; he let go and his hand fell to the ground.

Barclay saw no immediate danger. In his mind, the killer was gone and he'd left the property wide open. He could have waited for Scientific Support to arrive, to preserve any potential evidence, but Amanda could have been in there. Could have been hurt.

She could be…

He took the rooms one by one, de Silva at his side. The place smelled clean. Too clean. Like lemon-scented bleach. It was clean and there was no sign that anyone else had been at the property other than the suspect.

His bedroom looked as though no one had ever slept in it. The window ledge and any flat surfaces were lined with porcelain dolls in Victorian clothing, their white eyes shining. There were redheads, brunettes, blondes, all white faces. All smiling or with open mouths in the shape of an O.

'Jesus,' de Silva said. 'These things freak me out.'

'I definitely don't think they freak the suspect out.' He moved to the bedroom door. 'Maloret, you still here?'

'Yes, sir.' She bounded up the stairs, pushed her phone into her back pocket. 'D'ya need me?'

'What was this guy's name?'

'Er…' She pulled out a tiny jotter from her pocket. 'Jonathan Dunn. Twenty-seven years old.'

'Thanks. Could you wait outside and let me know when Scientific Support get here?'

Maloret nodded and left the landing.

'Bathroom next,' Barclay said to de Silva. 'I never got a chance to tell you. The PM found that there was perfumed water in Kelly Stack's lungs.'

De Silva started at him almost blankly. 'Bathwater?' she said. 'Why would he bathe her? Did he do the same with the others, with Lynsey and Danielle?'

'Yes,' he said. 'I know fluid samples were taken. They came back as tap water. Some sort of soap was used, probably bubble bath.'

The bathroom was small and pink. Very pink. The bathtub, sink and toilet all came from the same era. More porcelain dolls.

Well, some people collect house plants and some collect dolls.

The dolls in the bathroom were different from the others.

De Silva moved alongside him to have a look at the ones along the bath. All were in various stages of undress. Some with their shoes and socks off, some their dresses gone, some just in their underskirts.

'He's obsessed, isn't he?' Barclay said.

'I'd say so,' de Silva said. 'Whether it's with the dolls themselves or what they represent, I couldn't know without speaking to him.'

'What they represent?'

'Well, they're all little girls.'

Barclay felt a chill run through him. It was so obvious. 'There's another room over there at the back.'

The room was dark, cast in red from the light filtering through the closed curtains. Barclay found the light switch and flicked it, and his breath caught in his throat. 'Jesus!' Dolls everywhere. All naked. All with make-up painted onto their faces, sloppily. The heavy make-up, the kind he'd seen in drag bars or bad TV shows about prostitutes.

He leaned in close to look at one doll, larger than all the others with blonde hair and a shocked expression on her face due to the drawn-on eyebrows. There was a hole cut into her stitching between her legs. A shining silver thread, something like glue, across her body and face. Barclay realised what it was, could smell it.

'Look.' De Silva's voice pulled him away. She was stood near the window at a desk with three computer screens. On one of them, a paused video. 'These poor little girls,' she said. 'God love them.'

Barclay had to look away from the screen, but it was too late. He'd seen enough. He compared their sizes to Sarah to guess their age and that made him angry with himself. They must have been about four or five years old.

Four or five.

This isn't our man at all.

Chapter Twenty-Six

There had been some blood. In the car, up the stairs, on his bed. She was still passed out. He'd tied her down to the bed, put a sock in her mouth and tied it into place with rope. He watched her lie there, her arms and legs strapped to the bed, unable to move. He had to do that, he'd reasoned with himself. She'd panic. She'd fight.

She looks like she hasn't aged a day. Be careful.

She had changed since the last time he saw her, just days ago. The cuts and bruises and bites and the blood were gone. As though she'd been... reborn. Remade... for him. But she was her, was Lisa. He wanted to touch her, to stroke her hair the way she had done his all those years ago. But there was work to do.

He took a sponge and a bucket full of hot water and bleach, and cleaned off any spots of blood from the stairs. He'd do the car later. She slept on through it all, quiet and still. He removed the sock from her mouth and checked her breathing. He pulled an old rickety wooden chair to the bedside and watched. Waited.

When he was a boy and his mum had gone out, probably to suck some fella's dick around the back of the Cabbage, Lisa would come around with a carrier bag full of sweets and crisps and fizzy drinks she'd nicked from the corner shop. They'd sit on the couch, his head in her lap, eat and drink and laugh and watch whatever video she'd

brought. One time, she brought *A Nightmare on Elm Street* and when it had come time for her to go, he'd cried.
Like a little bitch.
She'd stayed until the morning that time.

His face burned with the shame of crying in front of her, and he wondered whether Lisa remembered. Whether she'd laugh at him when she woke up again.

The blood had dried on her head, had matted in her hair. He could have stopped and spoken to her instead of this, could have explained who he was; not the little boy he was back then. But she would have laughed, she would have walked away, she would have pretended she didn't know him. She'd played that game before. No, no, this was better. She'd wake up soon and he could speak to her and she would listen. She'd have no choice.

Then they could watch a film together, eat shit and laugh like when he was younger. He'd already been the shop for the cheapest juice – just 49p – Space Raiders and chocolate. Lisa loved chocolate.

When he was eleven, just before his mum sent him away, Lisa had stopped coming round because she got herself a boyfriend. He'd wank and think about her sitting on his thing. The first time he shot out the white stuff like those men did in that place, he cried. It felt wrong and disgusting and he hadn't expected anything to come out the end of it.

He was glad Lisa wasn't in that place to see all that happened to them. Him, and the others. But when he looked for her afterward, she'd moved. His mum said he shouldn't go looking for her, that she'd got on with her life. Married, had a kid. She wouldn't want to see his stupid face gawping at her. He'd felt so angry, so hurt. He tried to squash it down, but it came out that one time…

He turned on the telly and skipped to the news. Lisa would be all over it by now, if her parents or fella were arsed. Sure enough, her picture was there, on the BBC, but they called her Amanda.

What the hell? I told you to be careful.

Panic and shame rose in him, like a fire burning at his insides.

He flipped through the channels to the local one. The man there still called her Amanda. He spoke over photos of her, about how her parents were devastated. He doubted it; they left her alone as much as his mum did. No mention of her fella, maybe they'd broken up. The pictures changed to video footage, of a woman going into a building and tripping over her own feet.

The news fella said, '*Detective Chief Inspector Winifred de Silva, seen here entering a Merseyside Police building is thought to be in charge of—*'

De Silva. We know that name.

'Mum?' Lisa's voice sounded strange. It was a whisper, and as he looked, her eyes were still closed. Her accent was different, like one of those rich snob twats he'd always hated.

'Lisa,' he said. 'It's me.' He turned off the telly.

'Where's my mum?' Her arm jerked but stayed in place. He'd done good with the knots this time. 'What's happening?' Her eyes sprang open, wide and full of terror.

'Shh,' he said. 'Shh, I don't want to have to give you the sock, Lis.' He reached for it anyway. 'I just want to talk.'

'Mum!' She screamed. She struggled against the ropes. 'Mum!'

He pushed the sock into her open mouth until it was all inside. Her moans were muffled, but still she struggled against the ropes.

She'll give in. Tire herself out. She always does.

'Shh!' It sounded harder than he'd meant it to. He tried again, gentler this time. He stroked her hair and those big, wide eyes glared at him. There was a moment of… what? Almost like she'd recognised him. 'You'll be all right. The bleeding's stopped.'

She struggled and tried to scream. He picked up the telly remote and raised it above her head. She winced.

'I don't want to,' he said. 'But I will, Lisa. I just want to talk to you. Will you listen?'

She screamed through the sock, muffled. No one would ever hear her. Her eyes darted about the room between the white walls, the telly, and his clothes on the rail. There was nothing else there, nothing that could help her.

Later, when the sun had gone down and she'd slept through most of the night, he paced the floor.

She should be awake.

She should be listening to everything that had happened to him. He remembered the last time he'd seen Lisa before he went to that place. She'd passed him half a joint and stepped out into the flickering, buzzing light of the corridor. Her boyfriend took her hand and led her away. He'd thought of them so many times, of how hard he fucked her, the way he'd hear his mum through the walls. He wondered if she screamed like his mum did.

'Wake up!' His voice was thick with anger, with hate, with desperation. 'Wake up, Lisa! You've been asleep too long!'

Her eyes shot open and she struggled against the ropes again.

'Stop it!' he screamed. 'Stop it! Stop it! Stop it!' His face was hot and wet. 'Why?' He moved closer to the bed, got to his knees and stroked her face, wet too. 'Why do you want to leave? No one ever cared about us, Lis. All we had was each other.'

She tried to speak, but the sock made her words a jumbled, grumbled mess. She shook her head.

'Okay, but if you scream' – he picked up the remote again – 'you won't scream again.'

She shook her head.

He removed the sock.

'I'm not Lisa,' she said. She was breathless, her voice hoarse and low. 'My name is Amanda. Amanda Maclennan.'

She's lying.

'No, no, no.' He stood, his hands to his ears. 'No, you're lying. Sneaky, sneaky bitch. Why are you being like this, Lis? I thought you liked me.'

Do it. Do it now before she tells you more lies. Before she gets you into trouble.

'I don't know who you are,' she said. Tears ran from her eyes. 'I just want to go home to my mum and dad.'

Clock her one. Right there, across the mouth.

'Your dad?' His head hurt as his mind raced and spun, and he felt dizzy. 'Your dad legged it with some other woman.' Everything was confused. *He* was confused. 'Lis, don't you remember?'

She's playing games with you.

'My name isn't Lisa,' she spat. 'My name is Amanda.'

LIES! Do it!

'Your name is Lisa fucking McLaughlin! Don't do this shit to me. I thought we were friends.' He rested his head against her restrained hands, could feel her fingers on his scalp, but something was off. 'I'm sorry, I'm sorry.' There was no softness in her touch. No care. 'You used to play with me, stroke my hair, stay with me when me mum was out drinking. You used to like me. Until you met that dickhead.'

'I don't know what you're talking about.' She barely managed to speak through ragged breaths.

'How could you forget?' He wanted to tell her how much it had meant to him. How those few hours they spent together on days when his mum was out with random men had stayed with him all these years. Talking about feelings, emotions, things that had happened… that wasn't something he was supposed to do. Something his mum discouraged. She didn't hug, or tell him she loved him. Sometimes, she didn't even come home and he'd have to try to open a tin of beans with a knife so he wouldn't starve.

One sneaky little snake, this one. Do her in. Get it over with.

'We don't talk out loud about these things,' the deputy headmistress, Mrs Jones, had said in that place. 'We keep them to ourselves, and we do it in silence. Nobody needs to know, do they?'

'No,' he'd replied. He'd go to sleep sore, tears in his eyes, and praying. He'd beg for it to stop, for the men to go away, for Mrs Jones to die in her sleep. For someone to come and rescue them, rescue him.

No one ever came then. No one would come now.

'I'm not whoever you think I am,' the girl said. 'Just let me go home, I won't tell anyone who you are or where you are. I don't even know your name.'

'Lisa, please,' he said. 'I've loved you forever. I just want to be with you. All those nights in that place, I thought about you.'

She went quiet for a while. She didn't struggle against her binds. He didn't even hear her breath. He thought of leaning over to check her pulse again when she said, 'Okay.' She seemed calm. 'Okay, I'm Lisa.'

Careful now.

'Then why did you lie and say you're not?'

'Because you're scaring me.'

He put his head against her stomach, heard it groan and bubble. He lay there for what felt like hours. He could have fallen asleep there. 'We're going to watch our favourite film together,' he said. 'Do you remember?'

Silence.

See. Games.

He sat up and looked at her, wiped his wet face with his hand. 'Do you remember our film? Your Uncle Robbie lent it to you.'

She shook her head. 'No,' she said. 'No, I can't remember the film, but I remember Uncle Robbie.'

Lying slut!

His voice came out low, a growl. 'My Lis didn't have an Uncle Robbie. And our film? We watched it all the time.'

The girl cried.

'You should know.' He leaned right into her face and said, 'You should know.' She screamed. 'You should know!'

He stood and looked at her then, the girl strapped to his bed, whoever she was, and realised with that awful sinking of comprehension: Lisa wouldn't ever be scared of him, she'd never forget the film. She'd stroke his hair and make him feel safe, even for a few hours, no matter how naughty he'd been. These games they play. They look like her, wear her face, tell them they want him. Then, when they have him, they scream and cry and beg to leave. It wasn't fair.

It's not fair. Do it. Do it now.

'What are you doing?' The voice, shaken and ancient, came out of nowhere. For a moment he thought someone else was inside his head. He turned around and there she was. Phyl in the doorway, her shaking, wrinkled hand gripping the door frame. The door. In his panic, his excitement, his eagerness, he'd forgotten to lock the door.

She turned on her heel, tried to move fast toward the stairs. He was on his feet before he knew what he was going to do. He caught up to her and gripped her from behind, his hand clamped over her mouth. She scratched at his arm and he dragged her backward. Her slippers pulled from her feet.

'You shouldn't be here,' he whispered in her ear so soft, almost a hiss. He dragged her back inside.

He closed the door to his flat.

Someone came out from across the corridor and shouted, but Lewis could barely hear it behind his closed door. 'Turn the music down, you tit!' They slammed their own front door.

He turned off the TV and the place rang in silence.

Chapter Twenty-Seven

De Silva's fresh bedding smelled thick and sweet. She'd used the orchid-scented softener from the gold bottle, and it smelled like heaven, but even so, she couldn't sleep.

She felt bad for Barclay. His first major lead turned out to be a dead end; but, because of him, another predator was off the street and on his way to the nick. Though she wasn't convinced O'Brien would see it quite so positively.

The suspect had crashed his car on Queens Drive, out toward Old Swan. Must have been headed for the M62 when he lost control and it flew into a wall. He was scratched up and concussed, but they had him. That was some small solace. Carmichael on the other hand, the doctors had stopped some internal bleeding, but the following few hours would be critical. De Silva thought about his family, whether he had a partner or kids, a mother. They must have been in agony.

'We should have some patrols out along the river,' she'd said to Barclay earlier. 'If the worse comes to the worst, we catch him in the act of trying to dump her.'

'Do you think he will?' Barclay had asked, his hands on his hips. 'Won't he think we're expecting that?'

Truth be told, she wasn't sure. Should the blood sample from the pavement at the back of Walton Hall Park come back as a positive match, they'd know exactly where she was taken from, which was a starting point. But what had made him take her so soon after Kelly?

Lying in bed, she thought about calling Barclay and making him order the patrols tonight. With any luck, they'd have someone available, or at the very least be able to have them ready for the early hours. She looked at the clock. 10.45 p.m. Late in the night, and she didn't want to wake his daughter up. She picked up her phone regardless, because a call came through.

Sunview Home Calling.

'Hello?'

'Mrs de Silva?'

A knife to her heart. 'Yes.'

'It's Gina from Sunview.' She paused, waited for some sort of acknowledgement. 'Your mum's had a fall, love. I'm so sorry.' She didn't sound sorry. She sounded tired and fed up, her voice strained but soft. 'The ambulance has taken her to the Royal Hospital.'

'What happened?'

'Well, I wasn't on shift. Obviously, it's very late, but I came in soon as I heard.'

'So no one's told you what's happened? You're ringing me with half an update?' She was already out of bed, pulling on some jeans.

'I'm sorry, I only just got here myself,' Gina said. 'I rang you straight away.'

'Was anyone with her? Is anyone with her now?'

'We don't have the staff to take her in an ambulance…'

'So she's alone then?'

De Silva didn't wait for a response. She hung up and pulled on a hoody from a set of drawers, forced her feet into some already-tied-up Converses from the wardrobe and bounded down the stairs. She tried to call Laney, but it went straight to voicemail.

As she drove toward the Royal, de Silva realised she should have stayed on the phone. Should have asked more questions, like where she was in the hospital. De Silva slammed the steering wheel.

Fuck!

She should call Gina back, but she couldn't bear the thought of that woman's voice. Instead, she tried Laney again. *'This is the voicemail for Laney Brophy, please leave a message and I'll get back to you.'* Brophy. She'd gone back to her maiden name. Something had happened between her and David, and her sister had not even picked up the phone to talk about it. That cut de Silva deeply, but it wasn't entirely unexpected.

Why would she ring you? You made it clear to her, to everyone, that you wanted to be left alone.

De Silva knew she couldn't be pissed off that people did what she'd wanted. Her fractured relationship with her sister was older than Ritchie's death by a few years. Things hadn't been the same since their dad died.

She parked in the Q-Park across the road from the Royal, forgetting that the old building was mostly closed and so had to walk around to the new one a few minutes' walk away. She could have parked closer and saved time. She hadn't been thinking straight. She didn't know what state her mum would be in when she got there. Maybe it was just bruising, a sprained wrist at most.

The voice of pessimism chimed in: *Or a broken hip*. De Silva winced. She imagined her mum in pain, the nurses trying to treat her, Marie not knowing what was going on. She quickened her pace.

The automatic doors slid open, a blast of hot air from above like a curtain of warmth. Inside, the building looked so different from the old part of the hospital. Everything was new and shiny. There was a smell of wood and metal and harsh chemicals. She coughed and approached the reception desk and gave in her mum's name.

'Mrs Marie Brophy,' the man at reception, a large guy in a shirt branded with the logo of some security company, repeated. 'She's not related to Carl Brophy, is she?' The man smiled and de Silva saw how worn his face was, how deep the lines around his eyes etched into his skin.

'That's my dad,' she said.

'I worked with your dad years ago,' he said. 'The eighties. He was a good man was Carl.'

De Silva wondered how he'd ended up working security in a hospital, but didn't want to ask. Didn't have the time. 'He was,' she said.

'Your mam's up on the third floor,' he said. 'Do you know how to get there? I'm all turned around in this place.'

'I can find it.'

'The lifts are just behind me.' He pointed with a chubby finger over his shoulder. 'I was sorry to hear about your da, girl.' His eyes were soft, almost hazy. 'And I hope your mam's all right.'

Well, she's not all right, she wanted to say. 'Thank you. That's kind of you.' She walked off toward the lifts and felt instant guilt. That man was of a different era, where people spoke to each other without suspicion or anxiety. He'd known her dad, probably her mum too, and she'd not even bothered to ask his name.

The lift pinged as she stepped out onto the third floor. The corridors were quiet at this hour. She stepped out into the gloom and the lights popped to life as she walked down the corridor. She heard screams. Not screams of fear – she recognised those all too well. These were different. They were frustrated, they were tearful, and confused. They were her mum's.

She rounded the corner and pressed a buzzer at a locked security door. The voice that came through was tinny and the speaker fuzzed. 'Hello?'

'I'm DC— I'm Win de Silva, Marie Brophy's daughter. I was told she was brought in.'

'Push the door, love.'

The ward was hot, and de Silva took off her coat. There was a row of seats against the wall in a small waiting room. Laney sat there, typing at her phone with both thumbs.

She stood up when she saw de Silva, her eyes were red, her face wet. Her dark hair, their mum's hair, tied up in a ponytail. De Silva wanted to hug her, but Laney crossed her arms. 'Sunview rang me.' Laney didn't look at her sister. A scream from somewhere. 'They can't calm her down.'

'I'll go in in a minute,' de Silva said. 'Are you all right, though?' She touched Laney's shoulder. She expected her sister to wince or pull away, but she didn't move.

'No,' Laney said.

'Do you want to come in with me?'

'No.'

De Silva nodded and walked on toward the screams. Marie was in a side room off the main corridor. They'd fastened her to the bed with padded restraints, and de Silva felt sick. The room stank worse than outside. A nurse had a mop and was cleaning the floor. He looked up when he noticed de Silva.

'What are you doing to her?' De Silva flew at her mum and put her hand on Marie's head. 'It's all right, Mum. I'm here.'

Marie stopped struggling. Stopped screaming. Her voice was raw. 'Win. Oh, love, let me out. I want to go home.'

Anger surged in de Silva's chest and throat. 'Is there any need for these?' She pulled at one of the restraints.

'She attacked three nurses,' he said. He showed cuts up his arm.

'She's not an animal – undo these now!'

'We can't until she's calmed down,' he said. 'I'm sorry.' He took the mop and left.

Marie had a hefty black bruise across her cheekbone and her eye was bloodshot, so red that de Silva thought she was bleeding. She wanted to undo the restraints and carry her out, take her home and care for Marie herself. A rage boiled inside her.

She headed back out to the corridor and marched to the nurses' bank. Laney was already there. 'Who's in charge in here?'

'I am.' A tall woman with short, cropped hair and thick forearms. She pointed at her name badge and said, 'Ali.'

'Yeah, I can read, love,' de Silva snapped. 'Have you given her any pain meds?'

'Your mum has been too unstable for us to administer medication of any kind, even the stuff they brought in with her.'

'She's got dementia, you stupid cow.' De Silva couldn't help herself.

'I beg your pardon!' Ali's eyebrows knitted together. 'How dare you—'

'How dare *you* withhold pain medication from a sick woman! You've not even told us what happened to her.'

'I wasn't here when she was brought in.'

'Well, you're here now, so get in there and give her something so she can get some sleep.'

Laney's eyes were wide, her mouth open, fully engrossed in the exchange.

'I've told you, she's too unstable.'

'She's calm! I've just been with her.'

'I'll go,' the man who had mopped the room said. 'I'll sort it.'

Ali rolled her eyes and walked off, her shoes squeaking as she stomped down the corridor toward the security door.

De Silva slumped into one of the chairs in the small waiting room. Laney stood near her, arms folded, staring. 'Jesus, Win,' she said. 'Was there any need for that? You weren't here through the worst of it. I was. She wouldn't see me. Didn't even recognise me. But then soon as she saw you…'

'I see her all the time,' de Silva said. It was heavy with implication, with accusation, and she knew it.

'Oh.'

'Can we just leave this for tonight?' De Silva's head had started to pound. 'For Mum's sake.'

Laney sat down in a chair opposite de Silva. 'That's this family's motto, isn't it? Don't talk about the things staring you in the face. Don't ask questions.'

'What are you on about?'

'You and Mum never told me what happened to Dad,' she said. 'Then she got sick and you still wouldn't tell me.'

'He died, Laney! What more is there to know?'

'You didn't ring me to come and say goodbye. You robbed me of that, and I don't think I'll ever forgive you.'

A punch to the gut. De Silva and Marie had both thought they'd done the right thing. Those last few minutes of their dad's life were moments of sheer pain. He didn't look like himself, and in the rage of pain he felt, he said some awful things about his family.

'I don't know what to say to you,' de Silva said.

Laney stood up. She sauntered off and de Silva made no effort to stop her.

Laney left a silence so loud that de Silva's ears rang. The nurse's voice broke into it; Ollie, according to his name badge. 'Your mum's settled now. She'll sleep through the night, I hope. I'm sorry,' he said. 'Everyone's feeling the pressure here – you know, post-Covid. We're stretched.'

There were five of them stood behind the nurses' station, but de Silva chose not to address that. What did she know about nurse activity and running a hospital? 'It's fine,' she said. He stood there a moment too long. Maybe he expected an apology, too. It would never come.

'You're welcome to stay,' he said. 'But I'd say go home and get some sleep.'

De Silva nodded and looked at her watch. 11.15 p.m. She closed her eyes, rested her head on the wall behind her and breathed deep.

After what felt like just seconds, de Silva's phone vibrated in her pocket and she started. She fished for it and saw the time was 2.33 a.m. *Great*.

Barclay calling.

'De Silva.' His voice was light. 'Just got a call. There's been a body found near Marine Lake in Waterloo. Can you come?'

'Yeah,' she said. 'Yeah, I'll be twenty minutes.' She knew without any further explanation that the body would belong to Amanda Maclennan. She should have called Barclay in the car about those patrols along the river.

'Sound. See you there.' The line went dead.

Laney slept next to her, laying across three seats. She'd covered herself with her coat and she didn't wake up when de Silva moved. She'd send her a text on her way out.

—

De Silva drove up Cambridge Road to the junction with Brunswick Parade. Barclay waited there at the cordon, next to three PCSOs. De Silva assumed he'd been giving them instructions. He jumped into the car when de Silva arrived and she pulled onto the two-track road that stretched out toward the Marine Lake.

'Is it her?' De Silva lowered the radio. She'd found the constant chatter of early-morning radio presenters soothing on her drive over.

'Turn left here,' Barclay said.

They pulled into a pay-and-display car park; a hive of comings and goings. Scientific Support had already arrived. *Quick work.* She spotted Brennan removing his white suit at the side panel of one of the vans.

'I've not been down yet,' Barclay said. There were bags under his eyes, and a sort of distance in his voice. 'Was waiting for you.'

De Silva parked up on the opposite side to the Scientific Support vans, next to Barclay's own car, and walked over to Brennan. She nodded at his protective suit, scrunched up in his hands. 'You got any spares in that van of yours?'

'De Silva!' His smile was warm but respectful, given the circumstances. 'Long time no see. Barclay said you were on your way.'

'What're we looking at?' Barclay interjected.

'You mean, is it her?' Brennan replied.

Barclay nodded. His jaw clenched, hands firm in his pockets.

'I can't tell,' Brennan said. He pulled the coverings off his shoes – battered old black Reeboks. 'Not with the damage he's done.'

De Silva looked to Barclay. He looked down at the dusty car-park floor. 'Hey,' she said. 'We don't know anything yet.'

Barclay nodded.

Brennan dug about in the van and pulled out some suits in clear packages. 'Photography team are just getting started so don't get in the way down there.'

De Silva took the suit. 'Thanks. I'll see you around, Brennan.' She went back to the car, threw her coat onto the back seat among the old carrier bags and fast-food wrappers, all empty.

'I get it now,' Barclay said.

'Get what?' She pulled her legs through the suit.

'Why he wanted you back. O'Brien.'

'Stop it,' de Silva said. 'You're getting into your own head. Put that suit on and let's get down there.'

'No, it's more than that.' He leaned against the car and stared at the suit in its packet. 'I'm not good at this. I'm not you.'

De Silva stopped. She looked up into his face. 'You don't need to be me,' she said. 'Taking chances, putting people's careers at risk. You be you. You follow the rule book and you make it work for you.'

'I've messed this whole thing up from the start. I convinced everyone to move on the wrong suspect and now an officer is in intensive care.'

'You name me another detective that could do any better with grainy CCTV footage, hardly any evidence and not much of anything to go on. You're working through it all as it comes to you. I'd do the exact same.' She put her arms into the suit and zipped it.

'Except you wouldn't,' he said. 'You've got this… thing… like you see the victim, make choices based on your instinct, on that thing in you that knows what's happened.'

'A lot of that's horseshit, Barclay,' she said. 'I imagine myself in the victim's shoes, absolutely, but I can only base that on what's in front of me. What the evidence is showing. Come on, let's get down there.'

'De Silva…' He paused. His mouth open, like he couldn't find the words. 'What if they're right?'

'Who?'

'People at the station. The PCs and the detectives. O'Brien.'

'Right about what?'

'About me,' he said. 'That I was given this job, you know, to tick a box.'

'What are you waffling on about? Just come out and say it.'

'Well, they think I was hired because I'm gay.'

De Silva held the hairnet in her hand and studied him for a smile, or a wink, something that would tell her that Barclay was pulling her leg. Nothing. 'Barclay…'

'No, I mean it de Silva,' he said. 'I've heard the conversations in the corridors when they think I can't hear them.'

'Whatever job you're in, you're gonna meet homophobic pricks. They're also the laziest shower of shite and haven't got the drive to get where you want to get. Where you are. Your position now is their dream job. I'm sure you met people like that in the navy.'

'Yeah.'

'And I wouldn't let O'Brien catch you accusing him of hiring you because of your sexuality, you know? O'Brien watches. He has his eyes out everywhere. He's spoken about you for years. Well before you were asked to interview for the job.'

'Really?'

'Really,' she said. 'I get it though, you know. My dad was best mates with the DSI. You don't think that people talked about me? I had to work twice as hard as the men to get half the recognition I deserved. Add my dad's career and friendship with O'Brien into that, and it was tough.'

Barclay nodded.

De Silva knew that his confidence had been knocked when they moved on the wrong suspect. Another sexual predator was behind bars, true, but that didn't mean the dead girls would stop.

'You're doing a great job under the circumstances,' she said. 'And you've got to believe it. Even if they don't. Now put that suit on and let's get down there.'

He tossed his jacket into her car. 'Jesus, de Silva, get this thing cleaned. I'm considering leaving my jacket on the fence post. It'd be cleaner.'

'I'm scared what they'll find, to be honest.' She chuckled and pulled on the hairnet, then the hood. 'Put it in your own bloody car anyway!'

Brennan's van disappeared along the road back toward the cordon and the car park was silent. It had started to drizzle by the time Barclay had gotten himself ready. They walked from the car park onto a footpath that ran the length of Marine Lake and turned on their phone torches.

The light didn't make much difference. Boats were tied onto a small harbour near the sports centre across the lake, and de Silva could make out the reflection of white security lights on racked-up canoe hulls. Metal ground against metal in almost ghostly echoes from the working docks nearby and out in front of them; the eternal shush of the sea.

'Thanks for before,' Barclay said, his voice bright in the dark.

'Don't mention it,' she said. 'Seriously, don't. You know I don't like all that lovey-dovey stuff.'

He nudged her with his elbow and said, 'Shut up. But all right, I won't.'

'You feel how you feel, and that's fine,' she said. 'But people do have your back.' She left it there. The path seemed to go on forever, and finally, they could make out the dunes to the right, like giants sleeping in the sand.

'We need to keep following this fence,' Barclay said. 'The path goes right near the dunes and there's beach access. She's over to the left, right on the mouth of the river.'

'Who found her?'

'A dog walker.'

De Silva looked at her watch. 3.15 a.m. 'It's early for dog walkers.'

'The guy works late shifts,' Barclay said. 'He takes the dog out when he gets home to unwind before bed. So he says. I had someone take his statement. We'll follow up tomorrow.

'His dog was sniffing about near the rocks over there. Wouldn't come back when she was called, started barking. The guy, Leslie Francis, found her there. The way he described the body, nothing like Kelly Stack. He thought she'd been there for days, so he said. She could have been.'

'Definitely female?'

'He could tell that much.' Barclay's voice was grim now.

The bright lights of the crime scene crawled out of the black beyond the footpath, raked up into the clouds and reminded de Silva of a lighthouse. It would be seen for miles around, even across the water in New Brighton or Port Sunlight. *Beware*, it said. *Dead girls and rocks*.

Another cordon to duck and then they walked under the roof of the forensic tent without anyone paying them any mind. The drizzle sounded heavy under the tarpaulin and the photographers snapped at imprints from shoes and animals, tracks that could lead somewhere or nowhere. Another photographer hovered over a red rock, snapped shot after shot. Changed position and went for it again.

Barclay looked away when the flash went off. 'Where is she?' he asked one of the photographers. They pointed in the direction of the red rock.

De Silva whispered to herself, 'Oh my God.' Her gut wrenched and she held her breath. It seemed improper to breathe here, like any sound could disturb evidence or could wake the dead.

The rock was red from blood that had seeped out of the girl's body. From de Silva's estimations, it was a girl, early teens. She had seen some of this before. Deep lacerations to faces, split lips and missing teeth, dried blood caked to the inside of thighs, eyes so swollen she wasn't entirely sure there was any eye left. Yes, she'd seen it before, but not all in one place. Not all on one person.

De Silva took in the scene, everything in front of her, and closed her eyes. Barclay gave her a few minutes. 'I think we'll find that he's dragged her here, at least partially. Tried to hurry. It's all over the scene – look, all over her. This is a rush job. Not the usual care he'd take.'

'He's not cleaned her,' Barclay said.

'What does that tell us about this victim? Why is she different?'

'There was a sense of urgency with her. Something didn't go to plan. He had to dispose of her quickly. She's not even in water, but close to it. Maybe he was disturbed?'

'Right,' she said.

De Silva took herself out of the crime scene. She imagined Amanda being dragged along the dusty path toward the rocks; stones scraped at her back and arms. She went further back, to the boot of some car, stinking of stale things. Even further back, where the man held a hammer above her and struck; where he forced himself into her time and again. She had been gagged, barely conscious from pain.

'He's escalating,' she said. 'Losing control of himself.'

'The violence, you mean.'

'The other three victims.' She cleared her throat. 'The other three girls. There was evidence of violence, yes. Sexual. Bites. Strangulation. But this…'

Barclay got closer. 'Excuse me,' he said to the photographer, who stepped away. Barclay squatted and shone his phone's torch into the destroyed face.

De Silva knew what he would be thinking. The hair colour matched Amanda's, matched the other girls', but without a dental comparison, finger printing, or DNA test, there was no way they could know for sure. Her face was gone. Her parents wouldn't be able to make a positive ID.

A closed casket.

De Silva imagined her in her uniform, hockey stick slung over her shoulder. She walked down a quiet street, and he came out of nowhere. From behind her. The element of surprise always made victims that bit weaker. The lack of understanding about what was happening would have made her powerless against him.

'I've seen enough,' Barclay said. He stood and walked out of the tent. 'I'm going home.'

De Silva followed him out into the rain and the dark. 'Wait there, will you?' She caught up with him. She wanted to remove the hood and the hairnet, but they'd need to preserve this footpath as much as possible. 'You spent no time at all in there, what's going on?'

'Another dead girl,' he said. 'What else is there to see? I'm letting them down. If that's Amanda in there then we're back to square one and we know nothing.'

'No, we're not back to square one. Your team's working hard. You're closing in on him.'

'Come on, de Silva...'

'We don't even know if this is our guy. I agree that's Amanda out there, I know it in my gut. But we've not seen that level of aggression in any of the other victims. He's either escalating or losing control.'

'Or there's someone else out there.' He was serious. He pulled the hood down, took off the safety specs.

'You think he's got help?'

'Yeah,' he said. 'Too much doesn't add up. Too much coincidence. The killer avoids every one of the cameras on the network. The bodies are cleaned down before they're dumped. Mostly discarded in water, where even more evidence is destroyed. Think about it...'

In truth, she already had thought about it. Anyone who wanted to do a good job could find books on how evidence was collected, so they could destroy it; watch a Netflix true-crime series to understand police procedure. 'No, if there was a second killer, we'd know. On that CCTV footage, there was only him down at Canning Dock.'

'Just because we only saw one person on screen doesn't mean he was alone,' he said. 'Either way, she's dead.'

De Silva dropped the hood of her suit, the rain cold on her face and scalp. 'None of this is your fault. Just go home, Barclay. Try to get some sleep and we'll pick this up in a few hours.'

'I can't sleep,' he said.

She knew that already. He looked a mess. His skin was dry, and his breath reeked of old coffee. She couldn't imagine she looked any better. 'You should try,' she said, but it was useless. This was his first big case. His make-or-break, in his own eyes. She remembered the case that had almost broken her; how many hours she'd stayed awake and went over things again and again. Over the years, she'd learned to keep a professional distance. That case, forty-three-year-old single father of two little girls, butchered in his flat in Toxteth. She'd almost quit the police after that.

'I'm going home,' he said.

They walked in silence back to the car park, their torch lights bobbing ahead of them. When they got there, Barclay almost ripped the suit off himself and tossed it into the back of his car. He opened the driver side and said, 'See you in a few hours.'

He drove away.

De Silva moved slowly, removed each part of the kit piece by piece and folded it into the clear packet it came from. She'd dispose of it tomorrow at OCC. Barclay's jacket was there, among the debris of her life. She grabbed it, but his taillights were already far off. She'd give it to him tomorrow. It smelled like him, still. Citrus and black pepper and something else she couldn't name.

She removed the foot coverings last and threw them in the car and climbed in. She turned the key – even her car sounded exhausted. She flicked on the wipers and they squeaked against the glass. De Silva saw it, bright white in the night and spotted with rain, flapping in a light breeze.

She got back out and looked closer at the paper under the wiper. Not a piece of paper. An envelope.

4 DA SILVER

Chapter Twenty-Eight

Barclay planned to drive straight to OCC. He'd sent a text to Nick, got no reply. Barclay would need to explain himself later. Or tomorrow. Right now, there was only room in his mind for the case.

He was sure that O'Brien would boot him from the investigation, hand it over to the next up-and-coming detective; a smarter one who got shit done, who moved quicker and didn't play by the book. That or he'd give it to de Silva. Barclay didn't know what would be worse. Either way, he had failed the girls. Failed himself. Proved everyone who whispered behind his back right; the ones who said he was hired for the fact that he was gay, and not for his competence.

As he drove past the cordon on Cambridge Road, his phone rang through the car speaker.

De Silva calling.

'For God's sake. Just give me a minute,' he said aloud and declined it. She came straight back through and he declined that call, too.

Headlights blasted in his rear-view mirror. He pulled over on the path, just before the cordon, climbed out and waited. De Silva's dirty once-white Kuga pulled up behind his car and she bounced out.

'I know, I forgot my jacket,' he said. 'It's not the end of the world.'

She had something in her hand, enclosed perfectly in an evidence bag.

Old habits die hard.

'It's not your jacket,' she said. 'There was a note on my car.'

'From who?'

'I've not opened it.' She showed him the envelope. The writing looked to him like when Sarah practised her letters, her hand unsure of how to hold the pencil, not certain that the shapes she made would tell the story she wanted to tell.

'Not the killer?'

'Who else?'

'Well, that would mean that he's been here,' he said. 'He could still be here.'

De Silva put the evidence bag into her coat pocket.

Barclay thought of getting the helicopter. It might not get authorised in time, even if the budget allowed for it. *Nah, he'll be gone by the time it gets here.*

'What do you want to do?'

'I want to take a look around before I leave,' he said. 'Take that note to OCC. See if anyone's about who can process it. I'll ring O'Brien to get him to authorise it. We just need to hope it's not someone's shopping list.'

'See you in a bit.' De Silva ran back to her car and was gone before Barclay had collected his thoughts together.

There were still some PCSOs on the cordon up ahead, three of them. 'Good night, guys.' They didn't reply, and Barclay got into his car and turned left down Waterloo Road, left again onto Marine Terrace.

There were a few cars parked, all empty. None of them were the type of car he was looking for. Light blue maybe, a 4x4, partial reg *WL*. He glided past the massive houses, painted pastel colours that leapt out from the night. They reminded him of the *Mary Poppins* movie. Massive old things, remnants of the opulence of a different age. Some of them had been converted into multiple-occupancy properties. Barclay wondered what the previous owners would think of that. *Oh shut up. None of this matters. Concentrate!*

The road was quiet. Even at this hour, the usual boom and buzz from the bars, pubs and restaurants on South Road just up on the right was silent. He remembered all those early-morning shifts as a uniform, sometimes sat in areas like this, waiting. Watching. Sometimes sat in the bobby station, hoping that something would happen. For just a few hours in the predawn, it felt as though the whole world held its breath.

He drove down to Adelaide Terrace and found nothing. Turned left onto Blucher Street. There was a car park there that he and Nick used when they took Sarah to the beach. There was a footpath to the right that led straight down to the dunes.

As he turned the corner, headlights shone onto the grass verge before the dunes. His heart pounded and he held his breath. He turned into the car park. It was a tiny red Citroën. He approached it slowly and parked next to it. There was a man on his own in the car. A larger guy, the skin around his neck loose and hanging, and he stared at Barclay.

Not him. The car was all wrong. He'd struggle to get a dead girl in that tiny boot. *So that's how it is. Thinking of the dimensions of car boots and bodies.* He shivered. Thick Neck nodded at him and mumbled something Barclay couldn't hear.

He climbed out of his car and approached Barclay, driver side. Barclay lowered the window. 'What're you doing here?' he asked.

'Was gonna ask you the same thing,' the man mumbled. 'You here for the same thing I am?' The man touched himself, stroked the solid small thing in his trousers.

Barclay smiled and showed the man his warrant card. 'No, I don't think I am,' he said.

The man didn't move. 'Am I under arrest?'

'You seen anyone else around?'

'Some weirdo,' he said. 'Stared at me from his car. Am I in trouble?'

'Not if you go home as soon as you've answered my questions and don't come back here again.'

'What do you wanna know?'

'What was he driving?'

'Some old thing,' Thick Neck said. 'Looked like it'd been battered. Patchy paint, rusted. Absolute show.'

'A four-by-four?'

'Yeah, I'd say so.'

'Light blue?'

'Well, it's hard to see, isn't it? Couldn't tell at first, but erm…'

'But what?'

'Ah, nothing. Just forget it. Can I go, or what?'

'When you've answered my question, yeah.' Barclay was running low on patience. This man had information that Barclay needed, and he wanted it now.

Thick Neck looked around at the empty fields, the dunes beyond, over to the red lights of the cranes at Liverpool Port. Even from this distance, and even at this hour, metal ground there, things pounded. It was the only sound in the night.

'I'm already in enough trouble as it is. Don't want to bring the bizzies down on anyone else cause of me.' Thick Neck shook his head, his neck wobbled like jelly.

'If you don't tell me what you know, you'll be coming with me down the station. Do you want that?'

'Ah for God's sake,' Thick Neck said. 'Wait there, I'll show you.' He wobbled back to his car, and Barclay followed. 'I keep records of cars, colours, all that. Models, makes. This fella was a Toyota.'

'What did he do while he was here?'

'He headed off toward all those lights over there.' Thick Neck pointed across Marine Lake, toward the bright lights of the crime scene. 'Came back pretty quick and got off.'

'What did he look like?'

'Tall. Looked like he had an all right body underneath his hoody like. A bit like…' Thick Neck paused and looked away from Barclay, ducked his head into his car. '…Never mind.' He showed Barclay a small notepad. 'I like to just make a note so I know who's playing, who's watching, who's wastin' time.'

'I see,' Barclay said. 'Is there much going on at this time of night usually?'

'Sometimes,' he said. 'Some scallies, a few people walking their dogs. Well, you know it's late, isn't it? They're not really here to walk their dogs.' He smirked, his teeth small and grey.

Barclay stared at the scrawled, scruffy writing scratched out in pencil. Barclay took a photograph of it. 'I can't make it out. Which one is him?'

'Here.' Thick Neck pointed. 'M115 EWL. A Toyota. A bloody old one, like.'

Barclay entered the reg into his phone's notes. 'Can you wait here? Just fifteen minutes or so. I want you to give a description of the man you saw to one of my officers. Okay?'

He looked at his watch, and Barclay noticed the glint of a wedding ring. 'Well, er… Come on now, it's late. You said I could go,' the man spluttered.

'What's your name?' Barclay hoped his voice sounded authoritative.

'Cameron,' he said. 'Harry Cameron.'

'What do you do Harry?'

'I, er… I work in a bar.'

'Which bar?'

'One in Birkenhead,' he said. 'Is this important?'

'What do you do there?'

He spluttered and his neck wobbled. 'Why is this important?'

'It's just a question, Harry. Why're you getting so worked up about it? Is there something you don't want me to know?' An old tactic, one Barclay hated to use; he broke it out only in those times where he was getting nowhere fast.

'No!' Harry said. 'No, I'm just a barman, but please, you're not going to tell them, are you?'

'And you're married.'

Harry put his hand into his pocket and looked down at the gravel car park. 'None of your business.'

'Jesus, Harry.' Barclay shook his head. 'Look, you were going to hang around for whatever you were up to. Just fifteen minutes, then you can go. I've got your reg and I can find out where you work really easy. So if you leave, I'll get an officer to come to you. Understand?'

'No need for that, mate,' Harry said. 'I'll wait, I'll wait. It's fine.'

Barclay hopped back into his car and the tyres screeched as it careered out of the car park. He zipped between the cars on Adelaide and Marine Terrace and back around toward the cordon. He pulled up to the PCSOs, gravel clanging against the bodywork. 'There's a man in the car park just off Blucher. He's going to give you a description. When you've got it, I want you to ring me immediately. Don't wait. Ring me with it. I'll be back at OCC.'

They stared at him blankly, but he didn't wait for a response. They'd get it done or they'd be in trouble when he saw them again. He flicked through the screen on his dashboard until he found his most recent calls. He pressed on the incident-room number. The call was answered within one ring. 'That you, Maloret? Why're you still at work?'

'Couldn't sleep.' She sounded like the energy had been sucked out of her, lethargic and dulled by something. 'Mum took a turn last week and she's still at the hospital.'

'It's serious?'

'Yeah, I'm afraid it is.'

'Are you all right?'

'About Mum? Yeah, I'm used to it. But she needs full-time care, and I just can't afford that right now. But, we'll manage.' She went quiet for a moment. 'Sir, there's something else. Carmichael died, sir,' she said. 'About an hour ago. Internal bleeding. They thought they had it under control.'

Barclay didn't know what to say. He stopped at a red light and the click-clock of the indicator filled the quiet in the car. Barclay's chest tightened, and he swallowed repeatedly. It was inescapable now. The plans he'd put in place, the poorly constructed ones where people got hurt had led to someone's death.

'Are you still there, sir?'

'I'm sorry.' His voice cracked. There was so much to be sorry for. Carmichael, Amanda, Kelly. 'You should get home, Maloret. Is there anyone else around?'

'I can't sleep,' she said. 'I'm going through the lists. I ended up doing a VLOOKUP in Excel. I was going to ring you, still took some time like with a partial plate. But think I found a possibility.' Even at this, there was no excitement or anticipation in her voice.

'M115 EWL?'

'Yeah!' Her tone changed. Brighter somehow. 'How'd you know?'

'I got the reg from a dogger at Crosby beach.'

Silence. 'Oh,' she said finally. 'Well, I didn't expect that.'

'I was ringing for you to run it for us,' he said. 'But you've already done the hard work. I won't forget this, Maloret.'

'It's me job,' she said.

Barclay knew it was much more than that to her, to de Silva, and people like O'Brien. It was more than a job to himself. People talked of nursing being a calling, of taking holy orders. No one ever said it about the police, but that didn't mean it wasn't true. When Barclay left the navy, he was broken and carried his tattered reputation on his back. He'd needed order to his chaos.

'Who's the vehicle registered to?'

'A man called Lewis Lamond.' She took a breath. 'He wasn't on the sex offenders register. But it was the only vehicle I could find matching the CCTV from the Pump House. There's a spate of other misdemeanours. Theft.

Burglary. All when he was younger. Nothing like…' she trailed off.

Nothing like this. 'You got an address?'

'Yeah, in Fazakerley. Do you want it now?'

'No, I'm on my way back to the station,' he said. 'Is de Silva there yet?'

'I've not seen her.'

'Okay,' he said. His mind raced ahead of him. It was already back in the OCC, already pacing the office floor waiting for Forensics to finish with the note de Silva found, formulating a plan, the next step forward. 'I'll see you in fifteen,' he said. 'Good work, Maloret. I mean it.'

'Thank you, sir.' The tone in her voice was sharper now, more awake. 'I'll see you soon. And, sir, if I can say… I think you're doing a cracking job. I've never worked with… well, you know.'

He did know, and he appreciated it. His heart warmed to her, and he couldn't help but smile. Sometimes, when you need it most, you get the thing you need to hear. But it was fleeting, a temporary reprieve from the madness as the terrible weight of it all came crashing down around him.

Carmichael. He knew that Carmichael's death was on him. If he hadn't insisted on raiding the home of the wrong suspect, Carmichael would still be alive. He'd wasted time. Resources. Probably lost trust with O'Brien. And along with Carmichael's, the blood of any more of the killer's victims would be on his hands now, too.

Chapter Twenty-Nine

It had felt like weeks since Barclay had slept any longer than thirty minutes. His eyes stung when he blinked and ached when he didn't. He climbed into the cubicle of the staff shower at the OCC.

The hot water tingled on his skin, comforted him, and the potent lemon-scented face scrub pricked at his eyes. He'd rung Nick about nine that morning: he seemed fine, and Barclay even spoke to Sarah and promised, 'When Daddy catches the bad man, we're going to go on holiday.' She'd cheered and clapped her hands.

Nick hadn't mentioned the missed dinner that Barclay had promised. He had asked Barclay to stay on the line, and he listened as Nick dropped Sarah off at school. Heard him get back in the car and close the door. 'Are you all right, Ben? I'm really worried.'

'I'm sorry,' he'd said. 'There's a lot going on. I'm coming home tonight, regardless. I need my bed. I need to see Sarah. I need you.'

'You sound...' Nick had paused. 'You don't sound well.'

'Just tired,' Barclay had said. 'Promise. Can I ask a favour?'

'What?'

'Could you bring me some clean clothes? I smell like a bin man.'

Nick had laughed. 'Yeah, I'll be about half an hour.'

He'd met him outside, they'd exchanged a brief kiss and an overnight bag of clean clothes on the steps of the OCC, and Barclay felt as though he wanted to take him in his arms and sleep. Just sleep.

Barclay got out of the shower despite himself. He could have stayed in there for hours and scrubbed away the last few days like dead skin. Barclay hated to bother Nick, and knew he'd have to take a leaf out of de Silva's book and have spare bits in his locker for situations like this. He towel-dried his hair and applied some moisturiser from the tiny travel-size bottles Nick had brought for him. His toiletries were still in the travel bag Nick had put together for their trip to Sucina, the one they had to cancel when de Silva didn't come back to work.

He dressed and headed back down to the incident room. The place was quiet. 'Are we ready to go?' Barclay threw his bag onto his desk. 'De Silva?'

'I'm staying,' she said. 'I want eyes on the forensics report from the envelope soon as they've got it.'

'Fair,' Barclay said. 'Maloret, I'm going to pay a visit to Lamond's mother. You can come with me. Lawrence, I think de Silva had some tasks for you.'

'I do,' de Silva said.

'I need to use the loo first,' Lawrence said.

Barclay nodded at de Silva and headed for the door, Maloret in tow. In truth, he wanted to stay to know what was in the note addressed to de Silva. But he couldn't. There were things to do. People to visit. He'd made a decision to not go in hard this time. He didn't want backup anywhere near, no additional squad cars or PCs. He just wanted to scope the place out, get a feel for it and go from there.

In the corridor, Barclay noticed Lawrence shove her mobile into her pocket and turn into the small toilet on the left. The door locked.

Barclay turned to Maloret, looked her up and down. 'You got civvies in your locker?'

—

No road ran through Katherine Walk; it had a pathway, which was blocked off from vehicles by stone bollards. Barclay and Maloret sat in his car on Elizabeth Road. He'd rolled down his window and watched.

When they'd arrived, he and Maloret had split up. Maloret had taken the circular route onto Denise Road, and Barclay walked the length of Elizabeth Road until the junction with Field Lane. There was no sign of a blue 4x4 matching the plate they'd found. When she returned, Maloret reported the same.

Barclay checked his watch. They'd been there an hour already. There seemed to be no signs of life at all from the first house on the left, number one. The white PVC door was marked and scuffed, and a small window upstairs was open just a touch. He thought of the girls in there, their last horrible moments spent naked and cold in the winter air. He shuddered.

'Are we going to at least knock?' Maloret didn't so much sound bored as she did uncertain. Confused.

He was her once. Eager to move forward. *You still are.* Since he made detective, the work he did became more than work to him. It was as essential to him as drawing breath. As eating or drinking. It was important to him that he do a good job, to bring down the bad guys, to shine the light of justice on those dark, shadowed patches of the world. That's who he was. It was that need to do the right thing that led him here, after the HMS *Iron Duke*.

'You let me do the talking,' Barclay said. He got out of the car and headed for the front door of number one Katherine Walk. Maloret jogged to catch up.

The gate shrieked on rusted hinges. The grass in the small front garden was overgrown and brown in patches, and litter spun around itself in circles in the cold December breeze. He knocked loudly. 'The bailiff knock', his dad used to call it. It commanded an answer and demanded respect.

Behind the door, the tinkle of a security chain, and the click of a turned lock. A blast of heat when the door opened a crack. The small, slim face of an old woman, her straight white hair cut short. She looked frail and her cheeks were sunken where Barclay presumed her false teeth normally sat. He wanted to tell her that she shouldn't open the door before asking who it was. He told his mum all the time. She never listened.

'Morning,' he said. 'We're looking for Lewis Lamond.'

She blinked at him. She was in her dressing gown despite the hour, and she held it closed against the freezing air. 'Who the bloody hell are you and what do you want?' She summoned strength from somewhere and seemed bolder. Larger.

'I'm Detective Sergeant Barclay,' he said. 'This is Police Constable Maloret. We're looking for Lewis Lamond. Does he live here?'

'The bleedin' bizzies at my door.' Barclay couldn't tell whether she spoke to herself or someone else. 'And what d'ya want 'round 'ere like?'

'Lewis Lamond,' Barclay repeated. 'Are you Mrs Lamond? Is Lewis your son?'

She exhaled, sharp and with a hint of weariness. 'That lad. You'd best come in.' She moved out of the way of the door and let them inside. 'Before anyone sees.'

She led them through to the living room and turned the TV's volume down from forty-five to a comfortable sixteen. She went over to a black Calor Gas fire stood under a massive wooden clock and turned it to three bars, before sitting in the armchair next to it. Barclay's grandad had had one the same, and he remembered a man would deliver a new gas bottle and take the old one away at least once a month. His grandad had relied on the fire more as he got older, got sicker.

'Well, sit down then,' she said. She made herself comfortable in the pink and sagging armchair opposite the couch. She took a packet of cigarettes from her dressing gown and lit up. 'So come on, what's he done?'

Barclay didn't want to sit on the couch. It stank of smoke and there were dark stains and sticky spots he couldn't easily identify. He perched on the end of it and imagined the smell and stains clinging to his clothes. 'Sorry, I haven't asked your name. Getting ahead of myself, forgive me.'

'Margie,' she said.

'Does your son live here with you?'

'No.' She blew smoke out toward Barclay.

'Does he visit?'

'No.'

There was quiet. The Calor Gas fizzed, and the flame burned away the paper of Margie's cigarette. Ash hung on precariously, then fell onto her dressing gown. 'Lewis doesn't come round here.' She stubbed the cigarette out into a glass ashtray on the arm of the chair. 'Not for a long time.'

'But he is your son?'

'I gave birth to him,' Margie said. 'I raised him. Best I could.'

'Why doesn't he come around here any more?'

'None of your business.'

'We really need to speak to Lewis.'

From the corner of his eye, Barclay caught Maloret's head move from him to Margie and back, like she was watching a game of tennis, but she kept quiet and watched.

'Is there anything you can tell us?' Barclay's voice was even and flat. 'Has he been in touch? Contacted you in any way? Come around for any post while you were out?'

'I wouldn't give that lad a key to my home,' she said. 'And I've told you, he hasn't been around. We don't see each other, don't speak. Been that way for years.' She looked out of the window into her back garden, at the weeds growing through the pavement cracks. 'Probably wouldn't recognise him if I walked past him in the aisle at Aldi.'

Barclay glanced at Maloret. The conversation was going nowhere. Lewis must have purposefully registered his car here. No paper trail to him. *Another dead end.*

'He's always been weird,' Margie said. 'Especially after his sister died.'

'How old was she?'

'She was two. He was five, maybe six. He was a weird kid after that and probably an even weirder man now.'

'What makes you say that?' Barclay wished he had his pad and a pen with him. As he thought it, Maloret pulled out her notepad and wrote down the day's date and time, pen poised for more.

Margie exhaled sharply, rolled her eyes. 'There'd be fights with the other kids around here. He wouldn't hit back. He'd just stand there and take it.' She scowled. 'Took him for a queer at first, you know. Tried to knock some sense into him. But he just stood there and took it from me, too. Didn't make a sound. Didn't move. Didn't cry.'

'You thought he was gay because he wasn't violent?' Barclay fought hard to keep the incredulity from his voice and knew that he'd failed.

'Wouldn't you?'

'No.' Barclay stared at her and she stared back. She took another cigarette from the packet and lit up. 'So he was a passive kid. Was he bullied at school?'

'Don't know,' she said. 'Sent him to a special school in the end. Stole from me even then. Said he never, but he did. I know he did. That's how he was. He'd bring home skinny stray cats, half-starved with broken legs, birds with broken-up wings, shit like that.'

'Which school?'

'St Patrick's. No, that's not right. It was St Patrick's when I was a kid. A Catholic school, you know. Had a chapel and all of that. But it was run by the council when Lewis went. Church had nothing to do with it.' Her voice was thick with smoke. 'Closed years ago. But they had him assessed. Learning difficulties, they said, or some such shite. I know my son, I told them. I said he was just lazy and sulked.'

'When did you last see him?'

'I've already told you that.' She smiled, wide, pink and gummy. 'Trying to catch me out.' She tapped the side of her head. 'I've still got my wits, lad, even if I've not got much else. We haven't seen each other since school. When it closed, he came home and left the same day. That was that.'

'You didn't look for him?' Maloret chimed in. Barclay heard the real question in her voice: *You just left him to it. He could have been dead. Didn't you care?*

'No, I didn't,' Margie said. 'And he didn't look for me. Didn't come home.'

'Do you have any photos of him as a kid?' Barclay asked.

She sighed, but got up from her armchair and moved to an old, dark-wood drinks cabinet in the corner. The wood was chipped and one of the handles was missing. She slid it open. Inside was a half-empty bottle of Canada Dry and an old biscuit tin, silver where the shortbread print had come off. She opened it and handed Barclay a small red leather-bound photo album. He opened it.

In the first picture, a little blond boy stared back at him with eyes that had no shine about them. There was no smile, no happiness, and the picture itself felt cold. It made Barclay shiver.

'Rainford Lane School for Boys, it was called,' Margie said. 'They sent me that his first year.' She sat back down in her armchair. 'Told them not to bother after that. Didn't have the money.'

'Can we borrow this?' Barclay asked. 'I just want to take some copies and I'll get it back to you.'

She waved her hand. The gesture said, *Whatever. Don't care.*

Barclay turned the next page and she jumped out at him. Her blonde hair, those defined cheeks, the wide smile. It was Kelly. It was Danielle and Lynsey. It was Amanda. 'This girl here,' he said. 'Who is she?'

'Some trollop used to live around here,' she said. 'Gone now.'

'Dead?'

She shrugged. 'Don't know. Not seen her in years.'

'Who is she? What's her name?'

'Lisa Mc-something or other. I don't know. Years ago.'

'Can we borrow this photograph, too?'

'Take the album. I don't look at it.'

No, but you keep it. Barclay wondered what other things she kept in the drinks cabinet among the bottles and biscuit tin.

'Does he have any friends you know of?' Barclay clutched at whatever possible avenue he could. 'Any other family members he'd have kept in touch with?'

'There's no one else left alive,' she said. 'He never had any friends.'

That made Barclay sad. He checked himself. *This is a killer we're after.* 'Not even at school?'

Margie stood up and said, 'Wouldn't know.' She jutted her chin toward the living-room door. 'I've got shit to do and can't be raking up the past all day. Sorry. Can't help you.'

Barclay and Maloret stood and followed her to the front door. 'Oh, just one more thing if you don't mind,' Barclay asked as Margie opened the front door wide then turned to look at him. 'What happened to the hungry kittens and the broken birds Lewis brought home?'

She threw her cigarette out into the front garden, watched it smoulder and die. 'I twisted the birds' necks,' she said. 'Left 'em out in the garden. They'd rot or become a meal. Drowned the kittens in a bucket in the back. Best thing for them.'

Barclay thought of tiny paws reaching for the surface, wondered how she'd stopped the kittens escaping. Had she held them under the water, liquid filling their tiny little lungs. The thought disgusted him.

Like mother, like son.

'I don't know what you think he's done,' she called after them. 'But I always wondered about him. About those cats and birds with broken bones. Whether he'd done it himself.'

'Nice speaking with you,' Barclay said. He thought about monsters; about how they're not born but created when they're out of the womb. When they should be safe and in the arms of loving parents. Barclay closed the gate behind him and didn't look back.

They walked to Barclay's car in silence and somewhere a dog barked.

Chapter Thirty

De Silva couldn't sit in the incident room any longer. She went outside into the freezing cold, hoping it would wake her up. Her breath plumed in front of her as she paced and thought about going to the shop for a nice bottle of Malbec. Her hands shook. She could have been at home, her face in the biggest glass she could find.

You've made a choice. You're here now.

She went over it all in her mind. There had been an envelope jammed under the wiper of her car. It hadn't been there when she'd arrived, or when she got ready to visit the Maclennan girl's crime scene. She didn't remember seeing it when she and Barclay got back to the car park, but that didn't mean it wasn't there. She closed her eyes and tried to think straight. They'd been engrossed in their conversation. But it was there when she'd got into the car and started the engine.

They'd been down at the crime scene about twenty minutes. That had given the person who had left it a massive window. There were no patrols in that area. Just at the access points. So he would have to have been already inside the cordon when it went up. Which meant he didn't leave after he'd dumped the Maclennan girl. He'd stayed to see what would happen next.

Was that his usual habit? And why would he risk it now, or at all? She knew that sometimes killers liked to return to the scene of the crime, to try to relive or recapture the high.

'Slow down, you're gonna wear a hole in the paving.' Crosby stood just a few feet from her, his hands in the pockets of his thick, black woollen coat. He'd fastened it up to his chest and chewed some gum. Spearmint, as usual.

She hadn't heard him approach. 'What're you doing here?' She studied him. He'd shaved and had gotten himself some sleep since the last time she'd seen him.

'O'Brien asked to see me,' he said. 'With someone from IOPC.'

'Crosby, I'm sorry.' She walked toward him, put a hand on his arm.

'No.'

De Silva hadn't expected this. She and O'Brien hadn't talked about Crosby the other night, in truth they'd skirted around the subject. She knew that he'd done that to protect her. 'What happened?'

'He asked me to reconsider my resignation – pending an IOPC investigation, of course.'

'IOPC will see there was nothing you could have done differently. I'm made up for you.'

He looked away from her then, at the building, the skinny trees on the grey plateau of the entrance that never seemed to sprout. He looked anywhere but at her. His smile gone. 'Ann rang me.'

'Oh yeah?' She forced an eager sort of enthusiasm into her voice. She knew where this was going. 'She okay?' De Silva thought of Crosby's big hands on her, on her back or waist, the other tangled in her hair.

'She wants to meet up,' he said. 'Talk about everything.'

His mouth on her nipple, a hand pulling off her knickers. 'Does she know?' Her throat dry, she swallowed. 'About us?'

'No, I don't think so.' He looked at her then, his eyes narrow. 'She left because of this place. Work. What it was doing to me. To the marriage.'

Her teeth biting into his shoulder as he pushed himself into her. *Stop. Stop now.* She thought about telling Crosby of the conversation she'd had with Ann in the restaurant. She decided against it. Whatever Ann had told him was the truth behind her leaving, it had to stay that way. If their marriage could heal from all of this, then it should. She asked, 'How do you feel about that?'

'About what?'

'About your wife leaving you when things got difficult?' She hadn't meant it to sound so cold, but realised there was no other way for it to come out. Something in her wanted him to come to her, to take her into one of the rooms they could lock from the inside. She closed it down. 'I'm sorry,' she said. 'I don't know what I'm saying. It's good news, I'm happy for you. If that's what you want?'

'I think I do,' he said. 'I was no angel, you know.'

I know. She nodded. 'Yeah, neither was I.'

'We shouldn't have ever done what we did, Win. Look what it cost us.'

She wanted to ask what exactly it had cost him, other than a few days on his sister's couch. She wanted to say that she was the one who paid the price for what they'd done. And Ritchie. 'Yeah,' she said through gritted teeth.

'There was just too much temptation, wasn't there?' He rubbed his hands together and blew into them. 'You, me, the job. Not going home 'til all hours. Temptation was all it was.'

Was it? It felt more than that to de Silva. It always had. The guilt came when sleeping with Crosby became more than just sex. It had gone beyond that, become something more. She'd started to have feelings for him, and then when the urgent aggression of snatched sex turned into long hours of fooling around, exploring each other's bodies, she knew that she loved him. Guilt. Can't love two people at once, can't screw two people. The human mind is too complex to stick to that type of binary. She genuinely did love two men simultaneously and it hadn't felt too much. It was and always had been the other feelings that came with it: the sin, the wrongfulness, the delinquency that led to remorse.

Crosby touched her shoulder, lightly, and only for a second. 'You all right?' He put his hand in his pocket and de Silva wondered whether the temptation was still there for him.

De Silva cleared her throat. 'O'Brien's got me visiting a psychiatrist. But I'll be around while I'm seeing them. Light duties, probably. We'll go for a brew. I'll bring Barclay. Can't give in to your temptation then, can you?' She was aware she sounded icy, almost jealous.

'I turned O'Brien down.'

'You what?'

Crosby shook his head. 'O'Brien, that new Bradshaw woman I was reporting into, the police, all the people I work with; they all turned their backs on me through all of this. No one reached out to me to see how I was doing. I don't need that in my life. Time to move on.'

De Silva wanted to say she knew how that felt, but she didn't. Crosby had wanted people to be there for him, and she hadn't. They were different. Maybe too different. 'What'll you do instead?'

'I dunno.' He shrugged those broad shoulders. 'Private investigation, maybe. Not sure. I don't need to worry about it just yet.'

'Can we have a drink at least? Before I never see you again?'

'No,' he said. 'I'm sorry, but it's not a good idea, is it, given our recent history? Ann's gone to Wales, to her folks' house. I'm going to go and join her there. Who knows, maybe look for a house there. Big city isn't for me any more – can't hack it.'

'What's in Wales, though? Sheep and grass. There's nothing there for you.'

'My wife's there,' he said.

That stung. This whole conversation was an exercise in pain. She wanted out, wanted to be anywhere else. Jesus, she'd even prefer to sit in the incident room twiddling her thumbs, waiting. 'I see,' she said.

Crosby looked at his watch. 'I'd best get off anyway,' he said. 'Leave you to it.'

De Silva nodded, didn't know what else to do. 'I dunno how to say bye to you. Don't want to.'

'You don't have to,' he said. He leaned in and kissed her cheek. 'See ya around, Win.' He walked off out of the car park toward the main road.

De Silva wanted to chase after him, to flag him down and admit what she'd felt for him. The love she'd suppressed out of guilt for what happened with Ritchie. He'd seemed happy, though. Happier than she'd seen him in a long time. At peace almost. That peace was not because of de Silva; it was in spite of her, and she knew that. But somewhere inside her, she had always hoped, wished, that they would have been able to move through all of this and find a way to be together. She watched him and with every step he made, she willed him to turn back.

He turned the corner and was gone.

De Silva's phone pinged. From Lawrence:

> Forensics lab want to see you in IR.

That's it then. Crosby had walked off into the winter afternoon, his own sunlit ending, and de Silva would return to her life. To basements and Forensics and evidence bags, and a note potentially from the killer.

She made her way down to the incident room and every step felt heavy. Every yard she moved took her away from Crosby. From what she wanted to say to him. She wanted to run to the toilet and let it all out. But she couldn't. There was work to be done.

The incident room was quiet. Lawrence was busy with footage from traffic light cameras in the Walton Hall Park area. 'Oh, hello.' A woman with a bouncing blonde bob marched to de Silva. She held a file in her hand and looked perfect. De Silva didn't recognise her. 'I'm from the forensics team. Robertson,' she said. 'Felicity Robertson.'

'Oh,' de Silva said. 'I didn't think we'd hear from you for hours.' De Silva moved to the whiteboards, where school and crime scene photos hung side by side.

'Well, we're not finished,' she said. 'I know DSI O'Brien has asked for the evidence to be processed with haste, and we are working on it.'

'Right…' De Silva's tone was clear. *So why are you wasting time down here telling me stuff I already know?* 'Is there something I can do for you?'

'Oh, yes, straight to it.' The Robertson woman chuckled. 'They said you were like that.' Robertson handed de Silva the file. 'As I said, we're working on it, but O'Brien's instructions were to keep you and DS Barclay updated at all times. Where is he?'

'Not here.' She took the file to her desk and Robertson followed her in high heels. There were pictures inside, scanned and enlarged images of the envelope and of the note that was inside it. She recognised the scruffy capital letters from the front of the envelope instantly.

She looked up at Robertson, back down to the open file in front of her, took a breath to steel herself, and turned to the scan of the note, enlarged and printed on A4 paper, the original would still be in the lab.

> *You mite be wunderin why I am writin too you.*
>
> *I was not goin to but I saw you on the news when you fell over and that fella made a joke about you.*
>
> *I wanted you to no that he was a good man and he tried to stop this. He cud not. You can't either.*
>
> *I can not even stop myself.*
>
> *These girls need punishin for what they do.*
>
> *You need to stop lookin for me and if you don't I will look for you. I will punish you. You are a cryin slut just like the others. You all are. I am watchin all of you, watchin you do the nasty things you do.*
>
> *Stop lookin for me and tell that queer you work with to stop too. I know all about him and his fag husband and there daughter. She is too young to get hurt because of her daddy.*
>
> *I hope you like the present I left yous.*

She looked up to Lawrence and said, 'Get Barclay on the line now.' De Silva took out her own phone, found O'Brien on her most recent calls and rang. 'Sir, I don't have time to explain.' She was already picking up her car keys. 'You need to get a team out to Barclay's home address right now. Squad cars, uniforms, blues and twos.'

She turned to Robertson. 'Is this it? Is this the full note?'

'Yes,' she said. 'We still have some analysis to do on the original, bu—'

'Have you shown it to O'Brien yet?'

'Not yet.'

'I'll make sure it gets to him. I'm going to have to ask you to leave.'

'Oh, right.' Robertson's face was flushed. 'Yes, I'll get out of your way. We'll be in touch when we have more.'

De Silva nodded, moved around the desk and took the phone from Lawrence. 'Barclay, it's me. Where are you?'

'Just walking into the building now.' He yawned. 'What's up?'

'Stay where you are, I'm on my way up.' De Silva patted at her jacket pockets. Phone, keys, the copy of the note, that's all she needed. She darted from the incident room. The lift was agonisingly slow, that painful kind of wait when someone else is in the toilet.

When the doors slid open, he was stood there. 'You all right?' His eyes narrowed. That old look of detective suspicion.

De Silva nodded. 'I've got the note from the windscreen,' she said. 'You need to listen to what I've got to say. Okay?'

'All right?' His voice had the sharp edge of fear.

'You might get a call from Nick in the next few minutes,' she said. 'We've sent a team out to the house.'

'What's happening? Tell me!'

'The note made some very specific threats,' she said. 'But we're on it. We're going to make sure that Nick and Sarah are okay.' She could feel the conflict in him, could see it; he wanted to run, but wanted to stay.

'What did the note say?'

'Read it later, when we've sorted all of this out.'

He pointed at the paper in her hand. 'Is this it?'

She waited, and he stared. She handed it to him. 'Read it on the way.'

He held it in shaking hands, eyes wide. He threw the copy of the note back at de Silva and ran for the door. Barclay's phone rang as they got to the lift door. De Silva could hear the sobs from where she stood.

'Nick?' Barclay's voice shook. 'Nick, what's wrong?'

Chapter Thirty-One

Barclay knew he was driving too fast, almost recklessly. De Silva held on tight to the grab handle above the passenger-side door, the other hand holding her phone to her ear. That note on her lap. *He couldn't stop.*

He hadn't been able to get any sense out of Nick, couldn't pick out the words between the sobs. He'd had to hang up and put his foot down. That was all he could do, except to hope that everything was okay by the time he got home.

'Thank you, sir,' De Silva said. She hung up. 'The team are already there. Nick and Sarah are fine.' She stared ahead at the road as he weaved in and out of traffic. 'You need to slow down, Barclay,' she said. 'Getting pulled will just hold us up.'

He took his foot off the accelerator. She was right. 'I just want to get to them,' he said. He wouldn't settle until he knew for certain they were safe, until he saw it with his own eyes. He wondered whether Sarah was scared, whether she was crying and asking Nick why the police were at their house. 'Did he say what's happened? Why Nick couldn't speak?'

'No,' de Silva replied. 'He just said that they're both safe.'

The police presence would make Sarah nervous. She didn't like large crowds. She couldn't take the noise, the thought of so many people. Whenever she was invited to a school party, she'd ask how many people would be there first. At one party, they found her sat around the back of the bouncy castle, where the fan was, pale and quiet. What if she was like that now?

He needed to distract himself. They were still fifteen minutes away from his home. 'What else does the note say?' He glanced down at it in her lap then back at the road. 'Anything else about Sarah?'

'No,' she said. 'I told you everything it said.'

'That's all it said, that she's too young to get hurt?'

'Well, I think it's important that he didn't call Sarah by name, or Nick. He doesn't know them as well as he's making you feel he does.'

De Silva was right; he didn't use their names. Maybe he didn't know where they lived, either. But what was the alternative? That he'd seen them outside? In parks, food shopping on his day off, at the cinema, at another kid's party, or while Sarah was at school? He felt ill, like he could pull over and vomit at the side of the road.

Barclay gripped the steering wheel tight. 'We're gonna get him, de Silva. We'll get him and he'll pay for everything he's done.'

'I know we will,' she said. There was something in her voice. Some tinge of sadness or something. Maybe it was doubt. 'You never told me what happened at Katherine Walk.'

'His car's registered there, but his mum hasn't seen him for decades, since he left school. She sent him to some school out of the way. But look...' He leaned over and opened the glove compartment, handed the red leather album to de Silva. 'The second picture.'

'Jesus,' she said. 'This is it. This is the girl he's fixating on. Who is she?'

'The mum didn't say much, didn't seem like she cared. The girl's name is Lisa Mc-something. That's as far as we got.'

'This narrows things down quite a bit, but we need to find out who she is.'

—

They turned onto Barclay's road, usually a quiet little place. There were two police cars and six uniformed officers out in the front garden and street. Barclay wondered what the neighbours would think. Whether they'd have created a group chat on WhatsApp to talk about it. They knew he was police, but that wouldn't stop the rumour mill from churning.

Barclay bounced his car up onto the kerb a little too hard; something clanked underneath. *Great*. There was no time to worry about that now. He half ran inside and went straight to the kitchen, where he could hear voices. Nick was sat at the kitchen table, a hand over his mouth. When he saw Barclay, he sprang to his feet and cried. Barclay held him close and didn't want to let go of him.

'Are you all right?' Barclay stared into Nick's face, examined it for any visible damage. There were tears, there were red eyes, but he looked okay.

'I'm fine,' he said. His voice was strained and Barclay knew he'd been crying hard. 'Are you?'

'Where's Sarah?'

'She's fine,' he said. 'She's in her room.'

'What's happened?'

Nick sat down and Barclay dragged a chair next to him. He cried again, but tried to hold it together. 'The school rang me about two. I was just getting everything ready for dinner, so that when I got back, I could just turn the hob on.

'They said that someone had gotten into the playground. The gate had been damaged. They heard the kids screaming. The teachers on duty were looking after a little lad who'd fallen over and cut open his knee. When they looked up, they saw a man walking back toward the gate. Walking away from Sarah.'

Barclay swallowed the bile down that threatened to come out of his mouth. 'Had he...?' He couldn't get the words to come out of his mouth. 'Is she okay?'

'She's all right. But he gave her something.'

'What did he give her?'

'Look, here's Daddy.' O'Brien's voice. He held Sarah in his arms. 'I told you he'd be here soon.'

'Daddy!' Sarah leapt down from O'Brien and ran for Barclay.

He picked her up and held her close. Squeezed her a little too hard, maybe. 'Hello, princess.'

'Could I speak to you both?' O'Brien indicated de Silva and Barclay.

Nick took Sarah from Barclay. 'I'll be upstairs packing for Mum's.'

O'Brien closed the kitchen door when Nick left with Sarah. He shook his head. 'He can't go to his mother's house.'

'Well, he can't stay here,' Barclay said. He knew he sounded almost defensive.

'No, that's right.' O'Brien sat down at the kitchen table, slowly like an old man struggling with his hips or back. 'But his mum's won't do, either.'

'O'Brien's right, Barclay,' de Silva said. He'd forgotten she was even with him. 'If the killer has followed you and Nick around, then he might already know the places you might go, the people you'd turn to.'

'This is really serious, Barclay. Really serious.'

The world around Barclay narrowed. Everything faded into black, and all he could think about was the wording in the note. It was a threat. A promise. He'd come for her if Barclay got too close.

'They have to go somewhere,' Barclay said. *They*. He realised in that moment that he wouldn't be going with him. He'd have to let them go on without him.

'I've made arrangements already,' O'Brien said. 'There's a hotel we use sometimes, out in Cheshire. Middle of nowhere. I'll have some people escort Nick and Sarah. They'll stay there with them until this is all over.'

'Will I be able to contact them?'

'Yes,' he said. 'There's equipment there. Sarah won't have to miss much school. Maybe Nick could contact the head and ask for some online classes, like the Covid days?'

Nick had described to Barclay how difficult being at home so often was during Covid. Sarah hadn't understood why she wasn't allowed to go places as much, why she wasn't allowed to go to school. She knew there was a dangerous virus that could make her sick, but she didn't truly get what that meant for other people. Her entire world became the house and a walk around the park once a day.

It was about to happen to them again. *Because of me.*

'Okay,' Barclay said. 'I'll help them pack. Break the news.'

Barclay didn't wait for anyone to speak, but heard mumbles from the kitchen after he'd left. He took the stairs two at a time and went into the bedroom he shared with Nick. He was throwing clothes and chargers and skincare products into a massive suitcase. Sarah sat on the edge of the bed, kicking her feet and playing with a Barbie doll whose hair was matted and clothes were missing. It reminded Barclay why he needed to stay, why they had to go without him.

He looped his arms around Nick and pulled him close. 'I'm sorry,' he said. 'About all of this. I don't know how he knows who we are. About where we live…'

'Anyone can find everyone these days,' Nick said. 'You just need a name.'

Nick was right. Social media made everything so easy. A platform built for connecting people could have some serious and terrifying uses, too. 'We're going to sort this out,' Barclay said. 'But in the meantime—'

'It's not your fault,' he said. 'I've rang Mum and told her to expect us, so she's all excited.'

'Well, about that.' Barclay sat down on the bed. 'You can't go to your mum's. It's too dangerous.'

'Are you saying my mum and dad are in danger, too?'

'No!' Barclay grabbed Nick's hand. 'I promise you, no. But we don't know whether… Sarah, why don't you go and put some toys in a bag?'

'Can I take Mingo?'

'Course you can.'

Barclay lowered his voice. 'We don't know if he's been following us around or anything. We need to minimise the chances of him coming into contact with you, with Sarah. Do you get what I'm saying?'

'I do.' Nick huffed, sat down on the bed next to Barclay, rested his head. 'Will it always be like this, do you think?'

'No.' He kissed the top of his husband's head. 'This fella we're after, we have a name. It's a matter of time. I just don't want to take any risks, especially after today at the school. Sarah will be fine, I promise you.'

'Stefan rang me back,' Nick said. 'There's an opening for me at the gallery. He wanted me to go in tomorrow for a chat.'

'I'm sorry,' he said. 'Do me a favour, though, don't tell him where you are. Not him or your mum and dad. We're sending you out to Cheshire. A hotel there.'

'What's it called?'

He laughed. 'I don't even know myself.'

Nick looked up and kissed Barclay on the mouth. 'You'll be careful, won't you?'

'Yeah…'

The neighbours went back inside when the cars with blacked-out windows pulled out of the street. He waved at Sarah, at Nick, unsure if they waved back. Then he saw it laying on the floor. The black-and-white tatty mess they'd gotten her from Chester Zoo last year: the penguin, Mingo.

He picked it up and put it in the pocket of his coat. Every so often, as he drove back to the OCC with de Silva, he checked it was still there.

'You've done the right thing,' de Silva said after ten minutes, where the radio filled the silence between them. 'Probably doesn't make it any easier, but you have. They'll be safe.'

Barclay said nothing. He wanted to tell her that he felt like shit, like he'd abandoned them; told them the bad news and left them to it. They'd be out in a hotel in Cheshire alone, miles away from him if anything happened. *No*, he corrected himself, *not alone*.

There would be officers with them; protecting them and watching them and making sure no one gets near. He should have insisted that he drove them to the hotel himself.

He thought about the killer. *He's evaded almost every CCTV camera in the city and you think your family will be safe.* There were no other options, no way he could make things better or different or otherwise protect his family. He had to be here, on the case, in the thick of it with de Silva. He had to find the killer, and to do that he had to put his little family out of his mind as much as he could. 'Did anyone ask the school for CCTV?'

'O'Brien's on it.'

There were more cameras and journalists on the road outside the OCC. Cameras flashed at them as they drove past and one of them shouted, 'Is it true there was a note?' Barclay's heart could have stopped. This was the last thing Barclay needed, the last thing the case needed. He looked at de Silva, her mouth open and eyes wide.

'What the hell?' she said. 'How do they know about that?'

Barclay knew. 'There's a leak,' he said.

De Silva shook her head, looked out of the window at the OCC building as Barclay pulled up into a free space. 'It'll be all over the news, if it isn't already,' de Silva said. 'We should tell O'Brien. He'll want to get ahead of this.'

Chapter Thirty-Two

O'Brien's office smelled different. Not clean as such. It smelled like a normal office; the faint whiff of food, a hint of aftershave. 'Come in,' he said. 'Sit down.' A big mug of tea steamed on top of his desk. 'I'm sorry about all of this, Barclay. It's never easy when things get personal. Thank God Forensics got it to you when they did.'

'Yeah, thank God.' Barclay sounded almost sarcastic, maybe aggressive. De Silva would need to have a word with him later.

De Silva cleared her throat, eager to take the conversation in a new direction and said, 'We have another problem.'

'Go on…' O'Brien took a chug of his tea.

'On the way in, one of the journalists asked about the note.'

'I see,' O'Brien said. 'Who knows about it?'

Barclay looked to de Silva. 'Us two. PCs Lawrence and Maloret. And you.'

O'Brien smiled. 'I'll forgive your accusatory tone there. You look like shit and I want you to go somewhere and get some rest. You've got somewhere to go that's not home, haven't you? Of course you have.'

'I've just got here.'

'Yes, and I'm telling you to go back and get some rest. I've noticed you've been working all hours. Both of you are going home, and your little team downstairs.'

'We can't just stop everything—'

'What's next on your list?' O'Brien continued.

'Well,' de Silva said. 'We have a name. Checking employment history would be a good place to start, I think. If there is one. Any benefit claims made, maybe. That CCTV from the school would be helpful. We also have a potential name for a Lisa Mc-someone. We believe she is where this whole thing started for him.'

'Right, you leave that to me. Send your team home and I'll draft in a late shift.'

De Silva was already on her feet. 'Sir, can I ask a question?'

'If you make it a quick one, yes.'

'The note said something about "him being a good man", that "he'd" tried to stop the killer but couldn't.' She swallowed hard. 'Was my dad involved in a case like this back in his day?'

'Not that I know of.' He shook his head. 'I'll look into it. Leave that with me, too.' He took another swig of his tea, raised his eyebrows. 'I'm not certain why you're both still sitting in front of me looking like shit when you could be at home looking like shit. The only difference being, I don't have to see your faces if you're at home. So go.'

De Silva headed to the door. Barclay stayed in his seat, lost in his own mind.

'I'll get them to ring you if they come up with anything,' O'Brien said.

'As soon as they find something?'

'Scout's honour,' O'Brien said.

Barclay stood and they walked to the lift together.

'Where are you heading?'

'I can't go to Mum's,' he said. 'If he's following me, he could follow me there.'

'You're welcome to my spare room.' Even as she said it, she hoped that he would say no. Not because she didn't want to see him safe, but because her house was a temple to grief. A sacred space.

'No,' he said. 'I'll check into a hotel.'

—

De Silva felt for Barclay, and as she started the car, she exhaled, tried to release the tension of the day. Thankful to be heading home, as she needed the rest, she wondered whether Barclay would manage to get some sleep himself.

She thought of the note. The part about someone previously trying to stop the killer but failing. She'd assumed it was her dad, but if the note didn't refer to him, then who could it be? She couldn't expect O'Brien to remember every case he and her dad had worked on. But it'll be there somewhere, deep in the records, from the times before everything was on a computer or a cloud.

There was surprisingly little traffic along her route to the Royal, even with the roadworks that seemed to have popped up everywhere. She'd had a voicemail from the hospital earlier.

'We've X-ray'd your mum,' the man's voice had said. 'No fractures or breaks. She can go home tomorrow.' It had sounded busy in the background; people talked, someone yelled. It hadn't sounded like her mum and that was a comfort to her.

She parked in the quiet car park on a floor with three other cars. When she got out, she checked for any missed calls. There were none. She hadn't expected to hear from Laney, but she had hoped to.

The ward was baking hot. Not the comforting warmth of long summer days on Formby Beach, but an oppressive, sticky heat. De Silva fanned her face with her hand. Useless.

Her mum's little room was cooler, just about. She was sat up in the bed, propped against thin cushions and eating a yoghurt with a plastic spoon. Laney sat in the seat next to the bed and looked up from her phone when de Silva came in.

'Hello, Mum.' De Silva kissed her mum's head. 'How're you?'

Marie nodded.

'They said you can go home tomorrow,' de Silva said. 'That's good news, isn't it?'

Marie licked the spoon clean. 'Yeah.'

De Silva looked to Laney. 'You been here long?'

'Went home earlier for a shower and some food. Got back here an hour ago.' She didn't look at de Silva, scrolled on her phone instead.

'How's Bonnie?'

'She still doesn't know who her aunt is, if that's what you mean?'

De Silva glared at her and hoped the crack in her heart didn't show on her face. They needed to get past this, but she knew in her gut that the only thing that kept them interacting was the fact that their mum was alive. Once she was gone, they probably would never speak to each other again.

'She's fine,' Laney said finally.

'I'm glad.'

Their mum filled in the silence that sat between them, the scraping of the plastic spoon against an empty yoghurt pot.

'I'm gonna go,' Laney said. She took her thick, padded Barbour coat from the back of the chair she'd been sat on and flopped it over her forearm. 'See you later, Mum.' She walked out into the corridor and de Silva followed her.

'Wait, Laney.'

Laney groaned but turned around to look at de Silva. 'What now?'

'Mum isn't gonna be here forever,' she said. 'Do you think she wants her last years spent watching us at each other's throats?'

'She wouldn't remember even if we were.' A nervous laugh. 'I'm not at your throat, I don't know what you're talking about. I wouldn't give you the satisfaction.'

'Satisfaction?' De Silva laughed, too. 'Of what? You getting angry with me? Why would you think I'd want that?'

'You and Mum have always kept me at arm's length, always made me feel like I'm not one of you,' she said.

'God, and don't we know that's how you feel.' It was hard to keep the sarcasm from her voice. 'I don't know where that comes from, either. After Dad died, you pulled away. You even moved away.'

'The Wirral isn't that far to come and visit, Win, so don't give me that.'

'Laney, I haven't got enough hours in the day to go the toilet sometimes—'

'Oh, but I do?' Laney put on her coat.

'I think you fill the time with things you think are a priority. Like flower arrangement or supper with the

Joneses, or whatever it is you do now that you're a middle-class wool.'

Slap. Laney cracked de Silva across the cheek. 'You hateful cow!' She turned on her heel and stormed out of the ward.

De Silva raged, her cheek stung and there were so many other things left unsaid, perched on the tip of her tongue. Like how could Laney afford to not work when she'd gone back to her maiden name? Clearly, she and David had broken up. Maybe she got a good settlement in the divorce.

There is no falling-out quite like that between siblings; one will have known the other all their lives; there's a deep understanding of each other, usually, that no one else seems to get. And yet, de Silva wondered, how were they so different? How could she and Laney have possibly come from the same womb and been raised by the same parents?

When de Silva went back into her mum's bedroom and sat down on the still-warm chair that Laney had sat on, the anger ebbed.

—

Overnight, de Silva hadn't had any missed calls or any messages from Barclay or O'Brien. *Unusual.* She wondered how Barclay had slept in the hotel, in a bed that he wouldn't be used to. Whether it had been noisy or silent; the same silence she'd become all too accustomed to; the one she'd tried to fill with the clink of bottles, the thud of her headboard against the wall, with Crosby's moans and groans.

It can't ever be filled. Not properly.

The incident room was quiet, too. She didn't hear a single sound as she walked down the corridor from the lift. The late shift must have already left, but as de Silva entered, she found O'Brien staring up at the boards where the faces of the dead girls were.

'Morning,' she said. She hoped the tone of suspicion went unnoticed. 'You all right?'

'Look at you.' His smile was broad, and he seemed to be in a better mood than yesterday. 'Here early, looking like an actual detective chief inspector. Like the old days.'

She raised her eyebrows. 'Er... thanks.'

'Barclay not with you?'

'I've not heard from him.'

'Good, gives us some time to talk. Close the door and take a seat.'

She did as she was told and perched on the edge of the desk she'd claimed as her own. 'What's up?'

'Look, I know I asked you back just to offer your insight into this case and then I'd leave you alone until you were ready to come back on your own terms. But listen, I want you back properly. It's not that Barclay can't handle this – of course he can. He's a fine detective. I just think my concern goes much deeper than that. No, I know it does. Kath always says I should take ownership of what I think and feel, so here it is: I didn't think I'd ever see you recover after Ritchie. After where you went when he died. Thought you were gone.'

'Well,' she said. 'I'm still here.'

'Barely,' he said. 'Fingertips clinging to the edge of a cliff. But these last few days, here you are. You showed up for us, and I won't forget that. But I need to know now, de Silva: in or out?'

She took a deep breath and held it for what felt like the longest time. She let it out and said, 'I'm in.' She couldn't be certain what made her say it, she was so unsure about everything. Her future, her place with the police, everything. She'd wanted for so long to move away to an island, somewhere there were hardly any people, where no one knew her. Where nobody cared about whether she was sad or happy, grieving or just about keeping her head above water.

'Good,' he said. 'And the rest of it stands, the therapist, I mean. You have to agree to that.'

'I do.'

'That's good,' he said. 'That's fantastic actually, because I've already made an appointment for you. Next Thursday at five. Dr Emma Sharp. She's fantastic, so I believe.' He took a small white card from his trouser pocket and handed it to de Silva.

Her business card, address, phone number and email. The shining gold lettering made it look expensive. It seemed old-fashioned to her, almost ridiculous. *Just swap emails.* Still, she was grateful. 'Okay,' she said.

'I'll let you get on,' O'Brien said, moving toward the door. 'You and Barclay, come and see me when you've caught up. Little progress report would do wonders for me. You know how I like it.'

She nodded. 'We'll be there.'

'Oh, and as far as the note goes, I couldn't find anything like this related to your dad. I'm sorry.'

'The ramblings of a mad man.'

'Yes, I suppose so.'

A knock at the door. Holden, clutching his laptop at his side, peered round as he opened it. 'Is this a bad time?'

'No such thing,' O'Brien said. 'Anyway, I was just leaving.'

As he walked out of the incident room, de Silva realised he smelled like soap and shampoo, not like cigarettes.

'Come in,' de Silva said. 'It's good no one's here. I've been meaning to come and see you.'

'Oh, de Silva.' He flopped himself down on one of the chairs. 'I didn't have a choice but to speak to O'Brien. I didn't want to, but—'

'You did the right thing,' she said. 'What I asked you to do was wrong, and I shouldn't have put you in that position. I'm sorry.'

Holden fumbled with his laptop, almost dropping it. 'There's a lot of that going around. Apologies, I mean.'

'Yeah.'

'Who's in trouble now?' Barclay walked into the incident room and came slowly to the desk. He looked better. Sharper somehow.

'Oh, ho! It's Boy Wonder.' Holden clapped Barclay on the back.

'Please don't call me that,' Barclay said softly. 'Tell me you found something on Amanda's phone.'

'I've got some good news and some not-so-good news. Which do you want first?'

'Always the not-so-good news first,' de Silva said. After that, the only way was up. Barclay sat down next to her; he smelled of floral soap and aftershave.

'Well, we can't find anything about this Woulds app on Kelly's phone. Not anywhere. I'm not sure how they set it up or how it was downloaded to devices, but we do know that it was available on the dark web.'

'What do you mean "was"?'

'We were working on getting access to it, to see the process of downloading it, creating an account, all that. Then, it disappeared. That happens on the dark web.'

'So it's been deleted?'

Holden nodded and his cheeks wobbled. 'Yeah. Or moved. Renamed. I do have a contact with the National Crime Agency – lady I went to Oxford with.'

De Silva's eyebrows arched high on her forehead. Holden didn't seem the type to have gone to Oxford University. 'Could you contact her about it?'

'Reached out this morning,' he said.

Barclay sighed. 'So what's the good news?'

'Oh. Yeah.' Holden's fingers thundered at his keyboard. 'Well, the truth is that Amanda didn't have this app on her phone, so that's good news, isn't it?'

'It is,' de Silva said. 'Sort of.'

Holden grimaced. 'Why sort of?'

'Well, if only some of the victims had this weird app on their phones, then maybe we could have moved on. A coincidence rather than a link,' Barclay said. 'It means we've wasted your time, our own time, when we could have been focusing on something else.'

Still, the app stuck out in de Silva's mind as important. When Barclay had called them to ask, Kelly's parents hadn't known anything about the app, never heard of it, and were certain Kelly had never mentioned it before. But it was a mystery, and de Silva liked her mysteries resolved.

'There hasn't been much else to go on has there?' Holden covered his mouth. 'I'm so sorry,' he mumbled. 'I didn't mean it like that. I just know it's been a difficult case.'

Barclay nodded. 'I know what you meant.'

'I mean, there's still the question of what this app is,' de Silva said. 'It could still be important.'

'I'll let you know when I hear from my mate in NCA. But you know... could take months...'

'Nice one, Holden,' Barclay said.

Holden left without saying another word, closing the door behind him. Barclay moved to his own desk and slumped into the chair.

'Did you manage some sleep?' de Silva asked.

'After I spent a few hours down here, yeah.'

'You're joking! You should have gone straight home.'

He handed her a slim sheath of print-offs. 'I slept like a log after reading this.'

De Silva flipped it open. 'Whose file is this? Danielle's?'

'That's the case file detailing the murder of Lisa McLaughlin in 1999.'

Disbelieving, de Silva stared down at the file and clocked the date. It had read just like the file of one of the most recent victims. 'Jesus.' The bites, the strangulation, the water in the lungs. 'This is her. This is the one he's doing this to over and over again. This is the girl from the photograph?'

'Yeah, that's her.'

'So why her?'

'Something we'll have answered when we find him.'

Chapter Thirty-Three

Phyl hadn't spoken or moved in hours, even when he'd taken that rotten piece of trash out to Waterloo. She was slumped forward, her chin on her chest. Her breath was all Lewis could focus on. Sometimes it was quiet, sometimes it rattled around her chest like a broken tumble dryer.

You can't even get an old lady properly. You're just like they said you were. Feeble.

'No, I'm not.' Hot tears on his cheeks. He wiped them away quickly.

Do her before she gets you.

'No.'

Do it! Before she hurts you like those men did.

'No!'

Phyl raised her head just slightly. 'Wha…' Her eyes barely opened before they closed again.

'Are you awake?'

Nothing.

He got up from the bed and knelt down in front of her. 'Wake up!'

Phyl's head snapped back. Her eyes looked fuzzy, like she couldn't quite focus on him. A flow of blood slipped down her neck, curled around into the hollow of her collarbone and pooled. She spluttered and cleared her throat.

'I can't move,' she said. Her voice was ragged and quiet.

'Don't struggle or you'll hurt yourself,' he said. 'It's your fault.'

Hit her.

Phyl's head sagged again. 'Who... who was that...? The girl I saw...'

The memory that he'd gotten it so wrong about Lisa was almost too much for him. He winced at the pain of it. 'Someone I thought I knew,' he said. He steeled himself. 'But she's just like the rest of them.'

Phyl struggled to take a long breath. 'Where is she?'

Punch her. Right in the gut. Stop her going on.

'She's gone,' he said.

He looked away from her, at the splatters of blood on the wall still shining like the skin of ripe cherries. It would turn brown soon. Always did. 'You've seen what they made me do. You'll get me into trouble.'

'I won't,' she said. 'I just want to go home and lie down.'

Liar. Hit her.

He put his head on her lap and cried, bunched her nighty up in his big, heavy fist. He knew what had to come next, but couldn't bring himself to do it, to even think it. She was just an old woman. She'd been nice to him. 'Why did you have to come upstairs?' He sobbed and couldn't stop. 'Now we're both in trouble.'

He thought about his mum, and about that place. The shower block. The hands of men over his small body, the thwack of the cane when he'd done something they didn't like. The cries of the other boys lined up in the basement, where the pipes clanked and drip-dripped onto the cold concrete floor. The earthy smell of damp on his own knees. And through it all, the one thing that kept him going, kept him strong, was that after all of the pain was over, he'd get to see Lisa again.

'Untie me and we can talk a bit more.' Phyl tried to find some comfort on the chair but couldn't. 'These chairs are no good for me – I'll be crippled tomorrow.' She tried to smile, maybe to ease some of the tension between them, but couldn't. Her lip was split.

'You'll be dead before then.'

Her breath caught in her chest and she held it there. 'You don't want to do that to me. I've done nothing to you.' She coughed and he saw blood in the spittle on her lip. 'Why are… you doing…' She coughed again, like the bark of a dog. '…this?'

'I'll show you. She'll be out there now. Lisa, or someone wearing her face. You'll see.'

–

He left the engine off to save on diesel; it was stupidly expensive after Covid. Phyl shuddered beside him, her teeth chattering. He'd given her one of his old coats from the back seat, covered in black from when he tried to change the engine oil last month. Something else he'd messed up. It didn't quite cover her and, for a moment, he thought about turning on the engine to warm the car.

'There's not long to wait now,' he said.

The school bell rang; he could hear it from the car. When he worked there, it was the best sound of the entire day. Most of the kids were vermin; they scurried out like rats, but every so often, he'd see a shining gem. Sometimes they had black hair, sometimes brown. But one thing they all had in common is that they wanted him. He hadn't worked in St Mary's much, just once or twice. But he'd never seen *her* there before.

They spilled out into the streets in their blazers, the colour of the woods in spring. They scurried off in all directions, to bus stops, to parents' cars waiting on the main road. The light was on the cusp of night; soon darkness would hide everything.

As time wore on and she didn't come out, he began to panic. It was dark then, and the old lady shook with the cold. The kids had gone, the parents in their big, clean cars had driven home with their sons and daughters and probably made a nice tea. Something that would keep their bellies warm.

It was fine. He'd seen her at least, and now he knew that sometimes she would sneak out of school. Useful to know. He flicked on the headlights and turned the temperature right up. He looked across to Phyl, her eyes closed, face the colour of cigarette ash.

Do it.

'I will.' He couldn't do it right then; it would be too messy in the car. He'd take her somewhere on the way home and do it then. He couldn't lug her around forever.

'Did you... say something?'

See. Do it. She's listening to everything.

'No.' He smiled to himself; the old woman was on to everything.

Lewis lifted the handbrake and was about to set off when she came out of the school with her mate, that lad. She took a cigarette from the inside of her blazer and lit it, handed one to him. They'd have to speak about this. He would try to understand why she had him as a mate, and she'd do her best to explain it.

The lad went one way, and she turned to cross the road.

'You leave her... alone.' The old lady sat up, watching the girl.

He took his eyes off the girl and glared at Phyl. 'It's my Lisa. She wants me, you know. You might not see it. She looks this way and she begs me to take her.'

'No... she does-... doesn't.'

'She does.' His voice was calm. It wasn't Phyl's fault really; she didn't get it, and that was fine. She didn't need to. 'She wants me and I want her, and we'll do everything for each other.'

'She's a young... girl,' she stammered. 'She doesn't... want you... You're too old... for her.'

Hit. Her.

'She does.'

'And... if she doesn't?'

Then we'll make her.

'Then she'll be punished,' he said. 'For leading me on, for telling me she wants me and for lying. I just want to love her.'

'This isn't love,' she said. The car was warming up now. 'This is wrong!'

'That's what they said. The men. They told us that we led them on. Mrs Jones took us to the shower block to clean us up. Where we showered after PE. She'd turn the heat off and the water would come down on us, freezing. We'd hold our breath there as long as we could, trying not to shiver, and wait until she turned the water off. She gave us our clothes back and we walked back to our rooms dripping. I used to dry myself on the curtains when I got back to my room.'

'Why are you telling me this?'

'So you can see what I need, what I never had. What I focused on all those years. What they say they'll give to me and then don't. Lisa.'

'You need help,' she said.

Do it.

He lunged at her, grabbed her scrawny chin and held it. 'How dare you speak to me like that,' he growled. 'You don't know a single thing. How they all want me, how they all want to get me into trouble. I am not a queer like they said in that place. I'm a boy, and I will show them. Boys like girls. I like girls. My Lisa.'

'You're not a boy,' she managed through gritted teeth. 'You're a man.'

She's lying to you.

Anger surged in him like a rising tide, black in the dark of night. He leaned his forehead against hers and pushed. 'You're going to be in very big trouble.'

He pulled away from her and glanced out of the windscreen. The girl was on her way across the street. She jogged to get out of the way of a car coming from the right and headed for the side street where he was parked.

Oh, she wants you bad.

He hadn't expected this. He knew she wasn't coming to him, that would be too obvious, but she was playing with him. Walking right past him was part of the game.

He wound down the window to get a better look at her. She walked toward him now, slowly, eyes on the path in front of her. As she approached the car, his heart thundered in his chest. She looked up at him and he tried to swallow, but his mouth was dry as dirt. Her face changed, her brow wrinkled, and the scowl hurt him deep; just like the others. She'd lied to him since the day he'd seen her and he had believed her.

You stupid idiot.

He watched her in the wing mirror as she took her phone from her blazer pocket. Before he knew what was what, he jumped out of the car and was a few paces behind her. Phyl said something he didn't hear. He put his hand in his pocket and gripped the solid handle of his hammer.

It all happened so quickly. Too quickly. Somewhere in the evergreen trees above, birds squawked to each other. Shit fell down from the branches onto the path between him and the girl, black and white and wet. Cars roared past on the main road, but this street was quiet, barely lit.

His trainers thudded against the pavement, and he wondered for a split second whether she would hear him coming.

A car horn, loud and behind him. His car horn.

The girl spun around, her face full of rage. In her hand, her phone, the camera flash on. She shouted, 'Why are you following me?'

I knew you'd mess this up.

He'd meant to follow her for a few more weeks, get to know her. Keep playing her game, but now that was all gone. She'd scorned him with just one look, after all of these days of flirting.

He knocked the phone out of her hand and swung at her with the hammer. It made contact somewhere at the top of her head, he couldn't tell where. She fell, but he caught her. He swooped down to pick up her phone. She groaned in his arms.

There was wet on his face, it felt like warm rain. He looked about quickly. He had to take it on faith that because he couldn't see anyone, they couldn't see him.

He dragged her back to the car and flung her onto the back seat. He threw the phone onto the ground and smashed it with his heel. He looked into the back at her. Phyl had reached around her seat to put a hand on the girl's arm, gripped it tight. The girl was bleeding badly but breathing.

He turned to open the door and caught sight of himself in the wing mirror. The warm rain was red and it had splattered all over his face and neck and clothes, on his teeth. In his mouth.

He got into the car and pulled out onto the main road; someone beeped loudly at him. He hadn't checked for oncoming cars. Next to him, Phyl cried, snivelled, and snot glistened on her nose and lips.

Shut her up.

'Be quiet,' he said.

He turned on the radio and caught the end of a news story: 'Sources close to the investigation of three murdered girls on Merseyside have revealed local police are looking to speak with a man named Lewis Lamond in connection with the investigation—'

He turned off the radio. Rage boiled in him like a kettle about to steam. He banged at his steering wheel and screamed.

Beside him, Phyl cried harder.

The girl, her face pale, slept.

Chapter Thirty-Four

The school wasn't at all how Barclay remembered it. He'd only managed to pick up or drop off Sarah a handful of times, and maybe he'd not thought much about it. His head would have probably been full of murder, vanished people, dead things. This time he took it all in. His senses heightened by the fact that just a few hours ago, his daughter, his own little Sarah, could have been taken by one of the most dangerous men out there.

'It's been a long time since I set foot in a primary school,' de Silva said. 'They're so little, aren't they?'

Barclay grunted an acknowledgement. He didn't have the energy for chit-chat. He was there for one reason: to get the CCTV and to leave.

As they approached the school, a short and stout man, who wore his trousers too low at the back, removed the school gate from its frame. He leaned it against the railing and said, 'You two all right?'

Barclay presented his warrant card. 'We're here to meet Mr Burdekin at the main office.'

'Aye,' he said. 'Just follow the main path there. Straight down. You here about the man that got into the playground?'

Barclay's jaw clenched.

'Yes,' de Silva said. 'Did you see anything?'

'Me? No. No, I don't work here. Just putting on some new gates and fencing.'

'It's a little too late for that, isn't it?' Barclay's voice was a low grumble. It wasn't a question.

The short man held up his hands and smiled, his teeth off-white. 'They only called me today. I came out soon as I could.'

'Thanks for your time.' De Silva walked through the open gate, and Barclay followed her. 'I know you're angry, Barclay, but it isn't that guy's fault.'

'I know.'

He felt now, more than ever, that he should hand over the reins to someone else. Not because he'd failed his daughter and his husband, but because he knew that his emotions were compromising his objectivity. But true objectivity is rare. There are always emotions in the way, feelings that colour our hopes, our aspirations, the outcomes of any action.

He hated that he had to take the time out to collect CCTV footage when he could be looking for this Lamond character. He loathed the fact that he could no longer trust his own team. With Carmichael gone, his list of suspects was down to two: Lawrence or Maloret.

Can't be Maloret. She was keen to progress, he could see that. It had to be Lawrence, the cold, emotionless one. Calculating. Watching. Taking everything in. Listening. Had to be her. When they'd briefed the team on the girls, he'd found Lawrence just moments later in the corridor with her phone. She'd put it away when she saw him.

Mr Burdekin opened the door to reception wide and flew out to greet de Silva and Barclay. His hand outstretched, he took Barclay's. 'I'm so sorry this happened,' he said. His voice was warm and his accent placed him somewhere out near Southport way. 'I've got the CCTV all ready for you. How is she?'

'I had to send her and her dad away,' Barclay said.

'Dear God,' Burdekin said. 'I just can't imagine what you must be feeling. Can we get in touch with her? I know the kids would like to send their wishes, and the teachers… well, I've had to suspend the two from the playground this afternoon.'

Good. He'd always worked hard to forgive, to forget and move on, but as the years wore on, that became increasingly difficult. Especially after his short career in the navy. Some people didn't deserve forgiveness. Wildly protective of his family as Barclay was, he was unsure if he could ever forgive those teachers who didn't see a grown man climbing over the gate in broad daylight.

'The footage,' Barclay said. 'We're in a rush.'

De Silva shot him a look that said, *Pack that in*, or something along those lines. 'Yeah,' she said. 'We're really up against it at the moment.'

'It's in my office,' Burdekin said. 'Come on through.'

Barclay sat down at Burdekin's computer without invitation. There were streams from three different cameras. One on the front gate, and two from different angles on the playground. He took a USB stick from the pocket inside his jacket. 'Am I okay to copy these?'

'Yes,' Burdekin said. 'I've made a note of the timings where it all starts, and lined it all up for you. Just press play.'

Barclay started the footage on all the camera recordings.

'Thanks,' de Silva said to Burdekin.

The kids played on two of the screen windows, and on the third, a man paced beyond the gate. The two teachers in the playground were busy, devoting their time to a lad who'd fallen over.

The man at the gate pulled at it. He forced it down and back as though it was made of tin foil and climbed through the gap he'd made. He didn't need to look around, to search, to seek her out. He made a beeline for Sarah straight away. He'd known where she was since before working on the gate. Barclay imagined his eyes all over her, watching, taking her in. He leaned down on one knee, not bothered by the other kids, one of whom ran to tell the teachers. He whispered something into Sarah's ear.

'He spoke to her.'

'Jesus.' De Silva couldn't keep her eyes off the screen.

Moments later, the teachers rushed to Sarah, and the man, Lewis Lamond, slithered through the gap in the gate and ran off down the road.

'That's all there is of him,' Burdekin said.

'I'll take these for now, but I'm going to need footage of the gate, any outward-facing cameras that look onto the road and path next to the school going back the last few months.' Barclay took a breath and watched as his daughter was taken inside by one of the teachers. 'I want to see how long he's been planning this.'

'Are you all right?' De Silva put a hand on Barclay's shoulder.

He rewound the video and paused it just before Lamond knelt down, the clearest you could see him. They'd need to send it off to the Visual Evidence Unit for the footage to be enhanced. But Barclay didn't need any magnification or sharper image quality. He knew that the man was Lamond. This event, this show of strength, was sneaky. A little nod to Barclay that the game was on. A threat.

A promise.

Barclay inserted the USB drive into the computer and transferred three files onto it. He waited for the green bar to move.

'You all set?' De Silva was already at the door of the office.

The files had finished loading onto the USB drive. He ejected the drive and stood up. 'Yeah,' he said. 'I'm ready.'

–

The team had moved quickly. Barclay had asked Maloret and Lawrence to search social media and Google, while he would get onto the PNC. In his experience, sometimes social media searches were quicker. But they came up with nothing: two Lewis Lamonds in Wales and one in Bristol. All family men with no obvious connection to Liverpool. Still, Barclay knew he'd have to look into them, just to eliminate them from his inquiries. He'd get someone to call local constabularies for assistance.

He entered his log-in information for the PNC as the idea of Lamond at his daughter's school crept back into his mind. The VEU had promised to prioritise the CCTV footage and Barclay wouldn't forget that.

Things were different, things were changing quickly. De Silva sat at her desk, phone propped between her shoulder and jaw. 'I've already sent the Data Protection release form,' she said. 'Twice now. Give me your email address again.' She mm-hmm'd along. 'See, there's a dot there in the middle you didn't tell me about. Ah, I see the bounce-backs now, too. I'm sending again.' She waited a second. 'You got it? Good. Shall I wait or will you call me back? That's fine, thanks.' She hung up.

She caught Barclay's gaze and rolled her eyes.

Barclay smiled. 'HMRC giving you trouble?' The PNC, slow as always, continued to load.

'We got there in the end,' she said. 'We should have an employment history for any Lewis Lamonds in Liverpool soon. I gave his mum's address, but said it could be wrong, but we'll see what comes back.'

'Good,' Barclay said. He fidgeted in his chair, his fingers poised over his keyboard, ready to type. The PNC finally loaded on screen. His mouth was dry and he wiped away the sweat from under his nose. This was it.

Under *Licence Holder*, Barclay typed in *Lamond, Lewis*. Selected *Merseyside* and pressed *Search*. The little white bar turned grey slowly. Too slowly. As it moved, Barclay held his breath.

'Sir.' Lawrence was at the end of his desk, her phone in hand. 'I think you should see this.'

'What is it?'

She handed him her phone, open to her own Facebook account. The screen showed a headline from the *Liverpool Journal*: *Detectives Finally Have a Name for Local-Girl Killer. By Joel Matthews*. Above it, an image of the crime scene at Crosby Marina, taken from somewhere far away and zoomed in. Barclay felt sick.

De Silva got up from her desk and came around to Barclay's. 'What the hell?' De Silva's voice turned sharp, focused. Her eyebrows closed in over her eyes.

'Is it worth me even clicking on this story?' Barclay asked Lawrence. She nodded. He did. He read each sentence carefully, as though, at any moment, something might jump out from the dark of the ink. Then, there it was.

> Police have identified a possible suspect by the name of Lewis Lamond…

He couldn't read any more.

Barclay handed Lawrence's phone back to her. 'I'm sorry,' she said.

'Not your fault,' he said. But secretly, he wondered whether it actually was. Someone in that room, someone in his team, had leaked information to the press. Again. As Lawrence returned to her work, Barclay looked to de Silva. 'I can't believe this,' he said.

De Silva closed her eyes for a moment, as though trying to summon strength from somewhere deep inside her. 'There's been nothing to go on in this case for such a long time,' de Silva said. 'Since the beginning. As soon as we have something, the press know about it, too? I don't believe in coincidences. First, it was how similar the girls look. Now this.'

'It has to be one of them,' Barclay said.

De Silva looked across the desk at what was left of their small team.

Maloret headed toward them. 'I just took a phone call,' she said quietly. 'From a woman who says she had a Lewis Lamond working for her until recently. She heard his name on the news.'

Barclay looked around. Lawrence was listening, too. 'Can we talk to you in private for a moment?'

'Yeah,' Maloret said.

Barclay led her out into the corridor and closed the door. 'Who's this woman?'

'Jackie Flanagan,' Maloret said. 'She runs a cleaning company that contracts for schools. Flanagan Cleaning Solutions.'

Schools. Barclay wondered whether that was how he chose them, how we noticed them. His stomach gurgled. 'Okay,' he said. 'Thank you, we'll get on it.'

Barclay held open the incident-room door, let Maloret and de Silva go inside ahead of him, then went to his desk. He unlocked his computer, where the driving-licence photo of Lewis Lamond was open and waiting for him. Barclay studied his face. He seemed normal. His hair was blond and untidy, and Barclay wondered whether that was a stylistic choice. His eyes were blue, not the same airy shade as Nick's; Lamond's were colder, deeper, like pools of ice.

He sent the picture to the printer and quickly got up to get it before anyone else saw. He couldn't trust the team, and that hurt him for a reason he couldn't stop to think about.

He folded the paper and put it into his jacket pocket; he'd need it later. He double-checked the address on the driving licence: 1 Katherine Walk, Fazakerley. *Definitely our man.*

Barclay caught de Silva's attention and nodded toward the door. *Time to go.* They both left without a word. In the safety of the lift, Barclay showed de Silva the printout. 'See, it's him. This is Lewis Lamond,' he said. 'Registered to his mum's address, so doesn't help us out there, but we have a face. Finally.'

'HMRC got back to me,' de Silva said. 'The only Lewis Lamond in the Liverpool City region worked at Flanagan Cleaning Solutions until recently. They didn't send across his address, still working on it apparently.'

That didn't matter to Barclay. 'This Jackie Flanagan person could have it in her HR system, if he used his real address. But this is it, isn't it?' He smiled. It felt like it was all coming together, each piece of the giant jigsaw finding its place among the dead girls, the crime scenes, the evidence kits.

De Silva nodded. 'The only thing is... he already knows we're coming.'

—

Flanagan Cleaning Solutions was a tiny building, probably built in the 1960s, among the giant factories and pharmaceutical companies in Speke. The car park was a noisy gravel, which pinged against Barclay's car.

Inside, the office was cramped, four desks in a tiny space, and only two seemed occupied. The other two spaces were piled high with paperwork. Behind the other desk, a massive man, whose arms bulged out of his T-shirt, looked strong and capable.

Jackie rolled over two chairs from the other desks. 'Sit down,' she said. A steaming mug near the crumby keyboard said: *Good vibes only*. That made Barclay feel slightly out of place. *There are no good vibes here.*

'I'm sorry,' Barclay said. The two detectives remained on their feet. 'We don't have much time.' He unfolded the photo printout and handed it to Jackie.

Jackie shook her head, a smile on her face. 'That's him. Lewis Lamond,' she said. 'I let him go just a few days ago.'

'Why?'

'He'd turn up late, sometimes missed bookings with long-standing clients. Can't count the number of meetings I've had to convince clients to stick with us afterwards. And his attitude...'

'Do you have a list of the schools that he would have worked at?'

'Yeah,' she said. 'Davey, could you get a client list printed off?'

Davey, the muscle-man, nodded and stared into the screen of his computer.

'He came here the day I sacked him,' Jackie said. 'Spat in my face. Turned the air blue.'

'I noticed you have CCTV cameras on the car park,' de Silva said. Barclay hadn't spotted them and he could have kicked himself. 'Was that where this altercation happened?'

'Yeah.'

'Could we take a look?' De Silva sat down.

'Yeah,' she said. 'That's fine.' She looked over to Davey. 'Could you sort that too?'

Barclay leaned on the back of the chair, gripped it hard. 'Do you have his home address?'

'It'll be here,' she said. 'One sec.' She clacked at her keyboard with filthy fingernails and Barclay looked away. 'Here,' she said. 'Two-A Sybil Road, Anfield.'

Barclay looked to de Silva. 'Can we get those client names now?' he said. 'You can send the CCTV over later when you have it – I'll give you an email address to send it to. I'm sorry, we're really up against it.'

Barclay had to rely on luck – maybe Lamond hadn't seen the news yet. Perhaps he didn't know that his name was on the lips of every person in the city. There'd be phone calls from neighbours soon; Facebook posts calling him a nonce. Maybe one of those vigilante paedo-hunters would beat the police to it. Find him somewhere. Save the day.

Barclay's phone rang out so loud in the office that it startled him. *Maloret calling*. 'Maloret, I'm a bit busy right now, I'll call you—'

'I'm sorry, sir, but this can't wait.' Her voice sounded urgent, almost panicked. 'We've had a call from a Mr and Mrs Cole. They've called to report that their daughter hasn't come home from school.'

Barclay's heart pounded. 'Hold on one second.' He pressed mute on his phone and said to de Silva. 'We need to go. Now.' He unmuted the call. 'We're on our way back.'

Chapter Thirty-Five

The squad van was quiet as the grave. De Silva sat up straight, and as Barclay talked, she thought of the evidence boards in the incident room and the faces of every girl Lamond had taken and destroyed.

And now there's another one.

They had his address now, and with every minute that passed on their way to his home address, Barclay seemed renewed. Somehow, he seemed refreshed, ready to strike before another girl ended up dead.

From what Barclay had told her about Lamond's childhood, everything seemed to track. The neglect from his mother, the abandonment he must have felt as a result of going to a school away from home for kids just like him. The troubled ones; the ones they didn't know what else to do with. Had this Lisa been a source of hatred or a beacon of hope for Lamond?

Ritchie's school experience had been the same. He was always in trouble as a kid, and his mum sent him to this school that de Silva didn't even know the name of. He only came back during school holidays. He never once spoke about his school or his new friends, even when de Silva asked him outright. It had changed him, though she couldn't exactly say how. He was just different.

Barclay handed out some printed images of Lamond's face. 'This is Lewis Lamond,' he said. He passed about his work phone. 'And this is a video provided to us by the parents of Kim Cole, a local fourteen-year-old who never came home from school today. Kim had the foresight to go live on social media when she thought someone was following her.'

De Silva thought that that was very smart, but ultimately it had done her no favours. The video was graphic. When she turned on Lamond, he looked startled at first, then angry, his eyes predator-wide. The last thing on the video was the flash of something metal. Someone grunted, and de Silva hadn't been able to tell whether it was Lamond or Kim. Then, the video cut out. It had had thousands of shares and hundreds of comments within the hour or so that it was posted, before it was taken down for violating the social media app's terms of use. They were lucky someone had made a copy.

De Silva knew that what was about to happen next could go one of two ways. Lamond was unstable, and judging from the speed with which he was now moving, his MO had changed. He'd either slip up, make a mistake, and they'd catch him before any more harm came to Kim. Or, he'd decide that it wasn't worth the trouble and kill her outright. If he hadn't done so already.

Nobody spoke.

'We'll be joined by an enforcer team,' Barclay said. 'And an Armed Response team. We're not taking any chances. I don't want anyone in there that doesn't need to be there. I want the rest of you stationed around the property. The back entrance. We cordon off the road, no one in or out.'

His voice was authoritative, strong, focused. He was a natural at this kind of thing, even if he didn't see it in himself. The confidence would come. There was a fire in him now that shone in his eyes, lit by learning Lamond's name.

True, everything pointed toward Lamond, especially now with the video, but there was a niggle at the forefront of de Silva's mind. *What if we have this all wrong?*

The squad van had picked them up outside OCC twenty minutes earlier. De Silva had suggested the Armed Response vehicle should meet them there; if the media saw it leave the OCC, it'd be all over the news within half an hour. Barclay had agreed. De Silva had chanced a look over to where the reporters and camera operators were, a lot less of them, surprisingly.

De Silva looked at her watch. They'd be at the address in less than five minutes. Her chest was like a cave of bats, all beating their wings at once, and her stomach seemed to coil around itself. She wondered how Barclay felt. Excited? Overwhelmed? Relieved that this case could potentially come to an end with one successful raid?

Out of the back of the van window, de Silva spotted the Armed Response team's marked car pull in behind. Everything seemed to be going to plan. *A little too easily.* Things never went easily; if something could go wrong, it usually did.

The address could be wrong. Lamond had the vehicle registered to his mother's address, and this one at Sybil Road could belong to someone else he knew. They could be barging in on an innocent person's home. Or, Lamond could be there, but he could have already killed the Cole girl. She could be lying in her own blood while he prepared to dump her somewhere along the Mersey. He could have already done that and be out looking for his next victim. The possibilities were grim and endless.

De Silva's head hurt and the rumble of the van did nothing to soothe her roiling stomach. The van turned off Walton Breck Road onto Anfield Road. They passed the stadium, where tourists posed for their pictures under the Liverpool FC crest, and the black gates, *You'll Never Walk Alone* above in gold letters.

The van slowed as they approached Sybil Road. The ARV overtook and turned into the street, followed by two other squad cars. Then the van blocked the junction. No cars could get in or out.

Before the van had even fully stopped, Barclay was on his feet, sliding open the side panel. 'Fucking hell.' A camera flashed at him as he stepped down from the van, de Silva right behind him.

Joel Matthews was there, filming it all, speaking into the camera. 'Police have just arrived on scene—'

'Someone get him out of here!' de Silva shouted. Two officers swooped in and moved him and his cameraman on. But it was too late, it would be all over the news, and in a few minutes, the rest of the circus would show up. She wondered whether that was it: the operation blown before it had even started, and thought of the leak. How procedure required them to radio in their exact location when out in the field, and how that would have been heard by every officer in Merseyside. Whether Matthews's presence had tipped off Lamond – if he was even there at all.

De Silva looked around for the dirty blue, corroded shell of the car they'd been searching for. It wasn't there.

'What the hell was he doing here?' Barclay was at her side, his face flushed.

De Silva didn't need to say a word. She gave him that look, her eyebrows high. *The leak.* She opened her phone to Facebook and saw it straight away. A news article from Joel Matthews: *Teen-Girls' Killer Has a Face*, above it the headshot from Lamond's driving licence. She showed it to Barclay, who gritted his teeth and looked away, his nostrils flaring.

Neighbours had come out into the street. Young girls with rollers in their hair, already in their housecoats. Maloret and Lawrence set up a cordon from the lamp post outside the flats to the other side of the street where Matthews was trying to speak to them. Another officer that de Silva didn't recognise urged the neighbours to go back inside. They ignored him.

The four-person ARV team approached, their guns drawn. The armed team was essential; they couldn't risk the safety of anyone else. Onlookers had their phones out, and de Silva wondered whether they were going live on social media. This was a mess. Another three officers drew in close, carrying the red enforcer.

'We'll go in first.' Barclay indicated that he included de Silva in this. 'The flat is upstairs, first on the left. We'll try to get him to open the door as standard. If he does, you go in and we'll follow. If not, we'll use the ram.' He nodded toward the enforcer team.

The door to the building was unlocked, and the breeze that whipped through the concrete corridor and around the stair rails cried. The Armed Response team's heavy boots squeaked against the steps as they followed Barclay and de Silva up to the first floor.

The door to 2A was battered. The wood-effect melamine was chipped and flaked around the edges, the screws of the handle were loose, and de Silva doubted it would take much effort to get access. Barclay knocked at the door; three sharp raps.

It felt as though everyone in the corridor held their breath; as though if she focused, de Silva would see dust slip through the air like pond life. There were no sounds from inside – no scrambling to answer the door, or climb out of a window, or hide evidence. Nobody mumbling to themselves or to anyone else.

He's not here.

Something caught de Silva's attention. The faint whiff of metal, like when you've held coins for too long and your fingers smell of them; that sweetness. But there was another smell with it. An awful thing that smelled foul and made de Silva balk. From the way Barclay's lips curled back, she knew he could smell it, too.

She's already dead.

She couldn't help herself from thinking it. In a few hours' time, someone would have to call the parents of Kim Cole and tell them that they got there too late. That the media's coverage had probably spooked Lamond. That, just like Kelly and the others, their daughter was dead.

Barclay knocked again, heavier this time. Then de Silva heard it, so low she put her ear to the door. A definite groan, though she couldn't tell from what. It didn't sound human.

Could be the telly or the radio.

'Can you hear that?'

Barclay pressed his ear to the door, too. 'What is it?'

'It sounds like...' Her eyes locked on Barclay's. 'Sounds like there's someone in there.'

'Get this door open!'

The enforcer team moved in with the red ram and pounded at the door. It took just one thrust before the door crashed open. The ARV team moved in, quick and methodically, sweeping left and right.

De Silva could see into the flat. The bed was near the wall to the right, and from here, it looked to be stained brown. Dried blood. The carpets were stained too. They stepped inside as the ARV team leader called, 'All clear.'

The radio was on low, playing that song by The Police her dad had liked, the one about every move you make. She looked about her, at the blood stains, at the place she knew Amanda, and perhaps Kim, could have spent the last few agonising moments of her life.

It's empty.

Chapter Thirty-Six

The speakers on the car's old stereo crackled as he listened to the news, but the message was clear: another girl had been found and Lewis's face was all over social media. He'd heard the kids in the corridors talking about going live on these apps or whatever. He never thought for a second that she'd do it to him. That she'd try to catch him out, to get him into trouble. Was this part of her game, to make things more exciting, or had she already decided that she didn't want him? Lisa would never do this to him.

You've done it again. That's not your precious Lisa.

The girl lay there all that time, still and silent. Her chest rose and fell. He'd thought about getting rid of the old woman, dropping her back at her flat and doing what needed to be done. But they had his name, they had his face, they knew he'd taken her. The newsreader on the radio had read her name in a grim tone, the same one they used to read the register in that place he hated to think of. He knew he couldn't go back to Sybil Road. Too dangerous.

Nowhere left to go.

The old school looked different. He'd driven past it numerous times, but never dared get so close. It was just stacks of bricks in the shape of walls in the middle of a field of overgrown grass and weeds; nothing like it used to be.

It had once been where monsters glared out of every window and ivy grew up the sides, squeezing and threatening to choke everyone inside until they were dead. But now the windows were boarded up, daubed in graffiti. No monsters looked out any more.

He parked behind what was left of the old dormitory block, where he couldn't be seen from the road. The girl had stirred beside him, made some grumbles, but hadn't opened her eyes.

You hit her too hard. She might never wake up.

Phyl sat upright, her eyes shining like glass.

He'd brought her here, to this place, and he'd have to deal with her when it was time. He left his headlights on and climbed out of the car, the long grass up to his knees. There were still pieces of glass in the window frames, like mouths of ragged teeth.

He thought about what to do next. He couldn't risk leaving the new one in the car. She could sound the horn, or get out, even if he locked it. He turned to look at her through the window; she hadn't moved. Phyl eyed him.

Careful with her.

He saw his own reflection on the mucky window, the lined face, the bags under his eyes, the untidy hair that was quickly thinning. Lisa would want him how he was, as always. There were no airs or graces between them, before she met her boyfriend. And where was he now...?

He wanted to look around. See the place with his own eyes before he got them out of the car, but he needed the glare of the headlights to find his way inside. That meant leaving the keys in the ignition and being away from the car. Still, they were tied up. There was no way they could drive anywhere.

He went to the entrance of the old dorm block; there were heavy boards screwed into place over the door. Lewis pushed against it, but they wouldn't budge. He took out his hammer and smashed at it, where it was wettest. Softest. Finally, the wood splintered and gave way, and he pulled and kicked at it.

Good, you're in.

He went to the driver's side first, took the keys from the ignition and the place fell into the dark of early winter. Things would be more difficult in the dark, but he had no choice but to manage as best he could.

The passenger door squealed on its rusted hinges. Phyl moved as far as she could away from him, but he grabbed her by her bound wrists and yanked her out of the car. She fell down onto her knees in the grassy gravel and cried out. When he stood her up on shaking legs, blood poured from cuts on both legs.

He sat her down next to the front wheel and she winced at the pain. He should have finished her off when he'd had the chance.

He took cable ties from the glove box and tied the girl's feet and wrists together, pulling the cables until they zipped tight. Still, she didn't move. He shoved more ties into his pocket and left the girl there, the doors locked.

'Where are we?' Phyl's voice cracked and her bottom lip trembled.

He pulled her up to her feet and she cried out again. 'Just be quiet.' They had to walk slow, and every step was agony to him. He wanted to get back to the girl before she woke up, but Phyl could hardly walk.

She limped and winced and when they reached what used to be the dorm-block entrance, she crossed herself and cried. Lewis hadn't seen anyone do that in a very long time. He thought of Mrs Johnson and how she would cross herself before prayers at assembly and the shush of her skirts when she walked, like whispers at nighttime. She was fierce. Unstoppable. Just like the men.

And where are they now?

Inside, the dorm was the same but different. The roof was mostly gone and rain had gotten in, destroying almost everything. What had been their individual rooms now had no doors, and the narrow beds they had slept on were gone.

It was a long walk to the shower room, and Lewis knew he couldn't leave the girl in the car all that time, not at the pace Phyl was walking. 'Over here,' he said. He walked her over to a small room with an iron radiator on the left-hand-side wall. It was once painted green, but now all that remained of the colour were tiny flecks that the elements hadn't managed to get to.

Lewis fastened her to it after checking that it was still fixed to the wall.

Outside, clouds the colour of fresh bruises bulked against the black sky. It would rain soon. He moved quickly, hoisting the girl up onto one shoulder. As he locked the car door, he noticed the frayed edge of the piss carpet sticking up from behind the back seats and thought of Phyl. He threw the carpet onto his other shoulder. His back throbbed, but he managed it without falling once. He chucked the carpet onto the floor next to Phyl and she stared at it, eyes wide, mouth open.

'What are you going to do with her?' she said.

He put the girl down. If he didn't keep Phyl quiet, she would go at him all night. 'I said to be quiet.' He backhanded her across the face, a wet sound. She didn't look at him again. 'I'm sorry,' he said. He got down on his knees, felt sludge seep into his battered, faded jeans. He leaned his head against her chest. 'I have to move quick, and can't have you distracting me.'

Phyl's tears came again, and somewhere beyond that, a sound that reminded him of those nights when the men's friends came. The sound that reminded him of Mick, Ricky, Tommo and the others whose names he'd never remember. The girl had moaned, a whine almost. She went to touch the side of her head, where the blood matted in her blonde hair and found that she couldn't.

'I'll be back,' he told Phyl. He picked up the girl again, left Phyl there, and headed down a long corridor, turned right and down another.

The girl struggled against him, but he held on tight, and as he turned into the shower room, she screamed. The sound pierced his skull, made his ears ring, but didn't move him. He'd heard screams like that in the shower before, when he was a kid. They were nothing new.

It had remained mostly unchanged. The roof was intact but plants had grown up through cracks in the tiles, clung to the walls and pillars, and all around the place, which was smaller than he remembered, was a brown sludge. There was a hose pipe on the far wall which they'd sometimes use to clean the shower room. Sometimes they'd hit boys on the back of their legs with it for crying too much. The rubber of the hose would make a weird thwack sound.

He dropped the girl next to the old shower pipes and tied her to one with a cable tie from his pocket. She shouted and spat in his face and instinct kicked in. He punched her square in the face, a thud, and she fell into silence. Dazed, her eyes fluttered.

'You need to be quiet,' he whispered. There was to be no talking in the shower room, unless it was Mrs Johnson barking orders. *Take off your clothes. Stand under the water. Wash it all off, you dirty bastards.*

The girl shivered. 'Let me go!'

This crying! Just shut her up.

'If you be quiet, I won't have to gag you. Do you want me to gag you?'

'Fuck you!'

He looked at her, eyes narrowed, and contemplated. No one would come by here, nobody had a reason to, but still. There was a risk there. Someone could walk by with their dog and she could cry out at just that moment.

He pulled off her school shoe. It was heavy and scuffed, gravel stuck in between the treads. Her sock was a long, black thing, thin and with a sheen, and went up to almost her knee. He pulled at it and it came away from her leg easily. Softly. He wanted to put it to his nose, to inhale the smell of her. He jammed the sock into her mouth. He forced her shoe back onto her foot. Her eyes were wide, glasslike as she stared at him. She looked helpless. Powerless. That made him hard.

'I'll be back,' he said.

The corridor was cold, a breeze rattled around exposed pipes, and somewhere a low, gentle sniffle. Somewhere, someone cried to themselves. He couldn't tell if it was Phyl or a memory. He looked toward the classrooms and the entrance to the basement and wanted to go there. He couldn't say why. But he wanted to see where it had started, down there in the smelly basement, to see where he'd cried, to see if there were ghosts.

Behind him, the old bird was in the dorm. If they were both in one place, he'd feel better. He'd have to get her to the shower room. Then he could decide what to do next.

With every moment he spent in that place, he felt himself become the little boy he was back then. Frightened and nervous, sore and bruised. Every day, he wished that his mum would come back to take him home. She never did. He'd tried to make friends at first, but there was a sad truth in those early years: not one boy trusted anyone else.

Later, in his mid-teens, before the school closed, he and Mick, Ricky and Tommo were inseparable. They were a family they'd chosen for themselves when no one else seemed to care. Even that was ruined in the end.

He headed back to the dorms, ignoring Phyl's cries to be let loose, and kept walking until he reached one particular room. The door was missing, but he knew it had been his. His body remembered it. Stepping into it was like stepping back in time. The place where he'd sobbed, where his dreams turned to nightmares of clawing and pain, where he bled.

He could have curled up on that tiny bed if it were there. He moved to the wall, where sometimes he'd prop his pillows and think about home, about Lisa and her fingers in his hair.

Every time Mr Brendan and his mates touched him, every time they beat him with the cane, every time he'd gone to the showers and walked back to his room dripping wet, Lewis had made a tiny mark with his belt buckle on the wall and thought of Lisa. He managed to etch out five straight lines in his first two weeks. Those lines were countless before the school was closed, before that night in the woods with the other lads. Before his mum told him that Lisa had moved away. The marks were still there.

He made a new set with the edge of his hammer, a five-bar-gate. One line for each girl.

A shout shattered the quiet of his room, one of pain or horror, he couldn't tell, and for a moment he couldn't place it. Was it real or was it a memory, too? Then it came again, louder but almost like the rough voice of a man. He turned and was on his toes.

Phyl raged against the cable ties, blood dripping from her wrists onto the floor. 'Rats! There are rats.'

He hadn't thought she'd have had the energy to even move. She hadn't been fed in hours, hadn't drunk anything. Fear does things, he recalled. *Can make you do all sorts of things.* 'There's no rats now,' he said.

'That girl's done nothing to you. I've done nothing to you,' Phyl cried.

'You.' He spat the word out like phlegm on the pavement. 'You're the worst. The trouble you've got us all into. You're going to have to pay.' Lewis's phone rang from his pocket. He took it out: *MC Calling* on the screen. 'Where are you?' he asked. 'I need help. I'm in big trouble.'

Chapter Thirty-Seven

Barclay sat on the bottom step of the concrete stairs and waited while Scientific Support crawled all over the flat above. There'd been so much blood, in varying stages of drying and staining. That tracked. There had been Amanda, then Kim.

Lawrence and Maloret had started initial interviews with the neighbour on the first floor and those that lived above. De Silva had tried the only flat on the ground floor, the one the neighbours said belonged to an elderly woman, Phylis Dobson. There'd been no answer. One of the neighbours had said she hadn't seen Mrs Dobson for two or three days.

Nobody knew how to get hold of her son, and Barclay had ordered the enforcement team to gain access. There was nothing inside to indicate a struggle, or that there was any foul play. Maybe Phylis had visited a friend. Still, he'd have to arrange for someone to replace the door. Something else Barclay would have to justify.

There was one thing all the neighbours had agreed on: Lamond was a weird man, prone to loud music and shouting at all times of the day and night. Sometimes they'd hear him sobbing for hours on end.

De Silva came in from outside, closed the door behind her. 'Matthews's little stunt has caught the attention of every newspaper and channel. They're all here.' She sat down on the step above Barclay. 'What's up with you?'

'Nothing, I'm all right.'

'Tell your face that then, it might have forgotten.'

Barclay snorted a snigger through his nose. 'Just a bit stressed, that's all.'

'Because you thought you'd come here and get the bad guy?'

He'd promised Sarah that's what he would do. That he'd catch the bad man and they'd go away somewhere sunny and warm, as a family. He nodded. 'Something along those lines, yeah.'

'Look, we have a name, we have photos.'

'But we don't have Kim Cole. He does.'

'For now.' De Silva sighed. 'Look, I get it. He's not home. I already asked O'Brien for a couple of officers to go to Lamond's mum's house, just in case.'

'He wouldn't go there.' Barclay shook his head again. 'She wouldn't have him.'

She never wanted him, even when he was a kid.

'At least we'll know to cross it off.' Something caught in Barclay's mind, a thought half-formed that he couldn't quite bring to totality. *Lamond's mum said—*

'Barclay.' Brennan's voice from the landing above broke into Barclay's thoughts. 'We're ready for you.'

Barclay was on his feet, taking the stairs two at a time, de Silva following behind him. 'What are you thinking?'

Brennan picked up two clear bags containing white crime-scene suits. 'I'll show you. Come on in.'

Barclay had become well practised in the art of suiting up; it took him no time at all to get in it, slip on his shoe covers and get inside. The flat was worse than he remembered. Scientific Support officers took blood samples on cotton buds and put them into plastic containers. One of them did the same with a browning stain on the carpet.

The place was sort of tidy, but smelled bad, and not just from the blood. On the far wall were crude sketches of a building Barclay couldn't quite make out – they were childlike and colourless. Some large building that seemed to tower in every image, and in the centre, a room with what looked like shower heads and water. He took out his phone and snapped a photo. Brennan's voice broke Barclay's concentration.

'It all seems really strange,' he said. 'The blood on the bed. It's soaked through to the other side of the mattress and into the divan. Indicating the body was left to bleed for some time. Livor mortis – where the blood settles at the part of the body lowest to the ground – usually sets in around six hours after death.'

'So you're thinking she bled out a lot before she finally gave in?'

Brennan nodded. 'Without the body, that's my best guess, yeah.'

'What about this here?' De Silva pointed to the carpet.

'That patch has dried a lot quicker.'

That piqued Barclay's interest. 'An earlier victim?'

Brennan shrugged. 'Could be that, yeah. But it could also be that someone else was here at the same time. Less serious wounds. Didn't bleed as much.'

If no one had reported a missing kid, who else could the second person be? *Someone less conspicuous. A prostitute, maybe.* A lot of killers chose vagrants, hookers, or other people that would go unnoticed for the longest time. That didn't fit his MO though, his escalating thirst.

'There's one person we haven't accounted for,' de Silva said. 'Phylis Dobson from the ground floor. Neighbours said she's always popping her head out, saying hello. The man on the first floor said he'd heard a voice outside his door just before he came out to shout for Lamond to turn the music off.'

'What're you getting at?'

De Silva closed her eyes, seemingly to centre herself. Calm her breathing. 'She hears noises from the flat above, she comes up to see what's going on. Maybe she knocked on the door and told him to keep it down, or maybe it was open. She sees what he's up to.'

'That's a bit of a leap,' Barclay said. But how many cases had he seen her take a leap of faith on and be right? Scores of them. 'I'll ask Maloret to do some digging on her. Next of kin, all that. She may have gone for a holiday, visiting family, something like that.'

'I want to show you the bathroom.' Brennan led them through. Someone had covered the small window with a thick black sheet. It was dark when the door was closed. Brennan picked up a black light from the window ledge and turned it on. The room filled with a blue-purple glow. He hovered it over the bath. Black showed up first, smudges dark as shadows against the enamel of the bathtub. Then Barclay noticed the white patches too, glowing like stars. 'What is that?'

'The white, I'm guessing, is semen.' *Great*. 'The black,' Brennan continued. 'Well, that's blood. Judging by what we can see, there was a lot here.'

'He's used bleach on it, hasn't he?' De Silva had a smile on her face.

'Good memory,' Brennan said. 'Bleach is a sanitiser, not a cleanser. Good rule of thumb for getting rid of blood stains: clean first, sanitise second. We checked the bed. The floors. The walls. There's semen everywhere. There's a towel in there that's, er, particularly soaked. You won't struggle for DNA matching, I'll tell you that. And then this...'

Brennan shone his black light onto a shoe imprint on the floor next to the bath, black like the blood splatters he'd failed to clean properly.

'A shoe.'

'A boot,' Brennan said. 'And the size doesn't match any of the shoes we found inside. Not a single one. And he lived alone, I'm guessing by the size of the place.'

'So someone else was here,' de Silva said. 'Someone who stood in blood. They were here when one of the victims was here.'

'So he's not working alone.'

'This boot doesn't belong to just anyone. Look close.'

Barclay and de Silva leaned down and Brennan angled the light as best he could.

'See the lettering there?' Brennan asked. 'It's not exactly clear, I'll give you that. But there's a *P-A* there at the start. Second to last looks like an *O* to me. Last letter, a clear *L*.'

Barclay stood and caught de Silva's eye. He wondered whether she was thinking what he was. 'Patrol,' he whispered. 'It spells *Patrol*.'

De Silva nodded.

Barclay thought back to his days as a police constable, to the days he was so excited to slip on his standard-issue Patrol protective boots. He still had his in his wardrobe. He wore them sometimes when he went for a hike. Good ankle support.

His mind raced. Was this a coincidence? Had someone bought the boots online or at a charity shop, or was an officer involved?

'Is there anything else?' Barclay felt agitated and backed out of the bathroom. Ready to go.

'No, that's it for now. We'll get everything back to the lab and start work.'

'Thanks.'

Barclay and de Silva stripped off their protective suits as though they were dirty things that needed to go into the wash on sixty-degrees. There was a time when Barclay could have seen himself wearing that suit on a daily basis. Forensics fascinated him. But he couldn't imagine doing what Brennan and his team did, not now.

'We need to keep this to ourselves, Barclay,' de Silva whispered. 'We can't trust anyone.'

Barclay nodded. 'You read my mind.' He led the way downstairs and called out, 'Maloret!'

She appeared in the entrance, putting her mobile away into her pocket at the same time. 'Here, sir.' She smiled, wide and toothy.

'This flat here.' He pointed to the only flat on the ground floor. 'Phylis. Find out what you can. Speak to the neighbours again. I need to know where she is.'

Maloret was gone before Barclay had even finished his sentence. He liked her. She got stuff done, didn't wait. She was keen, eager, hungry. She reminded him of himself when he was in uniform.

He and de Silva walked over to the ground-floor flat's door, barely clinging on by its hinges. 'You've got me thinking now,' he said to de Silva. 'Her absence. Lamond's.'

It felt too coincidental, and he remembered one of the first things de Silva had ever said to him. 'I don't believe in coincidences.'

—

The incident room was cold, unlike the stifling heat of the squad van that brought Barclay, de Silva and the rest of the small team back to the OCC. O'Brien was there, perched on the edge of Barclay's desk. 'You lot can clear out, give us ten minutes.' Lawrence and Maloret left.

'I'm sorry, sir.' Barclay looked down at the carpet.

'Sorry for what?'

'I thought we'd find him there.'

'Oh Jesus, Barclay, enough with this, okay? The apologising and the looking at the floor.' O'Brien stood up directly in front of Barclay. 'I can't come down here every time you need a little pick-me-up. You're a detective sergeant. You've worked a case with little evidence, and yet managed to get us to the scene of at least one murder that we know of. We have a name, employment history. Now, if you'll just stop sulking and feeling sorry for yourself, you might just catch the guy.'

Barclay's face burned. He wished to God that O'Brien had asked de Silva to leave, too. He turned away, and then he saw it. Lamond's driving-licence headshot sat on the printout tray. But he'd picked it up. He'd handed it around in the van.

'I was coming down here to congratulate you, to ask what's next. Do you have a plan? Did you learn anything else from the scene?'

De Silva cleared her throat behind him. 'Nothing yet, but Brennan's working on it.'

Barclay knew why she'd not mentioned the standard-issue boot print. Not because they couldn't trust O'Brien, but because anyone could be listening just beyond the door.

'I'm working on it, sir.' Barclay looked up, directly into O'Brien's face and held his gaze. He wanted desperately to look away. 'We don't know where she is, where he is. He wouldn't return to work or any of the schools that he worked at...'

Then it dawned on him slowly, as he remembered Lamond's mum talking.

He quickly logged into his computer and brought up an image online and the others moved in around his computer. He opened his phone and brought up the photographs of the drawings at Lamond's flat. 'The old school. His old school. Rainford Lane School for Boys.'

O'Brien shook his head. 'Jesus, that old place. Closed in the nineties, I think. Surely it's been ripped down and made into student accommodation by now?' He chuckled. 'I'll leave you to it.' O'Brien headed for the door. 'But Barclay? Let's find this one, all right? Alive.'

That's all Barclay had ever wanted since the beginning. If he'd found one of them alive, then he could have stopped Lamond completely. This would have been over weeks ago.

O'Brien had been right. Barclay's own self-deprecation, his willingness to shoulder the blame for how the case had gone, was a challenge he needed to overcome. It had weighed heavy on him because of his own insecurities, his own view of himself, because of Nick and Sarah and the note on de Silva's windscreen. The threats Lamond had made.

'I'll go and get Lawrence and Maloret,' Barclay said.

De Silva sipped her coffee and hissed when it burned her tongue.

Barclay walked out into the cold corridor toward the lift, his mind a jumble of things he couldn't make sense of. The school meant something to Lamond, that was clear from his drawings. Barclay decided that he could waste time looking into Rainford Lane, or he could get in the car and go down there to scope it out himself. He looked at his watch. It was getting late in the day to be going off to abandoned buildings. He thought of Kim Cole. *It's getting late for her, too.*

One of the doors along the corridor was closed. He hadn't noticed that before. Probably wouldn't have noticed it, given everything that was going on, but he was sure that they had always been open. Under the door was a crack of light, low mumbles from inside. He pushed open the door gently and listened.

'...There was blood everywhere...' Maloret's voice. 'No, no, we don't know where she is. Phylis. Phylis Dobson.' There was a warm excitement in her voice.

Barclay's heart sank. It was her. The one he'd pitied and respected. The one he'd thought would go far in her career with the police. PC Maloret was the leak.

Chapter Thirty-Eight

De Silva heard Barclay rage from inside the incident room. She put away her phone, from which she'd been reading up on Rainford Lane School for Boys, and came out into the corridor at the sound of his escalating voice, where Maloret cried and pleaded.

'Ey, what's going on?'

'It's her,' Barclay said. 'She's the leak.'

De Silva's mouth fell open. She hadn't expected this. Lawrence, maybe. De Silva couldn't make sense of it. There'd been no signs, no indicators that Maloret would do anything like this. Finally, she managed, 'You what?'

'I'm sorry, I don't know what I was doing...' Maloret said. 'He rang here looking to speak to someone. Offered money. My mum's sick, I can't afford her care. It's just me.' She sobbed into her own hands. 'I gave just a little bit of info, nothing major. Just that the Maclennan girl was missing. But he kept calling, offering more, telling me I'd help or he'd report me for what I'd done.'

'I'll kill him,' Barclay said to himself.

De Silva moved to Maloret to put a hand on her shoulder. Her mum was ill and she needed the money, God knows the police don't pay well. De Silva knew how far she'd go for her own mum, how far she had gone for her dad; but nothing like this.

'You're going to have to go home now,' de Silva said. 'Don't speak to anyone about what's happened. Don't answer your phone to anyone from work, unless it's DSI O'Brien. Block Joel Matthews's phone number. Maloret, are you listening?'

'Yeah…' Her voice was soft and far away.

Everyone has their reasons. Money, some weird idea of glory or fame; to be the one to reveal the truth, to lift the lid, expose something. But there was nothing to show, no ugly truth beneath everything. Just a dangerous man with a sick mind, who Maloret had given the upper hand to every step of the way.

'I'll take you out,' said de Silva.

'No,' Barclay said. 'I'll show her out.'

Maloret looked to Barclay, whose face was set stern. 'I'm sorry, sir. I really am sorry.'

'Come on.' He didn't look at her, instead he walked toward the lift, waited for Maloret before he pressed the button. She followed, deflated and defeated, her arms loose at her sides.

As the doors closed on them and de Silva saw the shine of tears in Maloret's eyes, de Silva knew what Barclay was doing in taking her out himself. He was making an example of her. Showing everyone that such behaviour wasn't acceptable, wasn't wanted in the police. It had happened before, when de Silva was a detective sergeant: one of her colleagues had reported on the inner workings of a particularly violent case of sexual assaults across the city.

If she held back her own rage, kept it under wraps, she could almost feel sorry for Maloret's situation.

Almost.

She waited in the incident room for Barclay, where the time ticked away painfully. Lamond looked back at her from the evidence board, a big red circle around the printout of his driving-licence photo. What had changed? What had made Lamond go from an organised suspect to a disorganised one? Chance, opportunity?

We might never know.

Still, something had made him unravel. She looked at Amanda Maclennan's photograph on the board, one from a family Christmas by the looks of the bright-coloured paper crowns, the food on the table: turkey and potatoes.

A background check on Lamond had revealed no previous convictions. No earlier crime in the database that could serve as a flag to what was to come. No sex crimes, no violent assaults, no history of burglary or attempted thefts. Nothing in his childhood that would suggest he would become this monster, except his mother. But she didn't raise him. The school did.

Rainford Lane. A school for boys. There would have been no girls there, so who was Lisa McLaughlin to him? Why her?

She was shaken from her thought process by the slam of the door. She almost jumped out of her skin. 'Barclay, Jesus Christ...'

'Sorry.' He paced. 'I just can't believe her.' He bit the inside of his cheek. De Silva's dad used to do the same thing when he was thinking. Or overthinking. Turning things over in his head. It would drive her mum mental.

'God knows how much she's told that Matthews fella.'

Watching him pace the floor made de Silva dizzy.

'She was the one I was rooting for,' he said. 'The one I had hopes of progressing...'

De Silva had seen how much Barclay had liked Maloret, had watched his trust in her grow over the past few days. Those bonds hurt most when they break, the ones where there is complete trust and respect. Where suspicion hasn't yet crept in and ruined everything.

You can't believe it was her, because you don't want to believe it.

There was still an idealism in Barclay, something that let him believe in the virtue of people. That everyone is capable of goodness. The work hadn't ripped that out of him just yet. After this case was over, when he got his family back, and they moved onto the next case, de Silva wondered whether that optimism would stick.

'I'm sorry. I know you liked her,' de Silva said.

'My family had to leave their home,' he said. 'If I find out that anything she did or said led to that...'

'She'll be dealt with. But not right now.'

Barclay sighed and slumped into his seat, his head in his hands. 'I know, you're right.'

'I keep coming back to the school. This Rainford Lane place. I'd never heard of it before. I read a bit about it online. Award-winning reform practices and such like.'

'I need to look where exactly it is.'

'East of the city. I'd probably say it's on the border of Lancashire. Out around St Helens way. Off the A58.'

Barclay stood up. 'What are we waiting for then?'

'No, hang on a minute—'

'No point us sitting here. This place means something to him. We could be out there scoping it out.'

'No, no, no,' de Silva said. The suggestion made her nervous. What had just happened with Maloret had made Barclay reckless, careless, desperate to make a move on anything that seemed a positive lead. 'We can't just *go* out there.'

'Why not?'

'We're looking for a place where he could have taken his most recent victim,' she said. 'He could be there. We'd need backup, reinforcements, ARVs. We've just sent everyone home.'

'He might not be there, de Silva. Look, I'll shout on the radio when we get there. They'll know exactly where we are.'

It was true. The place was probably a ruin by now.

'Fine. We'll scope it out, if we see any sign, we call backup,' de Silva said.

Where was the detective sergeant who followed the rules, did things by the book, panicked when he thought he'd let someone down? He was gone now, replaced with someone who took chances, threw caution at the wind and said, 'Swallow it.'

It occurred to her hard and fast.

He's becoming me.

'All right,' she said. 'But I'm driving – I can see you're still rattling from your conversation with Maloret.'

—

De Silva was unsure when she started the engine, and she was still hesitant about going to Rainford Lane alone when she drove down Speke Boulevard toward the M57, where the rain fell in heavy sheets. Barclay had said, 'We're just scoping it out. We're not going in or anything, don't worry.' But she was worried. She couldn't help it. She had an uneasy feeling that wouldn't subside.

De Silva knew that the budget for the case was long gone – likely doubled from the deployment of the ARV team. It had been necessary, and they'd found a major scene in the case, but there was no Lamond, no Kim, no fruit on that particular branch. If they got into trouble out there, it could be a long time before anyone got to them with backup.

She wanted to turn the car around, go back to OCC and set everything up properly. Speak with O'Brien, ask for ARV and enforcer support. Pull a team together.

So why don't you?

She believed in Barclay, in his word that they wouldn't go inside if they suspected something was off. He'd live up to his word. He'd never let her down before, not like that.

The M57 seemed to stretch for miles, but in truth it was one of the shortest motorways in the area. The lane lines flitted by in her headlights, yellow-white like Kelly's skin as she lay on the banks of the Mersey.

She turned right at Switch Island onto the M58 and headed off toward Ormskirk and Wigan. Just a few more minutes and they'd be there. De Silva's stomach clenched and she wanted to be sick. Everything in her told her that this was wrong.

She drove on.

Barclay stared out of the window, elbow resting on the door, watching the orange lamp posts zip past. There was a calmness in his face that de Silva hadn't seen in days.

'What's on your mind?'

He didn't turn to look at her, but mumbled, 'Just thinking about Nick and Sarah. I haven't even had time to call them.'

'You've got a few minutes now.'

'No, no. I'd want to do it privately.'

'Behave yourself.' De Silva laughed. 'Just act like I'm not here.'

Barclay took his phone out of his pocket and looked at her. 'Are you sure?' There was a smile on his face now, that wonderful smile that had made her warm to him so many years ago.

'Go for it,' she said.

She could hear the ringing tone through his phone before she'd even finished speaking. For the longest moments, she was worried that Nick wasn't going to pick up.

Eventually, the video call connected. 'Daddy!' Sarah's sweet little voice. There was excitement in it, but it wobbled with emotion. 'When are we coming home?'

'Very, very soon. I promise. How are you? What've you been up to?'

'Well, we went for a walk. My teacher sent some spellings, and I didn't like that. But then we found the swimming pool and had a swim. I bet I can do it without armbands next time.'

'I bet you can, too.' There was a thickness in his voice. 'You're getting so big and brave. Is your dad there? I haven't got long.'

'Yep. Daaaad!' she called. 'So, are we still going on holiday when you get the bad man?'

'Yeah, when I get the bad man. Absolutely.'

'Okay, here's Dad.'

De Silva chanced a glance but returned her focus to the road ahead. Nick had come on screen. His hair looked a mess, which she guessed was unusual for him. His eyes were puffed and dark. 'All right?'

'Are you okay?'

'I've been better like,' he said. 'One second. Baby girl, you play with your dolls. I'll be back in a second.' There was a moment where de Silva could hear Nick moving about, the sound of a door closing. Then, in a quieter tone, 'How are you really?'

'I'm okay,' Barclay said. 'We're on to something. We're really close, I promise. I can come and get you soon.'

'I'm really scared, Ben.'

'I know.' He looked at de Silva but she kept her eyes on the road, coming off the M58 at Bickerstaffe. 'But you're safe.'

'Are you?'

A pause. De Silva's heart swelled for him, for them both. The wipers punctuated the silence.

'I'm all right,' he said finally. He covered his face with his massive hand. 'I'm all right, I'm just missing you both.'

'Well, you'll be coming to get us soon. Like you said.' Nick's voice cracked with emotion. 'My knight in shining armour. As always.'

'I thought you'd be mad at me.'

'What for? None of this is your fault. It's this sick...' he lowered his tone '...fucker's fault. You're the good guy, remember that.'

'Thank you.' There was a moment where they looked at each other and said nothing, but Barclay's shoulders shook. The pained, silent cry of someone whose heart was breaking. 'I'm going to have to go.'

'Me too. It's nearly bedtime for Little Miss. She's been good as gold.'

'She's an angel.'

'A Hell's Angel, maybe.'

They laughed. De Silva felt tears prick at her eyes. She'd never have that again with Ritchie. She wondered if she'd have that with someone else. She was surprised to find that she even thought of anyone else.

'I love you,' Barclay said. 'I'll see you very soon.'

'I love you too.' The line cut off.

Barclay covered his face with both hands, wiped at his cheeks and eyes. 'I'm sorry,' he said. 'I bet you didn't want to see any of that.'

'Are you okay?'

'Yeah.'

'Then that's all that matters.' She tapped his leg twice; good, hard and friendly slaps. 'I think this is it.'

Rainford Lane School for Boys was barely visible from the road. In the rain, the building looked like some castle or sprawling mansion from a horror novel about ghosts and things risen from their graves. The old metal fences were overgrown with long grass and weeds, and in the places where it was broken were wooden boards, spray-painted with names and obscenities.

The narrow road that led down to the school entrance was just a dirt track, lined with thick, overgrown shrubs that scraped the car doors. The gates ahead were massive old things that may have been painted black back in the school's heyday. One of the gates hung off its hinges, and the other was on the wasteland of the grounds. The place gave de Silva the creeps.

'Jesus Christ,' Barclay said.

De Silva stopped the car. 'Okay, we've seen it.'

'You're bloody joking, aren't you. I haven't come this far to just see it. I want to go into the grounds properly. Get a good look. If we see any lights on, we'll call for backup.'

'Lights on? This place doesn't look like it had electricity even when it wasn't falling apart.'

She was uneasy. She didn't want to go any further, but Barclay was right. They could see nothing from here, and besides, the place could give her further insights into the mind of Lamond. She sighed. 'Fine.'

De Silva turned her car around and edged it to the left of the dirt track. Barclay was out of the car before de Silva had turned the engine off. She joined him and moved around to the boot, handing Barclay a large umbrella and one for herself. She grabbed a torch and turned it on.

'What else have you got in there, de Silva?'

'There's snacks where the spare wheel should be.'

He laughed. 'I'll remember that.'

Barclay opened his jacket, pressed the green button on the side of his radio and said, 'This is DS Barclay. Could you put me at the old Rainford Lane School. Rainford Lane, just off the bypass.'

A crackled reply, 'Copy, DS Barclay.'

De Silva put up her umbrella; the rain pattered on it in heavy drops. From there, it was still a bit of a walk to the main building. Maybe five minutes. Finally, the dirt track gave way to loose stone gravel. It crunched under their feet and reminded de Silva of fresh snow in February. As they got closer, the façade rose up out of the night; a massive thing, almost monstrous in the rain and dark. De Silva wondered how many people had walked through its doors, how many people Lamond had interacted with during his time there. Whether he'd walked that very same path she walked now. She shivered.

'It's spooky, isn't it?' Barclay looked up at it, his mouth open in awe.

'That's one word for it.'

The main entrance doors were large, made of rotted wood with metal rusted studs. Barclay pushed against it, but even in its current state, it wouldn't budge. Maybe something was blocking it.

'Hang on,' de Silva said. 'You said we're not going inside.'

'I was just seeing. Come on, let's look around the back.'

The first thing de Silva noticed at the back was the newer-looking additional block or wing, fixed onto the school. The second thing she noticed was the blue Ford truck with rusted wheel arches, and filthy windows.

Barclay caught on to it just a moment later. 'Fuck.' He unclipped his radio and pressed the green button. 'DS Barclay, requesting—' There was a sickening crack, Barclay yelled and hissed as the radio flew from his hand. He held his right hand with his left, a mess of blood. De Silva thought she saw the glistening white of bone.

De Silva spun around and saw Lamond stood there in the torch beam. Bloody and glistening with sweat. His eyebrows arched over ice-blue eyes, his lips curled back over his teeth, like an angry dog. De Silva froze.

He held a hammer in his hand and it dripped with blood.

Barclay took out his baton with his left hand and flicked it so it extended to its full length. His other hand sagged at his hip, dripping blood onto the ground. 'Don't move.' His breath was ragged. 'Backup are on their way. It's over, Lamond.'

De Silva reached into her bag and took out the PAVA spray. Held it out in front of her like a gun. Lamond took a step forward and she released the cap, sprayed it into his face.

He screamed in agony, one hand at his eyes, and swung the hammer blindly with the other. It caught de Silva square in the side of her head and the world seemed to tip. She saw the building of the school, the gravel rushing toward her, Barclay swing with his baton but miss, Lamond running toward the newer part of the building, Barclay following him.

And then black.

Chapter Thirty-Nine

A ringing sound pierced through the darkness so loud it made de Silva's head hurt. She could smell the rain, sweet and earthy, and over that, the metal stink of blood. Someone was bleeding. She was soaked and cold. Beyond that, she couldn't sense anything else. Couldn't feel it or see it.

Am I dead?

She wasn't sure who she was asking, but was certain that no one would respond. Another shout. Barclay? He's in trouble. He sounded strange, muffled and far away. She remembered seeing someone go inside a building. It was Barclay. He'd gone inside.

Pain seared in her head; it came out of nowhere, so sharp. As her eyes opened, it hurtled back to her, hit her so hard it almost winded her. Kim Cole, Rainford Lane, Lamond. The hammer. She tried to sit up, but the pain made her want to vomit.

The old school building loomed in front of her, Gothic in the rain and night. She was soaked, and as she tried to sit up, the pain stabbed at her, rain dripped from her nose and chin and she shivered. She looked down at herself and saw that her top was red.

She needed to get up, to follow Barclay into the building. To ring through to dispatch. Next to her, her black handbag. The contents spilled out across the wet gravel. A lipstick she hardly used, the baton she'd had to engage only a handful of times, and a radio. Barclay's radio. Her PAVA spray was gone.

Get up.

She reached for the baton first, gripped it tight as she dragged herself toward the radio. She felt as though she might vomit from the pain in her head and neck. Wanted to close her eyes again and sleep.

In shaking hands, she gripped the radio and pressed the red button on top. She held her breath and waited for the mic to open her end. The mic would only open for fifteen seconds. She'd have to be quick. She heard the static. 'This is… DCI de Sil— Silva. Rainford Lane School.' Alarms would sound on every nearby officer's radio, on the screens at dispatch. They'd be there soon.

She pushed herself up, hoped that adrenaline would kick in. *Ignore the pain. Just get on your feet.*

She looked up toward the building and put the radio into the pocket of her coat and held onto the extended baton tightly. She needed to be ready to use it, ready to strike. With every step forward, her head rang with the pain from her wound. She daren't touch it.

She manoeuvred between freshly splintered wooden boards into the black of the building. She searched her pockets and found her phone – the screen now cracked – and turned on the torch. Rain poured through what was left of the roof, almost completely open against the elements. Time and weather had turned it to a stinking, slick mess. The old wooden floors were rotten and slippery. She walked carefully, the torch beam ahead of her hardly making a dent in the thick of the dark.

Open doors into empty rooms lined the corridor; small, cramped spaces. Some had a wardrobe, a bedside table, all thick with decay. Weeds clawed up from the ground and walls and trembled in the breeze – things that somehow managed to survive in that dark, terrible place. An old teddy bear stared at her with its one remaining eye, glassy and lifeless. Plant life had tried to reclaim that, too. These were bedrooms. Dorms.

The hairs on her neck prickled. She could feel eyes on her, watching her. Waiting. It could be Lamond. He could be ready to finish the job. Something shifted behind her; she spun, the baton ready at her side. The movement made her dizzy and woozy. The weak torchlight from her phone settled. Nothing there. She was certain there had been…

She moved on to the next room, and as the torchlight swiped across the almost-empty room, de Silva's breath caught. Fastened to a radiator was a woman.

'Who's that?' the woman screamed. Her voice was old, cracked. 'Who's there?'

De Silva moved in closer, putting away her baton and torch as she walked, and whispered, 'It's okay. I'm police. You're going to be okay. I'll get you out of here.' De Silva recognised the woman from the photograph they'd retrieved in the ground-floor flat at Lamond's building. 'You're Phylis Dobson, aren't you? We've been looking for you.' De Silva looked about for something to cut the cable ties.

'He's got a young girl with him, you know. You need to go and help her. Get her out of here first.'

'There's someone else with me,' de Silva said.

'Yeah, and there's someone else with him.'

De Silva felt cold at the old woman's words. 'Who?'

'I don't know who,' she said. 'A man. Lewis... You know, he's... there's something wrong with him. If he hurts her... Come back for me when you've got her out.'

There was nothing to cut the ties. She tried to pull them apart with her bare hands, but they wouldn't budge. Barclay could be bleeding out somewhere, Kim could be already dead, and if Lamond had another man with him... She knew she had to keep moving. 'There's backup on the way. Stay here and stay quiet.'

There. A piece of metal, blistered by rust, but with a sharp edge. It took some effort, but the cable ties snapped.

Phylis rubbed at her bleeding wrists and winced. 'Go and help her.'

'Don't move,' de Silva said. 'I'll come back for you.' She put the shard of metal into her pocket where it tapped against the radio's casing.

There was another door halfway up on the left side of the corridor and she headed for it. She had to take her time, but with each step she felt stronger. More aware. More able. The rain echoed off every wall and floor and de Silva could hear nothing else. Barclay could have been anywhere.

Still, she felt eyes on her. Not Phylis's. Someone else. She imagined Lamond watching her in silence from the shadows, his dirty blond hair falling over his narrow eyes, deciding when to attack. Or was it the man Phylis was certain Lamond had with him? Had Barclay been right about Lamond having an accomplice?

She shook the thought out of her head. There was a girl somewhere in there, frightened and cold and alone. God knows what Lamond had done to her. There was a rage in him. It was there in the post-mortem reports of the earlier victims, in the sexual assaults they'd suffered. It was there in Kelly Stack's autopsy. The abuse. The sheer violence. The horror they all must have experienced during their last few hours in the world.

Kim could be dead. She could have already undergone that same torture.

Though she was wounded and bleeding, tired beyond belief, adrenaline pushed de Silva forward. The morbid thrill of everything coming to its end. *One way or another.*

She walked out into another corridor beyond the dorms, where water streamed down the walls in torrents. It glistened silver under the torchlight.

A sound echoed down the corridor. The shuffle of feet? No, smaller. A sniffle. A moan. It could have come from anywhere. She spun around to check behind her. Nobody there. She could feel her heart in her chest; it banged against her ribcage like someone shouldering a locked door, trying to get out.

As she passed a room with no door, she heard it again. Low and gentle and constant. Cries. Someone was in pain. She turned into the room. A once-white tiled space with shower heads along each wall, as far as her torchlight could reach. In the centre, a small bath filled with water. Something they'd used after sports maybe. Rugby or football.

Something pulled at the edge of her mind: the water in the lungs of each victim. The contusions around their necks, wrists and ankles. She imagined Lamond holding them down in his bathtub until finally they had to breathe in. But nothing floated in the tiled sports bath, except a few brown leaves turning like the hands of a clock on the surface of the water.

The cry came again, from the back of the room. As de Silva approached, her torch caught the greening copper pipes. As she moved around the room, she saw her: pale and shivering. She looked so small, delicate. So different from the pictures they'd been given by her parents.

Kim.

'It's okay,' she whispered. 'I'm police. You're going to be all right, Kim.' De Silva put down her phone so that the torch shone up on their faces and knelt next to the naked girl. Her clothes were in a pile on the floor, soaked with blood and God knows what else.

Kim reached out to her, her eyes wide and imploring, but her wrists were secured to a pipe with thick cable ties. 'Get me out of here!' Kim's face was blue and purple from bruises, fresh. There was a cut on her forehead. It was deep; blood coursed down into her eye, half closed and swollen. There were bite marks across her neck and chest, and below her waist there was blood.

'Get me out of here!'

Da Silva put her index finger to her own lips. 'Shush, please.' She didn't want to scare the girl, but de Silva knew that Lamond or his partner could be lurking anywhere. Could be watching her right at that moment. The metal shard snagged on the lining of her pocket and tore the fabric as she pulled it out. She worked quickly, sawing away at the plastic cable ties on the girl's wrists and ankles, and put the shard back in her pocket when she was done. There were bloody lines where the ties had dug into Kim's skin.

The least of her problems.

'I'm going to get you out of here now, okay? Can you walk?'

'No, no, no.' Kim pulled away, moved closer to the cracked tiles.

De Silva knew. She hadn't heard them come into the shower room, hadn't heard the tap of shoes on tiles. They hadn't made a sound, but in that moment, she could feel them. Taller than her, broader, stronger and close. A man.

She spun around, swiped her baton into the dark and felt it crack against something. A cry of pain. She could see nothing in the dark. She scrambled across the floor for her phone and held it up into the darkness. Nothing. Someone moved out there, beyond the light of her torch. For an awful moment, she could hear nothing but her own breath.

He lunged at her out of the black. The breath heaved out of her as she hit the ground, him on top of her. The baton and her phone skidded out of her hand, she could see the light up-turned into the room, where dust hovered above it like flies or moths. He squeezed her neck tight, his hands rough and massive. And familiar. Something in the feel of the skin, a callous here, the smooth long outdent of a scar along the palm. Familiar, yes, but not in that way. Nothing like the violence they committed now.

She reached for the baton. The hands around her neck grew tighter and flecks slid across her vision, like dust in the torchlight. He grunted on top of her, pushed down on her neck. So heavy that she thought at any point her neck would snap.

Another sound in the room, footsteps.

Barclay. Thank God…

'You're in big trouble now.' His voice. Lamond's. He bent down to pick up de Silva's phone and shone the light into his own face. He took the hammer from his belt loop and held it loosely in his filthy, blood-caked fist. 'Should have finished you off properly.'

De Silva's mind ached. Throbbed. She couldn't make sense of it all. Who was on top of her? She couldn't see him. Barclay had been right. Phylis confirmed there were two of them. Was it him? Was it Barclay? No, she pushed the thought out of her mind. Couldn't consider it. The man on top of her couldn't be Barclay. She looked up, could see nothing but the silhouette of a man. Blood dripped down from him onto her face, and slipped down her cheeks into her hairline like tears.

Broad shoulders, ears that stuck out a bit too far from the side of his head. She knew before she saw him clearly.

My God...

Lamond stepped closer, she turned to watch him. She could see him better now. The skin around his eyes was red raw from the PAVA spray she'd fired off at him outside. He swung the torch around and aimed it at her. It stung her eyes, and for a moment, all she could see was white, until her eyes finally adjusted.

The hands on her skin, the weight of him on top of her. The smell of spearmint on his breath. She'd felt it all before. Intimately. He'd been in her bed. Inside her. He'd fallen asleep next to her and spent the night. She'd been alone with him in hotel rooms, in restaurant toilets where the doors locked.

'Mick,' she managed, her voice hoarse. 'You bastard.'

Lamond lifted the hammer above his head and roared, like some impossible monster.

Crosby held up his hand. 'Leave her.' He laughed. 'I'm sorry they got you involved in all of this, de Silva. You can blame O'Brien for that.'

De Silva grabbed his groin and squeezed, dug in her nails. He screamed, sagged and rolled off her. He held himself on the wet tiles and groaned in agony.

Lamond swung the hammer and de Silva rolled out of the way before it smacked into the tiled floor. Somewhere, Kim screamed. De Silva swung her legs around, caught

Lamond in the back of the knee and he fell down onto it with a crunch. De Silva was up and on her feet, she backed away into the shadows. If he couldn't see her, he couldn't find her.

She reached for her radio but found that it had been destroyed in her fall. The casing had come apart, and she could feel wires sticking out. She left it in her pocket and scrambled for her baton. Her fingernail caught on a broken tile and it bent backward. She hissed with the pain.

'De Silva?' Barclay's voice. The torch from his phone swept into the room. She tried to catch a glimpse of where Crosby had gone, but didn't see him. She needed that torch. Lamond got back to his feet, dragged himself away from the torch from de Silva's phone.

'It's Mi— It's Crosby,' de Silva said.

'Are you sure?'

'Yes I'm fucking sure!'

Shuffling somewhere close by. Could be Lamond or Kim. Or Crosby.

'Are you armed?' She padded softly to where her phone was, stayed low to the ground, then held it out in front of her. She swept it around the room and Lamond's face loomed out of the black. Her heart could have stopped and she wouldn't have been able to tell. She held herself perfectly still, like prey that knows the predator has found them, has locked on. Fight or flight.

She took a step back to get closer to Kim. She wanted to keep the girl as safe as possible, for as long as she could. Lamond stepped toward her, and as he did, Barclay threw himself on top of him and wrestled him to the ground.

De Silva could hear Kim's sniffling, could just about make out the shape of the girl. She reached into her pocket and found the metal shard there. It felt cold in her hands. The only thing she had left. She knew she needed to get Kim out of there, but she couldn't leave Barclay with Lamond, especially with Crosby somewhere out there.

She edged closer to the two men on the ground, grappling for the upper hand. She steeled herself and held the shard firmly in her grip. It cut into the palm of her hand. She ignored it.

Lamond spun himself on top of Barclay and delivered punch after punch. Barclay protected himself, his arms up over his chest and face as the blows landed on his forearms. De Silva brought the shard down into Lamond's back.

He screamed, deep and guttural, and arched his back in agony. He stood, lunged at de Silva, but Barclay hit him in the calves with his baton. Lamond crumpled and Barclay got a grip of him again.

'Where is he?' He was breathless. His chest heaved. 'Crosby.'

'I don't know.'

'Get the girl out of here.' Barclay held Lamond's wrists down to the ground, despite the searing pain in his hand.

'He could come back!'

'Go!'

'Come on.' De Silva helped the girl to her feet, but she could barely walk. De Silva half walked, half dragged her from the shower room into the corridor toward the dorms. Crosby. The man she slept with, the man she trusted, believed in, stuck up for. He was somehow involved in all of this. Helping that monster.

No, it's a mistake. Has to be. But even as she thought it, she knew she was wrong.

'Please get me out of here,' the girl said through shivers.

'We're going. Just keep moving.'

A deluge fell through the roof now. De Silva stopped, pulled off her coat and put it over Kim's shoulders. For the first time, she saw the blood on her coat, how it was completely covered in blood.

'Did you get her?' Phylis's voice from somewhere off to de Silva's left.

'I'm getting her out. I'll be back for you. Just hold on.'

No reply.

Light filled the dorm then, and de Silva froze at the sound of an engine. Was this Crosby?

A silhouette in the light, big and bulking, and it walked toward her. She tried to shrink back into the shadows, but couldn't manage it with the weight of Kim on her shoulders.

'Win?' O'Brien's voice.

She breathed out her relief. She looked him over. He was breathless, red in the face. 'Here.' She moved toward him, and he took on Kim's weight. 'How did you…?'

'You hit that red button.'

De Silva nodded. 'Get her out of here.'

He looked panicked, his eyes wide in shock. 'Where's Barclay?'

'He's still in there. O'Brien, Crosby's here.'

'What?'

'I think… I think he's been working with Lamond.'

'I can't believe this.'

'There's someone else here.' De Silva went into the room where Phyl was. 'In here.'

Phyl didn't move, and in the semi-dark, de Silva couldn't see her chest rise or fall. Her eyes were wide open, looking up through the ruined rafters of the dorm-block roof and into the sky above. De Silva didn't have time to check.

De Silva turned back to O'Brien. 'Just get Kim out of here and somewhere warm. Where's backup?'

'ETA four minutes.'

'Wait for them,' she said. She knew that having O'Brien in the mix could complicate things. He looked strong, but he was older now. Not the man he'd been just five years ago.

She'd have to go back in there herself.

Chapter Forty

Barclay hurt all over. He wasn't sure which part of that pain was serious, just a wound or something internal. Lamond was strong, and his punches had landed like lead. He straddled Lamond, held on to his arms so that he couldn't move, and with every second, the pain in Barclay's hand worsened. Barclay's thought was that Lamond would tire out eventually, but he showed no sign of weakness.

His eyes were wide, and in the dark, they flashed like the sharp edges of knives. Spittle flew out of his mouth. 'You fucking faggot. You wait. You wait 'til I get to her. Your pretty little Sarah.'

Barclay drew his fist up, ready to strike his face, to shut him up. He knew instantly that he shouldn't have. Lamond overpowered him, tossed Barclay aside and was on his feet. He kicked Barclay in the ribs over and over until the breath had gone from him.

Lamond leaned down, close to his face. 'You shouldn't have come.' He struggled to catch his own breath from the exertion. 'You're in big trouble. You all are.'

Something pricked at the edge of Barclay's hearing. A wail, up and down, in and out. Louder. Louder.

They're coming. Just hold on.

Barclay grabbed at him, wrapped both of his arms around his back and pulled Lamond to the ground. The weight of him almost knocked the air from Barclay's chest. He spun himself around and on top of Lamond, hoping his own weight could hold the enraged killer down. He looked down at Lamond, at the man that had caused so much damage. Could cause even more if Barclay couldn't keep a lid on him.

'Barclay?' De Silva's voice. He was relieved to hear it.
'Where's the girl?'
'She's fine. O'Brien has her.' She moved to his side.

Barclay whipped out his handcuffs from the holder at his belt, handed them to de Silva who fastened them tight around Lamond's wrists. He winced at the pain in his hand then said, 'Lewis Lamond, I'm arresting you on suspicion of murder. You do not have to say anything, but it may harm your defence if you do not mention when questioned something which you later rely on in court. Anything you do say may be given in evidence.' His lungs burned with every word as he struggled to speak.

Lamond made no attempt to resist. His whole body trembled, and for a second, Barclay thought he was having a fit. Then he heard the sobs.

'Are you sure you're all right?' De Silva could just about make out blood running down Barclay's face. 'That cut looks bad.'

'He clocked me one,' he said. 'I'll be all right. Crosby?'

De Silva shook her head. 'I'll get a team to do a sweep, but he could be anywhere by now.'

'But Crosby, though! He was involved in those initial investigations. Lynsey, Danielle, Kelly.' He looked de Silva in the eyes. 'I can't believe it. Are you all right?'

De Silva said nothing.

They hefted Lamond to his feet and walked him out through to the dorm block as the sirens blared somewhere outside. Red and blue lights shone through the ruins of the dorms, and it reminded Barclay of the colours of stained-glass windows, of Sundays singing 'How Great Thou Art' and 'Peace in the Valley'. They were, and had always been, the colours of comfort, of leaning against his mum's shoulder on hard-backed pews and smelling her perfume – sweet like almonds.

Outside, the scene was almost overwhelming. The ARV team were there, guns at the ready. De Silva held up her hand. 'Crosby might still be in there. We need him apprehended. Consider him armed and dangerous.' The team ran inside as two paramedics lifted Kim into the back of one of the ambulances.

It was difficult to take in, hard for Barclay's eyes to adjust to the lights and the noise of the activity. O'Brien was on his phone. 'Brennan, you best get down here now.'

Lawrence marched toward them, Barclay handed Lamond to her and watched as she put him in the back of the car.

'You need to see a paramedic,' de Silva said.

'I will if you will.' Barclay laughed despite how he felt. He thought getting to this point would offer him some relief, or release. Instead, he felt empty. Hollow. Except for the throb in his hand.

There was still work to do. He could go to Sarah and tell her that he had caught the bad man, but now he needed to make sure he stayed locked away. A prison cell, a psychiatric facility where he'd be studied and assessed, a basement room out of the way. A place where he could do no more harm.

A paramedic walked toward them. 'Let me see that hand.'

O'Brien opened his car door so that Barclay could sit down and the paramedic could get a better look. The woman looked worn out, pale with dark circles under her eyes, and he wondered how long she'd been on shift. Barclay felt as though he was looking in a mirror.

'So what are you thinking? Will he live?' O'Brien. Jovial as ever.

'We need to get your hand X-ray'd,' the paramedic said to Barclay. 'These bruises and cuts – well, you'll be sore for a few days.'

'There's someone else inside,' de Silva said. 'Phylis Dobson. She's dead.'

The paramedic nodded. 'We'll take a look.'

Barclay's head was too fuzzy to process anything. It almost felt as though he wasn't present in the moment. He put a hand on de Silva's shoulder and said, 'We got him.'

'You did.'

Just like her to say that.

She hated taking credit, even when it was due. He'd seen her sidestep it in the years they'd worked together, and had always admired it in her. How humble she was. They were so different in that respect. He craved the praise, the glory. As he looked around at the old school building, where the police lights made its shadows shift and twist; as the squad car splashed through muddy puddles to take Lamond away; and the ambulance with Kim inside headed for the nearest hospital, he realised there was no glory to be found in any of it.

The paramedic cleared her throat and looked to de Silva. 'Could you get over to my colleague there? Let him get a look at that head.' De Silva did as she was told for once.

O'Brien leaned in closer to Barclay, now that de Silva had walked away. 'Couple of painkillers and you'll be all right. You're sure it was Crosby you saw in there? Now you have to be certain. It was pretty dark.'

'I didn't see him,' he said. 'She did. And yes, she's sure.'

O'Brien shook his head. 'I don't know what to say. You work with a man for years and years, but do you ever really know him?'

'We'll find him, sir.'

'Yes, I bet you will.' O'Brien frowned, and spoke loud enough for all to hear: 'I'll stay here and wait for Brennan and his team. You two will want to be getting to the station, I imagine. After you're checked out, I mean.'

'I'm fine,' de Silva called over her shoulder. 'But he needs to go to the hospital.'

Barclay thought she looked anything but fine. Lamond had hit her hard. 'I'll be back in a few hours. If you're up for it?'

De Silva smiled, but it was half-hearted. She was in pain. The wounds Barclay could see looked bad, but he couldn't guess at what she felt about Crosby's possible involvement. 'I've wanted to get in a room with this fucker for days,' she said.

Chapter Forty-One

The interview room was silent, except for the hum of the heating system. Something up there rattled and clanked. Things had moved slowly since they made the arrest last night. Barclay had sat in A & E for hours alone. Things had changed since Covid, and no one was allowed in with him. De Silva said she'd check on the status of Lamond and Kim and come back to meet him at the OCC when he was done.

He had been seen by a doctor, a young lad with tattoos all over his arms. Mermaids and fish and an old-fashioned diving helmet the colour of brass. 'We've had your X-rays back,' the doctor said. 'Everything looks good, no broken bones. There is a tiny hairline fracture there on your middle metacarpal.' He pointed it out on a black-and-white image that Barclay couldn't make sense of. 'You said this was a hammer, didn't you?'

Barclay nodded. 'That's right.'

'Then you're really lucky. This could have been much worse. The swelling should go down in the next few days. Just use normal over-the-counter pain relief.'

Barclay didn't feel lucky. He drove back to the OCC after 2 a.m. and found the incident room dark and quiet; everyone was at home or busy. Even the night team had gone. Nothing more to do for now – they'd caught him.

The photographs stuck to the evidence boards fluttered in the false light and cast shadows over the handwriting, hastily scrawled in blue marker. He couldn't wait for the moment that he could erase it all – make all the questions, the lines of inquiry, the links and arrows and errant comments disappear with the swipe of an eraser.

He'd called de Silva on the drive to OCC. 'What have they said?'

'Nothing serious,' de Silva whispered. Barclay heard her moving, a change in her breath, and a door close. Her voice clearer then: 'Few cuts and bruises. Nothing broken, no serious wounds. What about you?'

'I'm fine.'

'Just fine?'

'Nothing's wrong, just going to be sore for a while. What about Kim?' He'd thought about her the whole time he was at the hospital.

'That's... I'll tell you when I see you.' De Silva's voice was low, serious. 'And they're going to release Lamond to us shortly, I think.'

'That's good.' Barclay couldn't wait to see the man eye-to-eye, to sit opposite him. To understand the reasons why he did what he did. 'Any news on Crosby?'

'ARV team searched the whole building,' she had said. 'Nothing. I, er... I just can't believe – don't want to believe – that he was any part of this.'

'I know,' Barclay had said softly. 'It must be difficult. He was your friend.'

'It was more than that.' A silence had passed between them. Then de Silva cleared her throat. 'We'll need an appropriate adult,' she had said. 'Do you have anyone in mind?'

'Julie Hardman?'

'That's who I was going to suggest. She was great when we worked with her last time, wasn't she?'

'I remember.'

'I'm heading back to OCC now. Will I see you there?'

'I'm a few minutes away,' he'd said.

De Silva had arrived just over thirty minutes later, and Barclay thought she looked different. Still exhausted, yes; still painfully thin, absolutely; but there was an energy about her, almost a glow from underneath her skin.

She lives for this.

She clocked the thick bandage around his hand and winced. 'Jesus, I'd hate to see what you look like when you're not fine.' She studied his face. The cuts and bruises and split lip; he'd seen them in the rear-view mirror himself before he set off from the Royal.

'It's nothing.' He forced a smile. He'd been worse, this was just a few cuts. There wasn't any blood, no shaking and being unable to speak. Nothing like the HMS *Iron Duke*. He shook his head, and those memories fell away like autumn leaves.

'I called Hardman,' de Silva said. 'She'll be on her way soon. She's got kids, so she's sorting them out with their dad.'

Barclay nodded. 'You were going to tell me about Kim.'

De Silva shrugged. 'She's had a rape kit. God, it breaks my heart. That hammer...'

Barclay looked away from her, away from the evidence boards, to the black screen of his computer. The dark of nothing was preferable over confronting what Lamond had done.

She's alive. He folded his arms across his chest and squeezed. *Wounds heal, but what's in her head never will.*

By 4 a.m., Barclay and de Silva sat in Interview Room A and waited for what felt like an agonisingly long time. Julie Hardman sat opposite them, her mouth a thin, straight line. She looked at her watch and sighed.

'I'm sorry, I don't know what's taking so long,' Barclay said.

'Have you contacted Social Services?'

'Yeah,' Barclay said. 'They're sending someone as soon as they can.'

'Good. From what you've said, he needs more than I can offer him. A social worker.'

'He'll be getting processed,' de Silva interjected. 'They said to wait, so he can't be too long.'

'That was half an hour ago,' Barclay replied.

'As if you've forgotten how long things take since you stopped wearing uniform.'

'I was one of the more efficient ones.'

De Silva rolled her eyes, mockingly. 'Yeah, I bet you were.'

He looked at his watch again. 'I'm going to see what they're doing.'

Just then, the door opened. Lawrence ushered in Lamond and sat him down on a chair next to Hardman. He looked smaller somehow. Maybe it was the fact that they'd taken his blood-soaked clothes. Maybe it was the thin polyester pyjama-type clothes they'd given him as replacement. His hair was slicked back, fresh from being washed. They'd have taken samples of his skin, hair, blood, fingerprints. His clothes would be on their way to the lab, and he hoped that O'Brien had marked them urgent.

Lamond was nothing like the terrible thing Barclay had built up in his mind, and certainly nothing like the wild man he'd met last night. There were tears streaming from his red eyes, and he wiped them away. He stared at the table, at the stain from a plastic cup, drained of coffee and discarded in the bin twenty minutes ago. The caffeine had done nothing to help Barclay; he still felt dazed, exhausted, and his head ached.

De Silva was the first to speak to him. 'Do you want a drink, some water?'

Lamond shook his head. 'No,' he whimpered.

Hardman glanced across the table at Barclay, frowned.

He was more emotional than Barclay had expected. Someone who'd caused so much harm sat in front of him now as a broken man. Barclay pressed *Record* on the digital box fixed to the wall. 'Mr Lamond, I'm Detective Sergeant Barclay, and this is Detective Chief Inspector de Silva.'

Lamond nodded.

'We're going to record this conversation, just to make you aware.'

A nod.

De Silva leaned forward. 'Do you understand why you're here?'

Another nod.

Barclay cleared his throat. 'For the benefit of the recording, Lewis Lamond has nodded, indicating he knows why he's here.'

Lamond looked up from the table and through sniffles said, 'I know why I'm here. I know I'm in big trouble. But you don't understand. They lied to me. They pretended.'

'These girls?' Barclay spread out photographs on the table in front of Lamond. The girls he'd taken and raped and killed.

Lamond sobbed and looked away. 'No, no, don't. Don't do that. I thought they were her. They made me think. They wanted me to take them, you know. It was their fault. They wanted to see me get in trouble.'

Lamond stood up slowly. Barclay's heart felt like an off-beat drum as Lamond pulled off the thin sleeveless top the police had provided.

Hardman was on her feet, but stayed clear of him. 'Mr Lamond, please be seated and dress yourself.'

'I want to show them.' He turned. His back, rippling with muscles, was a mess of long, skinny, white scars. 'Can you see? This is what happens when I get in trouble. This is what they did. And more. More down here.' He unfastened the drawstring trousers and pulled them down. He was naked beneath.

'Jesus,' de Silva gasped.

Hardman had been right, Lamond did need help. It was clear he was in no fit state. He thought about pausing the interview. 'Please get dressed,' Barclay said.

'I can't let this continue,' Hardman said. 'This isn't right. We'll have to terminate.'

'I'm sorry.' Lamond pulled up his trousers and pulled his T-shirt on back to front. 'I'll be good.' He sat down on his chair again and closed his eyes. He took a few deep breaths and opened them, his face creased with a pain Barclay could only imagine.

'We need to talk to you about Lynsey Renshaw and Danielle MacDonald.' Barclay took a breath. 'About Kelly Stack, Amanda Maclennan. Kim Cole.'

'I can't talk about them.'

'Why?'

'Because they've gotten me into trouble.'

'What did they do to get you into trouble?' de Silva asked.

'You're very tricky,' Lamond said. 'You're just like them, I can tell. You lead boys on, don't you? Get them thirsty for the wet between your legs and then turn your back.'

De Silva blinked, unfazed. 'Does that make you angry?'

'Yes.' He wiped tears from his face. 'It does make me angry.'

De Silva nodded. 'Will you speak to us about the girls? You see, we believe you murdered them. We believe that you raped them and tortured them and dumped their bodies.'

Lamond shrugged. 'I told you it's their fault. Sluts, all of them. They wanted me to do it.'

'Did Lisa?' De Silva placed the photograph from the leather-bound album on the table in front of him.

He stared at her, so much like the other girls. 'I loved her.'

'You don't love her any more?' de Silva asked. 'What did she do to make you not love her?'

'All through school, when they touched me and used me and told me I was a nasty queer, I thought about getting out. Getting back home. Getting back to Lisa. She always knew how to look after me.'

'So you killed her?'

He shook his head, fresh tears streaked his face. 'I found her. She'd moved on. A husband, said she didn't want anything to do with her old life. With me. She said she'd ring the police if I came around again.'

De Silva frowned. 'How did that make you feel?'

'She didn't want me. I thought of her every day, and she didn't want to know who I was. So what did I go through all of that for? I just wanted to talk to her. But she wouldn't talk, so I…'

'So you hit her. With your hammer?'

Lamond nodded. 'And I couldn't stop. I loved her, but she treated me like shit, and I wanted to show her how that felt. But after… she wasn't her any more. Her face was gone. The wet between her legs wasn't nice any more, it was red. I'd done all of that.'

Barclay sat forward. 'Do you know Phylis Dobson?' He held up a photograph they'd taken from the old woman's flat.

'She got herself into trouble. I didn't ask for that. She was always talking, always scheming. She got herself into it. But I always liked her… before…'

'She's alive,' de Silva said.

Lamond's face dropped and he became very still.

'She's going to be fine,' Barclay said. 'Her daughter is with her. She's very sick, but the doctors are hoping for a full recovery.'

'And despite what you did to her' – de Silva stared into his eyes when they shifted to her – 'Kim Cole is going to live.'

Lamond's face broke into lines and shadows as he sobbed again. 'I didn't mean to hurt them. They wanted me. Wanted me to want them and touch them and be inside them. They wore her face, and I thought it was her. Thought she'd come back for me. Then they turned their backs and I got s-s-so, so angry. I had to punish them.' He stuttered over his words, like a child who's been told off and can't quite catch their breath.

'Why did you punish them?'

'I told you!' he screamed. 'All through what they did, back then, in that place. To me. I only ever thought of Lisa.'

'Who did what to you?'

'The men. The teachers. Their mates. Mrs Jones.'

Rainford Lane.

Lamond wiped the wet from his face. 'They hurt. Every day and on purpose. Inside. Outside. In here.' He pointed to his head, then his chest. 'Everywhere. And it won't stop with me.'

Barclay's heart fractured a little, and he struggled with that. Here was a man who had done the most abhorrent things to girls. Here was a man who'd had horrendous things done to him as a kid. He knew then the answer to a question he'd asked himself: monsters are created; evil is born in the hearts of men, of mothers, of teachers, and supposed protectors. Now it was in the heart of Lamond himself.

Maybe Kim can break that chain.

'It will stop with you,' Barclay said. *For now.*

'Detective Crosby,' de Silva said. 'How do you know him?'

'We're old friends.'

'From school?'

Lamond nodded. 'He looked after me after... all of that.'

'He's older than you are.'

'I can't say anything else,' he said. 'Or I'll be in even more trouble.'

'How was he involved?' Barclay asked.

'He helped me.'

'To do what?' de Silva's voice shook. 'Find them? Kill them? Dump them? I need you to tell me exactly what he did and when.'

Lamond smiled. 'I'm not a grass. Ask him yourself.'

'We will,' Barclay said. *If we ever catch him.*

De Silva cleared her throat, shuffled some papers in front of her. Barclay knew she was buying some time to collect herself. 'Have you ever heard of an app called The Woulds?'

Lamond shook his head. 'No, I've never heard of an *app* called The Woulds.'

'Why do you say it like that?' De Silva's eyes narrowed. 'Why the emphasis on "app"?'

'I don't know what you mean.' He folded his arms and turned his head.

Barclay knew that Lamond had decided the interview was over.

Chapter Forty-Two

Three months later

'I remember, even before I got to the door, knowing that something wasn't right.' De Silva wiped at the tears on her face, long streams that slid down to her jawline. 'There were no lights on, no telly. He liked the telly on when he got home from work, left every light on in any room he'd been in.' She took a breath. 'It had rained that day, too. I'd noticed that the driveway under the van was dry. I thought he must have taken the day off sick or had no work on. I put the key in the door, and when I opened it...'

She hesitated. Held her breath in her chest, a bird in a cage. Emma nudged the tissues across the table and gave that weak, professional smile. The one that meant, *Go on*, that meant, *Continue raking up everything you've tried hard to suppress*.

De Silva let her breath go. 'I felt like everything closed in on me. Like my whole world had collapsed and that moment was the centre of it. Like there was gravity pulling everything else in on top of me. Like I couldn't breathe, didn't know if I wanted to breathe again.'

'Shock can be that way.' Emma's voice was soft like that gentle type of wool, not the kind that scratches. 'It affects everybody differently.'

De Silva shook her head. 'I don't think it was shock.' She knew shock. She'd seen it every day throughout the years of her career. It broke people, turned their faces pale, their knees to jelly, and sometimes their stomach to water. 'It was guilt,' she said. 'It was guilt and shame and the knowing, the understanding, that I was to blame. And it's anger. I'm so, so angry that he took his life without speaking to me. And I feel even more guilt because I feel angry at him.'

'That anger is important, so we'll circle back to it,' Emma said. 'But first, you've alluded to this guilt before. This shame.' Emma scratched out notes on her little pad. 'Do you want to talk about that today?'

'I was having an affair,' she said. 'Not just an affair. It wasn't just about sex. I mean, it started that way, but I ended up really caring for him. I think that I loved him and my husband at the same time. Do you think that's possible?'

'To love more than one person simultaneously?' Emma smiled. 'Yes, I do. But let's get back to you. Do you think that your husband, that Ritchie, found out about your affair? That this is the reason he committed suicide?'

'Yeah.' De Silva scratched at her upper arm until it turned pink. 'I think he knew it was happening, and he couldn't take it any more.'

'Was there any sign from him that he knew about it? Something he said or did, maybe? A change in his behaviour.'

'I didn't think so at first, no. But weeks afterward, when I logged onto the computer in our home office – I wanted to look at some pictures, you know... I remember charging my work phone on it once. And there they were, somehow. All our messages to each other, mine and the other man. He used that computer every day. I know he saw them.' De Silva cleared her throat. 'He kept all that to himself until the end.' She put her hand over her eyes, felt the swell of tears there, but swallowed them. She smoothed back her hair.

'And where is the other man now?'

'He's not around…'

'I see. Well, I understand that you feel this way about Ritchie's death,' Emma said. 'But I think you'll never know for certain why Ritchie did what he did.'

That hurt like a punch to the gut. 'I thought I was paying you to make me feel better?'

Emma laughed, but covered her mouth quickly. Forced her smile into a straight line. 'I'm sorry, forgive me,' she said. 'I'm just saying that all this guilt and shame you're feeling, you're putting it on yourself. You've described it before as like a black tide around you, threatening to drown you. It could be for nothing. Ritchie's reasoning for committing suicide could have been something completely unrelated to you.'

'Like what?'

-

De Silva's road was quiet, and inside every house lights were on. The place had a homely feel to it for sure, but this wasn't her place any more. Wasn't her home. Not without Ritchie. Headlights flashed at her from the side of the road.

Barclay. Again.

She pulled onto the driveway, past the *Sold in Seven Days* sign and climbed out of the car. Barclay had come around to see her every day since she'd made her decision.

'I'm going to have to take a restraining order out on you, aren't I? Does the DSI know you're here again, harassing me?'

'Who do you think sent me?'

She shook her head. 'Cuppa?'

'Gasping.'

De Silva opened the door and walked straight through the hall to the kitchen to make them both a brew.

Later, Barclay sat on the couch opposite her, his mug of cold tea in his good hand. 'I wish you'd reconsider.' The other hand had been tight since that night at Rainford Lane, and every so often he would flex it. 'It's not too late, you know.'

'What have they said about the pain?'

'Some nerve damage.' He shrugged. 'They're working on it. Anyway, pack it in. Stop changing the subject.'

She sighed. 'I'm done, Barclay. You should ask yourself whether your heart's still in it, too.' She knew already what the answer to that was. Barclay was born to be a detective. He was made for it, had the mind for it, despite what he thought of himself.

'You'll be back.' He smirked.

'God, don't wish that on me. Between my mum, the therapy, and everything with Lamond, I can't see myself doing that kind of work again.'

'What're you going to do instead?'

She shook her head, she wasn't entirely sure. 'There are a few options, I think. How are Nick and Sarah?'

He placed a coaster down on the coffee table from the stack of olive-wood ones de Silva had bought in Santorini when she and Ritchie went years ago; rested his mug on it. 'Sarah's fine. Kids are resilient, aren't they?'

She wanted to say that she didn't know, that she'd never had that opportunity, but nodded instead.

'Nick... well, he has nightmares sometimes. He's worried every time I leave the house. He'd always hated my work but now...'

There was something on Barclay's face. Something in the way he chewed his lip and stared off beyond the living-room wall. He became stuck in his head, turned something over in his mind. De Silva waited for him to continue.

'We'll be all right,' he said.

We, not he. That made de Silva sad.

'What about you?' De Silva sat forward, put a hand on Barclay's knee. 'I know you found it difficult after Lamond.'

Barclay shrugged. 'He's dead, what more can I say? No trial. No justice for the victims or their families. For Kim and little old Phylis. All that's gone, and they won't get the answers they deserve, because he took the easy way out. All they have is a court-appointed mental-health assessment to offer any sort of reason why.'

'Unless we find Crosby.' The air turned cold.

'There's no sign. Nothing. It's like he just disappeared.'

De Silva shook her head. 'O'Brien shared the details about Lamond with me.' It had never added up to her. The bruising around Lamond's wrists. She'd seen them in countless cases, numerous post-mortem reports, and they always indicated murder over death by suicide. She knew that Barclay would have felt the same. His apparent suicide, she had thought since the day of Lamond's death, had to be more than that. 'But you can't let anger over that consume you now. He's gone and no one will suffer at his hands again.'

'Except the families, and Kim Cole, and...' He looked down at his hand, flexed his fingers and dropped it to his thigh. 'Like you say, what's done is done.'

'And Lamond gave nothing more on what he was referring to in the note? About the person who'd tried to stop him?'

Barclay shrugged. 'I don't think we'll ever know, but my bet is he was talking about Crosby.'

That didn't sit right with de Silva. 'Did Holden ever hear back from his contact at the NCA?'

'About The Woulds app? As a matter of fact, he did.' He lowered his voice but de Silva wasn't sure why. Habit, she supposed. 'He was told to leave it alone. That was all he said.'

De Silva wondered about that. Lamond's reaction, the way he clarified just enough that he'd never heard of *an app* called The Woulds, and now this. There was more to it. *Stop it. This isn't your world any more.*

Barclay's phone rang. He held it up and said, 'Speak of the devil.' *O'Brien calling.* 'Yes, sir? ... I'm with de Silva... No, I've not managed to convince her... That's fine, I'll collect my P45.' He rolled his eyes at de Silva. 'I can be there in about thirty minutes...' He was on his feet. 'What have we got?' He stared at the coffee table and listened, index finger pressed across his lips.

De Silva could hear the cadence of O'Brien's voice, but not what was said. She knew the pattern of his speech so well that she knew that something had happened.

'I'm leaving now, sir.' He hung up and turned to de Silva. 'How can you tell me you won't miss this?'

'I won't, now get out my house.'

'I'm going, I'm going. You sure there's nothing I can do to convince you?'

She sighed. 'Look, never say never, ey?'

He beamed. 'I'll see you soon.'

She heard the door close behind him, the rumble of his engine and the screech of his tyres on the road. Then, her world was quiet again. How she liked it. There was a pang of jealousy in her gut that passed in seconds. She'd seen death, she'd looked into its ugly face almost daily for years. She'd sat with it, thought about it, brought it home, invited it into her bed. There was no real desire to revisit it.

Leave it buried.

She and Emma had spoken about the necessary things de Silva needed to do while she skirted around the subject of finding Ritchie's body and how it made her feel. The paperwork, the calling of insurance companies; all the stuff she'd shoved back into the box and left in the wardrobe months ago.

You can do it. One phone call at a time.

She took the stairs slowly, and with each step decided that she would only make a start, that nothing needed to be finished. On the bedside table, among empty glasses and a half-finished novel, the pages turned down and dog-eared, she noticed the packet of chewing gum. The silver foil winked at her in the light from the lamp. She took it into the en suite and flushed it down the toilet. She had to flush twice before it spun around itself and disappeared.

Back in her room, from the wardrobe, the box felt heavy, not with content but with meaning, importance; with everything de Silva had attributed to it: the end of something. She tipped everything out onto the bed. Swimming certificates, a football trophy from a Kirkby Sunday league when Ritchie was six years old, tarnished with the passing of time. Then her eyes fell on it and she smiled.

The back of a school report, signed by Mr Brendan in 1996, the second year that Ritchie was sent away.

> *I'm glad to see that Richard's behaviour has improved greatly this year. He's responding well to his lessons and physical education.*

De Silva needed to show this to Ritchie's mum; she'd likely forgotten about it, but it might spark in her some memory, some pride in him that she'd lost, misremembered. They'd not spoken in a long time, but she was sure that memories of their loved one could fix that. She turned it over to read more.

> *Richard does find mathematics difficult on occasions. He has a keen interest in religious studies, as proven in his most recent examinations. He has finally made some friends among the other boys.*

She saw the school's emblem at the top. An *R* in black cursive ink, overlaid by an *L* in the same style, faded almost to grey against the yellowing paper.

Rainford Lane School for Boys.

Acknowledgements

I can't believe that I'm finally writing acknowledgements for my first book. *Black Water Rising* was such a lengthy process; a labyrinth, if you like, full of dead ends, wrong turns, and finding myself right at the beginning again. It's been a novel I've loved and disliked in equal measures for various reasons, but I couldn't have got to this point without all of the special people who I've met, have supported me throughout, or have had direct influences on the book.

First and foremost, to all of my friends and family, you're too many to mention individually, but thank you for your support. Thank you for always being proud of me, for teaching me that hard work pays off. You've always spurred me on. You may have found that most of the character names come from our family tree, or from those I think of as family.

To my dear friend Sarah Maclennan, I don't know where I would be without your kind words (and the difficult-to-hear ones that made me work harder). You're a legend to me and I'll never forget everything you've done for me these last thirteen years – yes, it has been that long. I love, respect and appreciate you so much.

To Emma Carey – what an adventure! You've been there with me early mornings, late nights, through every phone call, every email, every bloody Google doc. You've played a massive part in me achieving my dream of getting this novel published, and I won't forget that. You next!

To the rest of "Write Club" (which also included Emma), I know the first rule of "Write Club" is not to talk about "Write Club", but here we are. Sarah Moorhead and John Thompson, both brilliant, talented, and passionate writers who pushed me to be a better writer and who shared their own brilliant work with me.

To Cathy Cole who told me my original concept for this novel (my own Merseyside version of Stephen King's Maine) should be a crime novel. Okay, okay, you were right!

To Taryn Preston, who has been a grammar detective for this novel, thank you so much!

To Jonny Cameron and Jon Dunn, who I can always turn to for advice on writing, and some very off-colour jokes to keep me laughing instead of banging my head against the keyboard. I love you guys.

To Karen Bradshaw, Vicki Spearritt, and Jenny Clark, thank you so much for all of your encouragement, for listening to me ramble on about my experiences getting to publication, and for your support personally and professionally.

To Jeff Young, whose amazing book, *Ghost Town*, was a huge inspiration for my novel, and for seeing Liverpool as something that lives and breathes and holds within it memories and poems.

To Melissa Grindon, for sharing great news all around, keeping us both going after it!

To Tori, who is evidence that our words can live on after they've left our mouths. I dropped a little present into this novel just for you. Emma is a therapist from a working-class background. I hope that scandalises you as much as it did in the first draft of this novel.

To my agent, the passionate (and patient!) Jordan Lees from The Blair Partnership, who took a chance on my novel, on me, and worked his socks off to get the novel ship-shape. I can't thank you enough.

To Siân Heap, Louise Cullen, and Alicia Pountney from Canelo, who have helped me understand what my novel would mean to a wider audience, taking it beyond my own mind and experiences and in turn making it more accessible. Special thank you to Rebecca Millar, copy editor, who I fully believe has superpowers – you've done so much to make this novel what it is today. You have all been so knowledgeable, so kind, so understanding, and you've made this whole process just lovely.

To Andrew Smith, who designed this beautiful book cover. I remember seeing this on the train back from London and nearly crying. I can't thank you enough for capturing perfectly the mood of this novel.

To Amanda and Jenny, the other two legs that make up our tripod. We've been together through thick and thin for longer than any of us want to remember. Thank you for always having my back, for always listening to me about my writing, and for always offering sage advice. I love you both so much.

Finally, to my partner, Matthew Stephen, my Frog, who has been a rock for me. Those odd moments when I need to get up and write, or go off for hours on end taking pictures for a scene I'd never use, for understanding that living with a writer is a serious business, and that you may be owed some sort of compensation for your pain and suffering.

Thank you.

CANELO CRIME

Do you love crime fiction and are always on the lookout for brilliant authors?

Canelo Crime is home to some of the most exciting novels around. Thousands of readers are already enjoying our compulsive stories. Are you ready to find your new favourite writer?

Find out more and sign up to our newsletter at canelocrime.com